The Sexton Blake Library

Published 2021 by Rebellion Publishing Ltd,
Riverside House, Osney Mead, Oxford, OX2 0ES, UK

ISBN: 978 1 78108 807 4

Copyright © Rebellion Publishing IP Ltd 2021

Sexton Blake is a registered trademark. All related characters, their distinctive
likenesses and related elements featured in this publication are trademarks of
Rebellion Publishing IP Ltd.

The right of the author to be identified as the author
of this work has been asserted in accordance with the
Copyright, Designs and Patents Act 1988.

All rights reserved. No part of this publication may be
reproduced, stored in a retrieval system, or transmitted,
in any form or by any means, electronic, mechanical,
photocopying, recording or otherwise, without the prior
permission of the copyright owners.

This is a work of fiction. All the characters and events
portrayed in this book are fictional, and any resemblance
to real people or incidents is purely coincidental.

10 9 8 7 6 5 4 3 2 1

A CIP catalogue record for this book is available
from the British Library.

Designed & typeset by Rebellion Publishing Ltd

Cover art by Crush Creative

Printed in Denmark

The Sexton Blake Library

ANTHOLOGY V: SEXTON BLAKE'S NEW ORDER

Selected, edited and discussed by Mark Hodder and Sexton Blake

BAKER STREET, LONDON

"I IS TO advertise you," Mrs Bardell said, as I entered the Blake residence, which from the outside didn't resemble a residence at all, "that Mr Blake proffers his apologists owing to it being that he is called away by an adenoidal circumference."

I hung up my coat, thought for a moment, then ventured, "Unavoidable circumstance?"

"Are you miscorrecting me, young man?"

She had a twinkle in her eye.

"Most certainly not."

"He'll see you upstairs in the insulting room."

What? He wasn't here but he was upstairs? As if her malapropisms weren't sufficiently confusing!

"But ... but if he's not here—" I stammered.

"Not him!" she snapped. "Off you go!"

So, bewildered, I left Sexton Blake's landlady, ascended the stairs and knocked on the consulting room door.

"Come in!" a voice called.

I entered. Pedro the bloodhound was sitting on the hearthrug. A young man, standing beside him, greeted me. "Hallo! We meet at last!"

A microsecond before crying out 'Tinker!' I managed to redirect my tongue. "Mr Carter!"

"In the beautiful flesh," Edward 'Tinker' Carter confessed. He lightly kicked the armchair that I'd occupied for the past four interviews to indicate that I should resume the position.

I did.

He settled into the one opposite.

"Sorry," he said. "The guv'nor's up to his neck in it, so you'll have to make do with me. And well done, by the way."

"For what?" I asked.

"I wagered Mrs B a fiver that you'd call me 'Tinker' the moment you saw me."

"I was on the absolute brink of it."

He grinned. "I really don't mind it as much as some of those later authors made out, even if the guv'nor suggested otherwise."

"He did. They were trying to 'modernise' you, I suppose?"

"Much to the disgust of the older readers."

There it was. The question of age. Tinker (I struggled to think of him as Carter) appeared to be, at most, twenty-four. He had blonde and somewhat curly hair, blue eyes, a snub nose, an infectious grin, and a boyish sprinkling of freckles across his nose. Handsome and friendly; exactly what a Sexton Blake reader would expect.

He had first appeared in the published stories, as a streetwise urchin, ten years old or thereabouts, in 1904. By the First World War, he was in his mid-teens. Now, in the 21st century, he was in his early twenties, just as he'd been described in the 1960s.

Plainly, it was impossible.

I, however, had met and chatted with Sexton Blake. The impossible was fast becoming familiar.

Tinker reached out and fondled Pedro's ear. "The New Order is the subject of the day, I believe?"

Straight to business.

"Yes," I responded. "Mr Blake and I have talked through the decades and reached the fifties." I opened my briefcase and took out a binder and my notepad.

Tinker said, "All right, fire away, old thing."

I consulted my notes. "Let's see. The Sexton Blake Library had been going since 1915. In 1925, after issue 382, it reverted to number one, beginning what came to be known as the Second Series. Seven hundred and forty-four issues later, the same thing happened again, beginning the Third Series. That continued until issue 526 in 1963. However, issue 359, entitled 'Frightened Lady,' brought so many changes with it that Blake aficionados call that one onwards the Fourth Series, which they also dubbed the New Order."

"Uh huh," Tinker agreed.

"It's generally accepted that the new editor of the Library—W. Howard Baker—shook it up in response to falling sales. What's the real story?"

"The guv'nor renting an office and hiring staff?"

"Yes, and moving into a penthouse suite at the top of his house while the lower floors were turned into offices." I stopped, looked around the room, and asked, "By the way, is this it, the original house?"

He shook his head. "No. That's the fried chicken place down the road, on the other side. Offices on top. The old penthouse is all storage rooms now. This place is built along the same lines, though. Most of them were, back in the day, before they became commercial properties."

I said, "So, why all those changes in Mr Blake's circumstances?"

"Eustace Craille."

I waited for him to elucidate. He obliged.

"During the war, Craille was a spymaster in the Secret Service, an organisation with which the guv'nor and I were already affiliated. He sent us on a number of missions. Some of them were subsequently reported in a highly juvenilised form in the Knockout comic."

I shook my head disbelievingly. "Yesterday, Mr Blake mentioned that those picture strips were based on truth. Frankly, I'm still struggling with the notion that the Rolling Sphere was a real machine."

"Me too, and I say that as a person who spent many a day being shaken about inside the confounded contraption. Anyway, after the war, Craille established a security agency that was even more clandestine than the Secret Service, and in 'fifty-six, the guv'nor and I were recruited."

I shook my head slightly. "But why did that necessitate the establishment of the Berkeley Square office? Why staff it with Paula Dane, Marion Lang, and Louise Pringle? And why were you, at least initially, so side-lined by Miss Dane?"

Tinker laughed and raised a hand, palm outward. "Slow down! It's all quite straightforward. By the fifties, new laws required us to adopt greater accountability. It was no longer enough for me to maintain the Baker Street Index and write up reports of our cases. We needed help with the bureaucracy. Also, I'd got it into my head that I wanted more independence, so I was undertaking quite a few solo missions. That's all there was to it, really."

"Miss Dane stepped into your shoes."

"For a little while."

I considered what he'd told me, absently clicked my ballpoint, and muttered, "More clandestine than the Secret Service."

"Did he explain his theory?" Tinker asked.

I nodded. "The Credibility Gap. Mass cognitive dissonance of such intensity that certain people are able to commit astonishingly audacious crimes which the law enforcement agencies can't even comprehend, let alone prevent. He claimed it struck in three waves: the first coming during the First World War, the second right afterwards, in the 1920s, and the third in the period we are now discussing, the late fifties and early sixties."

"Exactly so," he responded. "And that third wave required a particular sort of agency to cope with it."

"Particular, why?"

"Because it was weird," he said. "And brutal."

THE WORLD-SHAKERS

OUR CONVERSATION WAS interrupted.

Pedro suddenly looked at the door and emitted a happy-sounding snort. An elderly man stepped into the room. A small amount of blood was oozing down the side of his face. He raised a hand. There was an oddly designed pistol in it. I went cold and my scalp prickled as if my hair was standing on end.

"Hallo!" Tinker said. "Damaged?"

"Firing pin broke at exactly the wrong moment," the newcomer said. "I'll get them to revise the design."

"I meant you. Crack on the noggin?"

"Just a scratch. The matter is sorted. I'll fill you in later." He looked at me and smiled. "Hello there. My apologies. Give me a few minutes to clean up and I'll be with you."

He retreated, closing the door after him.

I stared at Tinker. "Who—?"

He laughed. "You didn't recognise the guv'nor?"

"A disguise!"

"Of course."

"And ... 'get them to revise the design.' Who's them?"

"Ah." In an exaggerated cockney accent, he said, "Them is

those what can't be named, ain't they!"

"Craille's organisation?"

He responded with an over-dramatic wink then pointed at the binder on my lap. "Shall we continue?"

With a frustrated sigh, I opened it, took out the first issue of The Sexton Blake Library that I'd selected for the anthology, and passed it to him. "Do you remember this case?"

Tinker gave a whistle. "Phew! I should say so!"

THE WORLD-SHAKERS

by Desmond Reid (Rex Dolphin)
THE SEXTON BLAKE LIBRARY
4th series, issue 457 (1960)

THE FIRST CHAPTER

Out of the blue.

OLIVER DE TRAFFORD was small, plump, dark, and bearded for effect. His features had a sallow cast. He was an aggressive, pushing and thrusting, devil-take-the-hindemost little man— like most little men who are bent on making their mark on the world. And, normally, he was bursting with self-confidence. It sprang out of him like sweat.

But not now.

At this moment, his self-confidence had utterly deserted him. At this moment he felt only deep, unreasoning, elemental fear.

He did not know why.

This fear was an inborn, instinctive thing. It plucked at his skin like the suckers of an octopus; it was a cold hand clutching at his heart—a sharp, sick, sudden squeeze of baseless terror. And there no visible cause for it.

The tree-dotted Buckinghamshire meadow in which he had paused by the side of his bigger, bulkier, burlier friend, Lewis Cochrane, was peaceful and empty. Dusk hung like a gold, gauze curtain over everything. The heat of the dying day still lingered pleasantly.

It was an idyllic, typical English scene.

The small sounds of eventide were very clear. Far off, the clock of the village church struck the hour. Distantly, rooks were busy with their vespers. Night was coming down gently, like a benediction. A fine end to a fine day.

Why should he suddenly feel so frightened?

And why—he shot a quick, questioning, apprehensive look at his friend—why had they halted here, in the meadow?

He started to put the last question into words, but Lewis Cochrane stayed him with an abrupt hand. "Wait!" The big man stood erect. His head was lifted, slightly cocked to one side. He was listening with grim intensity.

Listening—for what?

When Cochrane had invited him to accompany him this evening, De Trafford had been more than pleased to accept. For the plump little man was a successful journalist researching on his own specialist subject, and tonight he was being offered the chance of learning something of considerable importance about it. So much Cochrane had made very plain.

"Come with me tonight, and I'll show you something that'll help you decide the truth about the flying saucers."

Who could resist an invitation like that? Not Oliver de Trafford! But now, forebodingly filled with unreasoning fears, he was beginning to wish that he had.

Again he shot a quick, nervous look at his companion.

The big man had his own fears, his bitter thoughts, but his face did not betray them. It was a strong face, but something else outside the man was stronger: the power that had bidden him bring his friend out here. He knew that the order was a virtual death-warrant. He thought of the heavy revolver which weighted down the light coat so carelessly tossed over his arm. He stood some yards back from a small belt of trees that thickened the oncoming night, and he waited.

Oliver de Trafford waited, too. He waited because his friend waited—but he knew not for what. Cochrane had been very secretive. He had been unwilling to elaborate on that first statement of his—"something to help you decide the truth about flying saucers." It might be anything!

At first, De Trafford had thought his friend was taking him out to show him some observational apparatus. Then, when this idea had proved false, he had supposed that they were going to keep an appointment with someone Cochrane had persuaded to share Top Secret information.

But . . . an appointment at dusk—in the middle of a meadow—? The mind boggled at that.

What, then—? What were they waiting for?

The very last thing De Trafford was prepared for was the Shape that came dropping down out of the limitless sky!

It came down quickly, silently, invisibly—only slowing and becoming perceptible to the human eye as it descended below the level of the encircling hills. It sped across the wooded landscape to hover for a moment just beyond the belt of trees. De Trafford could only goggle at it. This was the real thing! This was a flying saucer! He dragged in a sharp, startled breath.

It was circular, of indeterminate size, giving off a faint but shimmering light whose wavelength seemed to oscillate so rapidly that all detail was blurred.

It was a phantom, other-wordly thing. A muted humming came from it. It dropped in an instant to ground level, and the trees hid it. Naked curiosity momentarily conquering his fear, De Trafford started forward to see where it had gone. He couldn't help himself.

But his friend restrained him.

"No! We must wait a little longer!"

"Let go of my arm!"

"Wait just a little longer—"

His friend still held him.

And, at that moment, as if appearing on cue, something big and bloated but undeniably animal advanced towards them out of the shelter of the darkly brooding trees.

IT WALKED UPRIGHT on two legs. It had a human, but bulbous outline. De Trafford found himself gasping at the sight of it, and then giggling nervously as a ridiculous thought sprang unbidden to mind.

I represent the Michelin Tyre Company . . .

Still the big and bloated creature advanced.

And now De Trafford could see that its shape was determined by some kind of inflated protective suit. In one massive, gauntleted hand it carried an object which looked like a heavy electric torch terminating in a circular network of wire. A cable trailed behind and away through the trees.

The creature came to within a yard of the two men, and halted. Through a sheet of translucent material let into the front of its globular helmet, De Trafford glimpsed a gaunt, bitterly-lined, almost human face and flat, empty, expressionless eyes.

It stood there motionless—but only for the smallest fraction of a second. Then, suddenly, it pivoted. It was a swift movement for all the bulk. It turned on Cochrane and pointed the torchlike object at him. Its other hand shot forward.

The hand fastened on the light overcoat the big man carried. It jerked the coat off his arm tossed it up, caught it one-handed, and found the heavy revolver which weighed down a pocket. It let the coat fall then—almost contemptuously. It had done with it. The gun was hard in its hand.

The muzzle of the revolver rose, jutting at Cochrane. De Trafford stared as if hypnotised, barely breathing. His friend shuddered as the gun lifted but, fantastically, made no move to stop the creature doing as it willed. He seemed powerless to do so. The revolver was pointed at his chest now. The hammer snicked back: a small, sharp sound. And still Cochrane did not move to defend himself.

It was then that something snapped inside Oliver de Trafford. He came out of his trance.

In that moment, fear took total possession of him. He knew he should hurl himself forward, that he should wrestle with the big, bloated creature for the life of his strangely helpless friend, but he couldn't. He just couldn't! Even as his reason demanded that he do so, his all-consuming fear was jerking him away. A wild cry escaped him. He turned to run.

He did not get far.

The creature merely gestured with the torchlike object in his direction, and Oliver de Trafford found that his legs refused to obey terror's urgent signal. He couldn't move any more. It was impossible—insane—but he couldn't move!

As soon as the torchlike object was waved in his direction, he was rooted where he was. He was fixed there. Frozen. Only his eyes retained their liberty of movement, and these scuttled this way and that in his head, like frantic mice.

He saw the heavy revolver that still menaced his friend. He saw one of the bloated fingers tighten on the trigger. Cochrane saw it too, and knew that the moment of truth had come. He prayed ineffectually for deliverance.

"No . . ." he prayed soundlessly but frenziedly. "No . . . no . . . !"

The big gun blasted.

The creature fired only once, but it fired accurately. The heavy slug threw Cochrane bodily backwards. He sprawled on the ground and now, suddenly, he was released from the invisible bonds that had held him captive and the unseen gag that had kept him silent.

He was free, and a wet scream bubbled out of him into the

gathering night. He was free—free to die. But he did not die instantly.

The scream sobbed away to a whimper. He looked down—almost in disbelief—at the ragged hole in his clothing. Arterial blood pumped out of it. He tried to cover the hole with his hands. The blood spurted through his fingers. He moaned.

It was a helpless, hopeless sound. He vomited and sagged over on to his face. He lay still. It was then, and only then that he died, and he left De Trafford waiting in horror for his own bullet, his own death. It must surely come.

But the creature looked at him with blank eyes, then tossed the revolver on to the grass beside Cochrane's drained corpse.

De Trafford felt the sweat of sweet relief start out on his forehead. No merciless execution for me . . . ? What, then?

As if in answer, the creature lifted the torchlike object and pointed it straight at his face.

Now De Trafford could see right into it; could see a network of bright wire filaments. And then—

Then—

The creature pressed a switch.

Instantly, a white-hot knife seemed to slice into the small, plump man's brain. His mouth opened, but the frantic sound born of the awful pain could not be uttered. The knife worked backwards and forwards, carving its dreadful way through brain-tissue and thought-patterns, chopping his consciousness into slices.

Fragments of his childhood sprang to life, to be mixed with the agonising present and visions of a fearful future. All time was rolled up into one piece.

Loathsome, obscene creatures from his subconscious were born in slimy reality and just as instantly died. Blazing patterns of unimaginable colour choked his optic nerve.

His sight was split, so that the immediate scene before him

was chopped into segments, a jigsaw with part of the scene in one corner of his vision and the adjoining part somewhere else. A blinding kaleidoscope. A ghastly television screen coming to pieces under violent interference. His nerves and muscles knotted. They died a death of their own.

But his legs were somehow made a part of him again. He could use them again. Truly, this was the one and only even semi-coherent thought that he had.

The power was suddenly switched off. The invisible, blazing knife had done its devil's work. He moved painfully, not even knowing who he was. He began to stagger back across the meadow away from the trees; back the way he had come.

The big and bloated creature watched him, satisfied, and then turned. The thicket behind it swallowed it up.

A moment or two later, there was a muted humming, a vague luminosity. The Shape rose in the sky and banked, accelerating.

Then it was gone.

THE SECOND CHAPTER

Seeds of doubt.

THE SEXTON BLAKE organisation occupied a modern suite of offices overlooking London's Berkeley Square, but it was a very rare day indeed when Blake himself was able to keep office hours.

This day was no exception.

At six, when he should have been on his way back to his penthouse flat high above Baker Street—going home to an excellent meal by Mrs. Bardell and to the long evening of ease he was continually promising himself—he was still hard at work at his desk. Something urgent had cropped up that afternoon, something pressing needing his personal attention, and once more the evening of ease had had to be postponed.

It was always the way, he thought ruefully. Events conspired to keep his nose hard against the grindstone. At seven, alone in the building, he was still working. At quarter to eight, he had only just barely finished and was thankfully pushing a clump of thick files away from him across his broad desk, when the telephone rang.

A sigh escaped Blake. More trouble? He hesitated for a

fraction of a second. It had been a long day. Let the telephone ring unanswered? He was tempted.

But no.

This was his life. Trouble was his business. He scooped the phone up. "Sexton Blake Investigations. Sexton Blake speaking."

He was answered by the dry, thin sound of someone clearing a very old throat.

The voice that followed immediately was equally dry, equally thin, equally old—but decisive none the less. It identified itself with a name. But identification was hardly necessary.

"This is Craille . . ."

Blake let his tiredness slip from him swiftly. It fell like a discarded cloak.

Craille . . . the indestructible Old Man . . . hardly known at all to the public at large, and then only as a rather shabby import-export agent with an office in Belgrave Square. Craille . . . Chief of Intelligence . . .

Blake found himself sitting up straighter. He was brisk; businesslike. Usually the detective was the Chief—but not when Craille called.

Blake said: "You'll want to see me, of course?"

"Naturally. How soon can you be here?"

Blake glanced at his wrist-watch. "A quarter of an hour?"

"Sooner than that," said Craille. "This is urgent."

The phone went back. The conversation had ended.

Blake moved then. Fast!

A TAXI TOOK him to a solid, old-fashioned block of flats in Belgrave Square. Four broad stone steps, hollowed out in the centre by the passage of time and countless feet, led up to a dimly-lit lobby where he gave his name to a porter. Less than a minute later, he was walking down a first-floor corridor to where a door stood open and a generously-endowed, rather beautiful brunette awaited him.

"Good evening, Mr. Blake, Mr. Craille is expecting you."

Her voice was soft and attractively husky. Her mouth was full-lipped, and avidly sensual. Blake smiled then, at the young woman and to himself. Craille certainly knew how to pick 'em!

And he knew how and when to replace them, too. Craille, the unchangeable, went out of his way to promote change, and not least in the composition of the group of very lovely young women who served him as personal assistants, round the clock.

Perhaps, Blake thought, if they stayed too long they got to know too much. Perhaps it was that. Close and continued contact with Craille was more than likely to make any beautiful girl rather too knowledgeable. In the way of business and otherwise.

The young woman stood aside to let him pass through the doorway first.

Beyond was an efficient-looking office, neat and tidy, functional with contemporary furniture. And then the brunette opened another door.

Now Blake walked out of an atmosphere of order into one of organised chaos.

"Hello, Blake. Good to see you. Sit down."

ILL-VENTILATION HAD PRESERVED the musty scent of Egyptian cigarette smoke with which the haphazardly scattered furniture and frayed curtains were thoroughly impregnated. Reference-books, documents, and papers of all kinds overflowed from despatch boxes and bookcases on to chairs and thence to the floor.

Dim lighting revealed the tall, hunched, skeletal shape at the desk in the centre of this paper jungle. Craille had just removed an Egyptian cigarette from his long, black ebonite holder and was stubbing it out in a rather preoccupied way on a corner of his desk. He had already lit another. His deeply-pouched eyes were inscrutable.

Blake found a vacant chair, looked at it with frank suspicion, and turned the dusty cover over. The old man's gaze lifted sardonically. "Yes, a pity to get dust into the weave of those beautifully-cut Savile Row pants."

Blake grinned. Then asked: "What's on?"

Craille's face didn't change expression.

It was as criss-crossed with fine lines and wrinkles as an aerial map of a wind eroded desert. He took a mouthful of cigarette smoke and blew a perfect smoke-ring which rose slowly upwards in the dead air.

"What's on? Something like that." He indicated the smoke-ring. "Flying saucers."

One of Blake's black, Satanic eyebrows inched upwards. "You don't usually joke."

"Nor am I joking now," Craille returned briefly. "Have you seen the Daily Post today?"

Sexton Blake shrugged. "Seen it, and read all of it that makes any sense. We seem to be embarking on yet another of what my friend Splash Kirby calls 'silly seasons'—when there's no real news, and the papers have to manufacture sensations."

Craille's amber eyes narrowed. "Like this, you mean?" He drew a crumpled copy of the Post out from under a litter of documents. His long, bony forefinger stabbed at the feature article on the leader page.

THE FLYING SAUCERS HAVE ARRIVED
— says Oliver de Trafford

Blake glanced at the article and looked up at Craille. "Yes, that's certainly the sort of thing I meant—until I heard you say you weren't joking."

The old man's lips narrowed grimly.

"As you know," he said, "I'm concerned with the safety and well-being of this country, and, believe me"—he tapped the article—"this really worries me!"

"But—" Blake began. Craille stopped him.

He said flatly: "I was never more serious about anything in the whole of my life!"

Sexton Blake was more than surprised. He said incredulously: "But I know De Trafford—by reputation, at least. Along the street they call him 'D.T.'s' on account of his crazy ideas!"

Craille leaned back in his chair. He said broodingly: "I know him, too."

He inhaled; he coughed. It was a dry, rasping sound. He said: "I'll tell you something, Blake. I used to go along with what they say in the street about Oliver de Trafford. I used to go along all the way. For my money, everything he wrote was ridiculous—everything! Little green men from Venus! Pah! I used to regard De Trafford as being just another smart, slick journalist: a man who jumped on the 'flying saucer' bandwagon in nineteen forty-seven and made it his own line of fiction, although his books and articles are all presented as fact. That, repeat, is what I used to think—until recently."

"You've changed your mind?"

"De Trafford has changed his material," Craille said sombrely, "and only in the last few months. He's gone from the impossible to the improbable, and that's not such a long way from demonstrable fact. He's become much more credible. And he's now packing his articles with information he shouldn't possess."

Blake's eyes narrowed sharply. "What do you mean?"

"I mean," Craille said bleakly, "that in today's article—to quote just one example—our friend Mister de Trafford

27

demonstrates to my satisfaction that he has lately acquired access to a source of Top Secret information. He must have! Do you realise that contained in the article—thrown in almost as make-weight—there are important facts bearing on space travel which our research engineers have only just found out?"

"I see . . ." Blake said slowly, and Craille looked at him—hard.

"Do you?" he said. "The alternatives are these. Either someone on the Anglo-American Joint Research staff has been blabbing to Mister de Trafford—and those facts printed today are Restricted, every damn one of 'em—or, judging from the casual way he dropped them in as being almost of no consequence, he's getting his information from some source, some group, whose knowledge of these matters is considerably in advance of ours."

Blake frowned. "But who—what—?"

"Exactly," said Craille. "The mind boggles a bit, doesn't it! Can you see Mister de Trafford getting his information from the Russians? Not on your life! So where is he getting it from? I've got to know!"

Again he tapped the newspaper article. "And there's another thing."

He said: "The possibility of the actual existence of flying saucers, whether of planetary or of earthly origin, is something that's been worrying Allied Air Force staffs ever since the end of the last war. You may know that research groups allied to N.A.T.O. Air Force Intelligence have been operating for years for the sole purpose of investigating every reported sighting of a flying saucer. A prolonged and determined effort has been made—and is still being made—to find out if flying saucers really exist and, if they do exist, where they are coming from."

And then he snorted.

"But De Trafford in this article says that he knows!

"He says that the 'saucer people' or creatures—or whatever they are—have established a base in an uncharted zone of the Arctic. He claims to know where."

Blake said: "He's just sounding off, surely."

"Perhaps . . ." But Craille was doubtful. He said ruminatively: "I have a first-class agent in Iceland who, oddly enough, holds exactly the same theory about an Arctic base." He eyed Blake keenly. "What would you call that? Just coincidence?"

"Bright boys frequently think alike."

"But my man's on the spot." Craille stood up slowly. "So many questions!" he muttered to himself. "So many damned questions!" He stubbed out his cigarette, and glanced at his watch.

He said: "De Trafford is giving a lecture at the old Gaiety Cinema off Tottenham Court Road tonight. It's a lecture on the same subject, and we're going along there. I want to talk to Mister de Trafford."

His old amber eyes narrowed.

"How much does he really know, and where is he getting his information from? It all comes back to that."

He moved, and he was resolute now: a man of decision.

"Believe me, Blake—I mean to find out!"

THE THIRD CHAPTER

Broken date.

THE OLD GAIETY Cinema had not known such a night in a very long time. The approaches to it were crowded. No sooner had the taxi in which Blake and Craille were riding turned off Tottenham Court Road than it was halted by a crash-helmeted motor-cycle policeman. Ahead, the street in front of the cinema was clogged with cars and milling with people.

Normally, perhaps, a lecture on flying saucers at an obscure venue would have attracted little attention beyond that of a few cranks and a handful of people at a loose end. But the Daily Post's sensational feature article had been the day's talking point, and this was the result.

To go farther in the taxi was clearly impossible, though the cinema was still some distance away. Craille paid off the cab driver and followed Blake closely as he ploughed a path through the throng.

They arrived in front of the cinema to find the crush there worse than ever. Policemen were attempting to control a far from orderly queue. It spilled over the pavement and into the road, pushing and shoving. Across the crowded foyer of the cinema, open doors to the stalls showed an auditorium almost full to capacity. Harassed officials flitted in and out, flustered and jumpy. Noise was continuous.

Blake and Craille looked at each other wordlessly. The detective shrugged, there was nothing else for it. He attracted the attention of a police-inspector then. A man he knew slightly. He spoke to him, and what he had to say produced the desired result. To the accompaniment of boos and sarcastic cheers and cries of "Blow you, Jack!" a way was forced for them through the pressing crowd. They entered the foyer, and there, momentarily, paused.

Blake looked around. Beyond the jostling throng round the pay-box was a small island of comparative calm near the manager's office. Here a long table carried neat piles of books, all by Oliver de Trafford. High on the wall behind the table was a large, framed, head-and-shoulders photograph of the author.

Blake eyed it interestedly.

It showed Oliver de Trafford as a plump-faced, sallow-skinned man with rather too clever eyes, sleek jet-black hair, and a carefully affected goatee. Blake's gaze travelled down. Immediately below the photograph was the real-life jet-black hair of a young woman standing behind the table. It fell in caressing waves about her oval, high cheekboned, and strikingly beautiful face.

Near her, a sour and dyspeptic-looking man moved irritably, looking at his wrist watch. The young woman glanced at him quickly, and her expression was troubled. At Blake's elbow, Craille murmured:

"I'll go and find De Trafford."

Blake stopped him. "No—wait." His eyes thoughtfully narrowed, he moved his head. "Who's the man?"

He already knew who the young woman was. She'd been pointed out to him in the street some weeks before by his newspaper columnist friend Arthur Kirby. She was Dorcas de Trafford—Oliver's sister.

"The man's De Trafford's lecture agent," Craille said, "and if I'm going to have my talk with De Trafford before he starts spouting—"

"Wait," Blake said again. There was something wrong here. He could sense it.

He moved forward slowly, seemingly casual. He reached the table. There, he made a show of interest in the books displayed for sale. He picked one up and turned over its pages. And all the time he was surreptitiously eyeing Dorcas de Trafford.

Her complexion was palely cream. Her eyes were finely shaped and of an unexpected and astonishing blue. And she was very badly worried. It was this which had captured Blake's keen attention right from the first.

Small lines of anxiety gnawed at her red-lipped mouth. The agent was looking at his watch again—for the third time in less than a minute. He muttered something explosively, half under his breath. Blake heard the young woman answer him. "He'll be here soon." But—oddly—it sounded as if she were seeking to reassure herself as much as the agent.

The words, though positive, betrayed a terrible doubt. Who was she secretly afraid wouldn't be here soon? And what was wrong?

"Damnit—" the agent grumbled, "—why does he have to cut it so fine!"

Then Blake knew.

For Dorcas de Trafford was speaking again—worriedly.

"I'm sure he never intended to be as late as this. He set out early enough. He left home hours ago. You heard what Benson said when I phoned. Oliver left with Lewis Cochrane soon after five."

One of Blake's black, Machiavellian eyebrows jerked upward

fractionally. De Trafford hadn't arrived yet. He was indeed "cutting it fine"!

The agent ground out: "Where the devil can he be?"

"He's got held up somewhere in the traffic," Dorcas de Trafford said—but she didn't really believe it.

The agent snorted: "For close on three and a half hours?"

"You'll see! He'll be along in a moment! He'll come soon! He must!"

But she said it with a certain desperation.

Still she sounded as if it was herself she most sought to convince. Still there was that odd note in her voice. Blake heard it plainly, but the agent didn't.

"I'll say he must!" he growled. "His lecture's scheduled to start in just another five minutes. Dammit, this is cockeyed! We've got the audience, but where is the lecturer? Where is he?"

Blake turned his head to speak to Craille.

And, at that moment, in the cinema-manager's office, a telephone began to ring—stridently.

SEXTON BLAKE FROZE. The sound was cut off abruptly. A voice spoke in the office, and then the door of the room was jerked inwards and a man in evening dress stood there looking out. His eyes fastened on Dorcas de Trafford urgently.

"The police. They want you."

"What's happened?" She couldn't get there quickly enough. "Is—is it about Oliver?" De Trafford's agent was hard on her heels.

They did not close the door.

Blake went rapidly around the table to get as close as he could to the office. There was so much noise in the foyer. Head bent, listening intently, he heard Dorcas de Trafford gasping into the phone.

34

"But—you must tell me what's happened! What sort of an accident?"

Then: "Oh, my God! And—and is Oliver—Mr. de Trafford—is he all right? You don't know? You must know! Yes—yes, of course I'll come straightaway!"

Blake heard the telephone clatter back on its rest. Dorcas de Trafford was breathing rapidly.

"They want me. The police. Next of kin—they said! Something horrible has happened to Oliver, and they won't tell me what!" Her voice was climbing. "Lewis Cochrane is dead!"

The agent burst out: "Damn! Something like this would have to happen when we've got a full house!"

The girl gave a choked, hysterical laugh.

The man said quickly: "Of course I'm sorry if something's happened to your brother—but what the hell do I do? The mob we've got in here tonight will wreck the place!"

"That's your problem—I've got mine." She blundered out of the office.

Almost blindly, she thrust into the crowd still thronging the foyer. Sexton Blake exchanged a quick glance with Craille. They followed her. Once in the street, she made straight for the car-park at the side of the hall. She wrenched open the door of a Riley One-Point-Five.

She got into the car, and she was shaking.

She released the handbrake; pressed the starter. There was a protesting whirr, and a jerk of the car. She bit her lower lip, switched on and pressed the starter again. The Riley jumped forward six inches and stalled.

Sexton Blake reached the car in four urgent strides. He flung open the door, and the interior light came on, striking cold blue flame from the young, startled and then indignant eyes.

She got out: "Who are you? What do you want? Go away—I'm in a hurry!"

Blake's retort was sharp. "And in no fit state to drive." He continued: "You've made two false starts already. What happens when you're out in the traffic? You're all set for an accident. You're jumpy; on edge."

"Who are you?" the young woman gasped. "What right have you got—"

Blake interrupted.

"I've been waiting to see your brother. I still want to see him, wherever he is. In some sort of trouble, is he? Well, trouble's my business—I'm a private investigator. My name is Sexton Blake.

"Now—" a ghost of a smile touched his lips "—do you mind if I take over the wheel?"

THE FOURTH CHAPTER

The Scrambled Man.

DORCAS DE TRAFFORD's blue eyes were angry.

"I don't care who you are! You've got a nerve!" She made to pull the door on him. He braced himself against it. She said furiously: "If you don't let me close this door I'm going to call the police!"

Blake said easily: "The ones in the street? I'll call them for you if you like. I know the inspector. Nice chap—"

Then his voice changed dramatically. It lost its bantering note.

He said quietly, persuasively: "Why won't you let me help you? That's all I want to do—help."

She stared at him.

"I'm quite a good driver," Blake continued. "I can get you wherever you want to go in double-quick time. Get you there in one piece, too. Why don't you let me?"

She hesitated, and then suddenly relaxed. "Oh—oh, all right. You can drive. I—I've heard of you, of course. I'm sorry if I was rude. But, please—please let's hurry."

She moved across to the passenger seat. Blake held the door for Craille. If the girl noticed the old man she gave no sign.

Blake slid into the driving seat. He glanced left at her tremulous profile.

"Where to?"

"Wendover," she told him.

He started the Riley smoothly, drove out of the car-park and headed north-east towards Tavistock Square. From there he would be able to strike through to the Euston and Marylebone Roads and thence west. It was a long way round, but better than trying to get back through the choked streets of the Tottenham Court Road area.

Thin rain came out of nowhere to drift against the windscreen. Blake switched on the wipers. A quick glance in the mirror showed Craille apparently asleep. The detective's lips twitched.

He said, in case she hadn't heard him the first time: "We really came to speak to your brother rather than listen to his lecture. Just why didn't he turn up?"

She shook her head worriedly. "I don't know." She said: "The Aylesbury police wouldn't tell me what's happened. All I know is that Lewis Cochrane—one of Oliver's friends, a Foreign Office official—called for him shortly before five. When I heard that, I naturally supposed they'd started on their way to London then. But apparently not. They drove to Cochrane's house near Wendover and there, somehow, Cochrane got himself killed. I don't know how. The police wouldn't say. And Oliver—I couldn't get anything out of them about him; just that if I was his next of kin I'd better get there as quickly as I could."

She shivered—and it wasn't cold in the car.

Sexton Blake slowed down, turned the Riley left into Euston Road, and settled down to a steady, suitable cruising speed. "You knew this chap Lewis Cochrane well?"

"Pretty well . . ." At first her answer sounded hesitant, then she enlarged upon it. "I was with Oliver when he met him, about a year ago at a cocktail party. Right from the first they

38

seemed to have a lot in common. After that, my brother and I visited him pretty regularly. They'd spend the nights playing chess and talking flying saucers—whenever Oliver could persuade him to. And when Lewis was ill recently I acted as his private nurse. I'm qualified."

Blake glanced at her. "Had your brother any particular reason for discussing flying saucers with Cochrane?"

She hesitated again; shrugged. "It's a subject he'll discuss with anyone."

A careful reply, Blake thought, and evasive. It didn't answer his question. But he didn't persist with it. Instead, he commented dryly, "From what I've seen of your brother's books I'd have thought there was nothing left to discuss. I get the impression he's pretty confident he already knows all the answers where flying saucers are concerned."

For the first time she really smiled. "Which books? Which answers? They differ, you know. It's hard to tell what he really thinks, and whether any particular one of his books is fact or fiction."

Blake said quietly: "And what do you think?"

The smile blanked out. "Me—? Oh, I'm—I'm not really interested. I'm just a kind of stooge for Oliver. I help him with the preparation of his manuscripts, but just in a secretarial capacity. I'd go crazy if I tried to make any sense out of them."

The detective said easily: "What kind of help did he get from Cochrane?"

He sensed a slight stiffening of the girl's body, but her expression didn't change. "He got no help, as far as I know."

Blake nodded, seemingly satisfied. And he was—that Dorcas de Trafford was lying!

So Cochrane had helped him. In what way? And if she knew that much, how much more did she know? The detective felt that she could have told him a lot more than she had, if only

39

she'd so desired.

The impression was obliquely confirmed by her next words. "Do you mind if I just relax for a while? And could you please lend me a cigarette . . . I came without mine."

So she didn't want to talk any more. Well, there'd be the opportunity for more questions later if necessary.

Blake passed over his cigarette-case and lighter. She took a cigarette, lit it, and returned the case and lighter to him. She leaned back in her seat, withdrawn and remote.

There was no more conversation for the rest of the journey.

Lewis Cochrane's house, West Towers, lay in a wooded hollow on the side of the Chilterns, a few miles from Wendover.

From the main road, the car turned off along a narrow country lane, and thence between tall, wrought-iron gates on to a private road which ran for a mile and a half. They came upon West Towers suddenly, after penetrating a thick screen of tall pines. It was a medium-sized Georgian house.

A few windows on the ground floor were bold with light. Two police cars and an ambulance stood in front of stone steps leading up to the entrance. Blake parked the Riley beside the other vehicles and, as he helped Dorcas de Trafford out, saw a man come striding from the rear of the house.

The man was big, thick-set, and squarely built. He filled out a raglan tweed overcoat. He looked at Dorcas de Trafford and then, questioningly, at Blake. "I'm Superintendent Brandon, County Constabulary," he said bluntly. "Who're you?"

"Permit me to answer that question." It was Craille speaking— dryly.

He had materialised from behind the car; a tall, stooped, skeletal figure. Now he laid a hand on the superintendent's arm and murmured something in his ear.

Brandon stiffened. He looked at first startled, then very

respectful. Craille finished speaking to him and drew back a pace with a thin smile.

"Of course, sir," Brandon said. "Certainly." He drew a torch from his pocket and flashed its beam back into the shadows behind the house. He called: "Sergeant Wetherby!"

Dorcas de Trafford said abruptly: "Where's my brother? Can I see him?"

"In just a few minutes, miss," the superintendent told her, speaking over his shoulder. "The doctor's still with him."

"What's happened to him? I've got to know!"

"We'll find out when the doctor's finished with him. It's no use scowling, miss. How can I tell you when I don't know myself?"

At that moment, light footsteps crunched on the gravel. A well-built but pleasant-faced young policewoman was approaching. She spoke to Brandon. "You wanted me, sir?"

"Yes, sergeant. Just look after Miss De Trafford for a few minutes, will you?"

"Yes, sir."

The policewoman turned to Dorcas de Trafford. "Will you come along into the house with me, miss? I'll get you some coffee."

The young woman hesitated.

At first it seemed she was about to refuse, but then Brandon said: "She's to be taken to her brother just as soon as the doctor's finished his examination."

"Yes, sir."

With that, Dorcas de Trafford turned and followed the sergeant into the house. And now Blake said: "What has happened superintendent?"

Brandon eyed him keenly.

"Cochrane was shot," he said. "Shot dead with his own revolver. Whether by his own hand, De Trafford, or some other person, we don't yet know. And the reason we don't know is, simply, that the one eye-witness of the shooting, De Trafford himself, is in a severe state of mental shock. He can't speak coherently enough to tell us how Cochrane came to be killed; he can't even stand. Our police surgeon had a look at him, but such extensive shock was entirely outside his experience. So we sent for a brain specialist from Stoke Mandeville Hospital. He's with De Trafford now."

"You're sure he was an eye-witness."

"Pretty sure." The superintendent nodded. "All the evidence points that way. I'll show you. Come with me."

At the rear of the house there were a number of outbuildings, a long stretch of lawn and garden, and, beyond that, a tennis court. Then came a tall wall which served as a windbreak.

The rough ground and meadowland immediately beyond the wall, Brandon explained, was also part of the estate. Five hundred acres of it. The Cochrane land sloped gently upward to the Chiltern ridge.

The superintendent led the way through the garden, skirted the tennis court, and went on through the gateway to the tall wall. Now he walked carefully, and cautioned Blake and Craille to do the same. Canvas covers blazed a trail over the grass.

Beyond the wall, portable floodlights illuminated a broad expanse of ground. Men were busy packing up photographic equipment. Others had lifted some of the canvas covers and were making plaster casts of the footprints beneath. A stretcher party stood sentinel near a small copse. Brandon walked towards it. "Cochrane's body is over here."

Blake and Craille bent down to look at the dead man as the superintendent drew back the sheet which covered the body. The cruel brown stain over the heart left no room for doubt as to the cause of death.

"He was shot with his own revolver at a range of not more than four feet," Brandon observed grimly. "We found the gun down there." He indicated the spot. "We know it was his because we've checked the serial number against the Firearms' Register. And we know the range was not more than four feet by the nature of the powder burns on his clothing."

"Good work," Blake commented.

"Now let me tell you what we know," Brandon said.

He moved. "Tracks lead out here from the house." He lifted a strip of canvas to show them. "Cochrane's and De Trafford's coming out—we've checked their shoes with the prints; De Trafford's alone going back, and it seems he wasn't walking back—he was staggering."

He straightened up.

He said: "The two men came out from the house together. Their footprints show that they walked side by side. They reached this point here"—his finger stabbed down, he stood near Cochrane's body—"and here they stopped for a while. A few minutes. Their footprints show that, too. They are fractionally, but measurably, deeper."

Blake nodded. "And then what?"

"Then," said Brandon, "Cochrane was shot with his own gun. Exactly what I think happened I'll go into later, but, for the moment, just take a look at these footprints here."

He bent down again, pointing.

"De Trafford's. A confusion of prints. Deep impressions. Seems he started for the house—running or very angry—and then after barely a couple of steps changed his mind. What do you make, of that, eh?"

Blake shook his head slowly, not speaking.

"Well, I'll tell you what I make of it—later," Brandon said. "But right now you can see that from the footprints alone it's pretty plain that De Trafford was the eye-witness I said he

43

was. I'd class it as a stone-cold certainty he was out here when Cochrane was shot."

Blake said quietly, "You think he shot Cochrane himself, don't you?"

The superintendent didn't answer immediately. He was nodding to the stretcher party to take the body away.

Then he turned back to Blake and Craille again. "That's the general idea," he admitted. Then he added slowly, "There's just one very odd factor in the whole set-up out here that I can't explain. Everything else fits, but this—"

He stopped. He levelled his torch. The beam slashed out over the ground. It pointed away from the spot where Cochrane's body had lain.

"See them—?" the superintendent said. "Slight disturbances of the grass, leading out from the spot where we found Cochrane's body. They lead out and then stop. One of the two men must have made them, but which one—and why? Where was he going? See—?"

Blake and Craille followed the torch-beam. The wet grass was bruised as if by large, soft carpet-slippers rather than shoes. Brandon commented on this. "That's another thing I don't understand!" The trail petered out after leading to a small screen of trees some yards away.

Blake cast around, puzzled. Then he caught his breath. "Shine the torch here a moment, superintendent."

"Why, what have you found?"

Blake had gone through the belt of trees, and was kneeling. Brandon reached him quickly.

The torch beam showed up a shallow, rounded depression in the ground, such as might have been made by some weighty spherical object of about two feet in diameter resting there for a short time.

Blake said: "Now what do you make of that? Whatever it

was, it didn't stay there long."

He borrowed the torch and shone it over the surrounding ground. Its beam moved . . . froze . . . moved again . . . froze again. "Come over here," said Blake.

He showed the superintendent and Craille a second, similar depression. "And here. . ." A third. His grey-blue eyes had a challenging look about them as he stared at his companions.

He moved again then, abruptly, to pace out the distances between the depressions. He returned to his starting point.

He looked first at Brandon, and then at Craille.

"Equal distances—of five yards," he said. "A perfect equilateral triangle. Now what are we on to?"

NOBODY ATTEMPTED AN answer. For a very long moment all three men were equally thoughtful. Then Brandon moved, breaking the spell.

"Whatever it was," he decided, "I can't see that it had any connection with Cochrane's death."

A Detective-Inspector came up at that moment, was introduced, and murmured to the superintendent that his presence was required back at the house. The brain specialist had finished his examination of Oliver de Trafford.

"I've got to go,' said Brandon.

"We'll come with you," Blake told him.

As they walked back over the meadow and through the gateway in the high wall, the superintendent summed up his suspicions. "I still think De Trafford killed Cochrane. And he's either badly shaken up by what he did, or he's shamming. We'll soon know."

"But what was his motive?" Blake asked.

"Trouble over the girl," Brandon said briefly.

Blake raised an inquiring eyebrow. "His sister?"

"Stranger things have happened. I had some inquiries made

before you arrived, and they disclosed a very close relationship between De Trafford and this sister of his. Unhealthy, if you ask me. There could have been insane jealousy. Dorcas de Trafford was here a lot when Cochrane was ill recently."

"As his nurse," Blake pointed out.

The policeman said simply: "Yes." But there was a volume of meaning in the inflection he gave the monosyllable.

Blake, thinking hard, said "You told us you had an explanation for that confusion of footprints where De Trafford was standing."

Brandon nodded. "I have. It's elementary. Cochrane and De Trafford went out there. They stood by the trees and they started arguing over the girl. Cochrane said something that made De Trafford mad—really mad—hopping mad. He made a threatening movement towards Cochrane. Cochrane produced his gun, and told him to get the hell out of it. De Trafford turned to go—what else could he do?—but then Cochrane had to sneer something after him. Those words were his warrant. De Trafford whirled around, somehow gained possession of the gun, and shot Cochrane with it. Then, aghast at what he'd done, he stumbled back to the house."

"It is elementary," Blake said, "and you could probably build quite a nice prosecution on it, but for one thing. That bit 'somehow he gained possession of the gun.' You'll have to do better than that. Defence counsel would drive a coach and horses through it."

Brandon was grim-faced.

"Don't think I don't know it. If it wasn't for that I'd have already formally charged Oliver Trafford with Cochrane's murder. But I'm working on it. Just give me time."

Craille, who had been walking silently, deep in thought, rasped, "Who reported the shooting?"

"Cochrane's housekeeper, sir. But she didn't actually discover the body. She heard the shot, didn't think much about it . . . then De Trafford came stumbling in, acting crazy, and scaring her stiff. He explained nothing—was in no state to—but the fact that Cochrane wasn't with him was enough. She 'phoned us. We discovered the body."

Craille nodded. "Did she see anyone else around, or hear anything other than the shot?"

The policeman glanced at him quickly. He said: "She didn't see anybody. But around the time that Cochrane and De Trafford went out into the grounds, she heard a humming. It could have been a freak of the wind—if there'd been any. But there wasn't a breath of it at that time." He eyed Craille curiously. "How did you know about that, sir?"

"Never mind. Go on."

"Well, sir, that's all there was to it. She heard this sound, but it soon went. But it gave her a bit of a headache, almost, she said, as if she was in for the 'flu. She was light-headed with it."

"She's still got the headache? She still feels light-headed?" Craille wanted to know.

"No, sir. It passed off. It left her after the sound died away."

The old man said "Ah . . ." in apparent satisfaction, and then closed up like a clam.

THE BRAIN AND nerve specialist from Stoke Mandeville Hospital was a short, elderly man inclining to corpulence. Normally, as almost a matter of policy, he wore a bland, professionally reassuring smile. But the smile had vanished abruptly when he had joined the police surgeon in Lewis Cochrane's warm, comfortable study and seen the wreck that was Oliver de Trafford.

He had dragged in a sharp, shocked breath. "What on earth has happened to this man?"

It was a question Craille and Blake were to echo when they

entered the study with Brandon a little while later.

They saw the journalist twisted almost into a knot in an easy chair. He was half sitting, half crouching, his body curled over the right, his small head hunched between high-raised shoulder-blades. His contorted, glassy-eyed face was slewed round, so that he looked sideways and up. His hands were down by his sides, one fist clenched as though with cramp, the other hand bent back with its fingers splayed out.

He seemed frozen in that position, every fibre and sinew iron-stiff. A groaning, moaning noise came from him which, every few moments, climbed to a crescendo and broke into a babble of meaningless syllables, only to die away again to a frightened whimper.

The specialist looked grim.

He told Brandon, "This man has to be hospitalised."

"He's genuinely in a state of shock, then? He's not malingering?"

"Malingering?" the specialist barked on a high note of sheer incredulity. "Great heavens, man! Just take a look at him!" With an obvious effort he brought his voice under control. He said: "Are there any relatives here?"

Brandon told him.

The specialist considered briefly. Then: "Sister, eh? Well it might help . . . if she can stand the sight of him. Get her in."

The superintendent gave a swift order, and bare seconds later Dorcas de Trafford entered the room.

Her nerves were on edge from the long time she'd been kept waiting, and she was trembling. The specialist took her gently by the hand and steadied her as her horrified eyes fell on the contorted creature deep in the chair.

"Go to him, my dear. Speak to him."

A tremor gripped Oliver de Trafford's tortured body. He tried to look at her. His eyes pleaded.

She dropped on her knees by the side of the chair, and took one twisted hand in hers. She uttered soothing, gentle, loving words in a voice which threatened to break at any moment under the near-unbearable pressure of her inner anguish. A sick, animal noise was drawn from the stricken man as he desperately tried to respond, and Dorcas De Trafford did break down then. She sobbed uncontrollably.

Quickly, Blake reached her side. He helped her to her feet. He held her, and calmed her. He took her out of the room. When he returned alone, some moments later, he spoke to the specialist in a voice cold with anger. "Was that little experiment really necessary, doctor?"

The other man's face darkened.

Craille saw all the signs of a first-class storm in the offing, and was quick to intervene. "Just what is wrong with De Trafford, doctor?"

The specialist's mouth tightened.

"Advanced mental shock . . . brain damage." He turned his back on Blake deliberately, and now spoke only to Craille and Brandon. "I've seen similar, but not so severe, cases where men have been accidentally exposed to ultrasonic radiation."

"What—!"

This from the superintendent. The specialist drew himself up.

"Gentlemen, in some way this man's brain has been virtually scrambled!"

"What—!"

It was Brandon again, incredulous and utterly bewildered.

THE FIFTH CHAPTER

No time to live.

COCHRANE'S CORPSE HAD been taken away in one ambulance, and another had come for the specialist and the shattered thing that had once been Oliver de Trafford, successful journalist and chronicler of flying saucers.

West Towers was still full of police.

Craille and Blake paced the private road, where the dark night gave them some semblance of privacy. Blake said harshly, "What in the name of Creation actually happened tonight?"

"There's always the superintendent's theory to fall back on," Craille suggested.

"It's bunk!" said Blake.

Craille stopped walking. He said slowly, "As far as I can see there's only one alternative to it that will fit all the facts."

Blake thrust his hands deep into his trouser pockets and looked up at the black velvet sky. "I suppose so. But the mind jibs a bit at accepting it."

Craille waited, and Blake continued: "I know what you think. You think that something struck at De Trafford tonight— deliberately subjecting him to a brain-scrambling treatment.

Some *thing*—" he carefully separated the words "—employing an ultrasonic beam as a weapon. The idea is fantastic—and inhuman."

"It's that all right!" Craille resumed pacing. "But, think, Blake! I believe that Cochrane had inside information on something. Maybe flying saucers—De Trafford's pet subject. The information was real, genuine, twenty-two carat, and somehow De Trafford got wind of it. After that, he wanted his share, and he bothered and badgered and kept after Cochrane until he got it.

"That made Cochrane a traitor to whatever cause he was serving, and he was liquidated as a traitor in the time-honoured way. De Trafford, being merely an outsider with a certain amount of dangerous knowledge, had his brain scrambled so that he couldn't pass on what he'd learned. Does that make sense, Blake?"

"It does indeed!" Sexton Blake nodded in time to his stride. "It makes a lot of sense. The spherical depression in the grass— they could well have been made by the landing gear of some saucer-like aircraft. The humming heard by the housekeeper . . . her headache and lightheadedness . . . she could have been on the fringe of the ultrasonic beam that struck at De Trafford. But if these things are possible, what in God's name are we up against? *Who*, and what?"

Craille chuckled drily, almost unpleasantly.

"You are excellent at stating problems, my friend. You've got this one in a nutshell, and it's all yours—if you'll take it."

The detective's mouth twisted wryly. "You wouldn't even ask me if you had any doubts." He squared his shoulders. "Right. So we need a starting point. Well, that's easily found. Plainly, we start with Cochrane himself. If he was liquidated as a traitor, he must have been working for the people—creatures— or whatever they were that killed him. To work for them, he must have had some means of maintaining contact with them. To find out how this was done is our first aim.

"So—" he continued "—it's back to the house, I think. And if we find nothing there, we'll have to probe into Cochrane's associations." His eyes narrowed thoughtfully. "He was a Foreign Office official, and a high-ranking one. We could rub up against some very big names."

"That—" Craille said precisely "—is precisely what worries me." He gestured. "I mean—we don't know what the hell is going on, except that it's considered important enough to kill for, and we don't know who is involved. We could have some nasty surprises."

His voice was grim.

"The sooner we can get away from theories and establish some facts about what's going on and the people concerned in it, the better I'll be pleased—so let's get started. Back to the house! And don't let's forget that it's possible Dorcas de Trafford could give us a lead of some sort if she wanted. She could know much more than she's told us."

"Yes . . . " Blake said reflectively.

TWENTY MINUTES LATER, all the police had gone from West Towers except for a constable patrolling the grounds and, before leaving, Superintendent Brandon had satisfied the housekeeper that it was in order for Blake and Craille and Dorcas de Trafford to stay for a while. The two men occupied the next forty minutes in searching the house.

They looked for evidence of Cochrane's contact with whatever organisation he might have been working for, and also for something to give them a lead as to how that contact had been maintained. But they found nothing. Nothing at all. It was very galling.

They returned to the drawing-room. There remained the

outbuildings to be thoroughly searched. But first to see what Dorcas de Trafford knew . . .

Craille held out his long bony fingers to the fire's warmth. He glanced up at the young woman, and his brittle voice took on an unexpectedly sympathetic quality, as though he were now using fine instead of coarse grade sandpaper for vocal cords.

"The specialist told me there's a good chance of curing your brother—with the right hospital treatment." Blake knew that this was just the old man's guile. The specialist had said no such thing.

"But to arrive at the right treatment," Craille continued cannily, "the medical authorities have got to know exactly what happened to him. That's where we—and you—can possibly help."

Dorcas de Trafford said nothing, and Craille cleared his throat. It was a sign that he had now finished sparring. He put the question bluntly. "You were in your brother's confidence, weren't you?"

"To some extent—yes."

"And what information had Cochrane given him about flying saucers?"

"Information? What information could Lewis have possibly given him?" She derided the very idea. "Oliver just used to air his opinions. Lewis would laugh at them and call them cranky."

"Young woman—" Craille said dangerously "—don't hedge with me!"

"I'm not hedging," she protested. "It's true!"

But, plainly, Craille didn't believe her. He rasped, "You'd be well advised to answer my questions honestly. We haven't got all night! And you're not protecting anyone by being evasive— least of all your so-called brother!"

She was suddenly very pale. The colour drained from her face. She stared at him. "What exactly did you mean by that last remark?"

"You know very well what I meant," Craille told her grimly. "You're not fooling me—not one little bit. I checked up on you some time ago."

His voice was hard.

"So let's get down to bedrock, shall we? Absolute bedrock. Absolute truth. I'll start the ball rolling. And the first item of absolute truth is—you've been lying to us all along about your relationship with Oliver de Trafford. He isn't your brother at all!"

SEXTON BLAKE WAS startled. This was a prime piece of knowledge which Craille had kept strictly to himself until now.

But— surprised as the detective was—he didn't show it. Dorcas de Trafford, however, lacked his strict self -control.

Her hand had leapt to her mouth, stifling a cry. Now, deathly pale, she gazed numbly at the old man as he went on: "You're first cousins, that's what you are. And you've been mutually attracted for years. But until you yourself reach the age of thirty, marriage to your cousin is out of the question, however much you might desire it—unless you're willing to forfeit a sizeable inheritance under your late father's will. At the age of thirty you come into one hundred and fifty thousand pounds— but only if you haven't married Cousin Oliver by that time.

"Your father held very definite views on the undesirability of first cousins marrying. I've also been led to believe he held equally decided views on the undesirability of Cousin Oliver." Craille said it dryly. "Not that you've let what your father thought influence you in the slightest.

"Both you and Oliver were determined to have your cake and eat it—to have each other and the inheritance. And, between you, you've managed to defeat the spirit of the interdict, if not its actual letter. But" —Craille's thin shoulders moved— "society has certain conventions which have to be given a show of respect, and so, for some time, being together, you and Oliver have been posing as brother and sister. Isn't that the truth of it—the whole truth?"

There was really no need for Dorcas de Trafford to voice an answer.

It was there, plain to see, writ large on her face. Blake saw it, and Craille himself saw it, and nodded.

And his voice softened.

"You see, my dear . . . ? I know your secret. And I'm not judging you. Don't think it. Frankly, I don't consider it any of my business what you and Cousin Oliver have been up to. But what he and Lewis Cochrane got up to—ah! That's quite a different kettle of fish! That I must know, and you're going to tell me! I want it all—the whole story—the lot! And I mean to have it! I warn you, I'll hound the life out of you until you do tell!"

The old man meant what he said, and Dorcas de Trafford realised it. She sighed.

Then: "All right," she said in a very small voice. "All right . . ."

And Craille leaned forward expectantly.

SEXTON BLAKE WATCHED and listened intently as the old man drew the story out of the girl.

She told of Oliver de Trafford's first meeting with Lewis Cochrane at the cocktail party she'd mentioned earlier—a casual affair.

But it had instantly ceased to be casual for her cousin when, talking to Cochrane on his favourite subject, he had suddenly realised with gripping excitement that here was a man who actually knew something about flying saucers. A man who knew something he himself did not know.

The discovery had turned on the smallest of things: the tone of voice in which Cochrane had made some of his seemingly amused observations. But De Trafford, as a competent, trained journalist, able to detect and interpret the slightest, smallest nuances of speech, had been absolutely certain that he was right.

Cochrane did know something! He had information about the saucers so far denied to himself!

From that moment, Oliver de Trafford had been determined to share the other man's knowledge, and he had tried to worm the facts out of him. But without success.

Then Cochrane had fallen ill with a severe bout of influenza which had left him very weak, and De Trafford had cunningly switched his line of attack. Now he had offered the Foreign Office man the trained services of Dorcas as a temporary private nurse, and Cochrane had been touched by this apparently disinterested act of friendship and had accepted. The other man had been secretly jubilant. He had a plan to make Cochrane talk, and this was a part of it. The foot in the door.

Craille said: "And did Cousin Oliver finally persuade Cochrane to tell him what he wanted to know?"

"Yes . . ." She said it unwillingly.

"How?" Craille asked sharply, and then shot at her: "By having you feed him drugs to loosen his tongue?"

The old man had guessed it, and she had to admit it. She did so miserably. "Yes."

Craille's thin lips tightened. "And what was this information Cochrane possessed?"

She moved uneasily. "He—he said a flying saucer base had been established somewhere in the Arctic."

"Did he say who had established it?"

"I—I don't know."

"The truth!" Craille snapped. "I want the truth!"

Her hands twisted one over the other. "That is the truth. I—I wasn't very happy about what Oliver had got me to do. I—I knew I shouldn't have done it—drugged Lewis—I—I didn't want to hear what he said. I left the room as soon as I could. I wanted no part in what Oliver was doing."

Craille said grimly: "A bit late for scruples, wasn't it? Your part had already been played."

She didn't answer, and Craille eyed her expressionlessly for a moment. "So you heard only a fragment of what Cochrane said under the drug's influence. You didn't hear all of it . . ." Then: "But Cousin Oliver must have made notes of what Cochrane said. If not at the time, then immediately afterwards. What happened to them?"

"They're in—in his safe deposit, I think. The key to the box is held by his solicitors."

Craille nodded. "At last we're getting somewhere. But there's something else—Cochrane himself. How did he seem while you were nursing him? I mean was he cheerful, depressed, or what?"

"He was tense and nervous."

"Making it easy for you to get him to accept the drug willingly," Craille said shrewdly. "I suppose you told him it was something to help him relax?"

"Yes . . ." She admitted it unhappily.

Craille eyed her again. "Tense and nervous, eh . . . ? As though something was weighing on his mind?"

"Yes."

"Something, perhaps, that he should have attended to—some duty that he'd neglected?"

"Yes . . . yes, I think so. Something like that could have made him the way he was."

Craille leaned back, pursing his lips with evident satisfaction. "Just one more question," he said, "but an important one. Think carefully before you answer. Did Cochrane keep to his room all the time he was ill?"

"Why, no . . ." She looked quickly at the old man. "As a matter of fact there was one occasion when—although he shouldn't even have been up out of bed—he insisted on leaving the house to go to his workshop"—she gestured—"out there, in one of the outbuildings."

"Did he now . . . ?" Craille was very interested. "Why? Did he give you a reason?"

"He said he'd left something there. Something he wanted. I tried to make him go back to bed, but he became almost violent. I had to let him go in the end, though he was so weak he could hardly walk."

"He wouldn't let you get this thing for him, whatever it was?"

"Oh, no!"

"Have you any idea what it was?"

Dorcas de Trafford shook her head slowly. "Just that it must have been something very important. Getting it seemed like a matter of life and death to him. I mean—"

But there she broke off, jerking upright, tense with nerves.

Sharply and suddenly, without warning, someone had flung open the door of the room.

THEY STARED, ALL of them, Craille and Blake and Dorcas de Trafford. But the man who stood in the doorway seemed harmless enough. He was about forty, with a pleasant round face, thick straw-coloured hair, an equally straw-coloured luxuriant moustache, and light blue eyes. He was dressed in a black overcoat, and he'd a bowler hat by his side in a pale, podgy hand.

Under the combined scrutiny of three pairs of eyes he shifted uneasily, and showed signs of considerable embarrassment.

"I say—I'm most dreadfully sorry. I was looking for Lewis. I thought he might be in here. Usually is. I just breezed round to collect my car pump, y'know. Didn't mean to intrude. I—"

"How"—Craille interrupted mildly enough—"did you get in?"

"Uh—?" For a moment the round face was blank. Then comprehension dawned in the light blue eyes. "Oh, I say—I see what you mean. Bit of a shock for you, eh? Me arriving unannounced. Sorry and all that. Lewis isn't here then, I take it. Where's he gone? Up to Town for the evening? You're relatives, I suppose. Staying here, are you? Lovely place Lewis has got. Lovely! Me, I'm a neighbour—well—sort of. Name's Lockwood. Have a house over the other side of this parkland of Lewis's. Always come over that way. Across the jolly old park, through the garden, and in through the rear door. It's always left open. Never bother the housekeeper. Lewis's own idea, actually. When will he be back?"

Craille said, still mildly. "He won't be. And we're not relatives."

"Good Lord! Y'don't mean to say Lewis has sold the jolly old place! You're the new owners? Why, he said nothing to me when he borrowed my car pump, and that was only a couple of days ago. Bit sudden, wasn't it?"

"It was sudden all right," Craille agreed, "but Cochrane hasn't sold up and gone away in the accepted sense. You see— he's dead."

"Dead—?" The man's jaw dropped. "Good Lord! What— old Lewis? Good Lord!"

Then: "What was it? Heart attack, I suppose. There's a lot of 'em about, and he was a big man, heavy man—"

"He was shot," said Craille.

"Shot—! Good L—" But before Lockwood could say it, Craille was going on. "And that's all I can tell you at the moment, I'm afraid. The police have taken his body away. This gentleman"—he indicated Blake—"and myself are—um— connected with them in their investigations. This young lady,

Miss de Trafford, was a friend of Cochrane's. If you're another, I've no doubt the police will want to ask you some questions later."

"Yes, of course. Help in any way I can. But—shot! Old Lewis! Fantastic! Accident, I suppose, but still . . . I didn't even know he had a gun. Not the huntin', shootin', and fishin' type at all, y'know. How exactly did it happen?"

Craille hesitated a moment. "I really oughtn't discuss it. My instructions from the police superintendent were very clear . . ." Still he hesitated, then said, "But I don't suppose it can do any harm for you to know . . ."

His eyes shifted to Blake.

He said: "I suggest you and Miss de Trafford carry on where we left off . . . while I'm talking to Mr. Lockwood."

Blake nodded, and stood up. He knew what Craille meant. He was to take a look at Cochrane's workshop while Lockwood was being kept out of the way.

He took Dorcas de Trafford's arm as she rose from her chair, and together they left the study. A few minutes later, they were crossing a cobblestoned yard at the back of the house.

It was dark in the yard: black as pitch except for a thin slit of light that knifed the night from an imperfectly curtained window in the housekeeper's quarters. Outbuildings hemmed the yard in. A thin drizzle fell. It was cold.

"This is the one," said Dorcas de Trafford, and gripped Blake's arm. "This was Lewis's workshop."

They came to a halt before a long, low single-storied structure with four square windows, two on either side of a central door. It was a door which the detective now opened. It wasn't locked. A strong, sweet odour of varnish and lacquer greeted them as Blake felt around for a light-switch.

He found one; thumbed it down. Lights sprang on overhead illuminating an interior filled with benches, machines, stacks of timber, and chairs and cabinets in various stages of completion. Shavings littered the floor.

One of Blake's eyebrows lifted as he looked around. "Well equipped," he commented. "More like a small factory than just a workshop."

And it was—giving him something to think about.

Dorcas de Trafford said: "Furniture-making was Lewis's hobby, and he took it seriously."

But, privately, Blake had already reached the conclusion that this superlatively equipped place needed rather more justification than that.

He moved around, examining the machines carefully. His expression became more and more thoughtful. Finally he stopped before a door at the far end of the workshop. He tried it. It was locked.

He said: "Any idea what's in here?"

Dorcas de Trafford shook her head. "I've never either been inside or seen inside. I suppose it's some kind of storeroom."

"Hmm. . ." Blake eyed the door very closely. He tapped it with a bent knuckle. "Maybe . . ."

Then his gaze crept down the face of the door to the floor below and suddenly he stiffened.

"What's the matter?" his companion asked curiously. "What is it?" she wanted to know as Blake bent down swiftly.

He straightened up with a few wood shavings in the palm of his hand. "Take a look," he invited, and now a strange note had entered his voice.

She looked. "Well—?" She was puzzled. They were just wood shavings. A little grubby perhaps, where someone had stepped on them—but still only wood shavings. The floor was littered with them, and she said so.

"But these are *wet*," said Blake.

And now, looking closer, she could see what his sharp eyes

had seen already: muddy smears of moisture drying quickly.

He bent down again. "And this one's the same." He had drawn another shaving out from directly under the locked door.

"Someone else has been here—and very recently. Someone to whom the lock on the door presented no problems."

"But—but who—?" the girl asked.

Blake didn't answer her. He was still crouched in front of the door, but now his attitude was a stiff, unnatural one. It was as though he had just fastened on the smallest, the faintest of sounds, and was straining to hear it again.

Then, suddenly, he was up on his feet. He whirled around. He was up on his feet, and running, and dragging the young woman with him. "What—?" she gasped. She never completed the question.

But in the instant that Blake threw her down behind a bench and flung his body across hers—a living shield—she never-the-less had an answer.

A muffled roar shook the room behind the locked door, building up instantaneously into an ear-shocking explosion as the pressure wave blew the door out.

There was an answering crash as part of the outer wall, torn bodily away, was blasted halfway across the yard.

The shock wave slammed across the workshop with hurricane force. It bulldozed everything in its path. It hit Blake and Dorcas and flattened them to the floor. It held them pinned there as the room disintegrated around them.

Windows shattered outwards in a million screaming fragments. Machines and benches and cabinets lifted, swung round, and toppled. Half-finished furniture was reduced in a trice to so much matchwood.

And then, with a sickening crash, the roof collapsed.

THE SIXTH CHAPTER

Against the unknown.

AFTER THE TUMULT of sound came silence.

An echoing, aching silence which hurt Blake's ears.

This was the very first thing he was aware of as he struggled back to consciousness.

Dust was caked thick on his face, covering his eyes. He fingered it away, blinking as he did so. It stung like pepper.

There was a weight on his back, pinning him down. Only feet away from him an electric light bulb still burned, incredibly intact amid the heaped wreckage of the roof timbers. A planing machine jutted up out of the debris, poised at a crazy angle, slanting across his field of vision.

Blake blinked again.

He was half-flung across something soft and warm—something that moved. As his senses returned, he realised it was the girl. A shuddering sigh escaped her now. She was recovering consciousness, too.

Blake braced himself against the weight that pressed heavily down upon him. With an effort, he turned over on to his side. Now he could see what the weight represented.

It was part of a bench, and a wall had collapsed to heap its bricks over one end of it. Carefully, Blake levered himself out from under it, supporting its weight all the time. On his feet, he dragged the bench to one side to free Dorcas de Trafford as she opened her eyes.

"What happened?" she said faintly.

Blake grinned briefly. A twisted grin. "Them's classic words! Let's not worry about what happened for the moment—are you all right?"

She moved, sat up, clasped her slim hands to her ears, and shook her head violently. She dropped her hands. "I think so. Bruised, battered—"

"But all right."

"Yes. Nothing broken. You saved me. You shielded me. Thank you."

He helped her up. When she saw the full extent of the desolation and ruin around them, she gasped. "What on earth—?"

"It was a bomb of some sort," Blake said grimly. "In the locked room. I heard the slightest, smallest sound—a ticking. And then it stopped. We were lucky to get as far as we did."

"Lucky to still be alive!" the girl said, and shivered. She looked across the rubble to where the locked room had been. It had vanished utterly; completely. It no longer existed.

And then her head turned sharply. Out of the darkness and into the thin, dim light two men came running.

The men were Lockwood and Craille, and as they panted up Blake thrust an arm around Dorcas de Trafford and helped her over and out of the ruins of what had been a very fine workshop. Craille greeted him with grim humour. "What've you been up to now, Blake?"

The detective ached in every bone, every joint. He jerked out: "What have I been up to? You should ask—" but there he broke off abruptly, second thoughts curbing his tongue. He waved a bruised arm. "I think that was where Cochrane kept the thing we were looking for, but a time-bomb beat us to it."

In the background, Lockwood looked stupefied. Craille moved quickly in the direction Blake had indicated. He stopped short where the locked room had been. "Here?"

"Yes."

The old man sniffed sharply; once, twice, head up, thin nostrils quivering. "Nitro-glycerine." Then he stopped and raked about the rubble.

His fingers fastened on scraps of wire and fragments of twisted metal. He found a small audio transformer, and some other bits and pieces that Blake recognised.

"Radio," the detective said quietly. "And neither you nor I imagine it to have been a hi-fi set-up."

Craille needn't have said it, but he did. "A transmitter-receiver, of course."

And then Lockwood and Dorcas de Trafford came up. Lockwood was still looking stupefied. "What a mess!"

"Yes, isn't it?" Blake returned, and then his voice hardened dramatically.

"You should be very proud of yourself, Mr. Lockwood—doing all this with one little bomb!"

"WHAT—?"

For a long second, the man just gaped at the detective, shock forcing the blood from his face.

Beside him, Dorcas de Trafford drew in a quick, ragged breath and held it. In the shadows behind Blake, Craille was suddenly very watchful, very still.

"A first-class piece of demolition," Blake told Lockwood bleakly. "Too bad you're not going to get away with it!"

Then the other man recovered. He began to bluster. "What the hell are you talking about?"

"You know damn well!" Blake rejoined grimly. "You planted that bomb before you came into the house!"

"Me—? Why—why you're crazy!" Lockwood appealed to Craille and Dorcas De Trafford. "He doesn't know what he's saying!"

"I know this," Blake said. "I found the muddy imprint of part of a rubber-soled shoe on some shavings in the workshop just before the big bang came. It was a man's shoe. And you're the only man wearing rubber soles around here tonight."

"The only man you know of—maybe," Lockwood got out. "But that doesn't prove anything!"

It was true.

But suspicions were very real, and he had a plan for deciding once and for all which Lockwood was; innocent or guilty.

He jerked his head towards Craille.

"We don't have to prove anything," he told Lockwood harshly. "Not at this stage. Suspicion's enough. I think we'll hand both you and my suspicions over to the police!"

He started to move towards the other man threateningly.

"There's a constable in the grounds. He could hardly have failed to have heard the explosion. He'll be here at any moment. And I'm pretty sure we can persuade him to take you in charge. I'm also pretty sure that my suspicions will be confirmed after a thorough search of your house!"

It was almost all bluff. A colossal bluff. And Blake held his breath. How was Lockwood going to act?

He didn't have to go on wondering long!

For Lockwood swallowed the bluff. All of it. He believed it—and showed his true colours. Sudden panic whipped at him. It was plain on his face. Still Blake advanced on him.

"Keep back!"

But Blake wasn't going to obey.

"Keep back!" Lockwood jerked into action, screaming the

words. A gun leapt into his hand. "Back, damn you!"

And Blake hurled himself forward.

He had been holding himself poised, tense and ready for just such a moment as this. He threw himself at Lockwood. The gun exploded.

But Lockwood had had no time to level it. Blake had given him no such opportunity. The bullet went wide, howling away through the night, and the next instant Blake had chopped the weapon out of the other man's hand.

Then Lockwood was running.

He wrenched away desperately, eluding immediate capture. He plunged across the cobblestoned yard. And Blake went after him. Out of the yard, around the house, and across the dark garden Lockwood ran, with Blake hard on his heels.

Proof—? What more proof of Lockwood's guilt did Blake need than this? His plan had worked. He crammed on a burst of speed to overtake the fleeing man, to grapple with him, and to shake the truth out of him. Who was he working for? Who had Cochrane been working for? What had really happened to Oliver de Trafford? What had scrambled his brain? Why had Cochrane been killed?

Pounding through the night, only feet behind Lockwood now, able to hear every ragged, rasping breath the man dragged into his lungs as he ran, Blake was grimly convinced that once he'd got to grips with him he'd wrest the answers to these questions from him, and more—many more.

But he never did.

Plunging through the tall, dark gateway from garden to night-shrouded meadow-land, the detective slipped on greasy mud, skidded, and fell. He was sprawled on the ground for only a moment, just a few savagely short seconds, but in that time the incredible happened. The utterly incredible. He saw it!

Lockwood was running—running—running like a madman—

away from him over the meadow when, suddenly, joltingly, he stopped dead in his tracks. Fantastically, for a split second, it was just as if he'd smashed into an invisible wall. And then—

Then there was a blazing flash of electric blue light. Blake was momentarily near-blinded by it. Lockwood was held by it. He was transfixed, contorted, in dense black outline, by the brief, searing brilliance. A scream was torn from him. And then—he vanished!

Blake leapt to his feet. He raced forward.

But where Lockwood had been only a fraction of a second before, there was now only a sick, sweet smell of incinerated human flesh on the damp night air. That, and a bald, charred, circle of earth, and a tiny heap of fine ash.

It was impossible—but it had happened.

Craille arrived by Blake's side just half a minute later. He had seen it, too. Lockwood had been utterly destroyed!

The wind stirred the fine ash, and scattered it, and Craille's amber eyes stabbed the dark night all around.

"What are we up against, Blake? What devilish, inhuman thing are we trying to fight?"

For the first time in his life, Blake heard the old man's voice tremble.

THE SEVENTH CHAPTER

Where in the world . . . ?

FOUR HOURS LATER, the false dawn laid its leaden light over the rooftops to the east of London's Belgrave Square, and beyond the thick curtains at the windows of Craille's paper jungle—through an atmosphere grey with the smoke of innumerable aromatic Egyptian cigarettes—Sexton Blake eyed the old man sharply as he returned a telephone to its rest.

"Good news?" he demanded.

Craille rubbed his skeletal hands together—a dry, rasping sound—and nodded slowly. "Pretty good. We seem to be making some progress."

"Tell me," said Blake.

Quite a lot of progress had already been made in the past four hours.

After the last incredible happening in the meadow at West Towers—after the complete and utter disintegration of Lockwood—Craille had recalled the police.

But this time he had summoned Special Branch men, a host of them armed with wide emergency powers, and a more than thorough search of Lockwood's house had followed. And a rare find—after the Special Branch men had practically taken the building apart!

The find had been a notebook small in size but great in the potential significance of some numbers inked on to a page. The numbers represented radio frequencies of an order of megacycles never employed for commercial transmissions, and the care and considerable cunning with which the notebook had been hidden betrayed the importance Lockwood had attached to it.

Could the radio frequencies represent channels of communication between the disintegrated man and his erstwhile employers?

Both Blake and Craille had thought so, and what had subsequently happened had seemed to confirm this belief. Craille had straightway phoned the suspect frequencies through to the Intelligence radio monitor station at Bagshot with instructions that a close watch be kept on these channels, and almost immediately the monitor station had begun to report results.

Encoded messages were being intercepted. Messages which the monitor station's sensitive direction-finding equipment plotted as emanating from Iceland.

Craille and Blake had looked at each other.

The messages had ceased after a while, cutting off abruptly, seemingly in mid-transmission, as though the senders had somehow discovered that they were being monitored. All the circumstances had been highly significant and suspicious—but that was all that Blake knew so far.

For, at that point, Craille had announced his intention of immediately returning to London and his own private nerve-centre in Belgrave Square, and he had asked Blake to escort Dorcas de Trafford safely home and then to rejoin him there. This Blake had just done—to find the old man busy with the telephone and looking passably pleased with himself as he set the instrument down.

"Go on—tell me your good news," the detective insisted now.

The old man leaned back and lit a cigarette with some deliberation. "I've just been on to Peters. You remember him? Perhaps I should have told you this earlier. He's the man I've had in Iceland for months."

"Go on," said Blake, nodding.

He certainly remembered Peters. Working for Craille, they had been thrown together more than once in the past. On two separate occasions, each had saved the life of the other. Honours were even—so far. What did the future hold?

"Go on . . ."

Craille exhaled with maddening slowness.

"As I told you earlier," he said, "for some time there's been a strong suspicion that a flying saucer base has been established in Iceland, but, needless to say, Peters has not been able to locate it, try as he might. If he had, the problem wouldn't be occupying us now.

"However," his amber eyes narrowed as he regarded Blake thoughtfully, "as the man on the spot Peters can say, realistically, where such a base might best be sited, taking into account what he knows at first-hand about the island—its geography, its people, its climate—all the local conditions."

"And—?" Blake said bluntly.

Craille gave him a wintery smile. He rummaged under a heap of documents to find a large-scale map of part of the Arctic regions. He spread it out and pointed with a bony forefinger, circling the fingertip round.

"Here, in the Greenland Sea, north of Jan Mayen, is a huge uncharted area," he said. "Ships go nowhere near it—it's covered with ice for most of the year. In the past, an occasional trawler has ventured that way, and some have been lost with all hands. There are rocks, reefs, and maybe the ridge of a sunken volcanic range, perhaps even a small island or two. The area is linked with the Arctic volcanic chain of which Iceland and Jan Mayen are a part. Aircraft avoid it: it's permanently covered by vast mists and fog. Besides, with the many better routes that exist, it's unnecessary to go near it. Because it's uncharted, avoided, a ghost sea, Peters believes it would make an ideal secret base."

Blake nodded thoughtfully. "And does Bagshot's radio fix do anything to confirm that?"

"Yes, indeed." And now Blake knew why Craille had been looking passably pleased with himself. "The bearing obtained went straight through it. I'm hoping that the transmission picked up was from the base, and not from an outpost."

Blake said slowly: "And you still think it's saucers and not—let's say—Russians?"

Craille's eyes were watchful. "I know what you think. If I told you all I believe, you might even consider me crazy. However .. . perhaps you should know this . . . it could have some bearing on the matter. Shortly after Cochrane was shot, and again after Lockwood was—uh—disintegrated, a radar station in Oxfordshire picked up a blip from the direction of Wendover. The object was unidentified, and it moved so fast that on each occasion it was gone from the radar screen almost immediately."

"Hmm . . ." Blake said reflectively. And then: "But why 'saucers'? Why 'unidentified flying objects'? Why not just 'an unknown type of aircraft'?"

The old man cracked bony knuckles. "I take your point. But the evidence for flying saucers is pretty strong, you know. Since nineteen forty-seven, when the first detailed records were started, there have been scores of reported sightings of saucers. Scores of them!"

He caught Blake's expression and added: "But, of course, the subject of flying saucers, like everything else these days, has its lunatic fringe."

He expanded his theme. "Some people have delved back into the past to associate saucers with all the mysterious, inexplicable phenomena of the ages. Some have even propounded that the burning bush of Moses was a flying saucer, and that Jacob's ladder was dropped from one. Such wild, outlandish theories have brought the whole subject into disrepute.

"The truth is that, so far, the cranks seem to have had their way to such an extent that level-headed technicians and flying men must now hesitate to report genuine sightings for fear of being thought cranks themselves. And yet the Americans maintain a vast organisation solely devoted to identifying, classifying, and tracking these things. D'you think they'd do that if, as Professor Jung has it, the flying saucer is just 'a modern myth'?"

"No . . ."

"Nor do I," the old man said. "And when you've eliminated the hoaxes, the balloons, the known types of aircraft, the hallucinations, the mirages, the birds and the meteors, and concentrated on what's left, you come inevitably to these conclusions.

"The flying saucers are real enough. They are disc-like objects capable of supersonic speeds, and possessed of amazing manoeuvrability. They are propelled by an unknown motive force. They operate both singly and in groups, and some seem to be piloted. Others are plainly under some kind of remote control.

"Sifting the reports, these are the facts, simply arrived at, but the larger questions remain unanswered. We've got to answer them, Blake! Where are the saucers coming from, and who, or what, directs their flight? I might add that, in this connection, I'm convinced that none of the major powers on this earth is responsible for the saucers, and, obviously, you can rule out the minor powers, too."

"You mean—you believe that extra-terrestrial creatures control the saucers, from an earthly base?"

"Can we rule that out?" Craille demanded. "Of course not! The affair at Kilbreck last year showed that such a thing is far from being impossible!"

"Yes, indeed." Blake nodded slowly, thinking back to those terror-filled days.[1] And then he said: "Yet the saucer people never attack . . ." and he said it almost wonderingly. "The creatures at Kilbreck had laboured under no such self-imposed restraint."

"Perhaps," Craille said soberly, "they consider their weapons so terrible that they're reluctant to use them—unless they're compelled to, as it seems they felt they were in the case of De Trafford and Lockwood."

"You could be right," Blake agreed.

"And what weapons!" Craille exclaimed. "A disintegrator and a brain scrambler! I don't mind admitting that the hellish possibilities of that unholy pair scare the living daylights out of me! Just think what the saucer people can do with them if they feel so inclined. Where's our defence against weapons like that? And these are only two items in their armoury. You can't even begin to imagine what the rest must be like!

"All right, so the saucer people haven't embarked on wholesale conquest and mass-murder—yet. But that doesn't mean that such isn't their eventual intention. What a threat to have hanging over our heads! And there's another thing that frightens me, too—

"These people seem to have some strange power to subvert men occupying positions of no little influence. Cochrane, as you know, was a highly placed official in the Foreign Office; Lockwood, I've discovered, held an equally responsible post in the Air Ministry."

Craille's voice was grim.

"Who's next, Blake? Who'll be subverted next? Who else

already has been? How far does this alien infiltration go? Where will it stop? And there's one thing more—

"Even if the saucer people have no aggressive intentions towards us, their continued presence on this planet undermines all hopes of ever establishing any kind of confidence between East and West. For despite all protestations of innocence, the Americans think the Russians responsible for the saucers, and the Russians believe that the Americans are. The sooner we can prove them both wrong—if indeed we can—the better for world peace."

"So where do we go from here?" Blake asked, but already he had a fair idea of the answer.

Craille smiled sardonically. "From here, I go nowhere. You go to Iceland. From Iceland"—the old man shrugged—"you go God knows where. Maybe by the time you've contacted Peters he'll have some more information to go on. I've an idea you'll be setting foot on terra incognita before very long. But wherever you have to go, and whatever you have to do. I want that flying saucer base located, Blake. I want it pinpointed exactly. I want all the questions we've thrown up between us answered—and another one, too. I'm curious to know if the saucer people have been responsible for the disappearance of certain top scientists over the past few years."

Blake stared at him. "You think that's possible?"

"Why not?" Craille said flatly. "Quite a few scientists have vanished without trace since nineteen forty-seven, when the first saucer was sighted. They've been men of all nations—Germans, Russians, Americans—Communist and anti-Communist alike. Where have they gone?"

"But the saucer people's technology is plainly in advance of our own," Blake said doubtfully. 'Why should they kidnap our scientists?"

"Who mentioned kidnapping?" Craille asked quietly.

"You mean—?"

"Maybe they were eliminated. Disintegrated like Lockwood, perhaps."

"But—but why?"

"I described them as 'top' scientists," Craille said. "I meant it. They undoubtedly represented some of the world's very best brains. All right"—he shrugged—"their technology hadn't advanced as far as that of the saucer people—not quite. But it might very well have done, given just a little time. Perhaps the saucer people saw them as a threat to their own superiority. It's possible, isn't it? Dammit, anything is possible! Just consider two of the missing men—Fedor Sergeyev of Russia and Murray Englefield of Britain. Brillant brains, both of them!

"Sergeyev was professor of abnormal psychology at Leningrad University—a man of international reputation. Murray Englefield was one of the backroom geniuses of the war, one of the finest scientists this country has ever produced. He hated war, but was responsible for several inventions that helped us to win it—some of them still on the secret list."

"Frankly," Blake said, "I've never heard of him. But I've heard of Sergeyev, of course."

Craille nodded. "That's understandable. The Russians saw to it that everything Sergeyev did got maximum publicity, whereas Englefield was always something of a mystery man. He shunned the limelight, and he worked alone. I mean really alone. I don't suppose that there were more than two or three men in this country during the war who could even have told you what he looked like."

"What—?" Blake was surprised. "He was as mysterious as that?"

"Certainly he was."

"Did you know him?"

Craille shook his head. "I never even met him—nor ever saw a picture of him. I should have told you: he shunned cameras, too."

Blake frowned, puzzled. "Why, for Pete's sake?"

Again the old man shook his head. "I can't tell you. Not with any degree of certainty. Not out of my personal knowledge. But"—he hesitated—"there was a rumour current that he was a sport."

"A what?"

"A sport. A spontaneous deviation from normal. It's a biological term."

"You mean he was born—well—deformed?"

"Something like that. It was said he was the scion of a very illustrious family which rejected him because of his deformity. So he became a complete recluse. At the war's end he could have had honours heaped upon him, but he declined them. In nineteen forty-six he vanished—just as if the earth had opened and swallowed him up."

Blake pursed his lips in a silent whistle, "You know, all this is news to me."

The old man smiled. "A well-kept secret—both his existence and his disappearance." His smile faded. He said seriously: "I'd like to know more about that disappearance, Blake. You must find out, if you can, if the saucer people did have a hand in it."

"You're giving me plenty to do."

"You can handle it," Craille said.

"But why me," Blake asked bluntly, "when for an operation of this importance you could write your own ticket. You could have all the resources of the nation at your beck and call."

"You're a part of those resources," Craille reminded him gently. "And the truth is, the smaller the investigating group the better its chances of escaping detection. The smallest practical group is one of three men. You and Peters—and your man Carter is an excellent operative, as he's already proved.[2] He goes too.

"You will locate the base and reconnoitre it. You will find out who, or what, is behind it. And you will examine one of the saucers if possible. If you are caught, or in the event of the saucer people proving friendly—well—you are one of the few men available who is as tough as any commando and yet possesses the intellect and personal stature to conduct negotiations."

One of Blake's black eyebrows twitched upwards. "Well, well! Appreciation at last!" He smiled. "Thank you for those few kind words!"

But Craille wasn't smiling.

He said levelly, soberly: "There's just one last thing . . ." and the tone of his voice caused Blake to look at him quickly.

"Yes?"

Craille spoke gravely. "In view of the extraordinary ease with which the saucer people seem to be able to subvert people in high places here, I think it will be best if we sever all contact as of this moment, until your assignment has been completed."

Blake stared incredulously. "You don't think—"

Craille nodded, his thin-lipped mouth tight.

"As of now," he said, "you will act entirely on your own initiative. Any further orders which come from me—or purport to come from me—you will ignore! Is that clear?"

Blake was serious now; deadly serious. "Of course, if you say so."

Craille spoke slowly, clearly, and with emphasis.

He said: "We just don't know the power of these people. We just don't know who they can reach and subvert."

The room was suddenly very quiet; very still.

"They might," Craille said, "even reach me!"

THE EIGHTH CHAPTER

Cold comfort.

THE R.A.F. TRANSPORT Command Vickers Viking flew high on a straight course, north-by-north-west, over the vivid ultramarine of the ocean. In the passenger compartment, Edward Carter awoke from an uneasy sleep and rubbed at his eyes.

He glanced out of the porthole on his left, squinting ahead, and then gently shook the arm of his companion. "Iceland's coming up fast, chief."

Sexton Blake opened one eye very slowly. "All right, Tinker. I wasn't asleep."

The long mountainous shape of the sub-arctic island already filled the horizon and spilled towards them as the Viking approached. Now the sea's surface was patched with white lace where the water broke over off-shore reefs, and it was a gleaming, glistening white echoed by the ice that topped tall mountains far inland, by writhing glaciers in the valleys, and by shining patches of snow sharp-etched against jet-black lava fields.

The Viking began to lose height.

It passed over a group of red-roofed cottages nestling close to a small fjord, then swiftly traversed the twelve-mile neck of land that separated it from its destination—the airport at Keflavik. Bare minutes later, Blake and Tinker were climbing down on to bleak, wind-whipped tarmac, and looking around.

Outwardly, the airport buildings were rectangular and singularly undistinguished. Inside, an attempt had been made at Americanisation. Blake and Tinker passed quickly through Customs, and then found an R.A.F. sergeant awaiting them. He fed them out to where a staff car was parked.

The car was a big one, and plainly intended for the transportation of high-ranking officers. Plate glass separated passengers and driver. The sergeant explained that communication could be effected when necessary by means of a small hand-microphone which plugged into a socket to the left of the car's rear compartment. With the microphone out of circuit Blake was satisfied it was impossible for anyone to overhear a conversation between passengers. He and Tinker made themselves comfortable in the car, the sergeant slid in behind the wheel, and they set off.

They still had a long journey in front of them. Reykjavik, Iceland's capital, was all of thirty miles distant, and from there they would have to strike north to the small coastal town of Akureyri where Peters awaited them—another hundred miles on. The road out of Keflavik led through desolate stretches of twisted lava—grotesque petrified fields where nothing grew. Snow lay in shapeless quilts over the landscape. The eternal mountains made a black-and-white backdrop against the sky.

Nearing Reykjavik, the character of the terrain fractionally softened, and here, for the first time, sparse grass was to be seen. Then they entered the capital itself and drove through streets which were spacious and cold. They found the city a curious blend of old Scandinavia and modern twentieth century concrete-and-chrome-steel America. Then they swung north.

Tinker took in the panoramic white-and-black of the bulk of Mount Esja away on his left, and then turned to Blake. "What's the set-up here now, chief?"

Blake took the hand-microphone out of circuit. "Militarily, you mean?"

Tinker nodded.

"Well, as you know, the Americans came here in nineteen forty-one," Blake said, "and they've been here more or less ever since. But, over the years, the size of their force on the island has been drastically reduced and, in fact, at the moment, only a few hundred American servicemen are stationed here. They are mostly Air Force men operating the radar warning system.

"Working with them is a small group from the Royal Canadian Air Force which, in turn, has a much smaller contingent of R.A.F. men attached to it."

"And how, and where, do we fit in?"

"As I explained earlier, we and Peters are ostensibly civilian scientific officers from the Royal Air Force Technical Research Establishment at Great Malvern. We're here to study the functioning of signals' equipment under Arctic conditions. For that purpose we'll be temporarily on the strength of the R.A.F. contingent at Akureyri."

Tinker was nodding his head vigorously. "Yes, I'd already gathered that much. But what do we do when we get to Akureyri? To support our cover-story I mean."

Sexton Blake shrugged.

"I don't think we'll have to do anything," he said. "Certainly not straightaway on arrival. So you can stop worrying about it. We'll be accepted as civilian scientific officers without question. And why not? Peters has been. In any case, there'll be little time for anyone at Akureyri to break our cover-story—even if it was likely. We shan't be there all that long. For us it's just a jumping-off point. Tomorrow we go on a three-day Arctic survival course that Craille has arranged for us."

"A survival course!" Tinker exclaimed, frowning. "But hang it, chief, we're both one hundred per cent fit!"

Blake grinned. "I knew that would be your reaction. I said exactly the same thing to Craille. I'll ask you what he asked me. How long since you roughed it in Arctic conditions?"

"Years . . . but what the hell—? We're nothing if not adaptable!"

"Again, you echo me, old son. But Craille insisted on it, and I saw his point. We're going straight from a temperate climate to a sub-zero one, and we don't know what conditions we'll be up against until we get out on the job."

Four hours travelling through the changing scenery dominated by glaciers, lava hills, and ice-capped mountains, brought them to the north-coast town of Akureyri; a pleasant little place on a fjord. They pressed on beyond the town and, reaching a camp set on coarse turf high up overlooking the sea, they climbed out of the car to be instantly made very conscious of a cold, biting wind. Here they were almost on the edge of the Arctic Circle.

The staff car had stopped outside a cluster of Nissen huts. Beyond were larger buildings, radar masts, and the criss-cross of a small airstrip. Their driver went on ahead to open the door of one of the huts for them. "Mr. Blake and Mr. Carter, sir," he announced, and inside the hut an officer got to his feet behind a desk and came forward to meet them. "Thank you, sergeant."

The officer was broad-chested, thick-set. He had rugged features, ruddy and weather-beaten. He wore the uniform of a Squadron Leader and his left breast was thick with ribbons. Very white teeth showed as he smiled and extended a firm, strongly muscled hand. "I'm Jim Roderick, Admin Officer here. Did you have a good trip?"

They exchanged greetings and sat down, and Roderick picked

up a telephone on his desk and ordered coffee and brandy to be sent in. But before the drinks arrived, there was a knock on the door and another man entered, limping slightly and thrusting back the hood of his fur-lined parka as he came into the warm air of the hut.

Blake smiled a welcome. "Nice to see you again, Peters."

"Good to see you." Peters grinned briefly. There was no need for the formal mechanics of greeting between these two men. They had shared the same dangers; their minds were attuned.

In any case, Peters was hardly conventional, and he didn't talk much. When he did speak, it was to the point. Like now— "I could do with a drink!"

Squadron Leader Roderick's rugged features slipped into a crumpled smile. "The drinks are on the way in, old boy."

LATER, BLAKE AND Tinker accompanied Peters to the small Nissen hut that was to be their temporary home. The hut was part bedroom, part office, and had that practical comfort which every serviceman knows how to achieve. There was the inevitable, almost red-hot, iron combustion stove, a table and chairs, and a scattered pack of playing cards sprawled on a bed. There were pin-up pictures of Brigitte Bardot and Anita Ekberg on the walls. There was a cleverly contrived wash-stand where a man could shave in warmth and good light.

Peters' mouth twisted sardonically. "Cosier than the Ritz, eh? But make the most of it. You won't have it for long."

"Off in the morning?" said Blake.

"That's right. And from now on, no shaving. You'll need your beards to keep you warm on that survival course."

The three men sat down around the stove, and Blake took out his cigarette case and offered it. "What's the latest news, Peters?"

The scar of an old wound quivered in the agent's cheek as

his mouth moved and the words fell out of him in staccato, nervous bursts.

"I've got around since I was last in contact with Craille. Found an old man from Jan Mayen. He talked of a ghost island he'd been wrecked on, donkey's years ago. Tied all that in with what I already knew. Took a plane over. Still no break in the fog. But I reckon I can pinpoint a place that has every chance of being what we're looking for."

"You think we can reach it?"

Peters nodded. "Yes, but it's landing—that's the trouble. You can't get a powered boat, even the smallest, in over the reefs. You can't go in all the way by air because of fog and the unknown terrain. Besides, we don't want to give the saucer people any warning we're coming, if we can help it."

"But you have a plan?"

"Yes, a natural. You may know that I trained under Lieutenant-Commander Wilmott of COPP back in nineteen forty-three—"

But this was news to Blake. He knew that Peters was versatile and tough, and that he had done Intelligence work during the war and since, but he didn't know that he had been a member of Willmott's Combined Operations Pilotage Parties. It was Willmott's organisation that, in two-man collapsible canoes and with the minimum of equipment, had reconnoitred the enemy coast and made the secret trial landings which had prefaced the Allied invasions of North Africa, Sicily, and Normandy.

"—And I reckoned we could use the same technique," Peters continued. "In fact, knowing there'd be three of us, I've already started work on a three-man canoe. By the time you've completed your course I'll have it ready. The cover-story for our trip, by the way, will be that we're going out to test a special piece of signals' equipment. We'll take a suitable transmitter-receiver with us. There are plenty of ice-floes in our target area and we'll land on one by helicopter, with the canoe, and make for the island from there. It'll be rough, but the canoe'll get through where nothing else could."

Blake nodded thoughtfully. "It could work at that. It worked in wartime against greater odds. Yes . . . but we need a trusty and reliable man to fly us out."

Peters agreed. "And I know just the chap. Not that we have to tell him any more than we want to. Squadron Leader Roderick. He's an ex-COPP character, too."

"Is he? Then that settles it." Blake said. The position of helicopter pilot had been satisfactorily filled—if Roderick would agree.

"I think so," Peters said. "I'm pretty sure, in fact. I've been sounding him out."

"Good," Blake said, and Tinker sighed.

"It's a pity we can't scrub round the survival course and get cracking right away."

Peters looked at him quickly, and smiled wryly. "It won't be time wasted. Every mother's son coming fresh into these parts needs the toughening-up the course gives you, to say nothing of the training in survival techniques. Besides, the canoe and equipment aren't ready yet, and if that's not enough there's another, better reason, why you should go ahead with the course just as planned.

"You've got to act normally—got to do what every T.R.E. scientific officer fresh out from Great Malvern does as soon as he gets here. Don't think we aren't being watched—"

He spoke flatly.

"—Believe me—Carter—we are!"

THE NINTH CHAPTER

The Brink.

EIGHT MEN WERE taking the survival course, and they moved off from the camp at six in the morning after a very, very early breakfast. They marched in an ordered formation. The tough Royal Canadian Air Force flight-sergeant in charge of the course was a disciplinarian and quite uncompromising. The fact that some of his pupils were senior officers and some civilians made no difference to him. In any case all outward signs of rank and status disappeared under the bulky weather-proof clothing.

Sexton Blake felt very much the new boy, and despite his original impatience with the idea of the course, soon had to admit that he was learning something. Fit as he was, and as he had always kept himself, the survival course under Arctic conditions required—and quickly brought about—an added toughness and alertness to match that which Blake had known in the war years.

Tinker had much the same feelings as Blake.

The flight-sergeant marched them out to a wild, hilly, snowbound part of the coast where, far below, they could see the bright blue of the ocean disappearing into a fog-shrouded horizon skirted by heaving patches of ice. He taught them the dangers of both heat and cold.

"Never give way to the cold, even for a second. Keep moving, get shelter if you can. The wind is a worse enemy than the cold. You, there—I can tell by your face that you're getting hot under your parka. You're sweating. That's dangerous. The chill-off can kill you. Keep an even temperature. Open your neck."

They carried small water-bottles and iron rations, but these were to be used only as a last resort. For water, they had to thaw land ice. As for food—

"Anything that walks or crawls you can eat, except toads. Anything from a seal to a beetle. You can eat leaves, moss, seaweed. Anything that has life is your life. When you can't see anything to eat, dig under the snow. You'll find something. The situation is nothing. Your brains and guts are everything."

He taught them how to avoid snow-blindness, and showed them how a man in windproof, fur-lined clothing won't sink immediately if he falls into water. Then he made each of them swim in the sub-zero sea until soaked, and then instructed them on how to dry out and survive. He taught them how to build shelters of snow, how to avoid frostbite, how to climb seemingly unscalable ice-bound cliffs, and what to do in all kinds of weather conditions.

"And if you want healthy faces when you get back, don't think it's pansy to use your lip-salve and face-cream. If that was all it was, you wouldn't have been issued with 'em."

For three long days, the flight-sergeant put his squad through every kind of frozen hell; but what they learned was worth a lifetime. At the end of the three days Blake felt twice as fit as at the beginning.

And Tinker was almost sorry when the course ended and they were back in Peters' comfortable billet.

THE FOLLOWING MORNING dawned cold and clear. Tinker looked

90

wryly at the washbasin in the hut, then at the mirror and a reflection of three days' growth of beard. Further back, the mirror image showed Blake seated at the table, telephone in hand.

Their glances met for a moment. Tinker turned.

He grinned. "Don't know whether I'm glad or sorry I can't shave it off yet." He took another sideways glance at his reflection. "I think it improves my looks."

Blake put down the telephone and cocked a humorous eye at him.

"That wouldn't be difficult—almost anything would." He fingered his own growth, the stubble just turning soft. "Stop admiring yourself for a moment, and listen. Everything's laid on. Peters has all the equipment ready. It's loaded in a truck in the yard of the small hotel in Akureyri he's been using these last couple of days. We're going down there right away. We'll move off from there. Squadron Leader Roderick will be waiting for us at a quiet place along the coast. We take off straight after lunch."

"Okay, I'm ready." Tinker shrugged into his jacket.

Blake had a jeep parked alongside the hut. The two men climbed in, Tinker taking the wheel. They drove off out of the camp and along the road to Akureyri.

It was a metalled road, and just barely wide enough for two vehicles to pass without touching. For some miles it skirted a fjord where, before, white-hot lava had flooded down to create a two-thousand-foot cliff of black pumice. Far below, jagged rocks reared their vicious heads high from the wind-whipped water. Tinker took a quick look downwards, and drew his lips back from his teeth in a grimace. "One helluva drop!"

It was, and there was no guard rail here, and the road surface bore a thin film of ice. All the same, with Tinker's sane driving, it should have been reasonably safe—if he and Blake had been

91

the only ones on the road.

But they weren't. Blake lifted his head quickly, listening intently and frowning. He could hear another vehicle coming towards them at speed. He couldn't see it yet, a curve in the road and a buttress of rock hid it from view, but—

"Sounds like he's going much too fast for this road," Blake said sharply. "He must imagine he's got it all to himself."

"Just what I was thinking." Tinker's eyes narrowed. Then— "Here he comes! A Yank, of course. It had to be! And, cripes, isn't he moving!"

A big American truck had roared round the curve. It bore down on them, hogging the middle of the road all the way. It showed no signs of slackening speed.

"What the devil does he think he's doing!" Tinker exclaimed. He punched the horn button.

The sound of the horn blared stridently through the air. Tinker had taken the jeep as far over to the right of the road and the precipice edge as he dared. But still the big truck came on; still it hogged the road's centre. "He'll hit us! He must!" Tinker braked. Again he thumbed the horn button.

Still the driver of the truck took no notice.

Blake could see him now, the driver, bent low over the wheel in his cab. And he could see a second man with him—a man crouched low in his seat, bracing himself.

Blake snapped, "They mean to hit us! They intend to!"

"What—!"

"They must be working for the saucer people! They mean to kill us!"

"But—but they're Americans—our allies—"

"Not any more! They've been subverted!"

"Cripes! Where will it end!"

"We'll end two thousand feet down if they hit us! How near are we to the edge?"

"Less than six inches! Look out, chief—"

The cry was almost lost in the roar of the truck's engine. It was on top of them now, filling the jeep's windscreen. And then—at the very last moment—its speed slackened fractionally. It swerved slightly to the left of the jeep.

Its angle-iron fender hit the smaller vehicle; tore into it. It screamed a furrow along the jeep's side. The vehicle shuddered under the impact. It lifted; swung. Its nearside wheels jarred over the edge of the drop. There was a sickening jolt as the axles took all the weight.

Tinker was overhanging the precipice with nothing between him and the sickening drop but a seat and a chassis. He could see straight down to the jagged pinnacles of lava.

He looked quickly ahead. His mouth was dry. He judged that the wheels had gone over the edge a good eighteen inches. Some part of the transmission or chassis was holding on to the road, but the jeep's centre of gravity must be close to the point of dangerous imbalance. At any second the vehicle might slip.

The American truck had stopped. Its occupants were looking back, their faces a blur at the rear window. The truck began to reverse.

Blake looked grimly at Tinker. "And they're not coming back to give us a tow!"

"We're sitting ducks, chief! We've got to get out—and quick!"

But both of them knew, and knew well, that the slightest movement on their part might send the jeep over!

THE TENTH CHAPTER

Death in the snow.

"WATCH IT!" BLAKE snapped. "We can't afford to be quick. That would have us over the edge for sure!"

And even as he spoke, Tinker was easing himself towards him, inch by inch, his whole nervous system alert for the slightest sign of movement from the delicately poised vehicle.

In the mirror, the image of the reversing American truck grew larger and larger. Now the driver put on a sudden spurt of speed.

Tinker was right up against Blake who had himself squeezed his body against the edge of the vehicle's interior. All their weight was now on the left, helping to maintain the jeep's balance.

But what was going to happen when they started to take that weight away? Could they both get clear before the slide started and the jeep plunged out and down into space?

Could they both get clear before the truck was on them again?

Blake spoke, his voice taut. "I'm climbing out now, Tinker. And I'm praying hard—"

LIFE HUNG BY a thread as with agonising slowness Blake put a foot to the ground.

It was Tinker's life that hung in balance, and Blake knew it only too well. The slightest mistake on his part would surely destroy his young partner. He felt the full weight of his awful responsibility.

Tinker had been like a son to him down the long years—and more than a son. Did it all end here, on a lonely Icelandic road, with a cold, cruel wind wailing a requiem?

No, by God! No! Not if it depended upon anything he did! But he must be careful, very, very careful. It needed only one jerk and the slight shift of balance would start the jeep on a fatal slide . . .

In the mirror, he saw the rear end of the big American truck looming larger and larger. It was reversing fast.

One of his feet was on the ground now. The other foot followed it. But he still applied weight to the jeep with his hands.

He had to. He mustn't disturb the vehicle's delicate balance. He straightened, still pressing down on the side of the jeep. He turned with care. There was sweat on his face. "Come on, Tinker! Gently now—"

The reversing American truck was almost upon them!

Still Blake leant his weight on the jeep.

Then Tinker was clear.

The vehicle swayed as their weight came off it—then settled again. In that instant, the oncoming truck braked sharply. A man leapt down from the back of it. In his hand he swung a two-foot length of lead piping.

The next moment, the truck's driver and his companion swung their doors open and dropped to the ground. Each had a weapon: the driver a long, adjustable wrench, his mate a short crowbar.

In a close quarter-circle, the three men advanced on Tinker and Blake.

They came in quickly. So quickly that Blake had only time for one swift injunction to Tinker, hissed through his teeth. "No mercy on them—but no guns if possible, Tinker. No traceable bullets—"

Then the three men were upon them. The one with the length of lead piping made a target of Blake.

The detective stood in a half crouch, hands low. He had moved so that his left side was flanked by the jeep. The heavy piping swung at his head.

He dropped quickly on to his left knee, and as he did so his left hand shot up to lock on his assailant's descending wrist. In the same moment he slammed his right hand under the man's crutch and thrust upwards. He jerked his left hand hard down.

The man gasped and went over head in a flying arc. He smacked into the road near the jeep and his legs went over and back . . . clearing the cliff edge.

Now he was screaming.

His scream crescendoed into a piercing shriek as his body plummeted down, down—down on to the jagged rocks far, far below. The sound and his life ended together—abruptly.

Blake swung round.

He turned to help Tinker, but no help was needed. Tinker was defending himself, and without recourse to judo. He had blocked a blow from the long adjustable wrench, and then pistoned a fist into his attacker's solar plexus. As the man doubled up, gurgling. Tinker slammed him full in the face.

The man made a horrible bubbling noise as he was forcibly unfolded. He smashed back against the jeep. The stem of the vehicle's exterior mirror was jutting out some two inches—two inches of steel that pierced the back of the man's skull and penetrated his brain as his head hit it.

He didn't even cry out.

The jeep swayed, and the man hung there—dead. In that

instant, the third and last and only surviving assailant dropped his crowbar and grabbed for a gun.

Blake lunged forward and fastened his hand on the man's wrist as he tried to level the weapon. They grappled with each other, fighting furiously for possession of it. Then there was a jolting roar, and the man pitched backwards. He had shot himself through the heart. He sprawled on the ground.

Blake stepped back, breathing heavily.

He looked with disgust at the two dead men, then thought of the other who had crashed to his death on the rocks. His steel-blue eyes were cold and angry as he looked at Tinker. He had no joy in causing any man's death, not even the death of such obvious enemies as these.

"Damned fools," he got out. He straightened his back. "Well, they wanted an accident. They planned to stage one. They shall have what they wanted!"

The road was deserted, and there was no sound of any other vehicle approaching. Blake walked up to the truck and climbed into the driver's seat. He started the engine.

He reversed carefully, taking the truck back as near to the jeep as he dared. Then he braked, swung down, and motioned to Tinker. Together they manhandled the two bodies into the back of the truck. Next Blake found a tow-rope. He hooked it between the two vehicles. He climbed up behind the wheel of the truck again, and pulled away slowly.

Gradually the jeep was hauled in, at an angle, its underside grating on the rock edge. There was a jarring bump as the dangling rear wheel mounted the road. Soon the rest of the vehicle followed it.

Tinker unhooked the tow-rope and threw it into the back of the truck. He drove the jeep out of the way.

Now Blake, in the cab of the truck, manoeuvred the vehicle so that its front wheels pointed straight at the precipice. He disengaged the gear and released the handbrake. He jumped clear as the truck began to roll. He stood there, watching.

The vehicle rolled slowly, gathered momentum, hung for a long fraction of a second on the edge, and then plunged over.

They watched it falling through free air . . . down, down . . . its bulk dwindling rapidly. Two thousand feet below it flattened itself on the jagged rocks. There came a seconds-late roar of an explosion as the truck disintegrated and the fragments of it flew into the sea.

The roar was repeated again and again as the hills bounced the sound from one to another until there was no noise left. Then Blake and Tinker slowly climbed into their jeep, and drove on.

"So," SAID PETERS, "they tried to stop you. I was right, wasn't I, when I said we were being watched? You don't think, in the circumstances, we ought to postpone this trip?"

Blake shook his head impatiently. "Of course not."

Peters grinned briefly. "That's what I hoped you would say. Carter . . . ?"

"We didn't expect a picnic, did we?"

Peters nodded, satisfied.

"We're solid on that, then. Now, this is the drill. First we're going to have a really heavy meal—as much as we can eat—at this hotel. That's our reserve. We shan't starve if we don't eat again for a day or two. We're not touching our iron rations unless there's no other food to be found and we're desperate with hunger. Water-bottles, the same.

"We've got windproof clothing, the lightest possible consistent with warmth. Equipment has been whittled down to a basic minimum: a knife, Service .38, a watch, compass, monoculars, nylon rope, climbing spikes, torch, benzedrine, and a small first-aid pack. We have one small service transceiver—ostensibly for testing, but really for contact with my chaps here. We have one very small transistor-operated beacon transmitter. This is for planting immediately we land. It gives an intermittent signal by which we can be located if we run into trouble and can't use the two-way radio.

"We're meeting Roderick at a pre-arranged spot on the coast. I'll navigate and direct Roderick to a suitable ice-floe in the target area. There Roderick will land us, and then return here, his part in the exercise over. From there on, our part of the operation is fluid, we improvise."

Blake nodded. "You've wrapped it up very nicely. The way I see it from then on is this:

"Although we shall be using what might be called commando tactics, our job is not to attack. We're strictly after information, so that, if necessary, a bigger force can go in after us. We've got to find out all we can about the saucer people, what they're like, what they're planning, how many craft they're operating, and what offensive weapons they have. We have to determine how best a larger force could land, what would happen if they did land, what strength would be necessary, and what weapons they'd need. We have to learn and map the geography of the place. All this is basic."

Tinker put in, "Always the little optimist, that's me—but we've got to consider the possibility of being caught. What happens then?"

Blake shrugged. "Who knows? If the saucer people will negotiate then we'll have to communicate with base by radio. If they won't negotiate, then at best we'll be prisoners, at worst we'll be dead. Craille's angle is that even if we fail miserably we'll at least have added something to his existing knowledge. Then there'll be another expedition. The beacon radio will furnish our position. If we're prisoners Craille will do his best to free us. If we're dead, he's promised us a hero's funeral."

Tinker smiled brightly. "There's a comforting thought!"

THIN SLEET WHIPPED at the bearded faces of the three men as they left the back door of the inn and made for the covered truck parked in the yard. But they were warm enough.

In Peters' private room they had put on string vests, flannel shirts, thick Icelandic sweaters, and fur-lined, zipped, nylon parkas. Over long woollen pants which would have provided some laughs in London they wore windcheater trousers tucked into supple, tough leather-and-rubber boots. Under the boots were special issue duffle socks. On their hands they had weatherproof but pliant Arctic mitts.

Blake swung up into the driving seat of the truck, and Tinker and Peters squeezed in beside him. He started the engine and nursed the vehicle out on to the road. He and his companions exchanged very few words as they drove towards their rendezvous with Roderick.

The weather cleared a little and, as they rounded a bend, they glimpsed a helicopter standing on the concrete plain of what had once been an American airstrip. It was now derelict. They pulled up alongside the aircraft, and the rugged Squadron Leader raised a cheerful hand in greeting.

Quickly, they manhandled the flat, collapsed canoe into the luggage-hold. The rest of their equipment was either on their persons or in their packs. Blake ran the truck into an empty shed, and then clambered into the helicopter to take his place, with Tinker behind Roderick and Peters who occupied the front seats.

The Squadron Leader started the engines and the rotors thundered overhead. The machine lifted gently, then slid into an easy climb.

Below, blue water lashed the northern shore, breaking white on black rocks. As the helicopter droned steadily through the sky, the sea began to show drifting of ice and, here and there, huge fields of it. Only an occasional trawler broke the blue and white monotony.

Their first landmark was lonely Jan Mayen, volcanic sentinel of the Greenland Sea. Soon the island appeared on the horizon like a mist-wracked mountain. Before it, heaving white pancakes of ice jostled each other in the blue-green water. Near the island's shore, the colour of the sea changed subtly to a clear blue.

As the helicopter drew level with the shore, little black figures darted out from the cluster of buildings forming the weather station and Squadron Leader Roderick tilted his rotors in greeting. The figures stood still for a while; then moved back to their shelter in obvious disappointment.

Lonely as Jan Mayen was, its isolation was as nothing compared to the vast unsailed sea that the helicopter was now to fly over. Once the island had vanished from sight, only an endless waste of drifting floes lay ahead. Peters was in constant consultation with Roderick about the course now. No landmarks existed, and in these latitudes the magnetic compass was unreliable. Peters took frequent bearings from the watery sun.

On they flew, and on, until a thick bank of mist appeared, blanketing the horizon.

Peters' voice was sharp, and very clear. "Target area ahead!"

HE CHECKED HIS bearings. "The fog-belt stretches for three or four hundred square miles. We certainly don't want to go through it, or even into it. We'll find a suitable floe, and land near where the mist begins."

Roderick glanced at him curiously.

"This is a helluva crazy set up! Are you sure that you really want to be set down hundreds of miles from nowhere?"

Peters grinned back. "Quite sure." Then he frowned slightly. "Drop her to about five hundred, will you? I've got to watch the colouring and configuration."

Below were several floes that were certainly large enough for the helicopter to land on, but size wasn't the only thing to be taken into consideration. The colour of the ice denoted thickness. A suspicion of darkness would indicate that a floe was too thin. And ice that looked flat from a height might show up ridged at five hundred feet, and unsuitable as a landing place.

The helicopter descended; hovered.

Peters finally selected a floe about a quarter of a mile square, with smaller ones jostling it. The Squadron Leader headed for it, and then gently settled his machine down.

All his passengers were very happy to climb out.

They were stiff from the long journey. The ice was a little lumpy, but reasonably easy to walk on. They unloaded the canoe, and unbuckled the retaining straps. They braced it, and made it ready for the water.

Blake looked up. Westward, the sun still shone, but the edges of the mist belt had reached out, dimming it. To the south there was the limitless sea and the endless ice. To the north-east, visibility was little more than one hundred yards. Beyond that, the mist formed a solid grey wall. And on the other side of the wall . . . ? Mystery!

All around, the ice masses ground and strained and groaned against each other—a weird orchestra playing a grotesque symphony in a minor key.

The helicopter stood waiting to make the return trip—for only one man.

Peters held out his hand. "Thanks for your help, Roddy."

Roderick shook hands with each of the three men. "Good luck. Keep in touch."

He turned, waved a brief salute, and walked back to the waiting machine standing some yards from the water's edge.

The others slid the canoe to where the sea lapped the clean-cut, slow-rocking edge of the floe. Blake turned briefly to wave again as Roderick climbed into the helicopter.

The Squadron Leader acknowledged his farewell, and then reached into his machine. He swung round swiftly.

Blake saw something in his hands. He saw it and recognised it and for a split second he could only register shocked disbelief.

Roderick was gripping a Schmeisser machine-pistol!

"Scatter—wide!" Blake yelled.

It was his companions' only warning.

Then Roderick jerked at the trigger of the gun, and death leapt out over the floe, cutting a murderous path through the cold, clear air.

THE ELEVENTH CHAPTER

Paddle your own canoe.

THE SAVAGE SOUND of the Schmeisser was an echoless voice made thin by the sponge of advancing fog.

On the run, Blake ripped at the zipper of his parka. His companions had scattered wide at his call.

But there was no cover; no shelter from the Schmeisser. Bullets beat the hard ice. Some bit into it; some ricocheted, howling away evilly. A semi-circle was being stitched into the ice. As the frozen chips flew, the advancing stitches gathered speed.

Peters was nearest the beginning of the arc. He saw the line of bullets leaping inexorably in his direction, and flung himself around in a wild effort to escape them. He couldn't. Slugs thudded into the casing of the radio transceiver he carried on his chest; bowling him over.

He fell, unable to hold back a cry of agony as something that felt like a circular saw tore through his flesh from ribs to thigh. He sprawled flat on the unsympathetic ice, writhing. His blood, spurting out, was instantly congealed on the frozen surface.

The Schmeisser's muzzle swung sharply to the left.

Now Blake was the target. Bullets ripped towards him. But, by now, he had his Service .38 hard in his grasp.

He hadn't much change left out of a second, and knew it. Yet he had to be dead accurate, or dead duck. No lucky chance shot was going to silence the snarling machine-pistol cradled in Roderick's murderous hands.

He used the slim margin left him between life and death to sight quickly but carefully, and fired.

The figure of the Squadron Leader, small over the sights, was punched backwards as the .38 exploded once. The Schmeisser tilted crazily, still chattering. Then, abruptly, the sound ceased.

Roderick had taken a bullet in the neck. He fell backwards against the helicopter's undercarriage. Blake shouted to Tinker: "Look after Peters!" but the instruction was really unnecessary. Tinker was already on his way.

Blake ran towards the helicopter, his revolver at the ready in case Roderick should make one last effort to steady himself and aim at a live target again.

And then—

Roderick tried. His death agony was upon him, contorting his features in a ghastly grimace, but still he tried to focus his eyes and fire at the oncoming Blake. But even as he jerked at the Schmeisser's trigger a spasm gripped him, and the machine-pistol's snout swung vertically upwards. Bullets punched into the plane's reserve fuel tank. Instantly, there was a billowing, blasting explosion.

Roderick and the helicopter both disappeared behind a wall of flame. A searing shock wave slammed into Blake, scorching his frozen face and wrapping itself around him. It hurled him back.

And now, where the helicopter had been, there was only a fierce ball of fire which lit up the ice with blood-red reflections and sent a ghastly smoke-signal skywards. It was Roderick's funeral pyre.

Nothing could survive in the heart of that holocaust. Nothing could approach it and live. Blake dragged himself to his feet. Roderick had perished utterly. The detective turned his back on the dead then, and returned across the ice to the living.

Tinker had already stripped off his parka, opened it on the ice, and laid Peters down on it. It made a bed, and Peters' own pack was his pillow. Blake knelt by his side.

The man was in great pain yet, as Blake looked at him, he managed to force the tortured ghost of a grin on to his face. "Fine mess . . . I got you . . . into . . ." he whispered. "I trusted Roderick . . . my fault . . ."

Blake said gruffly: "Don't be such a ruddy fool. We all trusted him, and why not? He had a fine record."

Tinker was shaking his head wonderingly. "And the saucer people can even corrupt a man like that! It's—it's almost unbelievable!"

But it had happened.

Blake took off his pack and got out the first-aid kit.

"Still . . . my fault . . ." Peters whispered. "What . . . what a mess . . ."

It was that all right, Blake thought grimly. Indeed a mess—marooned on an ice-flow with civilisation hundreds of miles away and no visible means of getting back to it! No means of communication, either, with the radio smashed.

There were now, he could see, just two alternative courses of action open to them, and both were equally bleak and uninviting. They could stay where they were and power the beacon transmitter, which would send a locating signal but no other message, and they could hope to be picked up—eventually—if they hadn't all perished first. Or they could press on to their unknown destination where an equally unknown enemy lurked, and trust that they could reach it and carry out their mission successfully when they got there—regardless of the fact that Peters, key-man of the enterprise, was in such a critical state.

What an unholy pair of alternatives to choose between, Blake thought as he prepared the morphine shot which was essential if his comrade was not to go into shock. As he gave Peters the injection, he looked down into his bearded, greying face. "Plenty of life in you yet," he lied.

What to do? Which alternative to choose?

He examined Peter's wounds as the morphine took slow effect. He swabbed away jellied blood. Straightway he saw that, in one respect, Peters had been lucky. Very lucky. There were no bullets in him. All had passed through. And there was only one fracture, simple not compound, which should mend if strongly strapped up.

Yes, he'd been lucky all right. But, just the same, his wounds were ugly and serious and he'd lost a lot of blood. He might yet die. As the morphine took over, and Peters slid into a coma, Blake and Tinker worked fast, cleaning the wounds, packing them with infection-fighting sulpha, and covering them with gauze and plaster. Despite the freezing atmosphere, the detectives sweated, and the cold only made itself felt once again when they had finished and Peters was re-clothed.

"Well, chief—?" Tinker wanted to know then. "What do we do?"

Blake had made up his mind.

"Go on," he said. "At least that gives us a fighting chance of survival." And it was true. "But we can't move right away. Peters has got to have rest for a while. We'll improvise a shelter for the night and move on in the morning."

But even as he spoke there was a sharp cracking sound from where the helicopter's wreckage still smouldered. Tinker's eyes lifted sharply—and then he jumped to his feet.

"Some hope!" he got out. "Look!"

A fissure had appeared in the ice-floe where the burning aircraft had melted the surface. It was a fissure that cracked wider and wider in front of their eyes.

Another split started outward in another direction. And another. And another. Crunching and crackling like thunder, the ice broke open in several directions at once. The floe trembled under their feet.

The ice was breaking up! All of it! Their one hope of granting Peters the rest and shelter he so desperately needed was coming to pieces beneath them.

Blake looked at Tinker with grim desperation in his eyes. "All right, old son, there's only one thing for it—"

"Don't say it, chief. 'Paddle your own canoe!'"

Blake nodded. It was like Tinker to joke in a moment of near-desperation.

"That's it. It's going to be rough on Peters, but we have no option."

They hadn't much time, either. The floe was already in the last stages of complete disintegration.

THE CANOE SWITCHBACKED crazily over the angrily heaving grey-black water. Blake and Tinker in the fore and aft cockpits, forced their aching muscles to continue the rhythmic dipping and pulling of the double-bladed paddles that alone kept them and their flimsy craft from being swallowed up by the ravenous sea.

They had thrown open their parkas to let the sweat escape. Despite the deathly chill of the foggy air, their bodies were clammy with heat. Their breath came out in grey-white bursts.

Peters, in the centre cockpit, alternated between coma and full consciousness. In coma he groaned and his breathing was weak. Conscious, his face betrayed the tremendous effort he was making to control his instinctive reaction to the pain he was suffering. His lips were thin and tight-drawn.

Although Sexton Blake had memorised the theoretical route outlined by Peters back in Iceland, Peters himself was the one man who had full and complete knowledge of the course they had to take and the instinct to know when to dispense with theory. In his conscious moments, biting back his pain, he managed to check their course with Blake and correct it when necessary.

For nearly two hours they paddled, and all of that time Blake held on to the idea of making a landing on another floe—if only they could find one large enough and strong enough to give them rest and shelter. But they never did. In fact, as they paddled the floes they encountered seemed to be getting smaller and smaller.

"Land . . .?" Peters gasped. "It's a sign there's land close by . . ."

Just how close was it?

Then through the fog they heard the sound of a colony of sea-birds, proof that indeed land was not far ahead.

But what kind of land? A large rock? An island occupied by hostile beings? Whatever it was, anything would be better than the cold, grimly relentless sea. Or so it seemed now. The very thought of land gave them new strength to paddle on.

Then suddenly Peters was sick. He had been holding himself in for a long time. But now he could fight his nausea no longer. He collapsed sideways, retching, only half conscious. The canoe nearly heeled over.

Blake and Tinker straightway threw all their weight to the left in a desperate effort to keep their craft upright. Blake looked back quickly to see what could be done for Peters. He took his eyes off the sea for only a second—but it was enough.

110

He missed spotting the sharp reef that appeared out of the fog ahead. Tinker saw it and shouted a warning—too late.

The next moment the bottom of the canoe was sliced open.

For a split second even the normally confident, imperturbable Blake thought: This is it! This, surely, must be the end! For a few moments, perhaps for a minute at the most, the air trapped in the canoe would keep them afloat. But no longer. And how were they all to escape in that time—?

Blake said urgently: "There's only one way. Tip her and fall out. Otherwise one of us may be trapped. Get ready to grab Peters. You're aft. You'll reach him quicker than I can."

Chilling water was already around their legs.

"Right!" Tinker jerked. "Give the word when you're ready."

"Now!"

The two men swung bodily over to their right, kicking themselves free of the doomed canoe. Tinker gasped as the freezing water enveloped him. Then he was lunging to reach Peters. He dragged his slackly inert body clear of the wreck.

Peters had swallowed water. He was blue in the face, and weakly gasping for air. But his windproof attire kept him buoyant.

Positioned on either side of him, keeping his unconscious head clear of the water, Blake and Tinker pressed on grimly, hoping against hope—praying—that they would soon reach the land.

AND THEN IT happened.

Tinker could hardly believe it when his feet touched bottom. He grunted something to Blake. Not words—he was beyond words. Blake grunted back. He had found bottom, too.

Both men accepted the knowledge with some reservation. The seabed might well fall away suddenly. They trod warily forward, and then, gradually, moved with increasing confidence.

For now, ahead, on through the mist, waves could be heard breaking over a shore. Blake forced a grin round chattering teeth, and gave a weary thumbs-up sign to his young partner.

So they struggled on. On to a grim, wave-swept beach. Above, sea-birds screeched. The fog was dense, but it moved under a strong wind, whirling and swirling and creating grey, ghostly illusions to harry the men's weary minds.

They made Peters as comfortable as possible. Then Blake left Tinker with the wounded man, and went on alone.

He did not go far. He sought only to reconnoitre their position. He did not like what he found. He discovered that the beach sloped gently upwards to the base of a sheer cliff, at once bleak, austere, and overhanging. He walked along it, first one way and then the other.

In one place—and in one place only—there was a very narrow fissure in the cliff wall. Elsewhere it was plainly unclimbable. And how far up did this one crack in the cliff-face go? Blake couldn't see. The fog prevented him from seeing. He had no means of knowing.

Now he began to look very worried.

For at each end of the beach, the cliff thrust its way into deep water. There was no hope of escape in either direction. Yet some way had to be found!

He could see the line of the high-water mark along the face of the cliff. When the tide came in, the beach would be drowned under twelve feet of water.

And the tide was coming in now. A quick check confirmed it.

It was coming in now—and coming in fast—and unless the narrow fissure in the cliff wall led upwards to safety they were doomed.

THE TWELFTH
CHAPTER

Human fly.

ON THE BEACH, there was nothing in store for them all but death by drowning.

Blake and Tinker acknowledged the fact grimly, and carried Peters gently, but swiftly, to the foot of the cliff.

The wall of rock might climb upwards for forty feet, or it might tower for all of four hundred. They could not know which. The fog hid the truth from them. And even if they did finally manage to reach the top, there was no means of telling what, or who, they might find there. Nevertheless, one thing was certain.

They had to scale the cliff if it was humanly possible, simply because it was the only thing that was left to do. It was their one way of escape—and, somehow, Peters had to be taken with them.

They set to work to make a sling.

They manufactured one quickly out of rope and pieces of webbing cut from their equipment, and they fitted it round the shivering, grey-faced man. Peters hovered on the rim of consciousness, every now and then slipping over into a coma.

"One of us will have to stay with him," Blake said, "while the other climbs up the fissure, sees how far it goes, and what's up top. Then the man on top will have to haul Peters up while the other man supports him from below to prevent him bumping against the rock. It's going to mean the second man climbing and supporting Peters at one and the same time. Some job! I think you'd better go first, old son."

"Okay," said Tinker.

Characteristically, Blake had accepted the harder job himself, but Tinker knew better than to argue. Blake would only have made it an order. Not that Tinker's own task was a sinecure . . .

He fastened a nylon rope around his waist, and reversed his pack so that it lay across his chest. He eased his way into the fissure in the cliff wall. It was little wider than twice the thickness of a man's body. Straddling his legs, he managed to find toeholds, and he reached up with his hands to gain purchase. Where there was nothing to support him, he took a climb-spike from his pack, and worked it into a crack in the rock. In that way he climbed the first thirty-five feet.

Then the fissure began to widen, and he was forced to bridge the gap with his body, pushing feet against one wall and his back and hands against the other. Still he worked his way upwards. But this was muscle-bruising, tough slogging to a sodden, dead-tired man.

Now the gap became too wide for even this method of climbing, and he had to scale the almost vertical face using what hand and toe-holds he could find, easing in spikes, and belaying himself periodically to regain his strength.

Then the angle of climb eased suddenly and, after that, it was just a matter of a simple but still wearying scramble up over the rest of the cliff.

A few more minutes, and he was close to the top. Tinker raised his head cautiously and peered into the unknown terrain. But there was nothing to see save a grey, grim, boulder-strewn field of rock. Fast-approaching night and the fog—not so dense here but still omnipresent—limited visibility to a few hundred yards.

Tinker eased himself on to the cliff-top. He took a few minutes out to recover his breath, and then began securing ropes to aid the ascent of Blake with the helpless Peters.

FORTY-FIVE MINUTES LATER, it was all done.

It had been a slow job and a tough one, getting Peters up the cliff-face. It had been a sweating agony for Blake and Tinker, and worse for the injured man, but now it was over.

There was still the need for shelter: a desperate need with the bitter cold wind sweeping along the rock-strewn cliff-top. Blake and Tinker were close to exhaustion, and Peters was sadly in need of careful attention and warmth.

Surely, Blake thought, in this rocky, volcanic region, there must be some sort of a cave to give them refuge . . .

On reaching the top of the cliff, Blake had straightaway found a suitable place to hide the beacon transmitter: a place from which its signal could beam out to Iceland with screening rock to impede its progress. Now, carrying the inert man between them, he and Tinker moved slowly from the cliff-edge into the unknown hinterland. It was a long and seemingly hopeless trek, but just as Blake was beginning to feel his tortured knees buckling beneath him his desperate prayers were answered.

"A cave!" Tinker croaked. "A cave!"

It was set in ground that had already started to rise steeply. The rocks outside the entrance were wet with half-frost, yet inside it was an entirely different story.

The cave floor was dry and gritty. Blake touched the rock wall. It was warm to his hand. He turned to Tinker, and managed a laugh.

"Our luck's changed. We've got central heating. Must be volcanic."

"Hmm," Tinker got out. "Very nice. Let's hope it's regulated, too. Cold as I am, I don't fancy being cooked."

They set to and improvised a bed for Peters, putting him in the warmest place. They stripped off some of their sodden clothing and laid it out to dry. Opening their packs, they got out rations and quickly prepared a meal from tins of self-heating soup, dried meat, and chocolate. After the meal they stretched out for a little hard-earned rest. An upturned electric torch gave faint illumination. Peters slept.

Tinker stretched; yawned. "Almost a home from home. But I'm going to complain about the beds in his place. Mine feels like it's got a rock in it. Not that that'll stop me sleeping . . ."

Blake glanced across at him. "You're not going to sleep. Not yet. Rest awhile but don't get too comfortable. We can't afford to sleep. We've got work to do."

"Moving on already, chief? What about our wounded friend?"

Blake frowned slightly. "He's the problem, of course. He needs warm bedding and clothing, better food, and soon more and better medical attention than we can give him."

"And where are we going to get all those things?"

"Well . . ." Blake said thoughtfully, ". . . if there's some sort of settlement here—hostile or otherwise—we should be able to lay hands on some of them."

"You mean—you mean raid the place?"

"Only if the inhabitants are hostile. And I'll do it. You stay here and look after Peters. I may be gone some little time. While I'm about it, I might as well scout around thoroughly, and get a good idea of the lie of the land."

He said it light-heartedly enough. He had no idea what he was going to find.

DRY AND WARMLY dressed again, Sexton Blake left the shelter of the cave and walked out into fog and cutting sleet. He went inland, climbing over boulders and shale. And all the time the land sloped upwards.

Far behind, he could hear the cries of sea-birds and the distant sound of waves beating the shore. From ahead, he could hear nothing. And visibility in the swirling fog was only a few yards.

Now the slope sharpened, and as he progressed the shale gave way to slippery ash and rough lava interspersed with patches of leathery vegetation. He did not attempt to circle the slope. He knew it for what it was—the side of a burned-out volcano—and somehow he had the feeling that if there was a settlement on the island he was going in the right direction to find it.

So he went on—climbing now, rather than walking—leaning his body forward. He used his hands to grasp the roots of the slippery vegetation and pull himself upwards. Sharp lava cut through his clothing and tore at his hands. His boots slipped on thin, greasy clay and the matted undergrowth.

Up here, the strong wind whipped him, ripping up gouts of lava ash and flinging them in his face to further irritate his already burning eyes. But he went doggedly on—upward ever upward—now and then losing ground as the slick, crumbling surface beneath his feet failed to give him purchase, but never losing heart. Every muscle in his body ached from the effort he was making.

But finally the fog thinned a little, and he saw that he hadn't far to go before reaching the rim of the volcano's crater. Another few minutes of hard climbing, and his hands touched the rough rock at the top. He pulled himself up slowly, wriggling forward until he was lying flat on a table of rock. He looked over the edge, and drew in his breath sharply.

The night was dark now, but, inside the crater, neither the night nor the thin fog prevented him from seeing that he had been right—quite right.

The punishing climb—everything he had endured—had not been in vain.

Looking down, he could see that the hand of an intelligent being had indeed been at work here—was, in fact, still at work. Someone had improved upon nature, there was no question of that.

But a much larger question remained.

Who was at work here?

It was the biggest question of all!

Were the intelligent beings whose settlement this was human . . . or alien?

Was he looking down upon the handiwork of man—or of creatures from Space?

THE CRATER'S INTERIOR was a sharp but rugged slope leading down to a narrow roadway which encircled the inside of the cone some two hundred feet below. It was like looking down into a basin fitted with a jutting ledge below the rim. Blake assumed that the road went right round although he couldn't see quite that far. The crater must have been half a mile in diameter.

Dotted along the road at regular intervals were small pools of light which seemed to spill out from sources in the cone wall. Inside the circle drawn by the road was a central well of deep darkness. A faint, faraway sound of machinery came to Blake's ears: a low, pulsating hum.

He edged along the crater rim. If he were going down to the road he would have to make for a spot between lights. He chose the place carefully, and then began lowering himself over the edge.

He felt like a fly on a wall, and at any moment expected to be swatted by the beam of a searchlight—and then by something more lethal. He went down quickly. Here the rock was rough, and although the slope was steep there were plenty of small projections to afford handholds.

He was less than twenty feet above the perimeter road, and descending rapidly, when, suddenly, it happened.

Without warning a sharp, loud, metallic sound slammed through the night. In the same moment, light leapt over the road, bright and rectangular. Instantly, Blake froze, crouching in a fold between rocks. What was happening? Had he been discovered?

What he saw next made him crouch lower. The sound he had heard had been that of a door in the cone wall being thrown open. Now a shadow was cast sharply across the road.

The shadow was that of a "thing." There was no other word to describe it. A huge, round puffball of a head doddered on top of a thin, grotesquely foreshortened trunk.

Was this one of the saucer people? Was this what they were like? The shadow was almost motionless now. Only the head moved, doddering round this way and that. The "thing" seemed to be listening intently and scanning the road. Blake held his breath.

Then, as suddenly as the rectangle of light had appeared, it was gone. The metal door in the cone wall was slammed shut, and on the heels of the dying echoes came silence. An empty silence. Blake wiped sweat out of his eyes and waited. He waited one long minute . . . two . . . three . . . four . . . five. Nothing moved.

He came to life again then. Cautiously, he descended the rest of the way to the road. He looked along it.

It was made of concrete, and was about twenty feet wide. There was no direct light here, and Blake took a chance. He crossed the road swiftly and silently.

On the other side was a concrete wall six feet in height. Blake pulled himself up and looked over it. He looked down into a completely black, blank pit. It must have been hundreds of feet deep. No light was reflected into it, and none came from it.

Blake slid back across the road then—a shadow among shadows. He found the metal door which the "thing" had opened, and hesitated momentarily before it. Then he put out a hand and gently grasped the handle. He tried the door. It was unlocked.

He eased it back a few millimetres. Nothing happened. He opened it a few millimetres more, and put an eye to the opening. Beyond the door there was darkness. He turned his head and listened and heard nothing. He pushed the door back a little way farther, and squeezed through the opening. He shut the door after him, and flashed a dim, hooded torch.

He was in a wide passage giving on to a cross-corridor after five or six yards. There were still no signs of life.

The corridor stretched many yards in either direction. There were doors. He tried one stealthily. The door opened.

And then—

Then with no warning at all the world seemed to fall in on him. Something struck him across the back of the head with furious force.

He knew only terrible shock and blinding pain and the hard floor leaping up to smash brutally against his face and forehead.

After that he was in the grip of deep, deathly unconsciousness.

TIMELESS AEONS LATER, light was bright in Blake's face. It seared through his closed eyelids. This was the first thing that he knew as consciousness slowly returned. The light hurt him.

He turned his head this way and that, still only barely sensible. But he couldn't escape the light. Whatever he did, it still penetrated his lids. He ran the tip of a dry tongue out over equally dry lips. He opened his eyes.

He opened them slowly, but even so he flinched away from the blazing brilliance which beat down upon him. He lay on his back on a cold, hard, marble floor. The light source was high above. He turned on his side to avoid the glare that hurt his eyes, and then froze.

Only feet away from him, a "thing" stood watching.

It was a bare five feet tall, and garbed in a strange dark blue uniform. Its spine curled in a terrible question mark. Its huge, puff-ball head doddered on the top of humped shoulders. In place of hair there was a scaly bald skull; in place of ears there were round, puckered holes.

The skull cliffed out to bald brows, below which a mere fold of flesh with gaping nostrils took the place-of a nose. All the skin of the face was wrinkled and dry and etched as though from some disease. The mouth was a wide, lipless slit.

The arms in the uniform sleeves were elbow-length only. They terminated in ball-like fists with only little bony protuberances jutting from them—embryonic fingers and thumbs.

The creature was looking straight at Blake, its huge puff-ball head trembling.

And then slowly, but deliberately, it moved towards him.

THE THIRTEENTH CHAPTER

The Thing.

TINKER WAS YAWNING.

And yawning not from tiredness, which would have been reasonable, but from inaction.

Sexton Blake had been gone nearly two hours now. Two hours in which Tinker had made Peters and the cave a little more comfortable; had manhandled a boulder to the cave-mouth as a defence against surprise attack; and had rested a little.

Now he was bored.

He yawned again, and then stood up abruptly. He must find something to occupy him! He turned around, and moved deep into the inner recesses of the cave. There he came to a halt below a hole which gaped in one corner of the roof.

He had discovered the hole earlier and had been tempted to explore at the time, but he had restrained himself. Then he had had other things to do.

But now—? Now was different. Now he had nothing to busy himself with. He crouched, tensed his muscles, and then leapt upwards, hands high. They clamped on to the edge of the hole. With a heave and a twist he swung himself up.

He found himself in another small, rocky chamber from which a natural chimney climbed like a tortuous tube. He wriggled himself up through its length. Then he was looking out of a narrow cleft some twenty-five feet above the cave mouth.

Cold foggy air swirled across his eyes. This would have been a good lookout point, he thought—if only he had been able to see anything at all through the dark night.

He tensed as a sound reached him from some distance away to the right. Could this be Blake returning?

The sound was small at first—but it grew. And then Tinker knew that this wasn't Blake. The sound was that made by a considerable body of men marching over the loose rocky ground.

Tinker crouched, waiting.

They came on fast, a blacker mass than the night, advancing from the right, making straight for the cave-mouth. They broke column as the ground gave way to piled rocks, but still they came on unhesitatingly.

Now they were directly below him, and now, too, Tinker had the first cold doubt. Were they men? He couldn't see them clearly. But . . . were they men—?

He began to edge his way back along the chimney as quietly and as quickly as he could. He could hear them in the lower cave now—where Peters lay helpless.

His mouth tightened.

He did not know yet what he was going to do. There were twenty, maybe thirty, of the marchers. And what were they—men . . . or aliens?

Tinker felt for his .38 revolver in its underarm holster. He thumbed off the safety catch.

What had happened to Blake—?

"Get up!"

There was no expression in the scaly face which looked down

124

into Blake's own. One felt that there never could be—with such a lack of normal skin and features. Only the eyes in the puff-ball head showed any emotion. They were blazing deep-red, demanding obedience.

"Get up!" the creature repeated.

And suddenly grey-clad armed men were there, jerking Blake to his feet. He wrenched away from them, and they would have handled him roughly had not the creature moved one of his stubby arms in a gesture which stayed them.

Blake looked around him.

He stood in the centre of a large, circular room. Electronic equipment was ranged round the walls. The eyes of the grey-clad armed men were hard upon him: grim eyes, and purposeful.

The creature spoke again. "What are you doing here? Why have you come?"

Blake faced the blazing, deep-red eyes, but didn't answer.

The huge head doddered on the hunched shoulders. "We are being investigated. I know that. You, presumably, are one of the investigators. Well—we shall deal with you in due course. But you could not have come here alone. Where is your companion?"

Now, for the first time in that great circular room, Sexton Blake spoke. "I haven't got one."

He was examining his questioner. The original doubt he had held as to the other's earthliness had faded by now—under rationalisation.

He acknowledged that this was a man. But a very, very unusual—and exceptional—one.

THIS WAS A man, but one such as rarely showed himself. It was astonishing how he had even survived birth.[3]

But survive he had, had overcome every handicap, and was plainly now in a position of power.

125

Power to what purpose?

He was obviously a leader. The leader directing the flight of the flying saucers, if this was their base. The grey-clad armed men had obeyed his every gesture.

And this must mean that he was an intellectual giant, a genius. It had to. Why else should men follow him?

But where was he leading? In what direction? What did his power portend? What was his goal?

Blake's mental questions were parried with an audible one. The red eyes burned.

"Where is your companion? You will tell us! Talk!"

BLAKE MOVED, FEIGNING impatience. "I told you. I am alone."

"You lie, of course."

Then the questions came fast, and to the point.

"Where have you hidden the radio? How did you discover this place? What were you hoping to find here? How much do you know?"

And it came for the third time—"Where is your companion?"

But now Blake hesitated.

He was suddenly nagged by the thought of Peters lying wounded and in danger from gangrene, battling for his life in the warm but damp cave.

He believed that these people would have the medical equipment and knowledge to look after Peters and ensure he got well again. Yet to tell where he was might, the more certainly, condemn him to death.

He wished he knew what to do for the best.

On the one hand, his captors could save Peters. He was sure of it. On the other, they might kill him. There had been murderous violence in Iceland, and more had been offered by Roderick.

What should he do?

Blake looked up to meet the eyes of his inquisitor. Eyes which suddenly seemed to shaft their gaze clean through his own. He had a strange, almost uncanny sensation of something probing about in his brain.

"You are concerned for the safety of your companion," the inquisitor said softly.

"I have no companion," Blake replied automatically.

Then a telephone buzzed.

One of the armed, grey-clad men reached for it. It stood on a broad, mirror-polished desk below a racked instrument panel. He lifted the receiver up off its rest and held it out. Blake's questioner didn't touch it. Just listened. And then—

Then he nodded briefly. The grey-clad guard dropped the receiver back, and pressed a push-button beside it. The outer door of the great circular room slid back with a faint sigh. Blake turned. No one prevented him.

Two more grey-clad men appeared in the doorway. They carried a stretcher between them. There was a body on the stretcher sheeted from sight.

Blake took a step forward. He couldn't restrain himself. Whose was the sheeted body? Peters . . . Tinker . . .?

The stretcher-bearers advanced to the centre of the room. They stopped and there was a faint click as the stretcher sprouted legs, becoming a kind of camp-bed.

Someone drew back the covering sheet.

Blake looked down. Looked again sharp.

It was Peters, and he was still alive.

Blake's inquisitor turned to him.

"You see . . . we knew you did not come alone. Our agents reported it. We knew of your mission. We have been following your progress. In fact, there is very little that we don't know, and that won't take us very long to find out—Mister Sexton Blake!"

THE FOURTEENTH CHAPTER

Turnabout.

SO THEY KNEW who he was!

The sudden ejaculation of his own name startled Blake for a moment, but not sufficiently for him to show any sign of surprise. Obviously, with their world-wide espionage system, these people were well equipped to obtain information.

He thought swiftly. They knew that he had not come alone—then Peters had been brought in. What of Tinker, then? Did they know about the third man? Had Tinker been killed or captured when Peters was taken? Had he tried to stop them taking Peters? If not, why not? What had happened?

The puff-ball head was nodding again: the slit mouth speaking. "Our organisation outside failed on this occasion. You and your companion should have been prevented from getting here. Now that you are here, you are a problem to us. Obviously, you cannot be allowed to leave."

Blake said: "Your agent, Roderick, tried to stop us all right. He tried to kill us, and he wasn't the only one. He ended up killing himself."

The other's voice sharpened. "That is a lie! No violence was to be used!"

Blake shrugged. "Not much! There was considerable violence, even murder, on several occasions. You have a strange attitude, my friend. You make war on the civilised world, then you talk of non-violence."

"We reserve the right to execute traitors in our midst, but outsiders are dealt with by other methods."

Blake's mouth set disbelievingly. "Roderick didn't attempt to use them."

The other man turned away sharply; abruptly. He spoke to one of the grey-garbed guards. "Have Number Two and Number Three come in immediately. I'll know the truth about this!"

The guard lifted the telephone and spoke into the mouthpiece. Blake waited, consumed with curiosity.

Number Two . . . ? Number Three . . . ? From the grotesque[4] man's tone of absolute authority, Blake deduced that he himself was "Number One" in this hierarchy. Who were these others?

Then footsteps sounded in the corridor outside the circular room, and he turned quickly—and knew.

The truth stunned him. For a moment he just stood—and stared.

For he recognised the first man into the room as being Fedor Sergeyev—the one-time Russian brain-and-nerve specialist and professor of abnormal psychology; the brilliant scientist who had disappeared without a trace from his homeland immediately after the war.

And the man behind him had been equally world-renowned for his brilliance before he, too, had vanished in the same year.

He was, without doubt, a famous German who had worked with Wernher von Braun on the V-weapons at Hitler's Peenemunde research base before being given a top-secret project all of his own.

130

His name was Haussman. Paul Haussman. And Blake knew it well, for Allied agents, of which he had been one, had combed all Europe for this man at the war's end. But to no avail.

It had been eventually supposed that he was dead, yet here he was. And here was Fedor Sergeyev. It incredible! Unbelievable! But it was true!

PAUL HAUSSMAN'S BLACK button eyes fastened on Blake grimly, then they jerked away. For the monstrous[4] leader was speaking—repeating all Blake had told him, word for word.

Then came the question, directed at Haussman. "Number Two, you are responsible for outside organisation. Does this man speak the truth?"

The German shifted his feet. The lids lowered over his black button eyes. "There had to be violence, Number One. There was obviously no other way to deal with the situation. What did you expect?"

The leader's eyes blazed suddenly. "Number Two, you are betraying all our principles, all our ideals. There are other ways, as you well know. Your violence failed, as violence always will."

The German stiffened.

"I am your equal—more than your equal—I am not to be reprimanded like a schoolboy. There was an emergency. Our people met it the best way they could."

Number One made a gesture with his stump of a fist. "It is over. But do not let it happen again. Remember our rules—our aims—our objectives. They should at all times be engraved on your mind."

Paul Haussman subsided, sullen-faced. The leader turned back to Blake. "As I said, you and Carter here are a problem."

So he thought Peters was Tinker. The spy system wasn't all that good, after all! It was beginning to look as though Tinker

131

had got clean away. Well, let them go on thinking they'd got him.

"But," continued Number One, in a thoughtful voice, "it is a problem which is relatively easily solved. Carter is injured. He will get expert medical attention. I have no use for dead men. Then you will both join our cause."

Blake laughed outright. "We came as agents of a World Power to investigate you—not to join you!"

"But you will."

"What makes you so sure?"

The deformed man was imperturbable. "We have the equipment to make you change your minds—literally. You will join the cause, have no doubt."

Blake shrugged. "Brainwashing?" he suggested sarcastically.

Number One's huge head nodded slowly. Something akin to a smile touched the grotesquely formed face. "You might call it that. You will see."

"And the 'cause'?"

The leader leaned forward. He spoke very clearly. "The cause, my friend? What the world has been waiting for—yearning for—hoping for! The end of all friction between nations! The precursor of eternal peace!

"World Government, my friend. World Government!"

BLAKE LET THE breath come out of him in a lingering sigh. So that was the answer! He had no doubt now that he was at the secret base of the flying saucers. This was the reason for the saucers, for the worldwide espionage system, for the grouping together of the V.I.P. scientists who had disappeared over the past decade.

Were they all here?

World Government . . . that was it in a nutshell. But there was a lot of background detail still to be explained.

And now he was to be forced by some mysterious means to

join the cause. He had a feeling that explanations would soon be forthcoming. And he knew that the leader[4], Number One, could be none other than the man Craille had mentioned—the Englishman who had disappeared, the backroom genius whose top-secret inventions had paved the way for Allied victory in World War II, the deformed child born to an illustrious family . . .

He said slowly, "You must be Murray Englefield."

The puff-ball head doddered agreement.

"Yes, I am indeed Englefield. But my name does not matter. It is what I am that matters. I am the leader of the movement that will save the world and bring peace to the nations."

"And yet you helped the Allies win a war."

Number One said with a harsh edge to his voice: "I helped them with one thought in my mind. The same thought I have now. The same burning desire. I longed for peace, and my warlike inventions paradoxically helped to obtain it. You might say that I gave peace to the Allies . . . and what did they do with it? They threw it away, a despised prize. They drift back to war!"

"And you are going to stop them?" Blake said. "You are going to bring the nations of the world into one camp? With this small island base and a handful of supporters in the outer world? Once this place is located, one medium-sized long-range missile could utterly annihilate you."

Englefield nodded. "I am aware of that. And maybe it will not be long before we are located and pinpointed. But we shall act first."

"With what?" Blake said bluntly.

"It is very simple, Mr. Blake. We have the power to control men's minds."

"The world over?"

"The world over. Listen. We have the supreme air transport vehicle—the 'flying saucer' invented by Number Two—"

"Paul Haussman," Blake put in.

"Paul Haussman, if you prefer. He was developing it for Germany. This island, with all its equipment, workshops, and barracks, was a secret German wartime base, for submarines as well as the saucer project. We have a fleet of saucers, all equipped with automatic cameras and other devices for surveying the earth.

"And we have, in fact, surveyed it. Our records are all preserved here on microfilm. We know the exact locations of all offensive bases and testing grounds. We know all the places where wealth in the form of mineral deposits is to be found. We know the places for crop growing. We have the biggest potential for world salvation that has ever been known, and when we form our World Government we shall eliminate want and starvation, disease and war, from all nations. Our survey is complete and action is imminent."

"You are going to make war on the rest of the world rather than ask the nations to co-operate?"

"They would not co-operate. We dare not let anyone know the power we hold. With the weapons we have, any one of the Powers would be able to conquer the rest."

"And that's just what you're going to do?"

"Mr. Blake, we have to operate from strength. We do not intend to conquer in the accepted sense—not using violence. At the given time, we shall land saucers in each of the seats of government and in the missile bases. We shall take the rulers and generals prisoner and give them an electronic treatment we have devised. There is no other way, for the generals and politicians have shown themselves to be truly incorrigible. After the treatment, they will have blank minds. They will possess no opinions. We will then re-educate them to seek friendship with their fellows, and world unity. There will be total disarmament and lasting peace."

Blake said: "An incredible scheme." And it was. But possible. Anything, apparently, was possible to these people. He had to learn all he could about their plans and equipment. So he went on now: "Incredible! And I thought you were a genius, Englefield. I know now that you are only a madman."

Englefield's red eyes blazed. "You think me mad? So others have thought! But you are as wrong as they were! My parents wanted to have me put to sleep at birth. Instead, I was allowed to live, but segregated from my fellows. But I received a training and an education such as few men have enjoyed. I was despised, rejected. The mere sight of me would have been enough to send normal people into hysterics. Yet millions of those same people will follow me along the path to World Government. You will see!"

He was in the grip of great emotion. He made an effort, and brought himself under control.

"But enough of that!" he went on. "I must not bring my own personality into this. You think our scheme is impossible, do you, Mr. Blake? Let me show you the machine that will accomplish it. Come!"

The grey-garbed guards were behind Blake, urging him forward. He followed Englefield, Haussman, and Sergeyev towards a battery of electronic instruments grouped in one segment of the room's perimeter.

The machine they approached stood six feet high, and had a matt grey surface littered with dials and control knobs. Cables linked it to sockets in the wall above. In the centre of the machine, about three feet from the floor, there was an eighteen-inch circular opening.

Englefield nodded to a guard. A switch was depressed. And slowly from the opening there emerged a bowl-shaped network of gleaming wire.

Englefield said: "This is the machine that can first wipe men's minds clear of every opinion, and then lay the foundation for new ones. It was developed jointly by Number Three— Professor Sergeyev—and myself."

He gestured towards it.

"As you may know," he said, "thoughts in the human brain take the form of minute electrical currents, and what we call memory is, in fact, a host of infinitesimally small electrostatic charges set up by shock, emotion, sensation—all the sensory perceptions—out of what we call experience. Opinion is created by the action of thought upon memory, real or imagined, conscious or subconscious. So much is basic. Now let me tell you how this machine works.

"It radiates a force which, in the first instance, equates the minute electrical currents we call thought. It cancels them out. We increase the force put out by the machine and at will—our will—the patterns of the electrostatic charges we call memory may be either merely re-arranged slightly, or utterly scrambled, or totally destroyed.

"And if we increase the force output still further, and modulate the beam of radiation from the machine—as we can do—electrostatic charges can be implanted in the brain cells in place of the old! We can give an artificial memory—firm recollections of events which never actually happened—and new thoughts from which to form the kind of opinions we want him to have!"

His voice rose exultantly. "Now do you see?"

The prospect excited him.

"With this machine, we can condition men's minds to peace and the ultimate sanity of one World Government. We can forever eliminate war! When the time is ripe for us to act—and it will be soon, very soon, I can promise you!—we will first seize the existing centres of government, as I told you, and we will then condition the minds of the world's leaders. This will

136

be enough to see us through the first stages of our humanity. Wholesale conditioning of all the world's peoples will be the next step. Do you still doubt the feasibility of our scheme, Mr. Blake?

"We have this master machine, and from it the conditioning force can be transmitted to 'slave' units operating anywhere in the world. We have already fitted such units in most of our saucer-craft fleet, and soon—very soon—we will have equipped them all."

His voice rose challengingly.

"Now what do you think, Mr. Blake? Do you still find our plans incredible?"

Dry-mouthed, Sexton Blake shook his head.

Incredible—no.

Diabolical—that was a much better word!

HE HAD LITTLE doubt that the machine was perfectly able to do everything Englefield had described. The brain-scrambling treatment meted out to Oliver De Trafford back in England had already provided terrible testimony to the more extreme of transmitted powers.

It could condition men's minds wholesale, expunge old memories, implant new and artificial ones, change patterns of thought. It could outlaw war from the face of the earth forever—surely a wonderful thing.

But Blake still thought it was the most diabolical and hellish machine he had ever clapped eyes on—and this was why.

Its use would rob man of all freedom of will, his endowment. The machine was designed to abrogate his one inborn prerogative, given him by God, and this was not all.

Blake had to believe that Englefield was fanatically sincere in his desire to do humankind nothing but good. But it was his own kind of good, and no man lived forever.

Who would come after Englefield, and what kind of "good" would the next Number One choose to do? Who would control the machine when the hideously deformed zealot was dead, and what use would they make of it? Whatever the theoretical structure of the World Government envisaged by Englefield, the fact would forever remain that he who controlled the machine would hold the true reins of power.

The machine was a force without equal for good and ill, but it could be no more beneficent than whichever man was its master. It would eternally give to its operator an authority hitherto undreamed of. It would permit him to impose his smallest whim or desire upon all mankind. Would not such absolute power ultimately obey the inexorable law and corrupt absolutely?

Fashioned to give mankind the freedom from the evil of war demanded by Englefield, the machine might spawn a greater evil still. It could be the instrument of the most all-embracing, and most vicious tyranny that this planet had ever known. It was more than possible. It was likely.

All this Blake thought as he gazed at the machine.

All this he knew—and knew equally well that he had to destroy it!

ENGLEFIELD SPOKE AGAIN.

"The wire bowl antenna you can see is for use in the immediate vicinity of the machine." He made a sign, and one of the grey-garbed guards turned a switch. "The pattern has now been set to equate all thought-currents in the brain of a subject. The bowl antenna has been put into circuit. We can now make any man give us the truth in reply to any question we ask him. He is incapable of evasive thought. He cannot lie."

He looked full at Blake.

"As I said earlier, we are going to persuade you to join our cause. But first we have to know the full extent of your investigations and what other people have assisted you with them, so that we can take counter-measures."

Blake stiffened inwardly. This was getting more and more dangerous!

Unless he did something—and quickly—he was about to be brain-washed. Under the machine's influence, he would certainly talk, and God only knew what secrets would spill out of him.

Somehow, he had to wreck the machine!

And the next few minutes were going to be vital!

HE THOUGHT OF his Service .38.

What had happened to it?

It wasn't in his possession now, so someone had taken it from him whilst he was unconscious.

Pity!

If he could only have had it in his hands for one moment, perhaps he himself could have provided the answer to another question which had raised itself in his mind.

Was the miracle machine vulnerable or invulnerable to copperjacketed slugs?

Then his eyes fastened on the grey-garbed guard nearest to him. His eyes slid down. The guard had a gun. They all had guns. Revolvers in buttoned holsters. If he could only reach one of them . . .

He looked up to find Englefield's eyes hard upon him. The hideous[4] man had moved away from in front of the machine. They had all moved away from it. He was left facing it. In a second it would begin—the brainwashing—and—

It was then that Paul Haussman spoke softly and sibilantly, his bright black-button eyes glittering with a strange light. "Perhaps we should start with the wounded man—"

"No!"

The word was jerked out of Blake.

"He will talk more easily . . ." Haussman said, and still he spoke softly. Too softly.

Englefield looked at him sharply, and then glanced at Sergeyev. The tall Russian shrugged. In a deep bass voice, he murmured, "It would serve to demonstrate to Mr. Blake the effectiveness of the machine."

"Exactly!" This from Haussman.

"No!" Blake said again. But no one was listening to him now.

Englefield made a signal. Two of the guards swiftly moved Peters on his stretcher into a better position in front of the gleaming antenna. Blake looked down at the grey-bearded, pain-racked face of his comrade. Then Haussman moved between Blake and the stretcher, and pulled back the sheet. He stripped it off Peters and let it fall. He stepped back. He turned his black-button eyes towards Blake.

Englefield stood by the machine, but one of the guards took over its operation. The gleaming wire bowl antenna was directed at Peters' head. The guard thumbed down a switch . . .

A shudder ran through Peters, and his tortured face twisted horribly—and then smoothed out. Blake's nerves were taut, as tight as piano wires. He had to stop this!

The others were watching.

Haussman said, "A little demonstration, Mr. Blake . . ." He almost purred the words. His little pink tongue played on his soft bottom lip. He said sharply to the guard operating the machine, "Make him get up!"

Englefield's eyes blazed with sudden anger.

"Stop that!'

He was too late. The operator had already swung a variable control. To Blake's horror, Peters, gravely injured and incapable of standing, sat up with blank eyes, sweat starting out on his grey forehead. His feet swung down towards the floor.

"Stop it, I say!"

The words leapt out of Englefield on a high note of fury.

The operator reversed the control. Peters sank back on to the stretcher.

Englefield turned. He moved ominously towards Haussman. He spoke in a voice which shook with passion. "That was entirely unnecessary, Number Two! I will have no cruelty!"

Haussman moved back involuntarily under the blazing ferocity of his leader's eyes. He came to within a few inches of Blake.

And Blake acted!

He slammed into Haussman, pitching him forward straight at the nearest guard. The man was knocked off-balance as the German blundered into him. His hands jerked upwards clutching at air—clutching at anything—to save himself.

In that same instant, Blake had his revolver!

He wrenched it out of the guard's holster. He moved so fast that no one had time to stop him.

In one swinging movement, he thumbed back the safety-catch, aimed at the brainwashing machine, and fired. The gun jumped in his hand. He emptied it into the machine.

Then the others were upon him.

He was beaten down to the floor by sheer weight of numbers. The empty gun was wrested away from him. He was dragged to his feet.

Haussman, white with rage, punched him full in the face.

"Stop!"

Englefield swung round from the machine. The damage it had sustained had been his first concern.

"Stop!"

Englefield's deformed body was shuddering with intense anger.

Behind him, smoke was coming out of the machine. Yellow

141

smoke, thick and acrid. The operator had hastily switched off the power.

Englefield advanced over the floor. His puffball of a head doddering furiously. He glared past Blake. His anger was directed at Haussman.

"The machine is badly damaged. It may take days—weeks even—to repair. Our plans will have to be put back in time. Consider yourself responsible for this, Number Two. It would not have happened if you had not indulged the sadistic streak that is in you! You—"

Haussman interrupted.

His pale lips spilled bitter words. His black eyes were beads of contempt. "All right, Englefield. I take full responsibility. And from now on, responsibility for the plans, also. I have had enough of you. This had to come, anyway. It was inevitable. World Government? To hell with it—and with you!"

Englefield's eyes glittered dangerously. His hand moved impulsively towards an ominous bulge in the pocket of his dark blue uniform.

But before the movement had been completed a tiny automatic had appeared in Haussman's hand.

It pointed straight at Englefield's huge, doddering head.

Then Haussman pulled the trigger.

THE FIFTEENTH CHAPTER

Divide and Conquer.

ENGLEFIELD WAS JOLTED backwards by the impact of the bullet. He staggered, and fell to his knees.

On either side of Blake, guards roughly restrained the detective's instinctive lunge forward.

Blood ran down into Englefield's eyes from the bullet-hole in his skull. He was gasping and swaying. He should have been dead. But somehow, desperately, he managed to hang on to life a few moments more.

He got out: "Treachery . . . now I know you for what you are . . . all of you . . . you must stop him . . . his ambition will . . . will bring ruin . . ."

Haussman's black marble eyes glittered as he laughed cynically. He gestured with the automatic. "Too late, Englefield. Most of them are already with me. Your dreams were too fanciful for them. I can give them something they understand."

Englefield stared in dulled disbelief. Death had its grip upon him. Blood sheeted his face.

"Look around you," Haussman said harshly. "Is anyone threatening you? Call on them again. Order them to arrest me.

No one will take any notice. You see—I command now!"

"Stop him . . ." Englefield whispered. "Stop him!"

His voice was but a faint, pathetic echo of what it had been. And in the great circular room, nobody moved.

Englefield died then. He died utterly disillusioned by the awful betrayal. He slumped to the floor, twitched once, and lay still.

Haussman's lip twisted. "Impractical fool!"

Blake looked hard at the German. "Whatever he was, he had principles. What does all this make you—a hero?"

The German's black-button eyes narrowed. "I'll tell you what it makes me. A leader. The leader everyone here has been waiting for—and everyone in Europe. World Government . . . ? That was Englefield's dream. A crazy dream. Between the dream and the reality too much could have gone wrong. We are strong, but we have nowhere near the size of force necessary to accomplish all that he planned. I tried to tell him, but he wouldn't listen to reason. Not about this, nor yet about anything."

His voice rose.

"If he'd got his world, what would he have made of it? A goody-goody heaven? Stupidly idealistic nonsense! Man is not yet ready for such high concepts."

He spoke with flat assurance. "My way, my plan, my target are all better than his!"

Blake looked at him sceptically. "And what is your target?"

The look angered Haussman. "Oh, you can sneer, but we will accomplish it! This is something we are quite capable of doing without over-extending ourselves. This is no dream!

"We are going to create a Third Force in the world. A United Europe. Europe one nation. The Third Force which European man desperately needs if he is to survive. Consider—

"In the world as we know it today, America and the Soviet

Union are bound to come into conflict eventually. They cannot fail to. They are twin giants greedy for ultimate dominion over every inch of the earth. Whether they admit it or not, they seek the same thing that Englefield did—World Government. But each seeks it only for his own ideology. Collision is ultimately inevitable."

The German spoke bleakly.

"And, meanwhile, they snarl at each other continually, like dogs over a carcass. That carcass is Europe. Between them, they have already torn it apart, and worse will follow—and soon—unless Europe unites as one nation to prevent it."

Blake nodded. He was forced to admit there was truth in what Haussman said. But, just the same . . .

He said, "Europe will have to unite, I agree. Many thinking people already know it. And the continental European states are already moving in that direction."

"With Eurovision—?" Haussman sneered. "What else have they come together on? Oh, they have plans—but they implement them too slowly. Even without our intervention it is likely that they will unite, it is true. But—when? That is the question. They don't seem to realise that time is not on their side. They talk, talk, talk—endlessly. And while they talk, the dogs take another two bites out of the carcass, and come nearer, ever nearer, to going for each other's throats for the last scrap of festering meat, the last bone.

"They talk, talk, talk—and all the time Europe is being swallowed up into tight little spheres of influence—the bellies of the two dogs. Our massive intervention will put an end to all that!

"We have the saucer-fleet and we have the conditioning machine which—despite your puerile effort to destroy it— Professor Sergeyev will quite soon repair. Then we will be ready.

"Overnight we will seize the centres of power throughout

Europe. We will compel unification. And with the morning there will be born a new nation larger and stronger than either the Soviet Union or America individually. Three hundred million Europeans will be on the march! The dogs will be driven off then, and the world will know peace.

"For after we have seized power and unified Europe, neither America nor Russia will dare to attack the other. If they were to, Europe would certainly side with the victim of the attack against the aggressor. Khruschev and the American generals in the Pentagon will know this. We will see that they know it. Any such conflict would be one an aggressor just could not win!"

"So you will have peace . . ." Blake said, and nodded. "But what is your price? You are no altruist, Herr Haussman. A few minutes ago, you made that quite clear. What do you and your men hope to get out of this?"

"We will get . . . whatever we want." Haussman said softly. "We will have the power."

Then Blake recalled Englefield's last, gasped-out warning, and he recalled other things, too. He remembered the rattlesnake swiftness of Haussman's act of treachery towards Englefield. He remembered the wanton callousness the German had displayed towards Peters.

He knew then that even although a united Europe would be an inestimable blessing he could not allow Haussman to unite it his way. He could not stand by while this man prepared to take whatever he wanted. He could not allow him to have the absolute power guaranteed by the diabolical conditioning machine.

He had to escape, somehow. He had to scotch this man's plans.

And he must do it soon. It was imperative!

HAUSSMAN WAS SPEAKING again, turning away. "I've wasted enough time on you." His gesture to the guards included Peters with Blake. "Take them away!"

Blake got out quickly, "What do you intend to do with us?"

The German glanced back at him. "I could have you killed . . . but it will be more fitting to have you work for the cause. So as soon as the machine is repaired, you and your friend will be properly conditioned. There are others, too, to be treated. They were Englefield's men. They'll join you in the cells."

"You are imprisoning this man with us?" Blake indicated Peters. "He's badly wounded."

"So—?"

"He needs care and proper medical attention—medicine, drugs, dressings. I am a qualified doctor. Will you let me have those things?"

Haussman looked hard at him, then momentarily his face softened and he nodded slowly. "All right. You can have what you require. Each day, at noon, you will be allowed out of your cell to go to the medical centre. Under escort."

Blake did not betray his elation.

To be allowed out, even under guard, was a valuable concession which might permit him to formulate a plan of escape.

Next moment, at another gesture from Haussman, grey-garbed guards closed in on him. They led him away.

It was a communal cell equipped with half a dozen metal beds fitted with boards and rough blankets. It was a cold cell, with no heating, and with high, smooth, grey rock walls which stretched up to a small ventilation grille just below an unreachable ceiling. The door was of heavy metal, solid except for a group of holes five feet up.

In the passage outside, guards patrolled at regular intervals.

Peters had remained on his stretcher bed. He was asleep. Blake took stock of his fellow-prisoners—Englefield's men. He wondered what use, if any, he would be able to make of them.

147

There were four of them. They sat on their beds dull-eyed, plainly stunned by the swift march of events.

One was an American: an ex-General of the U.S. Air Defence Command, no less! He was a rangy Texan with a long, lean, troubled face. His name, Blake soon learned, was Bradley Whittington. And he had a lot on his mind.

He said it again and again. "What's going to happen to us?" He told Blake, "I gave up everything to join Englefield. I believe in World Government."

He said it with a kind of sad, sick, desperation.

"I turned my back on my home and my family and my command in the Air Force. I even renounced my country. And for what?"

His voice was bitter.

"Englefield's dead, and the Concept is dead with him, and now his executioner is giving the orders. You think I can go along with that? Haussman murdered Englefield, there's no two ways about it. You think I can follow a murderer?

"I wouldn't trust Haussman an inch—never could. And what is there about a united Europe to excite me anyway? I go for 'One World,' sure. That's what I came here for. But if that can't be, why then I'm an American."

He said it again. "What's going to happen to us?"

Blake gave him an answer. "Join us. Come hell or high water. I'm going to break out!"

THEY TALKED ABOUT it; argued. Whittington could see no future for him here, but even less in the world outside.

He said with a kind of hopelessness, "I renounced my country. Can't you understand that? You think the Air Force would welcome me back—even if we could get out of this place, which we can't!"

"We've got to try to get out," Blake insisted. "What's the

148

alternative? Be conditioned? I don't care for that! Have a slice of Haussman's brave new world? I don't care for that either. His brave new world will just turn out to be a brave new tyranny, unless I miss my guess. The basic conception of a United Europe frankly excites me tremendously, but the thought of Haussman—a murderer—running it his way equally frankly repels. To tell you the truth, I'm dedicated to stopping him."

"But what can you do? What can any of us do?"

"Break out of here—for a start!" Blake said, and kept on saying it. The other men in the cell were apathetic creatures, almost numbly resigned to their fate. Blake had already mentally written them off as possible allies. Bradley Whittington was different, and two men would have exactly twice the chance of success than one had.

Blake kept hammering away at him. "Join me!"

Finally Whittington agreed. Blake convinced him there was nothing else he could sanely and reasonably do.

"Okay," he sighed. "Okay, Blake, I'll go along with you."

Blake grinned tiredly, and gripped the American's lean arm. "I thought you would never see sense! Good man!"

"How AND WHEN do we do it?" Whittington now wanted to know.

Blake countered, "How long before Sergeyev can get that infernal machine working again?"

"A couple of days at least. Maybe longer."

"Two days . . ." Blake echoed thoughtfully. "That's all the time we've surely and certainly got . . ."

Then he said, "I'm allowed out at noon tomorrow—if Haussman keeps to his word—and again the day after. So tomorrow I watch for openings, and the next day, at noon, we'll take a gamble and attack."

Even though he spoke with optimism, twin thoughts nagged

him. What about Peters? How were they going to get him away? And what about Tinker?

THE HOURS PASSED swiftly, every one bringing Blake's first break a little nearer. Whittington gave him a detailed description of the island and the men and machines on it.

The organisation Englefield, Haussman, and Sergeyev had created was almost entirely self-supporting, having its own sources of heat and power in the dormant volcano, and deriving food from the sea, from underground gardens, and from synthetics. Underground, too, were foundries and workshops, where the saucers had been built and where they were serviced, and submarine pens on the northernmost tip of the island.

The base had been planned and built by the Germans shortly before World War II as a refuelling and refitting station for the North Atlantic U-boat packs. Its use as a centre for flying saucer research had come later—after the Allies had finally won the Atlantic battle. At that time most of the U-boats based on the island had been withdrawn to other waters. But one submarine still remained, even now, and was still in use.

"What on earth is it used for?" Blake wanted to know.

"The secret transportation of heavy machinery," was Whittington's answer.

He went on to tell Blake that the circular room where Englefield had been killed was the island's nerve centre. Closely linked to it were other control rooms, and, opening off it, the small store where the microfilm records were kept. Here, on non-inflammable stock, the entire world was mapped, its strategic positions and mineral deposits. Also on microfilm were full details of the organisation, its internal personnel and agents throughout the world.

"What about the saucer-fleet?" Blake asked. "Where's that?"

Whittington told him.

The saucers were right in the centre of the island, deep in the crater, each in its own bay covered by a sliding roof. There were forty-eight saucers in all.

They were high altitude craft, Whittington explained, not space vehicles. Their ceiling was far in excess of that of any other aeroplane. They were twenty-five feet in diameter with a central control cabin twelve feet across and seven feet high—something like a squashed orange. They had sliding doors in the lower hemisphere, and were supported by an undercarriage of three, equally spaced, retractable globes.

The control cabin of a saucer was cushioned against gravitational forces by the nature of its suspension within its rotating circular wing. The seats were cushioned in their attachment to the deck. The occupants were cushioned in their seats besides wearing anti-g clothing.

The whole saucer was made of special aluminium alloy, double-skinned and pressurised. Its outer surface was coated with a silica-based plating which was virtually friction-free, so that despite speeds in excess of seven thousand miles an hour little heat was generated. In certain lights the plating gave off a peculiar scintillation.

An advanced form of completely automatic, transistorised, inertial navigation was used, the saucer's exact position being pinpointed at all times on an optically projected chart.

The saucers were powered and controlled by jets on the perimeter of the circular rotating wing. The fuel, a discovery of Haussman's, had a sodium base, reacting violently when meeting air, however thin.

The fuel was stored in special concrete and aluminium tanks set in the inside of the volcanic crater, surrounding and on the same level as the saucer bays. These tanks were very strongly constructed and under regular inspection, as no air had to be allowed to get in.

It was, said Bradley Whittington, like living on a powder-dump, for if any air ever did get into the tanks there could be an almighty explosion that might wreck the whole island.

Blake considered Whittington's information very thoughtfully.

"Can you pilot a saucer?" he asked.

"Oh, yes."

Blake's task, as he saw it, was principally to get away with a saucer with as big a payload of the microfilm records as the machine would carry. In addition, he had to destroy the brain-conditioning machine utterly, and he wanted Haussman and Sergeyev—dead or alive.

A pretty tall order. An alternative was to try and commandeer a radio transmitter and use it to contact the base back in Iceland, asking for a force to be landed. But a landing might not take place quickly enough to avert disaster . . . no . . . his first plan, desperate though it might seem, was the better one.

When noon came around, the door of the cell was thrown open. A group of grey-garbed guards stood in the corridor.

Their leader announced, "We have orders to escort you to the medical centre to collect essential supplies."

Blake said easily, "Okay, I'm with you."

He walked out through the doorway guarded on every side. He looked straight into the bearded face of one of the guards who stood waiting out in the corridor. A blank, blond-bearded face with light-blue eyes.

Blake's heart pounded.

The guard was—Tinker!

THE SIXTEENTH CHAPTER

Holocaust.

TINKER WAS SWIFTLY lost to view as the guards crowded close to Blake and shepherded him out of the cell-block and along concrete-floored passages.

How had he become a grey-garbed guard?

Outwardly, the detective's face was expressionless, but inwardly he exulted. He had found Tinker at last—or rather Tinker had found him. But what state was the young man's mind in? Had he been conditioned—or was he in full possession of his individuality?

The questions nagged at Blake, never letting him go. But he took stock of as much of the headquarters as he could, passing through. They were still in the section of the crater that housed the control room. The medical centre wasn't far from there. Bradley Whittington had already given him a complete mental plan of the whole island.

The detective was met by two assistants at the medical centre. They led him to the laboratory and store room and watched carefully while he selected his requirements. Then he was marched back to the cell.

Again in the corridor outside the cell-block he caught a brief glimpse of Tinker amongst the other guards. The young man gave no sign of recognition. Was it possible, Blake thought, that Tinker just didn't know him?

The idea was frightening, and it made Blake more determined than ever that Sergeyev should not be allowed to complete work on repairing the diabolical processing machine.

He manoeuvred himself as close to Tinker as possible. He looked into his eyes and formed silent words with his lips. Break at noon tomorrow.

There was the smallest, the slightest of nods from Tinker. So he had caught the message. But had he understood it, and would he be able to be on hand at the time?

Blake could not answer either of these questions with certainty any more than he could know how Tinker had managed to slip into the enemy's ranks.

Throughout the hours which followed, as he waited for one day to pass and another—the day—to begin, these questions worried Blake and gave him little rest.

Noon.

Zero hour had come at last.

Blake and Whittington were keyed up for action.

The other prisoners in the cell knew nothing of what was afoot. Blake doubted their mettle, and hadn't confided in them. They were cowed, subdued, and listless.

The cell door opened. The party of guards awaiting him in the corridor was only five strong.

And Tinker was one of them!

As Blake came out of the cell he glanced quickly to right and to left. There was nobody else in sight. This was the time, then. This was the moment.

One of the guards was behind Blake, locking the cell door.

154

The other four were paired, two on each side of him.

But only three of the four men were certain enemies. Tinker, he prayed, still not knowing, must be an ally.

He leapt into action.

He left Tinker to deal with one guard and, without warning, whirled round on the others. He uppercut one of the pair before the man had even time to register shock. The man reeled back—out on his feet. Blake sank his iron-hard fist deep into the soft midriff of the other.

Then there was the sound of a gasp and a blow from behind him and Tinker was there, standing shoulder to shoulder with him. He had dealt with his man. So he had not been conditioned.

Blake felt a sudden surge of inexpressible thankfulness. Together they went for the one remaining guard who, too stunned by the speed of events to cry out, stood key-in-hand, gaping foolishly, at the cell door.

He did not gape for long!

Tinker hit him once, then hit him again. The man fell as if poleaxed. Then Blake was grabbing his keys. "Into the cell with them all!" It was done in seconds. "Strip off their uniforms! Tie them and gag them!"

Tinker and Whittington worked feverishly at Blake's side.

The other prisoners in the cell stared as if stupefied—and then suddenly seemed to wake up to what was happening. Their voices became a babble of sound.

"Shut up!" Blake said savagely. "Quiet, all of you!"

He would give them their chance.

"We're getting out. Do you want to come with us? You'll run the same risks as we do. We may be shot down before we've gone twenty yards!"

Two made up their minds instantly. The others were hesitant, and there was no time for debate.

"Sorry!" Blake said briefly. "I hate to do this, but—"

He knocked the first undecided prisoner out cold. Tinker grimly dealt with the other. "Bind them and gag them along with the guards!"

They could not afford to take any chances.

SWIFTLY BLAKE DRESSED in one of the uniforms stripped from the guards. Whittington and the other two prisoners speedily followed his example. Meanwhile, Tinker explained breathlessly to Blake how, when the cave had been raided, he had been unable to prevent the capture of Peters. But one of the guards had dallied behind after the others had left and in the fight which had followed he had been killed. Tinker had then seized his chance, and the man's uniform, and penetrated the base . . .

"And no one questioned your bona fides?"

Blake was plainly surprised. But Whittington made a quick comment. "There are so many guards and technicians here, and they all wear the same uniform grey. It makes for near anonymity. They can't, and they don't, all know each other."

"But at night time—" Blake said, "—how did you manage? Where did you sleep? Surely, in the dormitories, each man knows his neighbour—"

"I slept rough," Tinker told him. "And I got around the base during the day by always appearing very busy—always looking as if I was going somewhere on duty in a helluva hurry. I must have walked miles—but it worked. And it led to me finding you. This morning I just joined the escort party as if I had a right to be there. There should have been only four men, I suppose, and the character in charge looked a bit puzzled. But he didn't question my right to be there . . ."

They were all dressed and ready.

Blake said, "Good work, Tinker. Damned good work. Got your revolver still?"

156

"Yes."

"I'll borrow it. You help Whittington with Peters. Make for the saucer bays—know the way? Whittington does."

"Know it blindfold, chief!' Tinker said.

"Good. See you there. You other chaps, come with me."

He pushed Tinker's gun into a pocket. He walked quickly out of the cell and into the corridor. The two other prisoners followed. They went down the corridor and turned sharp right at the end of it. They made for the control room. As yet they had encountered no one.

They rounded another corner. Now they could see the door of the control room straight ahead. There were two guards on duty there. Blake and his companions walked towards them.

The guards eyed them questioningly as they approached: a look which, too late, gave way to alarm. Blake hit one of them across the head with the butt of Tinker's revolver. His companions dealt with the other. Pressure on a button set in the wall made the door slide back silently. Blake stepped into the room beyond.

There was no one in it but Sergeyev, busily at work on the brain conditioning machine. His back was to the door and to Blake as the detective approached him. Without turning round, the Russian said, "It's nearly finished. A few more connections, and then to test it."

Blake smiled grimly. This was too easy. He took three swift paces forward. "Don't move, Sergeyev! This thing in your back is a gun!"

The Russian froze instantly.

"Put your hands behind you—slowly now!"

Blake jerked his head to one of his companions. "Tie his hands with some of that cable."

When it was done. Blake said, "Now you can turn around, Sergeyev."

The Russian did so. Bitter anger burned in his eyes. Blake kept the gun trained on him. "Stand clear of me, and clear of the machine."

Sergeyev obeyed, sullenly.

Blake tossed over his shoulder: "Either of you two understand this machine?"

"Yes—" one of them came forward "—I do."

"Can we dismantle the section that creates the control?"

"It is easy. This rack, you see? It comes free, like this." The man turned two catches and slid out one of the machine's sections. "This is its heart. The rest is simple electronics and radio transmitter technique."

"Smash it!" said Blake. "Destroy it utterly!"

Sergeyev jerked forward. The gun in Blake's hand snapped up. "One more step and you're a dead man," he told the Russian balefully. He kept his gaze hard upon him. "Go ahead," he flung over his shoulder, "smash it up!"

Soon it was done. The control rack lay in ruins. Valves had been pulverised, connections severed, components crushed.

"Good," was Blake's comment. Still he watched Sergeyev. "Now—" he tossed over his shoulder, "—into the storeroom. Find a box and load it up with the microfilms from the records."

Things were going well.

They were going too well, in fact, had Blake but realised it. Something just had to happen!

AND THEN IT did.

One of Blake's companions had disappeared into the storeroom. The other stood guard on the door.

Then, suddenly, the guard swung around. "Haussman!" he mouthed hoarsely.

Blake saw Sergeyev tense.

He reached the Russian in two strides, grabbed his shoulder,

158

swung him round. The gun slammed into the small of the scientist's back. "You're a shield and a hostage . . ."

And then—

Haussman stood in the doorway, guards on either side of him, all with guns levelled. Haussman had a Schmeisser machine-pistol hard in his grasp.

"All right—" he snarled "—you've had your fun. Now you pay for it! Come out with your hands up!"

He had seen the ruined control rack.

His voice was savage.

Blake's companions froze fearfully.

ONE, THE MAN who had given warning of Haussman's arrival, cowered away from the door, his eyes flicking this way and that, desperately looking for somewhere to hide.

The other had just come out of the storeroom with a big box brimming with microfilm spools. He froze where he was.

"Come out!" Haussman snarled again.

"Or what—?" Blake flung back. "You can't make us! Try, and Sergeyev gets the first bullet!"

His revolver thrust into the small of Sergeyev's back, using him at one and the same time as a hostage and as a shield. Blake felt the Russian begin to tremble. He could smell his fear-sweat.

Sergeyev was caught in the middle of two forces, either of which could, and might, kill him. He could feel the snout of Blake's gun boring into his spine; he could see the Schmeisser in Haussman's hands levelled in his direction. The trigger-finger was tight-bent, white, and bloodless.

Would he shoot?

Blake didn't think so. As long as Sergeyev lived, another mind-processing machine could be built. Haussman, he thought, would hardly do anything to negate that possibility.

159

So, in holding the Russian, he held a trump card—or did he? He wasn't sure. What could he do with it?

Use Sergeyev as a means of obtaining safe conduct to the flying saucer bays? Take the Russian all the way with them, the gun in his back?

No . . . Blake didn't think that would work. There were too many imponderables in a course of that kind. Anything could happen along the way to the saucer bays. It would be too easy for Haussman to lay a trap for them; with the German and his men hard behind, they might blunder into other guards lying in wait in front. And what could happen then?

Sergeyev was a trump card only as long as he lived. Dead, Blake well knew, the trump card became a death warrant. If the Russian was killed, by design or by accident, Haussman would be free to gun them down without mercy.

So . . . what to do?

Blake knew then, suddenly, that there was nothing he could do. There was nothing that Haussman could do, either. They were deadlocked. Blake and his companions couldn't get out of this room; the German and his men couldn't get in.

Sergeyev's body was the barrier.

Stalemate, thought Blake. No . . . Haussman wouldn't shoot. But he was wrong. Very wrong.

For, at that moment, the German did!

THE SCHMEISSER LEAPT to life in his hands. It flared sudden death. The bullets leapt out at Blake's two rebel companions, and cut them down.

The man with the box heavy with microfilms was practically sawn in half. The other, caught in the middle of the great circular floor, was flung bodily backwards under the bullets' impact. Flung backwards screaming. He smashed into one of the racks of control equipment lining the walls, and brought it down.

Everything happened at once.

There was the crash of the rack falling. There was an end to the man's screams. There was a blinding flash of blue light, and a sudden explosion. Acrid smoke filled the room in a trice. And Sergeyev was yelling, "—Out! We've got to get out!"

His voice was crazy with panic.

He jumped forward.

Blake couldn't even begin to understand what had happened.

The Schmeisser fired again from the doorway, orange tongues of flame stabbing the smoke. The doorway itself was invisible now. Sergeyev was invisible, too. Lost. Blake's hostage gone. Again the Schmeisser loosed off a burst. Bullets flew everywhere. Someone cried out in agony near the door: a sobbing despairing cry. Then, from outside the room, there was another explosion, a louder and more ominous echo of the earlier one. The floor quivered. Men were running—Blake could hear them. There was confusion everywhere.

Through the thick, yellow smoke, eyes smarting and watering, he caught a glimpse of the doorway. It was empty now. Where had Haussman gone with the guards? Running feet hammered the floor of the corridor, streaking away fast.

Blake made for the door, and stumbled over an obstruction unseen through the smoke. It was soft, yielding, and, when he crouched down, it was bloody. It was Sergeyev. He sprawled on the floor. Near him lay the Schmeisser, discarded, its magazine empty.

The last burst from Haussman's machine-pistol had caught the Russian high in the chest. The upper half of his body was like a ploughed field, splinters of bone showing through churned-up flesh and rags of clothing. He was dying, he was done for, and the mind processing machine would never be mended. He had only minutes to live, but still he whispered with dreadful persistence, "Got . . . to . . . get . . . out of here . . ."

His fingers scrabbled unavailingly at the stone floor.

Blake bent over him.

The dying man's eyes focussed on him with difficulty. There was no recognition in them. The end was near. But— "Help . . . me . . ." he whispered entreatingly. "Help . . . get . . . me . . . out . . ."

"What's happened?" Blake demanded.

"Got . . . to . . . help . . . me."

"I'll help you. But what's wrong?"

"Got to . . . get away from here." Sergeyev forced the faltering words out with a tremendous effort. "Air extractor control . . . saucer fuel storage tanks control gone . . . smashed entirely . . ."

The last word lingered.

And then a death-rattle started inside the Russian's throat. He made one last despairing effort to force himself over the floor. He failed.

He died then, and Blake jerked to his feet remembering what Whittington had told him.

The saucers used a sodium based fuel which reacted violently when it came into contact with air, however thin. The tanks were set deep inside the volcanic crater, next to the saucer bays, far below the level of the control room and barracks.

Life on the island, Whittington had remarked grimly, was akin to living on top of a powder magazine. For if any air did seep through to the tanks there would be an almighty explosion which would demolish everything.

Then Blake was running.

He left the box of microfilmed records behind him. There was no time for that now. With the air extractor control smashed, how long would it be before the tanks exploded? Not long, obviously. Haussman hadn't thought so—nor had Sergeyev—and they should know!

Everything was explained now—the German's hurried flight, Sergeyev's own attempts to escape, the minor explosions.

When would the major one come?

Blake raced through empty corridors, heart pounding, flat-out.

Tinker and Peters and Whittington had gone to the saucer bays. When the explosion came they would be caught right in the heart of it—if he didn't reach them first.

ON HE RAN. On. Then, suddenly, turning a corner at speed, he almost collided with another man running.

"Tinker!"

"Chief!" Tinker gasped, "I was coming to look for you, chief. We've got to get out!"

"Don't I know it!" Then Blake's voice was anxious. "Where's Peters? Where's Whittington?"

"We can't take a saucer, chief. The fuel tanks—"

"I know all about that."

"Whittington's got a helicopter. We've loaded Peters aboard. It's this way. Down here. Come on, chief! There isn't much time!"

They swung around; ran. Then they were out in the open on the edge of a small, flat, concrete plain overhanging the crater. A copter stood there, rotors slowly revolving. Whittington was at the controls. He saw them and waved furiously. He shouted, but his words were lost in a sudden ominous rumbling from under their feet.

"Quick, chief! Quick!"

They flung themselves over the yards which separated them from the machine.

The concrete plain shuddered beneath their feet as they ran. Then something exploded deep inside the crater—a sound like dull thunder. An appalling rushing noise followed. A blast of air nearly swept them back off their feet.

Then they had reached the helicopter, and Whittington was

there to grab them and haul them aboard. "Hurry! Hurry!" He was nearly frantic. "Hurry—or we've had it, too! The fuel tanks are leaking! It can only be a matter of seconds—"

They scrambled up into the machine, and Whittington jumped back to the controls. The helicopter started to lift. And then—

There was a huge, cataclysmic bellow of sound. The concrete plain on which their machine had been standing bare split-seconds before ceased to exist. In that same instant, the helicopter was literally hurled upwards as if by a leviathan hand.

The machine shivered and shook, threatening to disintegrate in the furious air. Blake and Tinker were flung from one side of the plane to the other. Somehow, Whittington managed to stay in front of the controls and fight for stability.

Up—the helicopter rocketed—up! Then it side-slipped. It seemed to hang motionless in the turbulent boiling air for an aeon of time while Whittington wrestled furiously for the lives of them all, sweated and swore, and—

Won!

The helicopter levelled off. Peters, strapped to a stretcher which, in turn, was strapped to the floor, worked up a grey grin and looked into Blake's face. The detective had been flung down only inches away from him. "I'm all right, Jack . . ."

They were all all right—now.

Blake got to his feet. He looked out of the cabin window, and down. Noise was still all around them, a mad, drumming thunder. Fog covered the island but, even as he watched, it was pierced by a red flash of flame which swiftly widened into an irregular glowing disc. The fog blanket was pushed outwards by giant, heat-filled force. The helicopter pitched this way and that, but remained under control. For a few moments, the island was seen in outline, its centre marked by great gouts of

164

fire and searing, spewing lava which bubbled and burst. Then the island split apart under Blake's very eyes. Incandescent lava swept into the sea, boiling water instantly and creating a turmoil of tremendous waves. Steam and spray blotted out the scene.

Whittington grimly fought to keep the helicopter stable and steady. They rode out the shock waves. Then he looked down lingeringly. His eyes sought out Blake's.

"Nothing left," he said tautly. "Just nothing."

And it was true.

The island was gone—erased off the map. It was just as though it had never existed.

It was gone.

Everything was gone.

There was nothing left of the island, nothing left of the saucer fleet, nothing left of the mind conditioning machine with which first Englefield then Haussman had planned to change the future of the world.

These physical things had been utterly destroyed. But what of the visionary ideas which had flourished here? World Government . . . United Europe.

They had been ideas in conflict but, Blake thought now, it was only the impatience of the men who had held them which had forced that conflict to life. Truly, each idea was a part of the other; and truly, some day, each was bound to pass out of the realms of theory and into practical reality.

And, in that day, the last should be first.

The unification of Europe was bound to come first, and bound to come soon. Blake hoped; as many men of New Thought hoped, that unity would not be long delayed.

But, when it came, the natural precursor to eventual world government, it must come in answer to the expressed desire of the European peoples. It must be something accepted voluntarily—never imposed. It must be something soundly based—in precept and practice—upon a new concert of freedom. No mind conditioning machines must be required.

It was on this he had taken his stand against Englefield and against Haussman.

Haussman . . .

At that moment, his eyes narrowed sharply. A thought had just entered his mind. He spoke to Whittington, telling him of what had happened in the control room. He ended, "Where would Haussman have gone?"

The American stared at him.

"To the submarine docks, I shouldn't wonder. I told you—there was still one U-boat there capable of putting to sea. You don't think—"

He broke off. This was just what Blake had been wondering.

Had Haussman perished as Englefield had perished, and Sergeyev?

Or had he escaped . . . ?

THE SEVENTEENTH CHAPTER

Who goes there . . . ?

The Meteorological Office reports—At 12.21 hours G.M.T. an earthquake of unusual force, believed to be the result of a volcanic eruption, occurred in an uncharted, ice-bound region of the Arctic, approximate latitude 75 deg. North. A tidal wave was caused, and considerable damage to shipping is feared. There are reports of widespread floods in Greenland, Iceland, Norway, and the Shetlands, with some loss of life. The shock was recorded at seismological stations all over the world. At Greenwich . . .

CRAILLE GRIPPED THEIR hands warmly as they stood up to leave his office after turning in a comprehensive report.

"Good work, Blake—Carter. A mission satisfactorily carried out. A very dangerous situation averted."

Blake said, "The understatement of the year."

Craille cocked a sardonic eyebrow. "What do you want—a big write-up in the press?"

Of course they didn't want that.

"A shiny new medal apiece?"

Blake said, "Too bad if we did. We wouldn't get 'em."

"Oh, I don't know . . . " Craille said, and grinned suddenly. "Maybe . . ." he said.

They left him then.

They aspired to no honour. They sought no recognition.

The knowledge of what they had done, and Craille's praise, was reward enough.

THEY ARRIVED AT the Berkeley Square offices of Sexton Blake Investigations just as Paula Dane, and Miss Pringle, and Marion Lang were all getting ready to close up and go home.

Splash Kirby was there, chatting confidentially to an amused but cool Dorcas de Trafford.

Blake and Tinker got quite a welcome. They monopolised all attention. Dorcas de Trafford hung on every word that Blake uttered. Kirby spread his hand in an exaggerated gesture. "I was doing all right," he complained, "until he came along!"

Blake said to Dorcas: "I've just had a report on your . . . brother. He's making some progress. I think he's going to be all right eventually."

She took his hand. "Thank you, Mr. Blake. Thank you—for everything."

Kirby pricked up his ears. "Oliver de Traford went missing . . . so did you. I smell a story, Blake."

Blake looked at him blandly. "Oh, no—no story, Splash. Just a temporary blackout. But he's going to be all right. I checked with a specialist just before coming here. I was able to tell him a few things he didn't know . . ."

"Come off it, Blake. You've been away well over a week, and you say no story—"

"Can't a man have a holiday? If you must know, Tinker and I went to Iceland. Invigorating air, marvellous scenery—you should try it."

"Iceland—!" Kirby said. He looked sharply disappointed. "You're sure it was Iceland?"

"Of course. Why—?

"Oh . . . " Kirby shrugged, " . . . nothing. Nothing now. I just put two and two together, but it seems I made five . . ."

"What on earth are you talking about?"

"Just this," Kirby said. He took a folded Daily Post out of his pocket. He opened it up. The headlines shrieked of tidal waves and disaster, but Kirby wasn't pointing at them. His forefinger stabbed down. "Thought you might know something about it . . ."

Blake looked at the paragraph his friend was indicating, and then looked again—sharply. He read it—and wondered.

An unidentified submarine had been reported in the Golfo Nuevo in Argentinian waters, seven hundred miles south of Buenos Aires. It had been called upon to surrender itself to units of the Argentinian navy, but, instead, it had crash-dived. It was now being hunted by depth-charging destroyers.

A submarine . . . a U-boat . . . ? Haussman . . . ?

"Of course," Kirby said, "if you really have spent this past couple of weeks in Iceland you can't possibly know anything about it."

"Sorry, Splash. We really have been way up in the Frozen North all right."

The journalist sighed. "Too bad. Well . . . it was just an idea . . . a wild hope. I know how you get around."

"Sorry." But still Blake wondered . . .

Then abruptly he turned to include the others. Forget Haussman—if it were possible! "What say we all go around to my place for a few cocktails? Then Splash can tell us some of his stories."

Paula slipped her arm under his, but looked suspiciously at Kirby. "What kind of stories?"

Kirby waved a hand airily. "Oh—anything you like," he said. "Murder, arson, divorce, society scandals . . . crime . . . take your pick!"

"Better make it crime," Paula said. "A real busman's holiday!"

"A crime at cocktail-time," Tinker mused. "Yes ... pedestrian but good to come home to . . ."

And, after all he and Blake had been through together —it was.[5]

THE END

Notes

1. A reference to TOUCH OF EVIL by Arthur Maclean (E. C. Tubb, with revisions by George Paul Mann), THE SEXTON BLAKE LIBRARY 4th series, issue 438, published in October 1959.

2. A reference to MISSION TO MEXICO by Arthur Maclean (George Paul Mann), THE SEXTON BLAKE LIBRARY 4th series, issue 445, published in February 1960.

3. The word "freak" has been replaced by more modern language.

4. Various instances of the word "deformed" have been removed.

5. Splash Kirby's newspaper account was inspired by a real one. The identity of the unknown submarine in Argentine territorial waters—reported extensively by the world's newspapers during 1958 and 1960—remains a mystery to this day.

THE BIG STEAL

TINKER LOOKED UP from the issue, grinned, but also raised his eyebrows as if challenging me to say, 'The whole story is nonsense, of course! It can't possibly be based on truth!'

I tried to be rather less confrontational than that. I said, "Amalgamated Press had become Fleetway Publications by this time, and Desmond Reid was a house name employed to disguise a number of its authors. In the case of The World-Shakers, it was Rex Dolphin. He was a long-time Sexton Blake enthusiast and I suspect that, with this one, he was paying homage to the exaggerations of the past when, for example, Cecil Hayter wrote of you discovering dinosaurs in deepest Africa or mammoths in the Arctic north of Russia."

Tinker snorted. "Ha! No, not really."

"Not really?"

"Not exaggerations. Apart from the dinosaurs. Maybe. Possibly. I'm still not a hundred percent certain on that one."

"Wait a minute! What? You're telling me—?"

I was interrupted by Sexton Blake entering the room. He dragged a third armchair over and plonked himself down into it. "Pour me a brandy, would you?" he said to Tinker. "And one for our guest."

He'd removed his disguise, washed the blood from his face, and was now attired in the same disreputable, acid-stained dressing gown that I'd seen before.

I said, "Tinker and I were just discussing your encounter with flying saucers. He said you've seen dinosaurs, too."

Inwardly, I cringed, having accidentally referred to Edward Carter by his nickname.

"Um—well—I didn't exactly say that," Tinker protested. He stood, crossed to a bureau, and retrieved from it a decanter and three glasses.

"Just a stray Ankylosaurus or two," Blake said. "Perhaps."

"Can't be sure," Tinker put in.

Blake nodded. "The conditions weren't ideal."

He leaned forward, took The World-Shakers from the arm of Tinker's chair, and passed it back to me. "Ah, I see. Yes, an exceptional case, that one. Others of the period were rather less ... bizarre. What's next?"

Brandy was distributed (it wasn't even lunchtime). Tinker sat down. Pedro stretched, yawned, and flopped onto the rug.

"A case in point, I guess," I said, holding up the next issue while forcibly but reluctantly shoving the subject of living fossils to the back of my mind. "Jack Trevor Story. Of all your authors, perhaps the one who wrote with the most style about the most mundane."

"Absolutely right," Blake said, with one of his fleeting smiles. "I gave him responsibility for relating the cases in which ordinary people got out of their depth."

THE BIG STEAL

by Jack Trevor Story
THE SEXTON BLAKE LIBRARY 4th series,
issue 464 (1960)

THE FIRST CHAPTER

Unmerciful release.

IN THE ANNALS of Sexton Blake's criminal investigations the O'Brien story was, in many respects, something quite different.

For one thing—unlike many cases of crime and detection which might involve Blake and his staff in forty-eight hours of dangerous adventure, and consecutive action, leaving little time for other jobs, or even relaxation and sleep—the O'Brien case lasted the full two years of the that simple, almost-innocent, Irishman's term in prison.

A large part of this time was spent in watching O'Brien's sweet and personable young wife Anny; a pleasant task, but regretfully, perhaps, a highly delegatable one. Blake could not afford luxuries of this kind, and therefore while Tinker, Paula Dane, Marion Lang and Miss Pringle took it in turns to relieve him of the duty, Blake himself kept the Berkeley Square menage on an action footing, and handled many other crises which have been dealt with elsewhere by other S.B.L. chroniclers.

The other great difference, besides the inordinately long time it took to write finish to the O'Brien case, was that Sexton Blake did on several counts place himself in a very false position.

Nobody could ever accuse Blake of being over-conventional in his handling of cases, and there have been occasions when he has placed himself, for a time at least, outside the law in order to meet, eventually, the ends of justice. But in the O'Brien story he came closest to making himself an accomplice; not this time for strictly judicial reasons, but—one might almost say—for sentimental reasons; certainly he jeopardised his reputation in the interests of chivalry.

The facts which Blake saw, and which are never a mystery to the reader, are that neither O'Brien nor his wife were criminals, though circumstances accrued that made both of them guilty parties.

Whether Blake was morally right in protecting Anny O'Brien is a question for the reader and his conscience.

But in judging for themselves, this chronicler humbly asks his audience to bear in mind the endearing qualities of a lovely, though misfortunate and underprivileged, young girl with a code of ethics entirely her own, fighting a gang of criminals entirely ruthless and willing to murder her husband without so much as a thought.

The O'Brien story must begin near the end, on the morning of the Irishman's release from prison, when the tragic events which led to a nationwide outcry and a Government inquiry took place right under Sexton Blake's nose.

THIS MORNING WAS going to be different. O'Brien told himself. He was excited at the prospect of freedom—even though he'd seen enough newspapers in prison, and heard enough radio, to know that the outside was not something to dream about any more.

O'Brien had served his two years rather in the spirit of a job to be done, and now he had done it. Anny was waiting for him just as they had planned, and the money was safe.

He honestly couldn't regret what had happened, for now he

would be able to do things for Anny that would never have been possible in the old days. And best of all was the fact that they could now have what they had always wanted—a child.

At nine o'clock the chief warder opened the door of the solitary confinement cell. This was an odd circumstance, considering that O'Brien had been a good-behaviour man and had earned himself a year's remission for good conduct. But the solitary confinement cell had been for his own protection. This is why happiness at being released was mingled with fear at what might happen when he got outside.

Even the newspapers had said that it was unlikely that O'Brien would survive for more than twenty-four hours once he left the protection of the prison cell.

"Ready, O'Brien?" the chief warder asked him.

"I am," said O'Brien.

And from their faces and the way they walked together to the administration block, and from the eyes which peered after them—some in pity, some in anticipation—an observer would have been forgiven for believing that O'Brien was on his way to the execution shed to be hanged.

OUTSIDE BRIXTON PRISON on this November morning, Sexton Blake and his colleague Edward Carter sat in a large Bentley Continental car, waiting and watching. Occasionally, Blake looked at his watch; occasionally, the young man beside him cleared his throat, nervously.

Neither knew quite what to expect, but they were fully alert and prepared for anything. As the prison clock chimed the hour of nine both became tense. Blake cast away a cigarette, leaving both hands free for action; Tinker started the engine.

What came next—although a tangle of noise, screams and fast action—impinged on Blake's mind in a mass of sharp detail which later he was able to draw on, and describe, at the inquiry.

The first thing to register, above the Brixton noises and the clatter of work-going people, was the strictly audible intrusion of a fast-revving engine. Suddenly, from a side-street beyond the prison gates, an ancient, shabby, though racy and powerful, Riley saloon car emerged to shoot down on the wrong side of the road for fifty yards, and stop abruptly with a squeal of brakes opposite the grim gates of the prison.

"Wait!" Blake said.

It was a word, and a decision, which afterwards was questioned in the highest of places—including Scotland Yard and the House of Commons. And it was to take Blake a considerable amount of time and talking to find a sufficient and convincing answer.

"Wait," Blake said again, softly.

The door of the Riley opened as a man came away from the prison gates. The driver of the car called out, in a friendly way, his words clearly heard by the watching detectives.

"Is that you, O'Brien?"

The man halted in his walk away from the prison, and turned eagerly towards the car.

"Yes," he said. "It is!"

The driver of the old car instantly brought his hand into view through the car-door opening, and there was a gun in it. He fired carefully, taking good aim, three times.

The shot man remained on his feet for seconds; his face at first showed shocked surprise, then a curious turning inward of his thoughts as he crumpled to the pavement . . .

As THE GUNMAN slammed his door and the Riley drew away, Blake's Bentley closed in to cut him off. The killer frantically swivelled his wheel, shooting out into the road at right-angles. A fast-moving omnibus coming behind ploughed into the Riley, rolled it over, and scraped the wreckage along for twenty yards before stopping.

There was a squealing and shrieking from passers by; a running and stopping and foolish staring; a gathering of a helpless crowd, all asking questions to cover their own panic and embarrassment in the presence of sudden death.

Blake pushed his way through the crowd and stopped, staring; there was nothing he could do now. An arm and hand were protruding through the torn metal, and the gun was still gripped in the leather glove.

Blake walked back to the pavement and saw Tinker standing there by the car, looking at the shot man. A young nun in her large black hood was kneeling by the body and slowly covering the face.

Blake was watching her walk slowly away as the first police car arrived followed by an ambulance with its bell ringing. Blake showed his card to a police inspector, and described briefly what had happened.

"Do you know who it was, sir?" the inspector asked, looking down at the shot man with the covered face.

"Yes," Blake said. "It was O'Brien—he just came out of prison."

"O'Brien!" The inspector stared down at the still figure. "I thought the Yard were putting somebody onto him!"

"They did," Blake said. "That's why I was here . . ."

"Did you see what happened, Mr. Blake?"

The question was put by Lord Quade, the Metropolitan Police High Commissioner. With him on the board of inquiry were sitting Commander Grimwald, Chief Detective-Inspector Coutts and Sir Martin Reynolds, a prison commissioner.

They had convened in a large, oak-panelled room whose long, curtained windows had the best view in the whole of New Scotland Yard of the Thames embankment and the river.

Sexton Blake sat at the end of the long table. He was dressed soberly, and well, in a dark-grey city suit, with just the tiniest wink of a crisp white linen handkerchief at his breast pocket. The only colour he had allowed himself lay in the blue diagonal Cambridge University tie; and that, perhaps only his friends Grimwald and Coutts appreciated, came from the honorary degree in law which had been conferred upon him at the Senate House some years ago.

Blake explained clearly what exactly had happened in the vicinity of Brixton Prison on the morning of the double tragedy.

Two days had passed, during which it had emerged that O'Brien's life had been in danger from the moment he'd stepped out of the prison gates. Why had he not been given police protection?

The question had crept into several newspapers during the past week. It had been asked baldly by Splash Kirby in the Post. Both the police, and London's underworld, knew that there were men waiting to kill O'Brien when he left the protection of his solitary confinement cell—why hadn't Scotland Yard done something about it?

The question had been picked up by a crusading back-bencher and tabled for a hearing in the House of Commons. With the knowledge that he would be summoned to the Home Office at any hour now, Lord Quade had set up this preliminary inquiry with the object of providing at least one or two relevant facts to tuck into his brief case. For, in point of fact, if there was one man who knew nothing at all about the two-year-old Dackworth Stores robbery, it was the up-and-coming Lord Quade. When the five-hundred-thousand-pound safe robbery had shaken London, Lord Quade had been concerned with housing, and that only as a junior minister. Lord Quade, until now, had never heard of O'Brien.

"Would you say, Mr. Blake," he asked now, "if your action

180

in driving in front of the gunman's car caused the accident in which he was killed?"

"Yes," Blake said, evenly. "I would."

"Then do you think that this kind of dangerous behaviour was justified—even though it was in the course of your assignment?"

Blake said: "It was not justified by my assignment for Venus Life and Property Insurance, sir—nor was it motivated by it. It was justified by my status as a citizen. Surely if you see a crime in the street, whether it's smash-and-grab or murder, then it is everyone's duty to do something about it if he can?"

Lord Quade nodded. "Yes, of course."

Commander Grimwald put in: "It might be argued that it was the gunman's desperate evasive action which brought about the collision with the bus."

Lord Quade accepted the point of view, and passed on to the more pertinent elements of the incident. Still addressing Blake, he asked the detective whether, at any moment after seeing O'Brien leave the prison gates, he was aware of the danger of what might happen; and, if so, could he have prevented it.

Before Blake could reply to this, the prison Commissioner, Sir Martin Reynolds, interjected in a thin, reedy, voice which matched his appearance and personality. "I would first like to know whether Mr. Blake knew anything of O'Brien's background, and therefore anticipated what happened?"

Blake looked at Grimwald; it was a glance which reminded that officer of the three-way chat he, Blake, and Coutts, had had in the Savoy Grill before coming to the inquiry. How much, Blake's glance asked, do I have to tell them?

Grimwald said: "Mr. Blake knows more about the O'Brien case than anyone else—he was assigned to it soon after the robbery, when Venus Life and Property had to indemnify the victims of the robbery."

"I see," Sir Martin Reynolds said. And to Blake: "Then the shooting outside the prison was not exactly a surprise to you—couldn't you have done anything to prevent it?"

"But it was a surprise to me," Blake admitted. "I had already seen the car waiting outside the prison, but I thought it had probably come to take O'Brien to his wife."

"Do you think that his wife has been hiding the money while O'Brien has been in jail?" Lord Quade asked.

Blake hesitated. "I can't answer that, sir, without telling you the story of the O'Briens—you may know that they weren't involved in this robbery in any usual way."

Lord Quade shook his head. "I know very little about them beyond what was given in evidence at O'Brien's trial."

"The true story never emerged at the trial," Blake said.

Sir Martin Reynolds put in: "How do you come to know the facts, if the police didn't get them?"

"Mr. Blake was assigned to recover the money for the company." Grimwald explained. "Our job was to apprehend the criminals—with, or without, the money. There's quite a difference."

Lord Quade said: "I can see that." Then, looking at Blake: "The only unreasonable thing about your presence on this case at this late stage, Mr. Blake, is that the insurance company should suppose that O'Brien's share of the money is still recoverable."

"But it is recoverable," Blake said. "I intend to recover it."

Lord Quade looked at him, shrewdly: "You sound confident."

"I am confident—and so will you be if I tell you the whole story."

Lord Quade frowned. "Is it going to help me with my report on O'Brien's death to the Home Secretary?"

Blake nodded. "I think so."

The Commissioner brightened: "Well, anything to get us out of hot water—eh, Reynolds?"

Commander Grimwald was looking thoroughly uncomfortable. "It may get the Home Secretary out of hot water," he said. "But I don't know where it puts us!"

Sir Martin Reynolds smiled: "It sounds intriguing."

"Let us be bold and hear the truth of the matter," Lord Quade said. He nodded to Blake. "You'd better start in the usual place—and make it brief . . ."

THE SECOND CHAPTER

O'Brien and the Angel.

THE WOMAN IN the case was Antoinette O'Brien. From the day she was given the name "Antoinette" on a shortened birth certificate, nothing had gone right for her. It was an ill-fated name, and particularly so in the Scotland Road district of Liverpool where she was brought up.

It was a name that her mother had thought romantic and a bit superior; she therefore liked to scream it the length of the street, as often as possible, in her broad scouse accent.

"Antoinette! Antoinette! Are y' ther?"

The girl, livid with embarrassment at such a name in such a district, got her friends to call her Anny. But her mother, who had known Antoinette's father for only a few hours at New Brighton beach, preferred to abbreviate the name to "Toin" when the mood took her.

"Run along and buy yourself a nice ice cream, Toin," she would say; and she made it sound like some lost noise from a renegade planet.

Altogether, for a woman sensitive about being an unmarried mother, no name could she have chosen in such an environment which sounded more rootless, meaningless, and sheerly illegitimate. Anny had left Liverpool at the age of seventeen mainly to get away from her name.

She had fallen in love with Tim O'Brien partly because his name, by Liverpool standards, was so ordinary. This had happened in Douglas, on the Isle of Man, where she had gone to work the summer season in an hotel. Another thing which had appealed to her was that he was on a week's holiday from a solid job in London. A plain, home-cooked man, already going bald at twenty-five; a sober, honest, highly-skilled tradesman, with twelve pounds a week, and one paid holiday a year. This, for Anny, was substance; romance, you could have. Right from the start she called him O'Brien; a good solid name with no trimmings.

O'Brien could overlook her single-minded attitude toward him—it was not every girl who questioned you about your prospects in the first hour—because she was beautiful; the one stroke of luck in her whole life; and because she loved him. Had he known that he was going to spend two years of his married life in jail, it would not have stopped O'Brien falling in love with her, and marrying her. In the ordinary kind of life he lived, and with the few chances that came his way, not to have accepted this dream of a girl would have been like winning the Irish Sweepstake, and declining the prize.

And what happened was not Anny's fault. Besides being beautiful, slender, fair-haired, with laughing blue eyes and a quivering, mirthful mouth, she was good, with all that that word meant. She was good because she was a fugitive from a harum-scarum mother and a home as shiftless as a bit of driftwood on the Cast Iron Shore—Liverpool's rat-ridden Cassy, where the little Antoinette had run with the rest of the dregs.

In a summer season on the Isle of Man, a girl as beautiful as Anny who would take no nonsense from the men with wallets was a rare gem indeed, and O'Brien had to look several times before he could believe it.

"Will you take me out and get me back by ten?" Anny had asked him at his first shy approach.

"I will!" O'Brien told her.

THEY WERE MARRIED from her home in Liverpool, and then he took her to London, where they made a home in two rooms of a big, tatty, terrace villa near Kilburn High Street. It was nothing very grand, but it was clean; and what sticks they had were paid for, cash.

"When the baby comes along," O'Brien told Anny one night, lying cuddling in the second-hand bed, "we'll put down a deposit on a little house with a garden, in the suburbs."

"No, O'Brien," Anny said. "When we've got the little house, and the garden, then we'll think about the baby."

It was against O'Brien's belief, but Anny could always convert him any time at all. He went on to full over-time and started a Post Office Savings account, and was always ready to do any little weekend jobs he could pick up. Once or twice more, O'Brien tried to persuade Anny to have a baby, for it would give her something to do while he was away all day at work, but Anny would never give in to the idea.

"What kind of a life would it be for a child?" she would say.

And they only had to look out of the window to see. The street was full of women like Anny's mother and full of children like Antoinette. And every morning there was a body in the street—in a box with flowers on it, but still a body—for there was an undertaker's establishment three houses along. Anny passed it each morning when she walked to Kilburn Park station with O'Brien, and went on to do her shopping. There would be a hearse and a box, and Anny couldn't stop herself from seeing inside it—a man, woman, or child, lying dead.

187

It only spurred O'Brien on to work harder and longer and save more, but it was no use saying that he could change anything quickly. It was going to be a long job. At the end of six months, they had fifteen pounds five shillings in the Post Office book.

"Well, I'm not complaining, O'Brien—am I?" Anny would tell him.

And it was a fact that she was very happy the way things were. The morning walk to the station, getting back and planning a meal, doing the housework, a bit of mending, cooking in the afternoon, and then walking to the station to meet him back from the city at night. Dull, stolid, regular, and supremely secure, with O'Brien to love her every night.

It was O'Brien who was unhappy. Anny didn't know how beautiful and good she was, and how much she deserved. And by his reckoning, even though he was the best craftsman in the firm, it was going to take ten years to save three hundred pounds for a deposit on a house. They had considered Anny taking a job, but he had agreed swiftly with her reasoning against it.

"That's the way marriages break up," she said. "Me working with all sorts of men, and you getting jealous."

"Yes," he thought, just watching the way she moved, "she's right!"

O'Brien was working his extra half-day Saturday job at the petrol pumps in Kilburn High Road when he first made the acquaintance of Sims; though it meant nothing to him at the time. A light-weight tropical man, in a light-weight tropical suit; his face yellow and wrinkled as a raisin, and smoking a cheroot. He had brought in an elderly Mercedes Benz for petrol and oil, and while O'Brien was doing the filling the driver had got out to stride up and down. When he tried to enter the car again, he found that he had locked himself out.

"It's the third time!" he said. He swore and asked O'Brien if he had a duplicate key. He spoke with the peculiar gutturals of a South African.

O'Brien laughed. He wouldn't have a duplicate key for a Mercedes, but it only took him half a minute to open the lock with a funny little silver needle that was jointed in various places.

"You want to keep that out of sight!" the driver told him.

O'Brien laughed again. He explained that locks were his real trade, and the South African was very interested. He soon learned that O'Brien had served seven years with Gallagher's Safes and Strong Rooms (London) Ltd.

"And before that, I was apprenticed in Dublin." O'Brien said. "But there's no money over there."

The man looked at O'Brien's overalls and his oil-stained boots. "And you find there's plenty over here?"

O'Brien explained that he got top rates for his job—twelve pounds a week, plus overtime—but you still needed the additional odd job to get by.

"There are some people who make more out of safes than you do," the man said. "And they don't know half as much about 'em, nor work a quarter of the hours."

O'Brien frowned. "They're not union men?"

The South African laughed. No, they weren't union men. And he gave O'Brien a generous ten-shilling tip, and complimented him on being a happy and contented man.

"Sure, I've a wonderful wife," O'Brien said.

The South African smiled again, and said that explained it. "I've got three," he said, miserably, before driving the Mercedes Benz away.

O'Brien stared after the car, still sniffing the cheroot smoke, and holding the ten-shilling note. Poor devil, he thought.

O'BRIEN ARRIVED HOME for his tea with a rolled-up carpet on his shoulder. Anny was delighted for a moment, going down on her knees and rubbing her hands across the deep red pile.

"But what about the baby?" she asked, looking up at him.

They always spoke as if they were saving up for a baby.

"Ah, it was only thirty bob," O'Brien said. "It's what you always wanted."

"It must have cost more than that, O'Brien!" she exclaimed. "It's brand new!"

"There's a flaw in it," he told her. And he got down on the carpet as if to look for it, but gave it up when she tickled him. They rolled together on the red carpet, like kittens; laughing and kissing.

"Now I know why you wanted a carpet!" he said, when she was quiet.

During the next few weeks, O'Brien brought in other splendid gifts for Anny which he had "picked up" or "knocked down" for a song. A new fireside chair, a radio, a clock that chimed; half a china tea service.

"But what about the baby?" Anny would say, her eyes shiny and cloudy at once.

"You can get anything for ten bob, if you know where to go," he would say. Or: "There's a flaw in it."

One Saturday tea-time he got home empty-handed.

"I thought we'd go to the pictures, instead," he said.

He had something to celebrate—his job at the petrol pumps had come to an end. "What the hell! After all, I'm a skilled man, really."

"I'm glad it's finished," Anny told him. "But we've got lots of nice things out of it."

There was a flaw in all of them, but she was not to know it until a few days later.

That night, they went to the pictures, and on their way home they bought fish and chips. They sat close together on the new

190

fireside chair, eating the fish and chips well-soaked in vinegar, with lots of salt and pepper; sublimely happy.

O'Brien watched her pretty face as she popped the hot chips into her mouth, wiped her lips on the back of her hand, solemnly biting with open mouth, as one does when things are too hot to eat.

"What are you thinking about, Anny?" he asked, softly.

She gave him little winsome smile, and shrugged.

"There's something in your thoughts, Anny?" he murmured, sparing a moment from a bite of fish to kiss her ear.

She swallowed, and wiped her mouth again. "I was just thinking," she said, "about these chips. Do you know it only takes one medium-sized potato to make sixpenny-worth of chips? They must make a fortune!"

"Oh," he said. "I thought you were thinking about the baby."

She suddenly giggled. "For heaven's sake, O'Brien! I'm only eighteen still!"

He looked at her in a startled way. It was something he was always forgetting. There was still time to build her a house and make her a garden, and then still time enough for the baby. Several babies.

When he got back from the city a few days later, Anny was not at the station to meet him. He hurried home, looking all around in case he missed her. He ran into the house, up the stairs two at a time, and burst through the door.

Anny sat by the window.

"What's the matter, Anny? Honest to God. I thought you'd had an accident! What's the trouble, Anny?"

She looked at him without smiling. "Nothing." she said.

He came towards her as if to hold her, but held back at the reserve in her eyes. "There is too something!"

"All right," she said, gazing out of the window so as not to look at him. "Can you think of anything?"

As he stared at her his thoughts probed inwards, and found something terrifying and wonderful. "Anny!" he exclaimed, and he went down on his knees, holding her arm. "It's not the baby, is it? I mean—well, you never know, but . . ."

She sighed deeply, still without looking at him. "No," she said. "It's not the baby. What's more there isn't going to be any baby."

He shook her. "What're you saying? Have you been to a doctor, or something—"

"I've had a letter," she told him at last.

"From your ma?"

"It says there isn't going to be any baby because my husband is a liar and a spendthrift, and"—she groped angrily for words—"and wrong in the head!"

She whipped the letter from under her apron and thrust it at him; and before he could start reading, she went on.

"Thirty bob, you said! A flaw in it, you said! This carpet was eighteen pounds ten shillings, and you're a month behind with your payments!"

"Oh, that," he said miserably, reading the letter. Then he brightened. "I've got the instalment—"

"That's not the point, O'Brien!"

He flinched away from the accusation in her pretty face. "It was just the one thing—I wanted you to have it."

She dwelt on this for a moment, and her face clouded even more darkly. "And what about the clock?" she said. And as he refused to meet her eyes: "And the radio? And the tea service?"

The enormity of it rendered her speechless for a while. He wanted to stroke her leg, but hadn't the courage.

"You've put us in debt!" she said fiercely. "That's what you've done! And I thought we were saving!"

"We are so!" he hastened to explain. "You can see the book. I gave up smoking to pay the instalments—"

"Don't lie to me!" she said. "I'm always clearing up your empty packets!"

"I know," he said. "I pick them up on the train—I didn't want you to know I'd given up smoking."

Anny stared at him for a long moment—seeing him, in her mind's eye, picking up empty cigarette packets and putting them in his pockets where she would find them. And just so that she could have nice things.

"I'm sorry, Anny," he said.

"You fool!" she said. "O'Brien, you big idiot!"

"Anny, I'm sorry!"

He knew she was going to cry, and she did. He still wanted to stroke her, but hadn't the courage yet, and his big hands were floating around her bent head.

"Anny, what can I do? Tell me what I can do!"

Her mother used to do things like that; that was the whole trouble. Anything she wanted—getting it for a down-payment. A dress, a bit of underclothing, a set of knives and forks; just cutting out a square from a newspaper, and sending off a five-shilling postal order, and letting tomorrow take care of itself. A life full of bailiffs, and county court summonses and threatening letters—just like the one O'Brien was holding now. Antoinette! a voice screamed in her ears.

And when things got too much, or there were too many knocks on the door, or too many strangers to hide from, it was the gas oven.

"The next feller that comes dunning at that door, I'll put my blasted head in the gas oven!" her mother used to say.

Ever since, Anny had been afraid of callers at the door, or unexpected knocks. That's why she had wanted a weekly-wage man like O'Brien, with everything paid for. He knew that.

"It won't happen again," O'Brien said. "I promise that."

She had stopped crying now and had gone silent and

thoughtful. Suddenly, she spoke without looking at him.

"This is what we're going to do," she said.

The money in the Post Office would go to pay off the carpet and a bit off everything else. Then, instead of saving each week, they would pay off the remains of the debts and get finished with them.

"It'll take a year," O'Brien said. A whole year, and then starting all over again from the bottom. "I tell you what," he said. "I tell you what we could do. You could cut out the meal at night—the meat for me, I mean. I get a meal in the middle of the day, anyway; an egg or a bit of toast would do at night."

Now Anny looked at him. "There's going to be none of that in this house. You're a skilled workman, and you're going to have proper meals. Besides, I like cooking for you."

"You're a wonderful cook, Anny."

"So that's settled," she said.

He said: "But a whole year and nothing saved . . ."

"And I may take a job after all," she added, dismissing his objections.

"You wouldn't do that—not after what you said. About the other fellers?"

She shrugged. "We'll just have to take the risk."

He looked hard at her—until her mouth quirked, and in his relief he hugged her. "Now I know you're teasing!"

"Only about that!" she said.

He held her closely, stroking her hair, the barrier gone. "Oh, Anny, darling . . . I brought a lot of trouble on you."

"No, you haven't, dear," she said. "It's just our first crisis."

"Is that what it is?"

She smiled at him fondly, and reached for her handbag. He watched her, puzzled, as she took out a half-crown piece and gave it to him.

"You'll take this down to the machine, and get some

194

cigarettes"—and stopping his protests with a hand on his mouth—"you're a craftsman, and an artist, O'Brien—and you won't do your best work without a vice or two. If you stopped smoking, the Lord knows what you might get up to."

He kissed her until she pushed him away breathlessly.

"Now go on—I'm not weakening, O'Brien! From now on, we'll do as I've just said."

He turned at the door, looking at her as she began to lay the table. "Is there anything else?" he asked.

"Yes," she said. "When you come in take off your shoes before setting foot on this eighteen-pound-ten carpet!"

"I will!" he said fervently.

THE THIRD CHAPTER

The shape of things to come.

Windy Willow's Silver Cloud Rolls Royce stopped outside the O'Briens' house on a Sunday morning, and was instantly surrounded by yelling children of all colours. Anny was attracted to the window by the yelling, for the car had made no noise. Her alarm grew by stages. At first sight of the Rolls Royce, she thought there would be the usual body in it; but then she remembered it was Sunday, and not a day for funerals. And when the door of the car opened and a man stepped out helped by a chauffeur, and looked up at the windows, she flinched back in fright.

"O'Brien—wake up!" she said in a hushed and scared whisper.

O'Brien sat up amid a tangle of sheet and blanket and pillow; yawning and rubbing his stubble.

"There's somebody coming!" Anny said. She was pacing nervously to and fro, plucking at O'Brien, then going back to the window to press herself against the curtains out of sight, and peer down. "It's a gentleman with a Rolls Royce and a chauffeur!" She came again to her husband, clutching a floral cotton housecoat to herself.

197

"There's nothing you haven't told me, is there?"

O'Brien—who had never been frightened of strangers, or had a mother who threatened to put her head in the gas oven—looked at Anny in a puzzled, and at the same time compassionate way; for she was really suffering.

"Told you about what, Anny?"

"You haven't done anything wrong, have you?" And she peeked down again and caught her breath: "For heaven's sake—he's coming in!"

"Well, let him!" O'Brien joined her at the window in his pyjamas, putting his arm around her. "I've got nothing to be ashamed of—"

But Anny was off on another wild, despairing tack of fear. "The room! Just look at the state of the room! Help me!"

They started tidying their small home with frantic haste; collecting stray articles of clothing; picking up cushions from the floor . . .

As the knock came at the door, Anny was trying to pick odd pieces of cotton off the carpet, while O'Brien was hurrying to put the cushions back on the chairs. Into the middle of this, the stranger opened the door and called in, at the same time noting their guilty activities and red faces.

"Does Mr. O'Brien live here?" he said.

"He does," O'Brien said, with a cushion in his arms, and strongly conscious that his pyjamas were slipping.

"And Mrs. O'Brien?" said the stranger, watching the girl retreat towards the bedroom in pretty confusion.

But at his look, and his tone of voice, Anny suddenly lost much of her timidity. "We're married, all right—if that's what you mean!"

"Ah, go and get dressed, darling," O'Brien said. And to the visitor: "Don't mind her—she's very shy."

"She's very beautiful!' said the visitor.

"D'you think so?" O'Brien said, warming towards the man immediately at this confirmation of his own opinion. "Will you come in and sit down—we're not properly up yet."

As the visitor came into the room, O'Brien called: "Will there be some tea, Anny?" And to the man: "Would you like a cup of tea?" And without waiting for an answer, he pulled the new chair round, and put the cushion straight; then he stopped to retrieve a wayward feather trailed in from the bedroom on his pyjamas. "I've put feathers all over her carpet—she's very fond of this carpet."

"It is a good carpet," the visitor said.

"Is that right?" O'Brien said. "I thought it might be—but I don't know much about them, meself . . . will you take this chair, now? It's very comfortable—the springs have a five-year life test before they let 'em go."

And, at last, the visitor was seated, and making himself comfortable. "It is a good chair," he said.

O'Brien rubbed his hands with delight at this all-round appreciation. They ought to have more friends calling. It was nice to have friends who appreciated the good things you had. A man could get too close to his own possessions.

"I hope you don't mind me calling on business on Sunday morning," the visitor said.

WINDY GAVE HIS name as John Hope, of Hope Brothers— exporters and importers with offices in Cheapside. He looked the part. A good-looking, smooth-featured, man of forty with a neat moustache, and greying hair. His suit was a hand-made brown tweed, and was set off with a red carnation which matched the silk handkerchief below it, and a red-striped club tie.

"I know the firm well," O'Brien said. "You've got one of our safes—the Impregnable Major."

"That's the whole trouble, Mr. O'Brien," the visitor said. "We can't get it open!"

Some urgent business had cropped up at the weekend, and although he had managed to rustle up a skeleton staff to deal with it, the cashier had already left for some unknown destination.

"Completely against the rules of the firm, Mr. O'Brien," the visitor said, aggrievedly. "Johnson knows very well that his keys should be turned over to the secretary if he's off for the weekend—but there you are, we haven't had a spurt of business like this for years."

O'Brien nodded, sympathetically.

"D'you know about our emergency number for cases like this?"

"Oh, yes—of course. I've already been in touch with your Mr. Hennessy, and he put me on to you."

O'Brien flushed with pleasure. "He did that, did he?"

"He said you were the best man for the job—'O'Brien will have it open in two ticks,' were his exact words."

O'Brien called out: "Did you hear that, Anny?" And turning back to the visitor: "He didn't mention Bert Wright, or anybody?"

"No—only you."

"Anny! Did you hear that?"

Anny came back into the room, smoothing down the dress she had just put on.

"Tell her what Mr. Hennessy said," O'Brien requested, adding to his wife: "They want me to open an Impregnable in the city, and Mr. Hennessy told this gentleman—"

"Will you be back for dinner?" Anny asked.

The visitor had got to his feet in honour of Anny's appearance.

"Now sit y'self down, Mr. Hope, and Anny'll get you a cup of tea while I get dressed, and collect some tools."

O'Brien went into the bedroom. The visitor sat down, and

watched the girl pull aside curtains covering the kitchenette. Anny filled the kettle, and looked into the shaving mirror above the sink. Her face flushed. She had seen that look from the men her mother sometimes brought home, and her only sixteen. A little cold fear began to grow inside her again. Her hand shook, and the water splashed over her.

"Can I help you?" the visitor asked.

"No!" Anny said, sharply. "Thank you."

Windy Willow sat back, his eyes ranging from the young figure in the cheap dress to the long legs; and then across the red carpet to a single white feather amongst the pile. It seemed symbolic. There was some innocence which seemed only to be preserved intact by an early marriage, and closeting from life, he thought.

O'BRIEN, WITH HIS bag of tools, rode eastwards through London into the silent Sunday city streets. He chatted with the friendly millionaire—for he seemed to be no less—in the sumptuous back-seat of the Rolls Royce. They stopped outside the Hope Brothers' office in Cheapside, and the chauffeur jumped out smartly and rang a bell. By the time O'Brien was out of the car with his tools, the big door was open, and a uniformed commissionaire was standing there ready to escort them in.

They passed through a foyer, and into an office from which sprang the clatter of busy typewriters. There were two girls typing, both pretty—but made up, and sophisticated, in a way which did not appeal to O'Brien at all. Still, he returned their smiles as he was led through into an inner office, and presented with his task—the familiar, blue-grey, monster of a safe that was Gallagher's pride and joy.

"This is Mr. O'Brien," the Sunday visitor told a fat, bespectacled, man behind a desk. "The man Mr. Hennessy recommended."

"Good!" the man said, with a heavy accent which O'Brien couldn't place. "Thank you, Mr. O'Brien."

They left him to it, closing the door behind them. O'Brien went to work on the safe door, quietly, methodically, keeping each tool in its right place on the leather folder. He knew that he was an expert, but it was nice to know that Mr. Hennessy respected him as well. It wouldn't do to have any slip-up on this job.

After half-an-hour, one of the typists brought him a glass of sherry and some biscuits on a tray.

"Are you getting on all right, Mr. O'Brien?" she asked.

"Yes—thank you, miss."

"We can't take out the ledgers until it's opened," she said.

"Nearly there now," he said.

She squatted at his side, and her tight skirt rode up over her knees, which upset him a little.

"You've got nice hands," she said.

"Well, I don't know," he said.

"Delicate, sensitive, fingers," she said.

O'Brien swallowed. "I've never been told that before."

"Rene!"

The fat continental man was standing in the doorway behind them. The girl stood up slowly.

"All right—only watching."

O'Brien smiled to himself as he worked. The way they talked to the bosses, these days! He took a swift sip at the sherry, a bite of a biscuit; he rubbed his fingers on his coat, and started the last stage, feeling that more than one pair of eyes were watching, and admiring, through the glass panels behind. The typewriters had stopped, and there was no sound but the satisfying lick, lick, lick of mechanical tumblers falling into their keyways.

Suddenly, he sat back. That was it! He was about to pull the safe-door open, when a hand did it for him.

He looked up to find four men and the two girls grouped behind him.

"I didn't know you were there, Mr. Hope!" O'Brien said.

"We like to watch the experts at work," his visitor told him. And then, with the safe door still only partly open, he added: "I'll get the chauffeur to run you home—and a little something for your trouble."

O'Brien stared at a bulky, sealed envelope—then looked up at the donor. "Oh, there's no need for that—the firm will charge you a small fee, I expect, and I shall get overtime."

"Open it when you get home," said the Sunday visitor. "It'll be a nice present for that beautiful wife of yours!"

"Thanks," said O'Brien. "I will!"

"TWO HUNDRED POUNDS!" O'Brien exclaimed. "Will you see this! Two hundred pounds!"

Anny stood staring at the forty five-pound notes, which O'Brien had laid out like a game of patience on the table. She was wiping batter off her hands with a damp teacloth. O'Brien let out a whoop of delight, picked her off her feet, kissed her, and whirled her around.

"That's what I call a real gentleman!" he exclaimed, his face turning red with excitement.

Anny stared at him as if he were mad. "Is that all you call him?"

He frowned, not quite with her; bewildered at her unexcited behaviour and expression.

She said, incredulously: "Now I believe everything I ever heard about Irishmen, O'Brien! Fairies, hobgoblins, leprechauns—they're all one to you, I've no doubt. You just stand there with a silly grin, and accept anything that drops from the sky. If I grew wings and flew round the room, or down into the street, you'd just say 'Well there's a real angel!' Now, wouldn't you?"

"I would!" said O'Brien, with enthusiasm.

"Now you'll pack up that money, O'Brien, and you'll take it round to the police station, and give them descriptions of the men—they weren't wearing masks, were they? Or didn't you notice?"

Now O'Brien began to see her line of reasoning, and it amazed him. "Oh for heaven's sake, woman—a man doesn't rob his own safe in front of the whole staff, and all! Now just sit down, and I'll tell you all about it—they gave me a glass of sherry!"

"That's a good start," Anny said. But she allowed him to pull her onto his lap and tell her all about everything. It was all very straightforward and convincing—except for the pattern of bank notes on the table in front of her. Why would a man pay two hundred pounds for a job he could have got done for a few shillings?

"Well, he liked me," O'Brien said. Then seeing that Anny wasn't impressed, he added: "And he liked you—he said you're beautiful. And you are. And the carpet, and the chairs, he liked. And, anyway, he's a millionaire—very eccentric they are, too."

"I didn't like him," Anny said. "I didn't like the way he looked at me when I wasn't looking at him."

O'Brien took hold of her hair and twisted her face towards him. "What kind of look was that?"

"You know," Anny said.

"Right!" O'Brien said, angrily. "Then we'll keep his money!"

"Well—I like that! I'd rather you took it for opening the safe, than for his looking at me!"

O'Brien was not up to her fine moral values, and he capitulated. "So we'll keep it, then?"

"I don't like it," Anny said. "Honest people don't have that much money—certainly not in cash."

O'Brien laughed at a thought. "There was this very tarty piece in the office, and she came and squatted right down beside me, and told me I had lovely hands!"

Anny looked at him, narrowly. "What were you doing to make her say that!"

"I was busy!"

"Right!" Anny said, her mind suddenly made up. "We will keep their money!"

He squeezed her and she said: "What'll we do with it?"

"We'll talk about it tonight," O'Brien said. "In bed."

"Two hundred pounds!" said Anny suddenly. "Just for opening a safe!"

O'Brien smiled, modestly. As he smiled, he remembered the South African and the Mercedes Benz, and couldn't think why.

THE FOURTH CHAPTER

The temptations of O'Brien

SEXTON BLAKE MET O'Brien for the first time the following morning, in the testing department of Gallagher's Safes and Strongrooms, Ltd. He was there with Chief Detective-Inspector Coutts, and they were both examining a big safe when the chairman of the company, Mr. Hennessy, brought O'Brien in. Hennessy, a big, shambling man with shaggy hair and eyebrows, and an untidy sack of a suit, did the introducing.

O'Brien stared at the two men, blankly: "Detectives?"

Hennessy said: "Yes, but there's no need for you to be alarmed, O'Brien—they just want the benefit of your opinion."

"Gladly," said O'Brien. "Anything at all."

He was shaken at that moment—not by anything he might have done, but what he had been in the process of doing when Hennessy had called him into the office. The trouble was the two hundred pounds which Hope Brothers had given him. Not that it was any problem, in itself; for it had given him the most wonderful night he had ever had with Anny—both of them spending it, and saving it, and investing it a hundred different ways. And there it had been, still intact, at breakfast time; with

Anny counting it three times, and then kissing him so much at the station that people had passed loud remarks.

No—the problem, which had only occurred to him in the train, was whether he should tell his boss about the present. His first inclination was to tell everybody he came to; and, in fact, he almost managed to impart the news to three people already, whom he knew only by sight and "good morning." But deeper reflection brought the possibility that Gallagher's would not look kindly on such a large tip to an employee, by one of their clients; or perhaps Hennessy might make the suggestion that part of it went into the Safemakers' Benevolent Fund.

O'Brien was not a greedy man, and he was ready to give a fair donation to any worthy cause; but Anny was the worthiest cause he knew, and he didn't want to risk upsetting all her plans.

Having decided that he would say nothing about it, he then discovered that he would have to put in an over-time chit for Sunday—or they would want to know why not. This seemed to O'Brien to be a very greedy thing to do, but there was no alternative, and he had been in the middle of calculating the time spent on the job, at time-and-a-half, when he was suddenly whisked into the presence of the two detectives. Naturally, it was unnerving. But not as unnerving as the ordeal to follow.

"This safe," Sexton Blake told O'Brien, "was broken into yesterday by a gang of thieves."

O'Brien gave the safe a cursory glance. "It doesn't look like it to me," he said. "They have to blow our safes apart to get anywhere at all."

Hennessy put in: "That's the curious thing, O'Brien—it appears to have been opened by keys and combination."

Blake said: "I'm sure there were no keys used—if you examine the lock carefully, you'll find tool-marks."

Inspector Coutts shook his head: "I say keys, Blake—but get the expert's opinion."

O'Brien gave a modest nod, and came closer to the safe, taking out his magnifying glass and inserting it into his eye. This was all very gratifying in front of Mr. Hennessy, and bore out the compliments of yesterday. With any luck there might be a chance of a managership later on, and a decent salary to go with it—

This happy train of thought was suddenly snapped by the sight of the lock through the glass. The marks he saw there struck a recent chord that he felt sure the detectives must have heard ringing around the room. With enormous self-control, considering the rate his heart was galloping, he kept his face close to the steel lock, and the glass screwed into his eye.

"Where was it?" he asked, as casually as he could.

"Well, never mind that," Hennessy said. "The police don't want information bandied around—"

"No, it doesn't matter," Coutts said. "The afternoon editions will have it, anyway—it was at Hope Brothers, in Cheapside."

"Well, come along, O'Brien—was it keys, or tools?" Hennessy asked.

"It was tools," O'Brien said, with a greater certainty than he'd ever said anything in his life. "It was a number one reamer and a sixteen gauge feeler, followed by aural manipulation of the tumblers—and a bit of luck."

Blake smiled, admiringly. "Well, that's excellent, Mr. O'Brien! You should be in my business."

Coutts shrugged, ruefully. "That's a drink I owe you, Blake."

Hennessy was smiling, proudly. "Does that satisfy you, gentlemen?"

Blake said: "Indeed it does—but it also starts another headache. For me, for the police, for Gallagher's, and for Venus Life and Property Insurance—there's a new peterman in business who's going to make all the rest seem like amateurs!"

O'Brien kept his face two inches from the lock—until his mouth stopped quivering like a baby's, and the colour started to return to his cheeks.

O'BRIEN'S EMOTIONAL DISTURBANCE could not go unnoticed by a man as perceptive as Sexton Blake. But it was not until the true facts had emerged from all that happened afterwards, that he was able to put that first meeting into its right perspective. Blake explained this to Lord Quade and Sir Martin Reynolds at the inquiry which followed O'Brien's death, over three years later. The story of the Irishman could never have been understood without it.

"When a big jetliner comes in to land at London Airport," Blake said, "there is a moment of decision."

Lord Quade hastily glanced at his papers in panic, lest he had come to the wrong meeting.

"It is a moment," Blake said. "when all the electronic aids are laid aside; when the autopilot is out, and air traffic control has put the machine into the hands of a human pilot, and that man is holding it six feet off the ground, at a hundred and forty miles an hour, with sixty people sitting behind him."

Quade now glanced at Sir Martin Reynolds, and the prison commissioner looked at Superintendent Grimwald. Grimwald and Coutts were listening intently.

"In the same way," Blake said, "there is an optimum moment for confession, when an innocent party is involved in a crime."

"Ah" said Sir Martin, with some relief.

"Quite so," Lord Quade agreed.

O'Brien's moment had come when he learned that he had helped to burgle a safe; and O'Brien's moment had gone, forever, when he'd said nothing about it.

"How do you explain that, Mr. Blake?" Lord Quade asked, with interest.

"Three reasons," Blake said. "One, he thought about it for a moment too long; two, his boss was there; and, three, nobody is entirely innocent." Blake looked round at them. "But, primarily, it was Hennessy. If Hennessy had not been there, O'Brien would have blurted the whole thing out to us. He was a conscientious craftsman, jealous of his prestige in the firm. It's asking a lot, for such a man—at the moment of great pride in his job, and with the boss looking on—suddenly to be called upon to confess that he's been stupid."

Quade nodded. "I can understand that."

"And, working on this, was his subconscious reluctance to give up that two hundred pounds. But this alone would not have stopped him from talking. It just gave him time to think—and thinking was fatal. Anny O'Brien told me, afterwards, that he was in a panic because he had not reported the enormous tip as soon as he got to work that morning. What he quite forgot was that, on his work-bench, he had a half-completed time-sheet for the Sunday job that could have exonerated him from all blame."

"But, of course!" Sir Martin said.

Blake said: "The first thing O'Brien did when we left the premises, was destroy that time-sheet. The moment of decision had passed, and disaster lay ahead . . ."

ANNY WOULD KNOW what to do. That was the recurring thought in O'Brien's head as he had travelled home by underground train, that evening. Anny would know what to do.

He would have to confess the whole thing—there was no doubt about that. But Anny would know the best way to do it. When he came to think about it—and he had had all day now—there was a very good case in his favour. The whole thing had been so convincing. The Rolls-Royce and the chauffeur, and the fellow himself—knowing his name and his job, and knowing how good he was at it. It was still a bit of a compliment, if you looked at it in that way; they hadn't gone to Wright or Jewson, or any of the other safemakers.

And then, knowing about the emergency service number, and quoting Mr. Hennessy's exact words—because it was just the kind of thing Hennessy would be likely to have said. And then, there was the thoroughness of it! Breaking into Hope Brothers' offices, and opening them up like it was an ordinary working day! How big was this gang, that they could provide typists, and commissionaires, and the like? And the sherry, too. A very endearing touch, that was!

A man sitting beside him in the train, opened a newspaper, and O'Brien caught the glaring headlines. Now, why hadn't he thought to get a paper? There it was, in big black-and-white, and with a photograph of the caretaker who had been tied up in the basement.

DARING CITY ROBBERY
Gang Move Into Cheapside Offices And Open Safe

O'Brien leaned closer to the man with the paper, and read on with a curious mingling of horror and pride. Phrases like "Expert job," and "Highly-skilled safe-breaker," caught his eye. When he got to the fold in the paper, the man at his side turned the sheet over, and he went on reading. There was a surprise at the end.

AND ALL FOR NOTHING

That was the sub-heading. After hours of work, the gang had got away with some un-negotiable bonds, and one hundred pounds in notes, of which the numbers had been recorded.

"Well I'll be—" O'Brien said, and stopped himself.

The man at his side folded up the newspaper, and glanced across the gangway to where a burly, pimply-faced, young man in a leather-jacket was sitting; there was a silent communion of glances.

O'Brien was tickled. It had cost them two hundred quid, and they'd got nothing out of it! Well that served them right! That served them right, all right!

As long as they don't come asking for it back, he thought. And, suddenly, he was alarmed. Anny had been alone in the flat all day with that money!

When the train stopped at Kilburn Park, O'Brien went running up the steps ahead of the crowd. Anny was standing in her usual place by the barrier, but O'Brien just looked at her—and ran on in growing fear.

"O'Brien!" she called, running after him.

"Didn't you see me standing there?" she said as she caught him up at the entrance.

"Was that you!" said O'Brien. And then, looking her up and down with amazement: "What've you been doing?"

"Do you like it?" Anny asked, twizzling round, and forcing the out-coming crowd to part and give her room.

There were smiles, and a few wolf whistles from the men.

It was a white, simply-cut, figure-hugging dress in some very revealing crepe material which brought out every pleasant curve of her body, right down to her knees. There were fascinating complementaries: a red belt at her tiny waist; sheer stockings, brown as suntan; small red shoes heels; and a necklace of ruby beads at her throat.

"Shouldn't there be a coat with it?" O'Brien asked.

"And what about my hair?" she asked.

"Smashing!" O'Brien said.

Her fair hair had been cut, and styled, and shampooed, and it shone in soft waves around her face, a shade lighter than her complexion.

"Is that all you can say?" Anny asked.

"How much did it cost?" he asked, anxiously.

Her eyes clouded as she looked at him. "That's a fine thing to say! Last night, you didn't care if I spent every penny on myself! That's men!"

She started walking away, and O'Brien fell into step alongside her, feeling embarrassed and shabby in his stained old mac and scruffy shoes.

"Anyway," she said, "the dress was only three guineas, and my hair was only fifteen shillings—and the whole lot was only five pounds, or less."

Holy smoke, he thought, it was going to be the red carpet all over again, for he'd have to put the money back. You couldn't go to the police with a story about two hundred pounds, and give them only one hundred and ninety-five. There was something not quite spontaneous about that . . .

THE MAN WITH the newspaper, and the pimply youth, came out of the underground station and walked across to a car parked nearby. Sims, the South African, sat behind the wheel; Windy Willow and Rene sat in the rear seat. They all watched the departing couple, but none as intently as Windy.

"I think we've got him," he said at last.

The girl gave him a sour glance. "You're not looking at him," she said.

Windy kept his eyes on the white dress, and the red shoes, as they walked away; but he patted Rene's leg, indulgently.

"We don't want any messing about," Sim said. "There's too much in the kitty." He looked at the man with the paper; a bony-faced man of thirty-five, with a slight cast in his eye. "All right, Baxter—jump in." And, to the boy: "Keep a watch on the house, Cyril." He handed the boy a pound note.

"Fanks," the youth said.

He watched the car drive away, before wandering slowly along the street in the direction the couple had taken.

THE FIFTH CHAPTER

The devil incarnate

ANNY WILL KNOW what to do, was still the thought in O'Brien's mind as they went up the stairs to their flat. It was no use telling her on the street. There was going to be a scene—there was no avoiding it . . .

"Now shut your eyes!" Anny said, before opening the door. "I've got a surprise for you—you don't imagine I just think about myself, do you?"

O'Brien shut his eyes, more in prayer than obedience, and allowed her to guide him into the room.

"All right, you can open them. Well, go on—open them!"

O'Brien, consumed with awful apprehension, opened one eye at a time. "Holy smoke!" he said.

Anny not only knew what to do, she had done it. The amazing thing was, he thought, that she had got it all into eight hours, single-handed. It was astonishing what a girl who had led an underprivileged life could do with two hundred pounds, on a sunny day in Oxford Street.

"Do you like it?" she asked, anxiously.

"I do!" said O'Brien.

And indeed if he could push the fact that they were ruined, and that he would go to prison, right out of his mind for a while, then he did like it. The table was the first thing that took your eye, with its crisp linen cloth and napkins to match, the flowered china dinner service, the silver cruet, and the Wedgwood blue vase filled with roses, and the bottle of champagne, and the smell of roast chicken coming from behind the curtains.

But that was no more than one eye and nose full. With the other eye you might take in a new television set and a portable record player with a pile of long-playing records, a bookcase filled with books, and framed splashes of Mediterranean colour on the walls.

"It's very contemporary," Anny said.

"It is," said O'Brien.

She gave him another anxious glance. "Are you thinking what about the baby?" And before he could reply: "Take a look in the bedroom!"

What's this? he thought. He put his hand on the bedroom door and turned to look back at her, wonderingly. Anything was possible with this girl, he had always known that.

"Go on," she urged, her eyes brimming with laughter. "Don't be frightened!"

Frightened? He was terrified. Two hundred pounds he could have taken away from her, but not all this! He opened the door and looked in. The bed had a new flame-coloured candlewick spread on it. And folded neatly on that were new sets of pyjamas for both of them; together with new shirts, ties, socks, flannels, and a sports jacket.

"You haven't looked at it yet!"

Anny had come to stand at his shoulder in the doorway, her hand around his waist.

"I'll be damned!" he said.

Beside the bed stood a baby's cot in bright pink paint with nursery transfers on it. In the cot were the small blankets and sheets and embroidered pillow cases which no baby could possibly appreciate. Slowly he looked around at her.

"With you earning this kind of money," she said. "I'm not going to wait any longer."

His mind was a jumble of mingled emotions. "I like the shirts," he said.

She was looking at him closely. "You're not angry, are you?"

"Of course I'm not angry!"

"You haven't kissed me."

"Is that right?" he said. He took her into his arms very shyly and gave her a swift kiss; then stood apart again. She was so beautiful in the white dress and everything. And at the uncertain look in her eye he covered up with: "And you got all this for two hundred pounds—"

"Well, of course not!" she exclaimed. "I wouldn't spend all your money. I've bought all this and paid cash and tipped the man for delivery and paid off all the bills with postal orders and put eighty pounds in the Post Office bank—what d'you think of that?"

"It's a miracle!" said O'Brien.

She was not quite satisfied with his reactions to anything, and particularly unsatisfied with the kiss. "Are you tired and hungry, O'Brien?" she asked him kindly.

"I am!" he said.

That was probably the trouble, she thought. "And I sent Mom a box of cigarettes and a bottle of scent," she added, as she went to the kitchenette.

"That was a good thought," he said.

He was staring at her now as he sat in the chair. It was the white dress that had held him off, but now she had covered the front of it with a little coloured froth of an apron, and it had suddenly put her within reach again. He went up behind her and embraced her, kissing her ear.

She laughed and warned him about the hot fat.

Still holding her, he said: "Have you seen the papers?"

She had not had time for papers or anything else.

O'Brien was relieved. He couldn't take all this away from her.

"You'll get the news on television if you switch it on," she said.

O'Brien ran his hands around her, nuzzled his nose in her hair. "We don't want the news," he said.

"Will you give over? You want your dinner, don't you?"

"There's plenty of time," he said.

She squirmed away from him and went to the table, picked up the bottle of champagne. "You'd better have a drink while you're waiting!"

"Better let me do it," he warned her. "It'll pop!"

"It popped when I set the table!" she giggled, and hiccupped.

She held him off while they drank together; toasting the future, and the baby; she held him off while they ate dinner, sharing the same chair and feeding each other—with the champagne getting lower and lower in the bottle, and O'Brien's brave resolutions dwindling with it.

WINDY WAS LOOKING up at the darkened windows of the O'Briens' flat.

"Are you sure they didn't go out?" he asked the youth Cyril.

"I don't fink so."

"You've been here all the time, haven't you?"

"Free hours, firty minutes," Cyril said. "Can I go now, Mr. Willow?"

"No visitors? The police—or Blake, or anybody?"

"Not frough the front."

As Windy stared up, a speculative expression came into his eyes. "All right—buzz off."

"Fanks," Cyril said.

The youth lit up a cigarette, cupping his hands around the flame of a match, then strolled off. Windy waited for him to go, then walked quietly up the steps of the house, through the open front door.

Windy knocked smartly at the O'Briens' door, then laid his ear flat against the panel to listen to all the hurried noises and whispers. He opened the door as O'Brien switched on the light.

"Mr. O'Brien," he said, with a pleasant smile.

O'Brien was again clutching a cushion, another of which lay on the floor, while Anny was again backing towards the bedroom in her stockinged feet, doing up a button with one hand and holding a bottle in the other; her hair was in pretty disarray, her face flushed.

"Will you come in, Mr. Hope—Mr.—will you come in?"

"I will," Windy said.

As the suave gentleman came into the room and closed the door behind him, Anny was holding a whispered conversation with her husband by the bedroom door.

"Doesn't he ever knock!" she hissed. "Tell him off for opening the door like that!"

"I'll get rid of him."

"But don't be too hasty," Anny added. "Perhaps he's got another job for you!"

O'Brien closed the door on her, and on heaven, and turned to face the devil.

"If it's the money you want back, you're too late!" he said. "She's spent it! And a good job, too!"

Windy sat down, and made himself comfortable, giving O'Brien a friendly smile. "I'm glad," he said. "You earned it, Mr. O'Brien."

"I'm going to the police!" O'Brien said.

"When?" Windy asked.

"Eh? Oh, tomorrow. That's right, tomorrow. First thing!"

"Why didn't you go today?" Windy asked.

"Well," O'Brien said, "I didn't know about it until I saw the papers tonight. On the train, coming home."

Windy pulled another chair round. "Sit down. Mr. O'Brien."

"Thanks," O'Brien said, taking the chair.

Windy said: "Didn't Mr. Blake tell you about it this morning? He was at your works with Inspector Coutts."

O'Brien frowned and shifted, uncomfortably. "He was there," he admitted. "And he did say something about a robbery— but I didn't know it was me. I mean you."

"Now don't you worry about Blake. He doesn't know anything about us."

"Are you sure?" O'Brien said, with great relief. Then, at the smile in the other's face, he checked himself. "There's nothing to know about me," he said. "But he's going to know all about you in the morning."

"What does your wife say about it?" Windy asked.

"Oh, she's of the same opinion," O'Brien said. "She wanted me to go tonight, only . . . She's of the same opinion—she thought you were a crook the moment she clapped eyes on you."

"Did she? Well let's ask her in, and let her—"

"Oh, no!" O'Brien put in quickly, lowering his voice. "She's very tired tonight."

"Well then let's drop the whole matter." Windy suggested.

O'Brien said: "There wasn't much of a profit in it for you, anyway."

Windy shrugged. "You can't always rely on information— but you have to take the rough with the smooth."

"Ah, you do that," O'Brien said. He took out some cigarettes, and offered one to his visitor. He was glad that the talk had shifted away from yesterday's business—which he wanted to forget, he had now decided, as quickly as maybe. "Do you have many like that?" he asked, politely.

"We hope to do better, now that we've got you with us," Windy said.

O'Brien looked at his visitor with growing alarm. "Don't talk like that! I'm not with you. I've got a job. A good job. You tricked me into opening that safe!"

"I don't want to depress you," Windy said. "But I can't think of a judge who would believe that."

"Would he not?" O'Brien said, aghast.

"You were paid well for it," Windy pointed out.

"I was," O'Brien said. "I'm not complaining about the money."

"And you've spent it," Windy said.

"Well Anny doesn't know—that is, she didn't know—"

Windy said: "She doesn't know, does she, Mr. O'Brien?"

O'Brien shook his head, miserably.

"She's so happy—I hadn't the heart to tell her. What am I going to do!"

"She need never know," Windy said, "if you do one more little job for us."

O'Brien stood up. "That I'll not do!" he said emphatically.

Windy shook his head regretfully. "It that your last word?"

"It is!" O'Brien said.

"The boys will be very unhappy," Windy said, sorrowfully.

"I'm sorry." O'Brien said, with genuine regret. "You've got the wrong man in me, Mr. Hope—Mr.—"

"Willow," his visitor said. "Windy Willow."

O'Brien said: "Are you a full-time crook, then?"

"Yes—I suppose you could call me that."

O'Brien said: "I've never met anybody like you before—I mean, a professional. Have you been to prison at all?"

"Several times," Windy said. "And it's not very pleasant."

"Haven't you ever thought of getting a good job?" O'Brien asked. "There's plenty of work about these days."

"I tried once," Windy said. "It wasn't a success."

"But aren't you terribly ashamed when you get your name in the papers, and your friends read it?"

"My friends are all crooks," Windy said, simply.

O'Brien sighed in despair. "It must be a terrible life."

"Not at all!" Windy said, cheerfully. "You'll be surprised how quickly you get to like it—there's no getting up in the mornings, you know."

"Is that so? I never thought of that." Then O'Brien gave Windy a suspicious look. "I'm not doing any more, you know."

"You'd better think about it," Windy said. "You see the boys are expecting you on this next job—and they're not ones to cross . . . Sunday was a kind of trial-run for you, really—it's a bit unkind to back out now you've passed the test."

"I'll not do it," O'Brien said firmly.

Windy sighed. "I don't want to alarm you, but they won't take it lying down. They'll probably shop you for Sunday's little effort."

"Shop . . . ? Hey—what does that mean?" O'Brien asked.

"Tell the police—get you put in prison."

"I'd rather go to prison," O'Brien said.

"It will be five years," Windy said. Then, reviewing the case in an expert way, he corrected himself: "No, four years."

"I'd rather go," O'Brien said.

Anny's voice could now be heard behind the bedroom door, singing to herself. Both men listened for a moment, then Windy said: "It's a long time to leave that lovely wife of yours all by herself, Mr. O'Brien."

And he looked down at the cushion on the carpet.

O'Brien's heart turned cold.

"What kind of job?" he said.

"I won't bother you with the details tonight," Windy said, "just wait for me to get in touch with you."

O'Brien said: "And how do I know there won't be another job after this one, and another after that?"

Windy sat up in the chair, and leaned close to O'Brien. "Because," he said, softly and confidentially, "strictly between ourselves, this is our last job."

"Then why not call it a day now and have finished with it?" O'Brien suggested. "A thing like that can get a hold on you— it's always going to be the 'last one'—and it never is. If you're not careful, it'll always be just one more—you'll never give it up at all!"

Windy waved the thought aside. "This is a special, Mr. O'Brien. If we pull it off, successfully—and we shall—there's fifty thousand pounds for every man!"

O'Brien boggled at the sum. "Fifty thousand pounds! I'd never explain that to Anny!"

Windy smiled, gazing around the room and noting all the changes. "You'd be surprised how women accept money."

"But why haven't you done this one before?" O'Brien said. "It seems the kind of thing you want in your line."

Windy gripped O'Brien's arm like an old friend. "We've been waiting for you," he said, warmly.

THE SIXTH CHAPTER

League of Gentlemen.

AN ATTRACTIVE YOUNG policewoman brought in a trolley of coffee and sandwiches, and Lord Quade was so absorbed in Sexton Blake's narration of the O'Brien story that he took sugar without a murmur; something he had not done since the war.

"There's a crowd of press men still waiting, sir," she told the commissioner.

"Well, they're wasting their time—not that that's going to worry them—they get paid for it."

Detective Superintendent Grimwald looked at the commissioner. "Do you want me to send them away, sir?"

Blake said: "I wouldn't be too peremptory with them— O'Brien sells papers, and has done for some time."

Lord Quade said to Blake: "Had these facts which you have been giving us become known at his trial I'm sure the verdict would have been very different."

Sir Martin agreed. "It seems to me that O'Brien was more sinned against than sinning—he was virtually blackmailed into the Dackworth robbery."

"And then betrayed," Blake said.

ON THE EVENING of the day following his second visit to the flat, Windy was waiting at the kerbside in a little scarlet Morris Minor when O'Brien came out of Gallagher's works entrance.

"What happened to the Rolls-Royce?" O'Brien asked as they drove down Ludgate Hill.

"I put it back," Windy said. Then as O'Brien dwelt on the disquieting implications of this, he added: "We pick the car according to the job in hand."

O'Brien stopped enjoying the ride.

"Is this one yours, then?" he asked.

"Oh, no," Windy said. "It's hardly worth running a car in London, what with all the parking problems."

O'Brien sat stiffly on his seat with a sharp eye out for every policeman. There came a yap from behind him, and he jumped; then turned to meet the aggrieved eye of a little white poodle, who sat in a basket on the rear seat.

"The boys are all very glad you decided to come in with us, Mr. O'Brien," Windy said, as they swung on to the embankment and headed west. "You made a great hit with Rene."

"Will that be the dark one?"

Windy nodded. "A nice girl—she needs friends." He spared a sorrowing glance and added: "A widow, you know."

O'Brien shook his head in sympathy, seeing in every widow a dark future for Anny. "She's very young. What would her husband say if he only knew what she was doing now?"

"Oh, he was with us," Windy said, "until he slipped up."

"Was it an accident?"

"That's what he tried to make out," Windy said, "but the jury wouldn't accept it—he was hanged."

O'Brien swallowed, and kept his eyes riveted across the river on to the gay frontage of the Festival Hall. "I promised Anny to be home by nine," he ventured. "She thinks I'm on over-time."

Windy sighed. "Innocence," he said, "is a rare thing."

O'Brien nodded. "You can't buy it."

Windy gave him a quick unobserved glance, then concentrated on his driving.

THE GANG MEETING took place in a luxury penthouse flat in Park Lane. O'Brien was badly inhibited by the luxury and formality of it all. No use telling himself that here was a gang of crooks—outcasts of society—dangerous, dishonest men; ex-jailbirds; common thieves. It was like a board meeting, and O'Brien sat on the edge of his chair, nervous and anxious to please.

There were nine men, with O'Brien making the tenth. There was Mr. Sims, the South African, whom O'Brien now realised must have been instrumental in bringing him into the gang. Sims was dressed in a black-silk dressing gown, which covered sartorial preparations for a dinner later that evening. O'Brien was fascinated by Sims' magnificent dress cufflinks which glistened at his wrists.

Introductions were performed on a polite and formal basis. There was Mr. Sims, and Mr. Willow; Mr. Tarrant, Mr. Lemon, Mr. Peel, Mr. Barratt, Mr. Featherstonhaugh, Mr. Hess, and Mr. Baxter.

"Then who's the boss?" asked O'Brien diffidently.

"I am," the nine men said, together.

Windy Willow smiled at the Irishman's confusion. "It's a very democratic organisation," he explained.

"It is," said O'Brien.

There was then a certain amount of preliminary and desultory conversation between the men—which might well have taken place in any professional man's club. During this interlude, the two girls, Rene and the blonde Margo, came in with coffee and drinks, and little parsley-sprigged canapes on silver platters.

The pace was leisurely indeed, and O'Brien had time to

survey them all.

Sims had been the man at the petrol pumps with the Mercedes Benz. Baxter, with the cast in his eye, had held the newspaper in the train so that he could read it. Mr. Hess was the Germanic gentleman, plump and stiff. He was dressed in black, with an old-fashioned shiny white collar and his short hair standing to attention. O'Brien remembered that this was the one who had sat at the desk where the safe was at Hope Brothers.

Mr. Tarrant could have been a middle-aged Yorkshire insurance man. He had been one of the clerks at Hopes, and Mr. Featherstonhaugh had been another—two very ordinary-looking men, O'Brien thought.

On the other hand, Mr. Barratt was elderly, and sat in a wheel chair with a blanket over his legs; while Mr. Lemon was an incredibly ancient, and very deaf gentleman who kept looking round as if wondering what was going on.

No wonder the police can't catch them, O'Brien thought. They were not the kind of men you would find in smoky Limehouse taverns and spielers, or Soho dives. They're just ordinary people, O'Brien thought. It must be the cost of living that's driven them to crime.

Rene came to O'Brien and held his hand as she offered him a tray. "Would you like another canape, Mr. O'Brien?" she murmured intimately. "I cooked them myself."

"Rene!" Mr. Hess called across the room.

Rene pouted. "I was only asking!" She wrinkled her nose into a farewell smile for O'Brien. "See you later!"

Windy Willow now banged on the table for silence.

The old deaf gentleman, Mr. Lemon, began to get to his feet, a few inches at a time. "Nice meeting," he quavered. "We must have some more. Jolly crowd!"

Mr. Sims sat him down again and bellowed into his ear: "We're just starting!"

Mr. Lemon sat down again with a grateful smile. "Very well, just one more of those little sausages then."

O'Brien looked at Windy Willow. "What does he do?"

Windy said: "He has the ideas . . ."

THE SAFE AT Dackworth Stores was the most eligible safe in the country. Every Thursday night it held half a million pounds in banknotes. The money was made up of the salaries of ten thousand weekly paid personnel, who worked in the giant Oxford Street multiple store, and in five hundred provincial branches; this, plus an enormous day's takings.

For this reason the safe was as large, strong, and as formidably situated and guarded as any bank vault.

It had taken the gang twelve months to infiltrate its members on to the payroll of the Oxford Street store.

"We can guarantee to give you four clear hours on the safe," Windy told O'Brien, as the others sat around listening, "with all alarms disconnected, and no interference."

"You must have put a lot of work into it," O'Brien said, admiringly.

Mr. Hess bowed his head stiffly. "We also are specialists, Mr. O'Brien."

Mr. Sims was watching O'Brien, closely. "Can you do it?"

"What type of safe is it?" O'Brien asked.

They gave him the size, the type, and even the serial number, of the Gallagher safe.

O'Brien clicked his fingers on a bright idea. "You know who you want for that baby, don't you? You want Bert Wright! He's the man for you."

He looked round at the unenthusiastic faces.

Windy said: "I thought you were the best man Gallagher's had?"

"I am," O'Brien said. "On the Impregnable Major."

Old Mr. Lemon looked around at his nearest neighbour. "What's he saying now?"

"He says he can't do it, Mr. Lemon!" came the shouted reply.

"Can't do what?" asked the old gentleman.

"The safe at Dackworth's!" somebody provided, at the top of his voice.

"Dackworth's?" said the old man, bemused. "But we did that last year!"

"No, no—that was Finnemore's!"

"Finnemore's?" bleated the old gent. "Well I never! No wonder I only got six months! Couldn't get that blessed judge to speak up!"

The old man peered across the table at O'Brien, as though seeing him for the first time. "Does he know all the details?"

Windy nodded.

"Oh dear," said Mr. Lemon, regretfully. "Then you'll be wanting an idea for another fatal accident. Pity."

O'Brien grinned; then, looking around at the regretful faces the grin faded. One of the men had crossed to the door, and locked it.

O'Brien cleared his throat. "I didn't say I couldn't do it," he ventured.

IN THE NEXT hour details of the robbery were thrashed out with all unpleasantness forgotten. Later in the evening Windy drove O'Brien home, this time in a Ford Consul.

Sitting in the car outside the house in Kilburn, Windy gave O'Brien a copy of the regulations by which each member of the gang had agreed to abide.

"It's the biggest job we've ever attempted," Windy told him, "and we don't want any post-operational complications."

Unseen by either of them at that moment, Anny was staring down from her window in fear and dread; in clearing out the pantry that afternoon she had made the most terrible discovery about Mr. Willow, and the two hundred pounds. Spreading an old newspaper on the newly-scrubbed shelves, she had come across the Hope Brothers robbery. She had almost fainted, and had to sit for five minutes with her head between her knees.

She had known right from the start that they were crooks. Hadn't she told O'Brien? But who had spent the money? She had. She couldn't blame O'Brien for that. Honest to God—if only she'd seen that report sooner!

Now here was poor, innocent, unsuspecting, O'Brien being led into heaven-knew what crime again. And the terrible thing was, she couldn't tell him. Not now she had spent the money— or most of it. O'Brien was a good, honest man. If she told him, he would be horrified. She had no doubt about the outcome. He would give himself up, and go to prison.

"O'Brien!" she called down at last. "Are you coming in for your dinner, or what?"

O'Brien craned his head out of the Consul, and looked up and waved. Windy also looked up and waved.

"You're a lucky man, O'Brien," he said. "Don't let me keep you from it."

He kept his eyes upwards as O'Brien got out of the car. He could still see that feather on the carpet.

It was not often you envied a married man. Where another woman might go home and take off her hat, Windy thought, this girl must take off even more. However, the light was not sufficient for him to be sure of this.

O'Brien watched Windy get out of the Consul, and drive away in a Vauxhall Victor.

"That's my old man's motor your friend just drove off in, mister!" exclaimed a small coloured boy.

O'Brien recognised the boy as having a basement father as big as a West Indian mahogany tree.

"Which friend?" O'Brien said.

He hurried in.

"You're not doing any more jobs for that man!" Anny said when O'Brien came in. "Promise me you're not doing any more jobs for that man, O'Brien!"

"Just one little job," O'Brien said.

"Not one!" Anny said, firmly. "If you do one more job for that man, I shall leave you—and go home to . . . I shall leave you."

O'Brien bit his lip. He couldn't stand much more. Anny could see how he felt, and she put her arms around him.

"I'd never leave you," she said. "Even if you did."

"This is the last one," O'Brien said.

"Then you must get out of it," Anny said.

"Wouldn't you like another two hundred pounds?"

"No!" Anny exclaimed.

"Three hundred?" O'Brien said.

"The more it is," Anny said, "the less I want you to do it!"

O'Brien said: "I'll do it just to get rid of him, then."

Anny set about laying a cloth and getting food out of the oven. If only she could tell O'Brien what he was getting into.

"It'll have to be something small, then," she said. "Cleaning his car, or something . . ."

"Just one more little job and that's the finish," O'Brien said.

He was re-reading the list of rules tucked inside the evening paper so that Anny couldn't see them. The rules seemed unduly strict to O'Brien: No car, no houses, no foreign travel, no free-spending . . . Did it also include no babies, he wondered.

"Then after two years," he said, as she busied around the room, "we'll go to Ireland, and buy a little farm with a few pigs and an acre of potatoes and raise a race horse or two."

Anny was tasting the gravy with her finger, her back to O'Brien. Race horses? It must be the Bank of England, at least!

THE SEVENTH CHAPTER

Crime of the year.

"MAY I INTERJECT?" Lord Quade asked, as Sexton Blake reached this phase of the O'Brien story.

Blake nodded, and sipped his coffee.

"Are you asking me," the commissioner said, "in a serious factual report to the Home Secretary, to state that although both O'Brien and his wife knew that he was involved in a crime at this stage—neither of them was aware that the other knew?"

"Yes," Blake said. "That's the truth."

"Very well," Lord Quade said.

Sir Martin Reynolds, the Prison Commissioner, shook his head. "I can believe it. I do believe it. It's the kind of ironical situation that can arise from too much mutual respect."

Quade said: "You needn't detail the robbery itself, Mr. Blake—I've read all the records. It went according to plan and they got away with half a million—of which, I believe, you have already recovered ninety per cent?"

"That's right," Blake said. "And nine of the gang are now serving prison sentences."

"Thanks to you, Blake," Commander Grimwald put in.

Quade acknowledged this: "A very creditable piece of work."

"The credit," Blake said, "should really go to O'Brien."

Ah!" said Lord Quade.

And Sir Martin squirmed into a more comfortable position, then rang the bell for more refreshment.

"You would think," Blake continued, "that the gang had managed to avoid all the usual mistakes."

Lord Quade glanced again at the set of rules. "You would indeed!"

"Indeed you would," said Sir Martin.

Chief Detective-Inspector Coutts, who had been silent, he felt, for far too long, now spoke. "If there's one thing I look for in any good safe robbery, it's the trademark of the peterman. You can rely on it. That's why the safecracker himself is always the biggest danger to a gang. He's the one man they have to provide with a good alibi—and good alibis are hard to come by. Besides, once we're on to a safecracker it's not difficult to find who he's been drinking with in the past six months."

"I appreciate that, Mr—" Lord Quade had to refer to his notes, before adding: "Inspector Coutts."

Coutts, undaunted, went on: "They avoided that by using a new man, an amateur. That was O'Brien's chief value to the gang."

"And the other thing," Grimwald said, "which you can look for after a robbery of this size, is for someone to start throwing his money around or shooting off his mouth—and the gang took care of that by drawing up these rules of behaviour."

"And now nine of them are in prison and one is dead," Lord Quade said. "I think the Home Secretary should bear that in mind in his reply to the Opposition."

Blake said: "I still have to recover O'Brien's share of the loot—fifty thousand pounds."

Quade said: "We're getting too far ahead, Mr. Blake—can

you tell us how it all came unstuck? What happened after the robbery?"

"Yes, of course, sir," Blake said. "It was then that I was officially assigned to the case . . .

THE DACKWORTH STORE robbery was the biggest, and the most financially catastrophic, in a series of five major robberies which the Venus Life and Property Assurance Company had been called upon to cover. Altogether, Venus had paid out nearly a million pounds in compensation, and a lesser company would have been bankrupted.

Therefore when Paula Dane took the call summoning Blake to a meeting at the Venus offices in Moorgate on the Monday the Dackworth robbery was discovered, Blake dropped everything and went.

"It must be a Royal Command," Paula told Tinker while the door was still swinging.

Tinker was peering down into Berkeley Square with a worried frown as Blake drove swiftly away. "It'll be a Royal Raspberry if we don't soon get a lead on this gang," he said.

Paula joined him at the window. "I'm always ready to take a wage-cut," she said, gloomily.

Tinker sighed. "I was just thinking of asking for a rise."

Paula patted his shoulder. "You'd better do something to deserve it, first."

If only he could! Tinker went back to Blake's big desk and sat behind it with his feet up, as if seeking inspiration. Over the past few weeks he had been through all the files and criminal records, searching for a clue to this new series of robberies. Already there were characteristics beginning to emerge giving a pattern which linked the robberies together. They seemed to be a happy, casual and audacious lot—usually they stopped for a drink, or stuck a bawdy pin-up on the safe; and in one excess of good spirits, they had left the safe closed but filled with the kind of things one puts into a refrigerator.

Tinker and Blake had at first considered the possibility that it was the work of the Syndicate, but had dismissed the idea. For one thing, the crimes lacked the hallmark of a Syndicate job—smuggling, counterfeiting, drug-running, and murder, came into the Syndicate's history—with not much lightheartedness about it.

Paula went towards the door, and cast an amused but sympathetic glance at Blake's young colleague. "If I think of anything helpful," she said, "I'll let you know."

Lost in speculation, Tinker offered no reply.

But when the telephone on the desk buzzed ten seconds later he was instantly on the ball.

"Is that Sexton Blake Investigations?" asked a high-pitched, muffled voice.

Tinker said: "Take that handkerchief away from your mouth and I might tell you."

"Do you suffer from overwork, eye-strain, sore feet, biliousness, spots before the eyes?" asked the muffled voice. "If so, try Gallagher's. Gallagher's will do you good."

"Ta," Tinker said.

He heard the telephone receiver replaced. He put down his own receiver for a moment, then picked it up again.

"Marion?"

Marion Lang's voice came absently from the switchboard, as if from the depths of some intriguing novel. "Hm?"

"Get me back to Paula," Tinker said. And when her voice came on the extension, he stuffed his handkerchief into his mouth and spoke in a high-pitched, nasal voice: "Ees zees Mees Dane?"

"Yes, Tinker," Paula's voice said.

"Gallagher's Fallaghers," said Tinker, and hung up.

In the next office, Paula stared at the receiver for a moment, then re-rang for the switchboard.

"Marion—if you're not too engrossed in your book take Tinker a cup of tea and an aspirin, will you?"

When Marion went into Blake's office with the tea-tray, Tinker had his head buried in his hands. She put down the tray and slid her hands around his neck, kissed his ear.

Tinker slid one eye up to meet hers, suspiciously. "Now what are you reading?"

"That was just for you," Marion said. "To cheer you up."

He pressed her hand. She was very nice, but what he really needed was some kind of clue.

MEANWHILE SEXTON BLAKE was in the vault of Dackworth's Stores, in Oxford Street. With him—stern, tense, unhappy in various degrees depending upon their own particular grievance in the robbery—were Mr. Phipps and Mr. Marks, of Venus Life and Property; Commander Grimwald and Chief Detective-Inspector Coutts, of the Yard; Mr. Hennessy, of Gallagher's Safes and Strongrooms; and Gordon Dackworth Junr., of Dackworth Stores.

"Gallagher's safes I would not give to my child for a money box!" Mr. Marks was saying, bitterly.

This was unjust, and everybody—including Mr. Marks—knew it; but it did express the kind of feeling in the air.

"They open them without explosives even," Mr. Marks complained.

Hennessy said: "That's because Gallagher's safes can't be opened with explosives. If you remember, the last time they tried gelignite on one of our safes, we found a hand amongst the debris."

Blake said: "This is a repeat of the Hope Brothers job—the same craftsman, the same tools."

The police detectives looked at Blake with interest.

"You mean the new man?" Coutts said. "In that case, I don't give you much for our chances of catching them—not until he's got a record."

Mr. Marks turned to Blake, nervous and edgy: "Never mind what the police say—you catch them. We don't want any defeatism. On top of your retainer you get another ten thousand pounds if you recover this money."

"I shall do my best," Blake said.

But his heart was heavy. It was another clean job. There were plenty of fingerprints on the safe, but none with a record.

Hennessy said, including Blake and the Scotland Yard men in the question: "Would you like me to get my man O'Brien to give you a report on the locks?"

They shook their heads, glumly. The locks had been turned and half a million pounds taken in negotiable currency, and they needed no report to tell them that.

THAT NIGHT, BLAKE took Tinker and Paula on a round of clubs, dives and spielers, throughout London's West and East ends. It was hectic, tiring, expensive, and unrewarding, with only Paula—who had not been on the town for goodness knows how long—really enjoying it.

However, enjoyment was not the object, as Blake pointed out rather bitterly once or twice. He was looking for information, renewing old friendships with old lags, dispensing fivers, getting only negative replies, shrugs, rumours and gossip.

"Don't say I told you this, guv'nor, but the boys think it's an American crowd, fresh over . . ."

"Don't let this go any farther, Mr. Blake, but I got it on good authority it's a gang from Tangier—they've been turfed out since they nationalised crime over there . . ."

"Listen, Mr. Blake—this is worth a tenner—thanks—what you're looking for is a gaggle of Debs' Delights—society types—doing it for kicks . . . and they'll get 'em, when the boys catch up with 'em . . ."

A large, bulky, haggard-looking, man propping up a club bar in Park Lane at two in the morning, summed up the whole depressing night for them.

"The truth of it is, Blake," he said, "nobody knows a thing."

"Thanks, Splash," Blake said. "That's what I gathered."

"Dance?" Paula said, brightly, to their favourite columnist. Splash Kirby of the Post was taken by surprise.

"Well," Paula explained, "nobody else has asked me for the past hour . . ."

THE PENNY DROPPED while they were sitting in the *Brush And Palette* coffee house in Bayswater, taking a quiet coffee, and watching the life class and their blonde young model who posed unselfconsciously in front; listening to the quiet conversation around them, and the soft laughter. It was relaxing; it was a way to end an evening. The penny dropped quite by accident.

They were discussing the robbery—Blake and Paula on one side of the table, Tinker and Splash on the other.

"There may have been five robberies, in all," Blake said, "but only two of them involved opening a safe. The first three were furs from a shop, jewels—also from a shop—and the cargo of cigarettes they stole by kidnapping the lorry driver, and taking his place."

Splash said: "I don't see that it helps us. They were probably working up to this one big job."

"It indicates one thing," Blake said. "Until they tackled Hope Brothers they had nobody capable of opening a safe. They obviously didn't want to employ any one of the known petermen."

"That means they've recruited somebody recently," Paula said.

"Or else," Blake said, "they've been waiting for him to train—Hope Brothers might have been an apprentice effort, and they were not interested in the proceeds."

Splash nodded. "They must have had their eye on Dackworth's for months."

Paula was puzzled. "Where do safecrackers train? Is there a school somewhere?"

The question hung in the air unanswered as they all watched the nude model, and sipped their coffee.

Tinker yawned and stretched, inelegantly.

Paula looked at him. "You're going to have a hang-over."

Tinker spared her a narrow glance. "I should try Gallagher's," he said.

Blake looked at him, sharply. "Why?"

"Gallagher's does you good," he said. Then: "It's a private joke between me and Paula."

"Hm?" Paula said, mystified.

"You may be joking," Blake told his colleague, "but you may also be right."

It was Tinker's turn to be mystified.

"May I?"

"I was thinking along the same lines," Blake explained. "It seems such an incredibly unlikely possibility that I dare hardly to put it into words."

Paula was looking at Tinker as though for an answer. "Gallagher's Fallaghers?" she said.

Tinker shrugged. "You started it. You tell me."

Blake was looking from one to the other; he exchanged a glance with Splash, who was also out of his depth.

Tinker said: "That silly telephone call this afternoon—"

Paula said: "But you made that—'Gallagher's Fallaghers', you said."

"But that was after you called me, and asked if I had any

240

spots before the eyes!" Tinker exclaimed, growing red.

Paula was looking blank. "Spots before the eyes?"

"Didn't you?" Tinker said, uncertainly.

Blake put in: "You'd better tell me what happened."

Tinker sat up, losing his yawns and becoming alert, and a little shamefaced. "There was this telephone call," he told Blake. "Just after you'd gone out this afternoon. I thought it was Paula using a silly disguised voice . . ."

As Blake listened his brow cleared.

"It was a tip-off," he said.

"Good lor!" Tinker said. "And I missed it!"

"I see!" Paula exclaimed. "If Sexton Blake Investigations has any problems they should try Gallagher's—Safes and Strongrooms!"

Splash smiled round at them. "Aren't you lucky? Gallagher's is the place to train safecrackers. I'd better stick around."

Blake called for the bill. "You go home to bed, Splash. We don't want any publicity at this stage. If there's any joy you'll know about it." Then to Tinker: "Go and get Grimwald on the line for me."

"He'll be in bed," Tinker said.

"Good," Blake said.

"He'll grumble at me," Tinker said.

"Good," Blake said again, "You need grumbling at. I've worn myself to a shadow tonight looking for a tip-off—and you had one all the time."

It was not only a tip-off. It was a tip-off in the direction Blake was already beginning to look. He was remembering that moment in Gallagher's factory, after the Hope Brothers robbery. The moment when the safemaker kept his face to the lock.

THE EIGHTH CHAPTER

A print for framing.

GRIMWALD WAS NOT angry at being dragged down to the Yard Records Office at three in the morning. He was glad to do it.

"You don't think I was sleeping, do you?" he told Blake.

Tinker had taken Paula home, and Splash Kirby had taken the model from the life class. Blake and Grimwald were with the Records Superintendent in the fingerprinting room.

"First of all," Blake said, "I want to see all the prints photographed from the Dackworth safe."

"There were plenty," the Records man said. "We've had a busy day."

The enlarged fingerprints had been assembled into a file. Some were full and round, others just small fragments; others again, so faint and blurred that a magnifying glass was necessary to trace the characteristic lines.

The Records Superintendent used a pointer, and read out the captions. "These are the chief cashier's at Dackworth Stores, these belong to Gordon Dackworth, this one is the detective sergeant who took the prints; this, Marks of Venus Life and Property; this one Detective Inspector Coutts; this one is yours,

Commander Grimwald, and these are yours, Mr. Blake."

"Are they?" Blake said. He looked at Grimwald who became a little sheepish.

The Records man explained: "We got everybody to give us their prints—co-operative lot."

Blake said: "I didn't give you my prints."

Grimwald cleared his throat. "The fact is," he began, and stopped. "Well, we happened to have them by us."

"All right," Blake said patiently. "How long have my fingerprints been in Criminal Records?" And as the Commander hesitated, he added: "You may as well tell me, Grimwald."

Grimwald shrugged. "I inherited them."

The Records Superintendent nodded. "I've been here ten years, and they were here before I came."

Blake sighed. "All right—give us the rest."

"Only one other—unidentified," the Superintendent said. "It was on the lock itself."

Blake examined the solitary print very carefully through the glass. Without looking up at his two companions, he said: "I can identify it."

Grimwald and the Records man looked at each other, then watched with acute interest as Blake took an envelope from his breast pocket and drew out a glossy photoprint.

"Snap!" he said, laying it alongside the print in the file.

It was unmistakably identical.

Grimwald said: "Where did you get that?"

"I took it off this," Blake said.

He had obviously come prepared to find the print he wanted. From his jacket pocket he had taken a handkerchief, and, carefully folded inside the handkerchief, was a Sherry glass.

"One sherry glass," Blake told them. "From Hope Brothers' office in the city."

Grimwald stared from the glass to Blake. "I didn't see that."

"I know you didn't," Blake told him. "I saw it first."

Grimwald breathed hard. "And then you get huffy because you're in Criminal Records!"

Blake shrugged. "Give a dog a bad name . . ."

The Records Superintendent said: "It proves that the same man was on both jobs—but do you know who that man is?"

"Not yet," Blake admitted.

Grimwald grunted disparagingly. "If it's not in Records I don't see that we're any forrader. We know the same gang did both jobs by the technique."

Blake said: "I haven't finished yet."

And as they waited for his next request, he said: "I want all the prints off the Hope Brothers safe."

"You're getting tired, old man," Grimwald said. "There weren't any prints on the Hope safe. It was as clean as a whistle—you know it was."

"I know the gang didn't leave any prints on it," Blake said. "But I want it finger-printed now—you've still got it, haven't you?"

"It's here at the Yard," Grimwald said. "But everybody's been handling it—what's the use of that?"

"Let's get it covered," Blake said.

Grimwald yawned. "I don't know what you're after, Blake— but won't it keep until after breakfast? Some of us have to be up, and on the job by ten o'clock."

Blake said: "How would you like to make an arrest before breakfast?"

Commander Grimwald met Blake's steady gaze for a moment. Then he picked up a telephone.

THE RED SUN was rising over the Pool of London and sending half-hearted beams through a dawn mist on the river, by the time all the prints had been photographed and mounted ready for inspection.

"Twenty blessed prints!" Grimwald grumbled. "Most of 'em policemen!"

Blake settled down at the desk. "You know what we're looking for."

The unidentified print found on the Hope sherry glass, and on the Dackworth safe, was now mounted in a projector, and its image shone clearly on the surface of a screen on the wall.

With three of them searching, it was not long before the right print was found. Grimwald held it up.

"Housey-housey!" he said. Then, puzzled: "Are you saying that one of our chaps is in with this gang?"

"No," Blake said. "One of Gallagher's chaps . . ."

The night's work was not yet done. The print they had now found on the Dackworth safe must have been left on the lock after it arrived back at Gallagher's for examination. Blake had a very firm idea whose it might be—but a final check was necessary, no matter what trouble it caused.

Mr. Hennessy, shaggy, tumbled and tired, met them at the factory gates. "Is this strictly necessary?" he asked.

"Tell you in ten minutes," Blake said. "I want to examine your Mr. O'Brien's tools for prints."

As THE TRAP closed, the victim was at home, in bed, snoring peacefully.

A door opened softly, and Anny stood there looking down at him; she was dressed in a nightie and her hair was all anyhow. The daylight was filtering through the curtains and the room was chilly.

"O'Brien—are you awake?" She knelt down and began to arrange the covers over him. "Look what you've done with the pillows!" she muttered. O'Brien, in his sleep, was hugging one of the pillows to his cheek. Carefully, she slid down beside him and snuggled close. Suddenly his hand closed on hers.

"What's the matter, Anny?" O'Brien asked.

"Nothing!" Anny said. "I'm cold."

He began to cuddle and stroke her.

"And I'm worried," she said.

O'Brien kissed her.

"I've got a terrible premonition," Anny murmured.

"You're cold all over," he said.

"Will you listen to me, O'Brien! I've got a terrible confession to make."

"Will it keep till the morning?"

"You know that two hundred pounds?" Anny said.

"What about it?"

"And you know the fifty thousand pounds?"

"Don't mention it!"

"It's all stolen property," Anny said.

"Is that right?" O'Brien said.

"He's not an eccentric millionaire, at all!" Anny said. "Didn't you guess?"

"I wasn't sure," O'Brien said. "And I didn't want to worry you once you'd bought those nice dresses."

"It's all my fault," Anny said. "I should never have spent it."

"Sure, you deserved nice things."

"You'll have to go to the police," Anny said.

"I will," O'Brien said. "But how will you live, if I go to prison?"

"I shall manage on the fifty thousand pounds," Anny said.

"But shouldn't I give it up?"

"Not if they send you to prison anyway," Anny said. "That wouldn't be fair."

"You're right!" O'Brien said. "Will you know how to take care of it, Anny?"

"They'll never find it," Anny promised him, "if they look forever."

247

She was asleep in his arms when the noise of the cars outside woke them up. They both went to the window, and looked down.

"It's the police!" O'Brien said.

"ARE YOU TIMOTHY O'Brien?" Commander Grimwald asked, though he knew very well from their previous meeting that he was.

"I am," said O'Brien.

"And Mrs. O'Brien?" Grimwald asked.

Anny was backing towards the bedroom door. "Are you saying I'm not?" she snapped.

Blake was standing just inside the doorway, looking at the girl and the man and the room, and feeling sorry for them.

"I have a warrant to search these premises," Grimwald said.

"Will you let me get something on, first?" Anny asked.

Blake, Grimwald, O'Brien, and Anny, sat silently in the room while three C.I.D. officers searched the flat. Not until the search was finished with nothing found, did Grimwald speak again. Then he addressed himself to O'Brien.

"I want to know where you were on the night of Thursday last, the fourteenth."

"I was at Dackworth's," O'Brien said.

"Can you prove it?" Grimwald asked.

"There was nearly a dozen of us there," O'Brien said.

Grimwald turned to Blake: "We'll have a job to shake an alibi like that!"

Blake smiled, sympathetically. "You're tired, Grimwald. That wasn't an alibi—that was a confession."

"It was!" O'Brien said.

And he slipped an arm around Anny's shoulders. She smiled at him.

"I feel better already," she said.

"You'll look after the carpet while I'm away?" he said.

"I will!" she told him.

"And you'll be able to come and visit me—" he turned to Grimwald "—do you happen to know the visiting days?"

Grimwald, tired and bemused, looked plaintively at Blake, then said: "Do you mind if I arrest you first?"

"I'm sorry," O'Brien said. "Anny likes to have things settled."

Anny gave Blake an apologetic little smile which went right to his heart.

"You'll have to be patient with us," she explained. "We've never done anything like this before. We don't know the ropes yet."

Blake nodded, understandingly. "You can come down to the Yard with him."

"Oh, I'd rather not leave the place unguarded," Anny said, "if it's all the same to you."

The C.I.D. men who had searched the flat looked sour.

"Don't worry about that, Mrs. O'Brien," Grimwald told her. "From now on you can be sure it'll be well-guarded."

"Wear your blue suit and the spotted tie," Anny was telling O'Brien as they prepared to leave. She turned to Grimwald again. "Will he need any clean shirts and underclothes?" And to Blake she added: "He's got six new shirts unworn . . ."

THE NINTH CHAPTER

Out of harm's way.

LORD QUADE SNIFFED and touched his eye. "A thoroughly nice couple," he said.

Sir Martin Reynolds nodded. "What I should call decent people caught up in a maelstrom of crime and passion."

He reads too many thrillers, Blake thought.

Grimwald said: "But there are inconsistencies, Blake. I said so at the time, and I say so now. I mean, for a gang as meticulously careful as they were, and who went to such extraordinary lengths for the sake of security—and then leaving the fingerprint on the sherry glass at Hope's and again on the safe at Dackworth's. A bit odd, surely?"

"They," Blake said, "were deliberate mistakes. They were planted in the hope that we should find them. But when it became clear that they were not sufficient on their own, then I had the telephone call."

Lord Quade groped. "You mean O'Brien deliberately left those clues, and then phoned you? He wanted to be arrested?"

"No." Blake was surprised that a Scotland Yard Commissioner could take so long to catch on. "Windy Willow did all that. He made certain that O'Brien held the glass of sherry, and that the prints were not cleaned off. He was probably entrusted with the job of cleaning the Dackworth safe, too. And he certainly made the telephone call to Tinker."

Sir Martin said: "He wanted to see O'Brien arrested, then?"

Blake said: "Windy coveted his neighbour's goods and his neighbour's wife. With O'Brien safely in jail he thought he would get both Anny and another fifty thousand pounds."

"It was a dangerous thing to do," Detective Inspector Coutts put in. "O'Brien would naturally have shopped the lot straight away if he knew about it—he was always crazy about that wife of his. On visiting days at the prison it took four strong men to separate them."

"Yes, yes, Coutts," Lord Quade said, "don't spoil it for us." And to Blake: "You are going into all that?"

Sir Martin said: "But didn't you tell O'Brien that he had been betrayed, Mr. Blake? I mean as soon as he was arrested? You could probably have rounded up the lot straight away?"

Blake said: "It wasn't my job to tell O'Brien anything—my assignment was to recover the money in my own way."

Lord Quade looked at Commander Grimwald. "Then what about you? Didn't you tell him?"

Grimwald gave Blake an aggrieved look. "I didn't know, sir. We helped to make the arrests once Blake gave us the information, but we didn't know how he was getting it. We're only just getting the true facts, the same as you."

Coutts said cheerfully, "It makes it more interesting for us now."

Grimwald gave his subordinate a pained glance.

"All right, Mr. Blake," Lord Quade said. "Carry on—"

THE O'BRIEN TRIAL had been one of the Old Bailey's cut-price jobs. When a man pleads guilty the law is only too ready to believe him, and get on with something more profitable.

He was sentenced to four years imprisonment.

"It's more than we could have saved in the time," Anny told him, before he was driven away.

"It is," said O'Brien.

Blake had given his evidence, then sat at the back of the court to watch its inevitable effect. Neither of the O'Briens appeared to bear him any malice for his part in apprehending the safe-breaker. The trial was curiously lacking in drama, tragedy, or pathos, and the modest sentence, Blake thought, was partly due to the friendly, cheerful, and helpful attitude of the prisoner. Indeed, once the law had caught up with them, the O'Briens seemed to view the whole thing not as crime, punishment, and disaster, but as part of a long-term budgeting plan.

O'Brien had refused to incriminate or identify the "other unknown persons" mentioned rather bitterly by the Prosecution, nor had he given any clue as to the whereabouts of his share of the spoils. This was understandable, because when O'Brien said he didn't know, he didn't know. He had handed over the fifty thousand pounds to Anny, just as he had always handed over the money he earned to Anny. He didn't know what she had done with it, and he didn't want to know. She certainly couldn't put it behind the clock, for even in five-pound notes it was quite a parcel.

Mr. Marks of Venus Life and Property had followed Blake out of the court, now his face was dark with anger as he saw Anny O'Brien drive away in a taxi.

"That's five shillings she needn't have spent!" he exclaimed. And then vehemently: "I hope you will watch that girl night and day, Blake! Night and day!"

"I will," said Blake.

And, indeed, wearing yet another new dress, a crisp blue shirt-waister with a wide, rustling skirt and a show of pretty white net at her knees, Anny was not a difficult girl to watch. But it was not her money that Blake was thinking about when he accepted Mr. Mark's instruction, for like every other person in the court—including possibly the judge himself—Blake half-hoped that the O'Briens would be allowed by fate of circumstances to keep their share. One got the feeling, wrong though it might be, that the fifty thousand pounds had gone to the right home.

But what Blake hoped to find, by watching Anny, was a lead to the other four hundred and fifty thousand pounds. O'Brien had not been shopped for nothing. Sooner or later somebody was going to come forward and claim the prize. And from what Blake had seen of Anny O'Brien so far, it was not going to be an easy job for anybody. There was a girl in love with her husband, and fanatically loyal to him; seduction and persuasion were therefore out; force might work, but it was doubtful; stealth, wile and a clever confidence trick, was more the kind of thing she would have to guard against.

"I will," Blake said again, almost absently, as he got into the Bentley and told Tinker where to go.

THE TENTH CHAPTER

Lady in Distress.

DURING THE NEXT six weeks, Anny settled down to her grass-widowhood. It was not easy, with the police dashing in and searching the flat every other day, and even in the middle of the night. She always made them tea or coffee, but they were always grumpy. Particularly Detective Inspector Coutts, who always seemed to come when she was immersed in travel brochures, or housing magazines, or furniture catalogues. He seemed to take it as a personal insult that she was planning for the future, and for O'Brien.

Then there was Sexton Blake, who had taken a room directly across the road; she could never do anything personal without drawing the curtains, for there was always somebody perched at the window with a telescopic lens. And when she travelled, twice a week, to Wandsworth jail—for that was O'Brien's first resting place—she was followed by goodness knew how many people.

It was an irritation, but it didn't seriously worry her. In a way it was nice to have company, and now there was never any fear of being alone, either out of doors or in the flat.

"One good scream," she told O'Brien on one of her visits,

"and the flat would be crowded."

"It would!" O'Brien said, sharing the laugh.

When the need for screaming came, however, it was not such a joke.

It happened at midday while Anny was preparing to make her Wednesday visit to the prison. She had collected details of a Mediterranean tour to show O'Brien, and the picture of a beautiful old Elizabethan mansion which was for sale on the Sussex Downs. Having packed her bag, Anny went to the wardrobe to select a dress for the day.

It was a wonderful selection she now had, and she liked to wear one of O'Brien's favourites. Before changing, she remembered to pull the curtains together, and shut out the telescope across the road. But what she did not realise was that by this time drawing her curtains was a sign, well known to others besides Blake, that she was about to put herself at a disadvantage in one way or another.

Anny had the new dress half over her head when a pair of strong arms enveloped her, imprisoning her hands to her sides, and her face in the folds of the garment so that her screams were muffled.

She felt herself thrown back on to the bed with a heavy weight on top of her. Now with a tremendous effort, she freed her face of the dress to find a tough, young thug panting foul breath two inches from her mouth.

"You'll not find the money this way!" she gasped.

"What money?" asked Cyril.

Heaven help us! Anny thought. If it wasn't the money, then— And with the awful thought she exerted all her strength and brought her knees up. The youth gasped with pain, said something foul, smacked her across the face, and took another grip on her body.

Anny screamed twice before he rammed a piece of the bed quilt into her mouth. But twice was enough, for the door burst open, and Windy Willow come rushing in. In one fierce movement he swung Cyril off the girl, twizzled him round and punched him in the face with a force that sent the youth spinning through into the living-room.

"I'm much obliged!" Anny gasped, scrambling off the bed.

But Windy was not finished. He followed the youth through, grabbed him by the scruff of the neck and seat of the pants, and hurled him out of the open door.

There was a wild cry followed by the crashing of a heavy object down the top flight of stairs, and then silence.

"Good Lord!" Anny whispered. "Have you killed him, Mr. Willow?"

Windy closed the door. "Don't worry—they're tougher than that, Mrs. O'Brien."

"I'm glad you came when you did," Anny said, gratefully. "There was nothing else I could do."

Even as she said it, she was thinking it was a funny thing to be saying to this man. If she had had any qualms about unwelcome visitors it was in relation to Mr. Willow and his warm, raking eyes. What came next only made her realise how she had misjudged him.

"You'd better put something on," he said, turning his eyes away from her.

Well now! Anny thought. Those were the very words she would never have expected him to use to a girl.

"I will!" she said.

And while she was getting into a dress, he continued: "I came to warn you about this kind of thing—but it seems that I was only just in time."

"Better in time, than too late," she said. "I shall tell O'Brien this afternoon. I'm sure you'll have his thanks."

"No, no," Windy said, brushing the whole thing off inconsequentially. "It will only worry him. Just keep your door locked and bolted, in future."

Windy walked towards the door as if to leave her.

"Would you like a cup of tea?" Anny asked, anxiously as she buttoned up her pink shirt-waister.

Windy had to grip the doorknob tightly to retain self-control. "No, thank you—I'm sure you want to get going." He half-glanced at her, then quickly away. "If you want any help, at any time, you must let me know—ring this number. I live in the country with my daughter."

"Thank you, Mr. Willow," Anny said.

As he went out she scanned the card. She had been very wrong about him. And him a family man, too.

CYRIL WAS ROUND the corner, nursing his bruises, when Windy came by and stopped, briefly, and passed him a five pound note.

"Fanks," Cyril said.

Sexton Blake witnessed this transaction through the powerful lens of the telescope from the window of his room across the road.

"One confidence trick just accomplished," he said, without turning round.

"And about time!" said Tinker.

Tinker was cooking sausages on an oil burner. The Blake staff had been camping out in this tatty bed-sitter, on and off, for six weeks, and it was just beginning to get tedious, except when Marion was there.

Down in the street, Windy opened the door of a Bentley Continental and slipped behind the wheel.

"Don't mind me!" said a voice.

Paula Dane—looking beautiful although a little surprised, and wearing a ranch-mink stole over a new cocktail dress—was sitting in the back seat.

Windy smiled at her. "So sorry! But they do all look very much alike until you examine the interiors, don't they?" he apologised.

She smiled at him and watched him get out and go to a baby Fiat which he drove away in a cloud of dust. What a very charming man! she thought.

Next instant Blake was behind the wheel and revving the engine.

"Which way did he go?" he asked.

When Blake's car had driven off a police car jerked into view from a side turning and followed the Bentley.

Detective Inspector Coutts sat beside the police driver, his face grim. It was always galling to have to follow Blake in order to keep up with his job.

Five minutes later when Anny came out to hail a taxi, Tinker was already behind the wheel of the Jaguar. Another police car was parked around the next corner.

Anny cupped her hand to her mouth to save everybody a lot of bother.

"Wandsworth Prison!" she called.

Tinker smiled at her and touched his hat.

BLAKE FOLLOWED THE Fiat from Kilburn, down through the western outskirts of Paddington into Notting Hill Gate, and thence over the hill of Hill Road into Kensington.

"I must say he seemed a Kensington type," Paula remarked.

"He's one of the gang," Blake sounded annoyed with her.

Paula smiled at his tone and expression. "I doubt it. He's not the breaking-and-entering type. Too smooth altogether."

Blake grunted. None of them were the usual gang type—that's what made them different and hard to catch. They were now two cars behind the Fiat, with the police car behind them, all travelling down the Earls' Court Road.

"Another half mile," Paula said, "and I shall be terribly

disappointed in him."

The destination turned out to be a small but classy hotel in the Boltons. Blake was watching their quarry enter the hotel when Detective Inspector Coutts joined him.

"Know who it is?" Coutts asked. He was wearing a horribly obviously-deadpan expression.

Blake shook his head.

"I do," Coutts said.

"Good," Blake said. "That saves us a bit of work."

"He's not one of the gang, you know," Coutts said.

Paula smiled. "There! That's what I said."

Blake, in the minority, looked up at Coutts. "How do you know?"

"That's Windy Willow," Coutts said. "He's a con man."

Blake's expression changed; he looked at the Scotland Yard man with respect.

"I see," he said.

The point was a good one. Criminals kept very much in their own categories; it was unlikely that a pick-pocket would rob a safe or a smash-and-grab man work in the protection racket; but most unlikely of all was that a confidence trickster should join a gang for whatever purpose. Your professional con man might work in partnership, but he always kept his hands clean. Brain, charm, and psychology were his tools. He went in for painless extraction, rather than robbery, and if there was a safe to be opened then he would insist that his victim did the opening.

"You remember," Coutts said now, "He was in that rent extortion case—ran a mobile permanent-estate office for years. Letting flats he hadn't got, and taking key money with no keys."

Blake nodded. "I've heard the name."

Coutts said: "He must have read about the O'Brien girl, and just called to give her some advice about investing the fifty thousand pounds."

Still watching the entrance of the hotel, Blake considered this. It was sound reasoning. Sending a hoodlum in to frighten the girl, then performing a big rescue act. But Blake was disappointed. He had hoped that he was at last onto a member of the gang.

"Well, he'll bear watching," Blake said. "He might succeed in finding the money where you've failed."

Coutts frowned. "We haven't failed, Blake—we just haven't looked in the right place yet."

Paula, still sitting next to Blake, suddenly pointed: "Look— he's moving out already!"

Windy Willow had appeared at the hotel entrance with two large suitcases, and followed by a pretty schoolgirl, carrying another large case. Windy looked along the street at a number of parked cars, selected a large Bentley, and piled his luggage into it.

Coutts said: "That's not the car he came in!"

Paula laughed, lightly: "Apparently he's got a bad memory for cars—he nearly got away in this one."

Coutts brightened: "That gives me a chance to pick him up—"

Blake had a restraining hand on his arm. "I shouldn't," he advised. "Not yet."

"Ah!" Coutts said, as though he understood. "I get you."

They watched Windy drive away, the schoolgirl waving a handkerchief back to the hotel manager, who stood on the steps looking dazed. Now Blake got out of the car, and followed by Paula and Coutts, he walked over to join the bewildered and worried young man.

Coutts showed his card, which seemed to worry the young man even more.

"I didn't know she was a child!" he said.

Blake said: "What's the trouble?"

Now the young man gave them a shrewd and withdrawn look. "It doesn't matter."

Coutts said: "Did they pay the bill?"

"Who—Mr. Willow? Oh, yes. A most generous gentleman."

Blake said: "Then what's worrying you?"

The young man appraised Blake, then looked at Paula, and showed very white teeth in an even smile. He had obviously decided that he could confide in them.

"Well, we're both men of the world," he told Blake. "But one can slip up occasionally, especially these days." He glanced after the car, wonderingly. "You see, I'd never seen her dressed—I mean, she stayed in her room practically the whole three days!"

"What about it?" Coutts asked.

The young man wrung his hands: "Gosh! And then to see her come out dressed in a gym slip."

Paula was trying to hide a smile.

"Of course," the young hotel manager said reflectively. "Now I see why he was in and out of her room at all hours of the night—" he shrugged, bemusedly "—glasses of water!" Then he said: "Phew!" and wiped his brow, at some remembered narrow escape.

Coutts said: "Did he say she was his daughter?"

"Only just now," the young man said. "A bit unfair, y'know."

"What was her name?" Blake asked.

"Rene, apparently," the young man said. "That's right—Rene!"

Paula laid a friendly hand on the young man's arm. "Let me put your mind at rest," she said. "It would take more than a gym slip, a yo-yo, and a pair of spectacles to make that young lady a juvenile."

The hotel manager smiled his relief. "That's what I thought!"

Coutts said to Blake: "I've got the number—shall we have them tailed?"

"It's not necessary," Blake said. "Let's just keep a close eye on Anny O'Brien and I'm sure we'll meet them again . . ."

THE ELEVENTH CHAPTER

"Anny doesn't live here any more."

"AND THAT'S WHAT happened?" Lord Quade asked.

"Not immediately," Blake said. "In fact, I doubt whether Anny would have fallen for the Windy Willow trick at all but for an unfortunate circumstance some two weeks later."

Sir Martin Reynolds now leaned across the conference table. "May I recap, and clarify things a little, Mr. Blake? Is it true to say that you did not know at this time that Windy Willow was a member of the gang you were after?"

Blake nodded. "I didn't know until later."

"I see," said Lord Quade. "Therefore you also didn't know that he might well have been carrying his share of the Dackworth robbery in one of those suitcases?"

"He was," Blake said, ruefully.

Commander Grimwald said: "But who would expect a con man to rob a safe?"

"Damned unethical!" Coutts complained.

Lord Quade waved him to silence and looked at Blake in some anticipation. "Tell us about this new circumstance."

Blake said: "It may not show me in a very favourable light, sir.

You see, I found out where Anny had hidden the fifty-thousand pounds, and said nothing to the police."

"Did you really!" Lord Quade said, warmly; he turned to the prison commissioner: "This is what fascinates me! All that money—" he broke off, remembering the seriousness of the purpose of the inquiry. "No doubt you had your reasons, Mr. Blake."

"I'll try to justify it," Blake promised.

THE VISITORS ARRIVED on a Wednesday morning. When the taxi drew up outside the O'Brien place in Kilburn, Blake was on duty at his window, but the police were absent. Content that Blake's organisation was keeping a twenty-four watch, Commander Grimwald had withdrawn his forces.

"If you catch the gang you get ten thousand pounds," Coutts had said, enviously: "We only get cold feet."

But it wasn't the gang stepping out of that taxi down there. Or was it? A hard, high-blonde, over-dressed woman with cheap jewellery flashing, a mock-fur stole flung across the shoulders of a mock-silk blouse; a large toughie, half her age, wearing black-white check, and Italian pointed yellow shoes, was putting mock leather cases on to the path.

Not the gang! Blake thought. These were too provincial.

"Ther y'are wack!" called the flashy young man, spinning a coin to the taxi driver.

Liverpool, Blake thought, shifting his glasses to take in the woman who was now standing, legs inelegantly astride, looking up to the top of the house.

"Antoinette! Antoinette!" she shouted, raucously. "Are y' ther?"

THE HIDEOUS SOUND of the name ringing through the Kilburn air came to Anny like an old nightmare. She was sitting comfortably on the red carpet, surrounded by travel brochures and property clippings. On her last visit to Wandsworth prison, O'Brien had been full of enthusiasm for the West Indies; apparently, a man who had run a highly successful trading schooner between the islands and the mainland, and who was full of ecstatic praise for the climate and the golden beaches, was now in the next cell.

Judging from the literature which Anny had amassed, the man had not exaggerated. There were houses to be had if you had sufficient money; wonderful big white houses with green-lawned terraces down to the blue sea; there were sweet-natured, brown-skinned people ready to take all the work off your hands for the price of a bottle of rum. Anny could see herself tanned as a berry, wearing a flowered sarong, and with a white hibiscus blossom in her hair, waiting for O'Brien to come leaping over the verandah railing with another turtle on his back.

"Toin! Toin! Toin!" came her mother's voice, echoing metallically through the old house as she came clumping up the stairs.

"Antoinette! Are y' ther?"

When the woman finally burst open the door and came in, the burly cretin at her shoulder with the cases on his head, Anny was sitting amid the ruins of her dreams, clutching both hands to her ears.

"Ther you are, Toin! Why didn't you answer? Are y' poorly?"

THE AWFUL MISTAKE had been that one generous-hearted gesture of Anny's, when they had got two hundred pounds and she had sent her mother the box of cigarettes and the bottle of scent.

"You could've knocked me over when I got it!" her mother said, a little later, having settled herself in the armchair holding a cup of tea with her little finger well out.

"Aye, aye, I thought—didn't I, Rudolph—aye, aye, I thought meself, O'Brien may have looked a bit of a simpleton but he's starting to do right by our Toin . . ."

It emerged, without a great deal of subtlety, for Rudolph was already searching the cupboards, that they had left Liverpool one jump ahead of the bailiffs, and were expecting Anny to make a three-way share-out of the fifty-thousand pounds.

Anny didn't argue with her mother. She had already made up her mind what to do from the moment she heard that dreaded word broadcast through the street. She had left Liverpool to get away from that name, and now she would have to leave Kilburn.

"Would you like a drink?" Anny asked.

Rudolph swung round from the bookshelf, where he had been quietly prising off covers in a quick search for the hiding place. "Got a drop of Scotch?"

"I'll have gin," said her mother. "Neat if you don't mind, Toin."

Anny said: "Well there's a pub down the road—why don't you two go and have a quick drink while I get the dinner ready?"

She gave them a pound note and listened for them to descend the stairs, craned out of the window to watch them walk up the street. Then she looked directly across the street and called for help.

It is disconcerting to have a magnified figure in a telescope lens suddenly stare directly at you and beckon, furiously. Blake lowered the telescope and glanced back into his room to see if perhaps the girl was waving to somebody behind him. But then her voice came to him:

"Mr. Blake! Mr. Blake! Help!"

"She's in trouble," Blake exclaimed.

"Shall I come?" The question came from Paula, Marion, Tinker, Miss Pringle and Splash Kirby, all talking together.

"You stay here—I'll shout if I want you."

He laid aside the telescope, took out his small Browning revolver and checked it for bullets, then hurried out.

Paula wiped a spot of glue from her nose, sniffed. "I hope nothing happens to her just as we've gone to all this trouble!"

"How about this?" Tinker said, sitting at the top of some wooden decorators' steps.

"Very pretty!" Marion said. "How about this?"

They had spent the last two weeks redecorating the room in a do-it-yourself fever of activity. It had been started reluctantly, so grimy and forbidding were the decorations, but soon they had been swept away on a wave of enthusiasm; as people who spend most of their time working with their minds are swept away once they get a paint brush in their hands.

The ceiling had been whitened twice, the walls had been papered with an expensive embossed design, the woodwork stripped, under-coated and finally finished in glossy lilac eggshell lacquer. Splash Kirby had scrubbed the floor and laid new lino-tiles—four days of back-breaking work—partly on the promise of an exclusive story, and partly to impress Paula and Marion.

"I like that floor!" Paula told Splash.

He smiled, fatuously, and regarded the transfers which she had just applied to the cupboard door. "And that looks wonderful!" he exclaimed.

Tinker looked at Marion: "You've made a smashing job of the frieze!" he told her.

"Do you really think so! I like your lampshade," she said.

"Tea up!" said Miss Pringle, unbending from the oil stove.

"Marvellous tea, Pring old thing!" said Splash.

They sipped their tea and smiled at each other, foolishly

proud and happy at something accomplished, something done.

WHEN THEY HEARD Blake returning, Paula stood by the door and stopped him on the threshold. "Close your eyes," she instructed.

"Why?" Blake asked.

"We've finished," Splash contributed. He waved a proprietary hand around the smartly painted room. "Don't you think it looks terrific?"

"Terrific," Blake agreed, looking round. Then he said: "Now pack everything up, and get it out to the car—we're leaving."

The Blake staff looked at each other, dismally; Splash seemed about to burst into tears, regarding his floor with possessive pride.

Paula said: "Why? What did Anny want?"

Blake said: "She just wanted me to help her pack."

Tinker said, blankly: "Help her pack."

Blake nodded: "I don't blame her. She wanted to get away before her mother and the boyfriend got back from the pub."

Marion frowned. "That's not very kind. Doesn't she love her mother?"

"You only get one mother," Splash Kirby said, gently stroking the floor with his suede toe-cap.

Blake said: "You'd only want one mother if she's anything like Anny's—she's been telling me all about it."

Tinker wandered to the window, and looked down. "Has she gone, then?"

"She's gone," Blake said. "And now we've got to go—I've given up the room."

Paula bit her lip, vexed. "Just as it was beginning to look like home—"

There came a tap at the door and a wrinkled, grizzled head in an oily cap with broken peak looked in; astonishingly, it was a woman. "Can I show a gent round?" she asked.

There was a silent communion of disgust between the home-decorators. As they picked up what was rightfully theirs the landlady ushered a gentleman into the room.

"It isn't much," she said, "but it's got a front view what you wanted and I can always get Fred to do a bit of decorating."

"It'll do very nice—thanks!" said the newcomer.

He began pacing the room, politely ignoring the outgoing tenants. Blake was watching him without appearing to, and counting the number of steps he took in each direction.

Not until they were outside and stacking their belongings into the three cars did Blake mention the stranger, and then only casually.

"What nationality would you say he is?" he asked.

Tinker said: "South African."

"Notice anything else about him?" Blake asked.

Paula said: "He wanted a front view—probably another Anny watcher."

"Very good," Blake said. "Anything else?"

The columnist said: "He didn't appreciate the decorating. In years to come, that floor will probably have a plaque on it—laid by Splash Kirby of the Post."

Tinker was looking at Blake, seriously. "What was it, chief?"

Blake said, looking up at the window they had just vacated: "He's spent quite a lot of time in prison."

"All right," Paula said. "How d'you know?"

"Never stops pacing." Blake said. "Four steps each way. Just the length of a cell."

"That's clever," Tinker said. "Want me to watch him?"

"No," Blake said. "Just show Coutts a photograph and try to get it identified."

"What photograph?" asked Tinker.

Blake took a small instrument as big as a watch from his

wrist, handed it to Tinker. "You'll find three in there."

Paula said: "D'you think he's one of the gang?"

"Another con man, I'd say," Blake told her.

"Well, he's too late to con Anny out of her money." Splash Kirby was looking across the road.

A voice came floating out to them: "Antoinette! Antoinette! Are y' there?"

Paula held open the door of the Bentley for Blake to enter. "Back to the office?"

"Yes," Blake said. "I think you can tell me where Anny keeps that fifty thousand pounds."

Paula's mouth opened in surprise. Then she closed it. If Blake said she could, then she could . . .

THE TWELFTH CHAPTER

Silver lining.

DETECTIVE INSPECTOR COUTTS was able to identify the new tenant without much difficulty.

"Walter Sims," he told Blake on the telephone, soon after he and Paula had arrived back at the Berkeley Square offices.

"Confidence trickster?" Blake inquired.

"I'm afraid so," Coutts said. "Not the man we're after. Having some bad luck, aren't we? You'll have to try again."

Blake looked up at Paula, who was standing by the desk watching him. "Tell me some more about Sims," he requested.

Walter Sims had always specialised in promoting phony companies; a bucket shop man, fishing the small unwary investor-fish. Operating chiefly from South Africa, he had dazzled his victims with gold and diamond mirages which needed only a little warmth, comfort, nurturing, with a few dollars or pounds to give them rich substance.

"Eight prison sentences," Coutts continued. "Five for false pretences, embezzlement, fraud, and the like; three for bigamy, non-payment of maintenance, and desertion—got a whole host of illegal wives which he tries to support apparently. Not vicious."

"That follows," Blake said, drily.

Coutts chuckled: "But no safebreaking, old chap—sorry."

"That's all right," Blake told him. "Tell Tinker to bring my camera back . . ."

"It's very odd," Paula said, thoughtfully.

Blake, who had been looking depressed since he had hung up on Scotland Yard, now looked at his secretary hopefully.

"What is?"

"Well—you know."

"These con men, you mean?"

"Yeah," Paula said, vaguely.

Blake was staring at her. "What's odd about it?"

"I dunno . . ." Paula shrugged. "It's just odd."

Blake persisted, trying to make her vague thoughts articulate. "You mean that they should all come flocking around Anny?"

"Well," Paula said. "Yeah."

"When they must know she's surrounded by police?" Blake said.

"Well," Paula said, "well, something like that."

Blake smiled his relief. "Well, I'm glad you think it's odd, because friend Coutts seems to think it's the most natural thing in the world."

"I think it's very odd," Paula said, owl-like. "Very, very odd."

"I'm glad," Blake told her.

"Very odd," Paula said.

Paula now started twisting a piece of lace at her neck, under something of a strain. "I suppose you're going to ask me where Anny's hiding her money now?"

"I just want to try an idea on you," Blake said.

The girl expelled a breath of pure relief. "I've been thinking you expected me to have an idea."

"'You have plenty of ideas," Blake told her. "Sometimes I

can't keep up with them."

"But I'm always obliging," Paula said. "Now fire ahead."

Blake said: "I helped to pack her things."

"I know," Paula said. "She shouted for help because she wanted help."

Blake said: "She wouldn't let me touch her dresses or underclothes."

Paula just looked at him steadily.

Blake said: "I mean she let me pack anything else but not her clothes."

"Clothes are personal," Paula said.

Blake pressed on, stubbornly. "She was nervous every time I laid a hand on her dresses—the ones we were packing." Then, slowly: "She acted as though I might be getting warm."

"Really," Paula said huffishly; "it sounds to me as though she acted right."

"Stop being a woman for a moment," Blake told her. "There were these six or seven new dresses—very crisp and colourful, buttons from the neck down to the waist."

"Shirt-waisters," Paula said. "I've noticed. She wears them all the time—in bright cotton colour-prints."

"The skirts," Blake said, "are stiff and they rustle."

"Paper-lined," Paula said.

Blake stared at her, blankly, for a moment. "That's what I thought—paper-lined."

"Okay?" Paula said brightly.

"Yes, thank you."

Paula said: "I'm afraid I can't tell you where she keeps that fifty thousand pounds, though." She walked towards the door. "Better go and catch up on some work, I suppose. I must say I did enjoy that decorating. I wonder what brick-laying is like—"

She petered out. Blake was not listening. He was busy at his desk, making calculations, drawing, jotting down figures.

Paula Dane came back, and stared down at what he was doing.

Blake muttered: "How much material in an average skirt?"

"A full skirt? About a yard—a square yard."

Blake looked at her suddenly and asked a straightforward question: "How many five-pound notes in a square yard?"

Paula screamed as it hit her.

"WILL YOU TAKE it away from her?" Paula said, when she had sufficiently recovered.

"No," Blake said.

Paula said: "It would be a terrible shame if you did. Imagine how happy she's been feeling with several thousand pounds swinging around her hips."

"A good idea on her part. Simple and clever."

"Do you have to tell the police?" Paula asked anxiously.

"I suppose I ought to."

Paula said: "You realise that besides losing the money, and with O'Brien gone to prison for nothing, they'd put Anny on trial for receiving."

Blake nodded worriedly: "She'd probably get four years."

Paula said, with barely controlled emotion: "Then when they came out, starting all over again—no home, no money."

Blake nodded gloomily. "And nobody would give him a job."

Paula put an entreating hand on his arm: "You won't tell the police, will you?"

"No," Blake decided, "I won't tell the police."

Paula said: "But supposing the police find it?"

"They won't find it in her skirts," Blake said. "Coutts is too much of a gentleman to even think of looking." Then he frowned at a new thought. "I wouldn't say as much for her new host—it might be one of the first places he goes to."

Blake looked round on this note of alarm, snapping his fingers. "Get me the AA guide book," he said.

"London area?" Paula asked.

"No, Sussex," Blake said. "There's a millionaire's private estate called King's Gorse near Angmering on the coast—"

THE THIRTEENTH CHAPTER

Poor little rich girl.

BALLS WITH PINK spots! Rene muttered to herself furiously, her eyes narrowed, her bottom lip pushed rebelliously out. She sat there on the lawn, picking the rubber covering off the ball with pink spots which Windy had given her to play with while he entertained the visitor. She sat cross-legged on the grass wearing a little pink pinafore, little white socks and sandals. Her eyes were fixed unswervingly on the long legs trailing from the swinging hammock, and Windy who sat also watching them and giving the hammock an occasional push.

"I don't want to know what you've done with your share of the money," Windy was saying. "In fact, I prefer not to know. But you must keep a sharp eye out for certain people."

Anny, wearing a brief sun suit, nodded dreamily in the sun, her eyes closed, her hair falling back over the hammock.

"Oh, brother!" Windy thought, with every push.

Anny could imagine that she was in the West Indies, and it was O'Brien doing the pushing.

"So be sure it's perfectly safe," Windy said. "Like mine."

"Oh, yes, of course," Anny said. "You've got fifty thousand

pounds, too."

"I've got much more than that, Anny," Windy said. "I've been in the business longer." He sighed. "And after all, there's nobody to spend it on now that Rene's mother is dead."

"But it's not so bad for you," Anny said. "You're not being watched the way I am."

"It would make no difference," Windy said. "My money is in a safe deposit—it's the only safe place."

'What's that?"

"It's like a bank," Windy said. "You have your own safe, and nobody has the key but you."

"Couldn't the police inspect them if they wanted to?"

"Oh, no! Nobody's allowed to open that safe except the person who has signed for the key."

"It's a very good idea," Anny said.

She had never heard of it before. Why should she have done? The most money she had ever had in her life was twenty-five pounds, which she won as beauty queen of Bootle, and which went to settle some outstanding bills of her mother's. Faced with the prospect of hiding the fifty thousand pounds, she had only the minimum of ideas. It was apparently too much to put into the Post Office book, and had she bought Premium Bonds somebody would have got to hear about it. The obvious thing seemed to be a biscuit tin buried in the garden, if she had had a garden, or a parcel stuffed up the chimney.

As things turned out, with the detectives searching every inch of the flat, even taking up floorboards and using some kind of electronic detector on the brickwork, she was glad she had put the money where it was. But now it seemed to her that the safe deposit might be a better long-term answer, especially as Mr. Blake had seemed suspicious about the dresses.

"Do you get any interest on it?" she asked. "Or a dividend like at the Co-op?"

Windy looked at her to see if she was joking, but she wasn't. "You mustn't declare it!" he said. "They'd be on to you like a shot if you did. Nobody but you knows what you've deposited in your private safe—and the police won't even know that you've got a deposit."

"Oh, I'm not saying I'm going to do it," she said. "It's very safe where it is."

He's a nice fellow, O'Brien had told her when they had been discussing Windy on one of her visits, but I wouldn't trust him too far.

"I'm sure it is," Windy said now. "I wouldn't presume to advise you—that's for your husband."

It wasn't much of a comfort; O'Brien knew little about what went into a safe, even though he knew all about their workings.

"Look," Windy said now. "There's a ship on the horizon."

And I wish me and O'Brien was aboard it, Anny thought wistfully. It was going to be a long, hard, four years.

"Come and play wiv me!" Rene called.

Windy smiled at Anny. "The child's jealous of visitors. She's always afraid that I'll marry again."

Anny sat up on the hammock. "Well, no fear of that with me!"

Windy caught her hand for a moment. "You are very beautiful, Anny," he said.

Anny felt that breeze of panic which had engulfed her on his first visit to the flat. She jumped down from the hammock.

"Here comes your father," she said. "Have a talk with him while I play with your little girl."

Old Mr. Lemon was tapping his way across the garden with a cane. As he passed Rene he gave her a playful pat on the bottom and she brought him a resounding clap across the face which nearly knocked him over.

Anny caught him and set him back on his feet.

"Playful child!" quavered the old man.

And when he had passed on, Anny told the girl: "You mustn't be rough with your grandad, Rene!"

"He gets too familiar," said the girl. "Catch!"

WINDY AND THE old man went into the house, leaving the girls playing in the garden.

"I've been to Shoreham to see about the boat," Mr. Lemon said. "It's a fast luxury yacht, ready to sail."

"What do they want for it?" Windy shouted.

"Fifty thousand—but we don't have to pay."

Windy frowned at the old man. "Have you been working the treasure hunt again?"

"Subterranean Trojan ruins," said the old man, pouring a whisky. "The maps have just come into circulation again." He sighed. "Funny how the fashions go full-circle." He had done his first term, in nineteen-twenty, on the Troy legend. Then looking out of the french window at the girl bouncing across the lawn in the bright playsuit, he added: "Any luck with the girl, yet?"

Windy sipped his whisky, and said, rather sadly, "It'll be like taking candy from a kid."

THE FOURTEENTH CHAPTER

Painless extraction.

"THERE HE GOES," Tinker said.

It was the following morning, and Blake's assistant was watching Windy depart, dressed for the city, carrying a brief case, and riding in a local hire-car.

"Think he's got the money?" Tinker added, handing Blake the glasses.

"No." Blake watched the car depart along the private road. "Not in a case that size. He's going to town, probably by train. Follow him in the Jaguar, and leave it at the station—be sure it's locked."

"What are you going to do?" Tinker asked.

"There's an old man there with the girls," Blake said. "I want to get close enough to get a picture."

Tinker departed and Blake wandered along the top of the shingle bank which separated the gardens of the big houses from the sea. It was not easy to get close without being observed, for King's Gorse was a private and secluded place, hostile to strangers, and built to repel day-trippers.

As a beauty spot, its own fortifications despoiled and

inconvenienced it. It was bristling with notices:

PRIVATE ESTATE—NO THOROUGHFARE
NO PARKING
NO THROUGHWAY
NO ROAD TO SEA
NO LOITERING
NO PARKING
RESIDENTS ONLY

And in keeping out the dreaded common tripper-bird it had also kept out all signs of life. Big houses with large blind eyes staring towards the horizon of the sea; enormous gardens slumbering unwatched and unsmelt in the sunshine; roads and paths unused, the air empty of sounds; a big, expensive, and dead ghost-town by the sea.

With such a sparse population Blake found it difficult to get close to Windy Willow's garden without being observed. He could see the old man taking his ease in a deck-chair on the front lawn; he could see the dark girl playing sulkily on a garden swing. He could not see Anny.

Blake got down behind a clump of gorse, and peered at the battlements of the mansion. The glint of something shining in the sun caught his eye and he turned his glasses up towards the roof. There, sitting astride the stone balustrade, sat Anny O'Brien with the wind in her hair and a pair of binoculars to her eyes. She gave Blake a gay[6] wave.

Blake waved back. He lowered his glasses, pink-faced, looked furtively either side before walking away. What a blessing Tinker and Paula had not witnessed it.

TINKER FOLLOWED WINDY Willow to London by train, then from Victoria to Queen Victoria Street by taxi. He watched him go into the tall portals of the Victoria Safe Deposit and Trust

Company. Tinker followed him in, wishing that he also was dressed for the city, and not for the beach in tweed sports coat and twill trousers, with his toes showing through open sandals.

He stood close behind Windy when he made his request for a safe-deposit box and key, made a mental note of the number. Now, Tinker thought, if I can just get down there into the vaults, and get a look at what he deposits.

"Yes—sir?" the clerk was asking with a noticeable delay on the title.

"I'd like a safe-deposit box," Tinker said.

"I see," said the clerk, looking him up and down.

That was odd, Tinker thought. He hadn't said "I see" to Windy Willow, the con man!

"I'm in rather a hurry," Tinker said. He looked round to see if Windy had gone below.

"Ah," said the clerk, as though Tinker's haste clinched matters; which it did, for a different formality swung into force.

Tinker found himself surrounded by three large, dark-suited gentlemen. One of them gave Tinker a very forced and polite smile, showing a gold tooth.

"Will you step this way, sir—we'd like to ask you a few questions—"

And to cap it, as Tinker was led away for interrogation by the security officers, he saw, to his chagrin, Windy Willow walking smartly out of the building without depositing a thing!

"That was a very indifferent piece of detection, Tinker."

"I know it."

They sat, together in the lounge of a private hotel at Angmering, that same night. Blake had taken his picture of the old gentleman, using a telescopic lens, and had had it identified as Ernest Lemon—yet another con man, specialising in marine frauds of one kind and another. He was an ex-sea captain who had lost his ticket for conspiring to defraud his own line by faking a breakdown in the Irish Channel, and arranging with a pal to cash in on the salvage operation.

"How did you manage to get all that without going to town?" Tinker asked.

Blake had had the picture tele-wired to the B.B.C. from the Brighton Post Office, and Coutts had co-operated from the other end.

"He still thinks we're working up the wrong tree," Blake added.

"I think he's right," Tinker said. "If they're safe-crackers, then I'm a Dutchman."

"Don't be too sure," Blake told him.

Tinker looked at his chief over his mug of ale. "Have you got an idea?"

"I don't know yet. I only know that when sheep are being rounded up for slaughter, it's a useful thing to be a goat."

"Ah!" said an old man from a nearby domino table.

FOUR MILES AWAY, on the terrace of the house in King's Gorse, Windy sat with Anny taking a drink. Rene, to her fury, had been sent up to bed at nine o'clock.

"Are you sure it was Sexton Blake?" Windy asked Anny.

"Ah, yes. He waved back to me."

Windy smiled confidently. "There's nothing to worry about. They couldn't find your money in London, I don't suppose they'll find it here. And mine's safe enough."

Anny said: "Could they get a search warrant, and go through all my things again?"

"Yes, they could. But they won't. Blake hasn't the least idea where it is, or he would have found it before now."

Windy was watching Anny's face, unobserved; he was pleased to notice her worry and uncertainty.

Anny said: "Could I put it in a safe-deposit if I wanted to?"

"Yes, of course."

"How would I do it?" Anny asked. "Supposing I wanted to?"

"You just go along and ask for a safe-deposit."

"Yes, but where do I go?"

"Oh, there are several of them in the city."

"Where do you keep yours?" Anny said. Then, at the cloud on his face she added: "You needn't tell me! I didn't mean to pry!"

Windy smiled at her. "That's all right. But I wouldn't tell just anybody. It's at the Victoria Safe Deposit and Trust Company in Queen Victoria Street."

Anny was impressed. "It sounds very safe."

"As the Bank of England," Windy said, comfortably.

"Would you take me there tomorrow, Mr. Willow?"

He hesitated. "Shouldn't you consult your husband first?"

"I should," Anny said.

She was glad that the suggestion had come from Windy Willow, for it banished any remaining vestiges of apprehension about him. But with Sexton Blake outside, and the memory of the way the detective had fingered her dresses, Anny could delay no longer.

"I've made up my mind, Mr. Willow," she said, at last. "I'd be much obliged if you'd take me tomorrow."

"I will," said Windy.

AND HE DID.

He took her for the best part of the fifty thousand pounds. It was a smooth operation by a smooth operator. They travelled up to London on the city express, and breakfasted on the train. At the Safe Deposit and Trust Company, he insisted that Anny hired her own safe deposit and signed for the key. He accompanied her into the vaults, and let her deposit two large parcels in the box allotted to her.

"Now lock it up," he said.

Anny locked the safe deposit.

Windy withdrew the key from the lock and held it up. "Now," he said, "your future depends on this key, young lady. Keep it in a very safe place!"

"It'll never leave me!" she said.

She never got it. The key Windy put into her hand was the one he had hired yesterday—the key to an empty safe.

She laughed light-heartedly as they left the premises. "I feel that relieved!" she said.

Windy took her arm and hailed a taxi. "We'll lunch at the Berkeley Grill," he said, "and celebrate."

IF THE TRANSACTION was a relief to Anny, it was even more of a relief to Windy, whose reserves of self-control had been steadily running out with the continued necessity of being a gentleman while Anny remained essentially a woman. The warm raking look returned to his eyes over lunch, and heightened in temperature over liqueurs and coffee. On the train back to the coast he so far forgot himself as to place a hand on her knee, and she had to reprimand him.

"Sorry, my dear," he said. "Tired. We'll get to bed early tonight."

And when Rene passed Anny that evening, on her way up to her room, she whispered: "Goodnight, Anny—if you want anything, scream."

By the time Anny had locked the door of her bedroom she had already resolved to get herself an hotel room somewhere in the morning.

Windy, nicely high on whisky, came into her room from the balcony window at midnight.

"Ssssh!" he said. "Don't want to wake the child or the old man, do we?"

286

Anny sat up in bed, clutching the cover around her. "I'll wake the whole estate, if you don't get out of my room—I'm a married woman!"

Windy sat on the edge of the bed. "Without a husband," he reminded her.

She kicked him, and he sat on the floor, but rested his head tranquilly against her hand.

"Anny," he murmured, "I'm a lonely man."

"I'm not surprised!" she said. "This isn't the way to treat your friends! Get out before I scream!"

"I've loved you,' he went on, "ever since I first came into your flat and found the feather on the carpet."

"You're a bad one," Anny said. "I thought so at the time."

"I thought you liked me," he said.

"I hate you," Anny told him. "Wait till I tell O'Brien about this."

"I've been kind to you," Windy said.

"I'm beginning to wonder," Anny said. "Is it the key you want—because you're not getting it!"

Windy began to climb to his feet. "It's you I want, Anny!"

Anny waited, holding herself tense as a tiger; she had fought bigger men than this on the Cassy and remained undefeated.

Windy slid an arm around her back and leaned over her.

"I hope you won't hold this against me," Anny said. "You've only yourself to blame."

And with her other hand she brought over the china bedside lamp, and smashed it on his head.

IT WAS HALF-PAST twelve at night when Anny left the big house carrying a heavy hold-all, and with the roll of red carpet— the only possession she had brought from the flat—on her shoulder. It was a dismal prospect. The estate roads were unlit, there was a chill wind from the sea, and the nearest main road was three miles away.

She was passing the big Mercedes Benz before she actually saw it. Breaking all the laws, it was standing parked on the grass verge, without lights. As she stared at it, a match flared, and the man behind the wheel lit a cigarette.

"Good evening," Anny said.

"Good evening," said the man.

"Would you be going anywhere?" Anny asked. She hoisted the roll of carpet to ease her shoulder.

"Are you leaving?" asked the man.

"I am!" said Anny.

"I'll take you to London if you'd like to share the cost of the petrol," said the man.

"I will," said Anny. "Gladly."

And when she was in, with the roll of carpet poking out of the rear window, the man said: "I'm Walter Sims—I'm a good friend of your husband's."

"It's lucky you were here," Anny said.

She had grown so accustomed to being watched, accosted, and searched, since O'Brien had gone to prison that nothing really surprised her any more.

They chatted pleasantly as they drove northward on the Horsham-London road.

"Have you any cigarettes?" Sims asked her as they came on to the Dorking By-pass.

She found him cigarettes from her hold-all, but she was puzzled. "Are you one of the gang?"

"I was," he said. "But I resigned."

"But didn't you get your money?" Anny asked. "We all got fifty thousand pounds. You want to put in for it."

Never fully aware that she was embroiled in one of the biggest robberies of the decade, Anny's mind was still permanently keyed to the old penny-watching way of life. Without really

288

knowing it herself, she saw the whole thing as some slightly illicit lottery, a diddleums club; she thought of the gang as a shady firm who had employed O'Brien and paid him a dividend. She had never completely disassociated Windy Willow from Hope Brothers, what with the Rolls Royce and everything.

"Oh yes," Sims said, "I got my cut—but it went."

"You spent fifty thousand pounds?"

"I have a lot of responsibilities," Sims told her.

To pass the time as they sped along the Kingston By-pass Sims told Anny all about his various wives in different parts of the world, and he showed her a photograph, switching on the dash lamp so that she could see it.

"My eldest boy," he said, proudly.

Anny was a sucker for families—though, unlike Windy's, this one was quite genuine—and was really interested. The photograph showed a shiny-faced, curly headed youth wearing a cap and gown.

"Witwatersrand University," Sims said. "Studying social philosophy."

"You must be very proud," she said.

"But it's all expense," Sims said. "I can't keep up with it. By the time I get a bit of money, it's all spoken for—over-due maintenance, alimony, mortgages, hut fees, school fees, clothes, pocket money."

Anny tutted sympathetically. "It's all spend, spend, spend, these days," she agreed. "Still, it's nice to meet a man who can face up to his responsibilities."

"It's not easy," Sims said.

"It's not," said Anny. "How old is the youngest?"

"I don't know yet." Sims concentrated for a moment. "She'd be about two, I suppose. I haven't got back yet."

"Well, it'll be a long time before she's off your hands," Anny said, chattily. "They're a burden to keep—but I bet you wouldn't be without 'em."

"I would not," said the con man, and he brushed his eye.

IT WAS SUCH a sociable, chatty, ride that Anny was not aware of the true calamity which had befallen her until they arrived at Sim's flat in Park Lane. The journey had taken two hours, and they were both tired. Margo, the blonde member of the gang, was soon making them hot coffee; she had been asleep when they went in, and she was the only one there. Anny drew her own conclusions about this, but was ready to forgive Sims; there was no doubt about it—he was a lady's man, and suffered accordingly.

Anny had known this instinctively, as women do. The shyness in his eyes when he looked at you, knowing that you knew all about him; the gentleness in his voice, and the comradeship in his manner, and the gratitude and reward in the blonde girl's eyes as she gladly waited upon him at two o'clock in the morning. He was one of those men who belonged to womankind, rather than woman: he would never take unfair advantage of a girl, nor leave her in the lurch; but you had to be prepared for his falling deeply in love two or three times a month.

In the balance of nature men like Sims amassed responsibilities as swiftly, and easily, as men like Windy threw them off. If Anny had been completely honest with herself, she would have admitted that she'd known all along that she was going to have to hit Windy on the head, in the end.

But what she didn't know, because it was not implicit in the first look a man and woman exchange, was that he was also after fifty thousand pounds.

"I think it's a dirty, stinking, shame!" Margo said, when she handed Anny her coffee.

"Oh, he didn't touch me!" Anny said.

"But all that money!"

Anny dipped a hand into her bosom and took out the key. "Don't worry about that—that's safe enough. He'll not get his hands on that!"

Margo looked at Sims: "Doesn't she know, Walter?"

Sims shook his head. "I just kept her talking," he admitted, miserably. "I hadn't the heart to tell her."

Anny looked from one to the other, fearfully, like a patient who's safely negotiated an appendectomy only to find that somebody's noticed a carcinoma.

"It's the old safe-deposit trick," Margo explained. "I could see it coming a mile away. He did the same thing to Rene after he'd shopped her husband—only you're lucky, her husband was hanged, and now she's stuck with Windy . . ."

Anny listened with a sinking heart, all her dreams of the West Indies draining away.

"What shall I tell O'Brien, tomorrow?" she said.

"Tell him that I had nothing to do with it," Sims asked.

"I will," said Anny.

But already she was pondering a way of getting the money back. The sheer injustice of it stuck in her throat. She could see now that O'Brien had been the patsy of all time. He was serving the prison sentence while the others got away with the money.

"What are the police doing?" Anny said, now that she no longer had anything to lose. "That's what I'd like to know."

Sims pointed out that she couldn't go to the police, or they would arrest her for receiving, whether she still had the money or not.

"Then what about that Mr. Sexton Blake?" Anny said. "He seems a nice feller."

"But he's trying to get the money back," Margo said.

"Well, that doesn't matter to me now," Anny said. "And it doesn't matter to you, if it's all been spent."

Sims shook his head. "I don't know—they're a funny crowd. I met Blake and his staff when I was looking for you—I wanted to warn you about Windy."

"What's funny about them?" Anny asked. "They've a very good reputation."

Margo said: "But they're on the wrong side!"

"Besides," Sims said, "they're not altogether respectable. There were these three men and two women, all going in and out of this one small room for weeks on end."

"Is that right?' Anny said. "I would never have thought it of them by looking at them. Still, it proves they're human. I'll have to see what O'Brien's got to say."

"If he's got any sense," Sims said, "he'll put us all behind bars, and I wouldn't blame him."

"I'll see that he keeps you out of it," Anny promised.

Sims gave her a touching smile. This was really the reason he had been trying to help Anny; the reason he had followed her down to King's Gors, and—when he knew that it was too late to save her money—had waited patiently until she needed help. Sims had broken the gang rule about not touching the money as soon as he knew that Windy had shopped O'Brien. They'd expected the Irishman to betray them all in the dock and—he hadn't. But there was nothing to stop him doing so now.

"I can't afford to go to jail, just now," Sims explained to Anny. "There'll be more bills, and demands, and claims, coming in before I can turn round, and I've got to start another job."

Anny looked at him, sympathetically. "It's a pity you couldn't have given yourself a bit of a holiday first."

"There's no rest for the wicked," Sims said, ruefully.

"What I don't understand," Anny said, pondering, "is why the police haven't made some arrests already. They seem to have been knocking into you all for weeks."

"They're looking for a gang of thieves," Sims explained,

"and we're all confidence men. That was Mr. Lemon's idea. We're not in the right union. You'd have to rub their noses in the proof before they'd do anything to us."

"O'Brien could do that," Anny said.

"He'll have to work fast than," Margo put in. "If I know Windy, he's already making tracks."

"I have a lot of faith in Mr. Blake," Anny said, "whatever his personal habits may be."

THE FIFTHTEENTH CHAPTER

Up the creek.

LORD QUADE BANGED the conference table with his fist. "It was a dirty rotten trick!" he exclaimed. And to Blake: "What were you doing to allow it to happen?"

Blake said: "If I had stepped in at that stage we might never have seen either the gang or the money again."

He explained that the gang felt quite safe, were living openly, and feeding on the greenest of pastures; but the least snap of a finger and they would all vanish down dark, deep, and impenetrable burrows which stretched from Winnipeg to the South of France.

"This is why I couldn't even tell my old friends Grimwald and Coutts here what I knew. Oh, they could have made their arrests—but that wouldn't help me or Venus Life and Property. Remember, O'Brien was already in jail, and we had not got his share of the spoils."

Sir Martin Reynolds, the prison commissioner, pointed out: "But you could have got that money before Windy Willow stepped in."

"And Windy Willow," Blake said, "would promptly have stepped out—for good."

They were not dealing—Blake reminded the inquiry—with a bunch of Bermondsey Boys, who would run no farther than the top of Lavender Hill.

Commander Grimwald said: "When did you first realise that these con men were in fact the gang we were searching for?"

"At the moment I found Anny O'Brien packing to leave—and when she showed me Windy's card of invitation. She was willing to let me know where she was going—I think she was secretly glad to have my protection—but she didn't seem to realise that it gave the whole thing away. In fact," Blake went on, "it was obvious that Windy was an old acquaintance, comparatively speaking. He had not just moved in on her as a stranger."

Coutts shook his head: "I was on a completely different track by that time—"

His superior officer, Grimwald, shut him up quickly: "It was brilliantly conceived," he said. "No wonder our usual channels in the underworld were foxed. The gang might well have come from Jupiter, or Timbuctoo, as from the ranks of our leading con men."

"All right, Commander," Lord Quade said, gently: "We have the point."

Sir Martin said: "Luckily, Mr. Blake's views are not as stereotyped as Scotland Yard's." Then looking at Blake: "But surely by the time you had seen Windy rob that poor girl and then followed her back to Sims flat, you had enough evidence to start rounding up the gang? After all there was Windy, the girl Rene, the old man Lemon, Sims, and his girlfriend Margo—you were bound to crack some information out of one of them."

"No," Blake disagreed. "I had to go on making a gamble by doing nothing. You see from my point of view the risk was in capturing the gang without recovering the money—that's where my duty and the police duty parted company."

Lord Quade nodded. "I can appreciate that. They are clever men, used to handling big sums of money—they would not find it difficult to disperse five hundred thousand pounds, have it salted away until they had served their terms."

"Exactly," Blake said. "I couldn't take that risk."

Lord Quade said: "Then what was your plan?"

"The only chance I had of recovering the money," Blake said, "was to try to get every member of the gang to put all their shares together in one place at the same time—and then pounce!"

Lord Quade's eyebrows shot up. "What an excellent plan!" And turning to Commander Grimwald: "Why didn't you think of that?"

"A policeman could never have thought about it, or done it," the Commander said, pithily: "It would take another con man."

"Thank you for the compliment," Blake said.

The Metropolitan Police Commissioner and the Prison Commissioner, shared the joke. Then Sir Martin Reynolds said: "How on earth did you ever accomplish such an unlikely set of circumstances, Mr. Blake?"

"With a slip of paper," Blake said. He took another document from his pocket and laid it on the desk. As they all peered at the scribble of handwriting, he explained: "O'Brien's Ultimatum!"

"O'Brien's Ultimatum!" Lord Quade echoed.

"O'Brien's Ultimatum!" Sir Martin said, in a different tone. "I shall never forget that!"

There were few people in the world of crime, or crime prevention, or crime punishment, who would ever forget O'Brien's Ultimatum. It had caused three prison riots, one break-out, and four attempted murders, in the course of a single week.

"Getting him to write it," Lord Quade said, "was a stroke of genius!"

"But I didn't get him to write it," Blake said.

And as the four men stared at him, he added, simply:

"I wrote it myself . . ."

"IT's NOT LIKE O'Brien!" Windy Willow said, in an injured tone. "I'm disappointed in him."

Mr. Hess the German shook his head in a depressed way. "Please—read it again."

Mr. Barratt, the elderly man in the wheelchair, had the paper in his hands. The gang meeting was taking place once again in Sims' Park Lane flat, and all were present.

"Unless," Mr. Barratt read out, "my share of the money is replaced by noon on Friday, I shall give the police a full list of the names of every man involved in the Dackworth Store robbery. It is signed: T. O'Brien and written on prison notepaper."

Windy said: "How did he get this note out?"

Sims said: "He smuggled it to his wife, who brought it to me."

Old Mr. Lemon said: "We've all got friends on the inside— we could have him put down."

"Why not just restore the money to Anny?" Sims said, looking at Windy.

"So that you could get it?" Windy said. And then: "I fully intended sharing it between us all—that goes without saying."

Mr. Peel, a quiet man who said very little and made most of his money out of elderly widows, put in: "You've put us all in jeopardy, Windy—you'd better give it back."

Windy shrugged off the idea. "Do you think he wouldn't give us away afterwards to get his revenge?"

Mr. Lemon said: "I have a better idea. We have three full days to get away—"

Mr. Hess said: "What about our rules? Were they drawn up for nothing? They are still watching seaports and airports. Between the Customs, Scotland Yard, and Interpol, we should not get very far carrying all that currency."

"Which is why I have found myself a yacht," said Mr. Lemon. He smiled round at them. "A big yacht. A luxury yacht. It can be ready to sail within twenty-four hours."

"Where from?" asked Mr. Barratt.

"Shoreham," said Mr. Lemon. "We can be round Cap Finisterre by Friday noon, and heading for the sun."

Windy said: "There's still port clearance."

"I've thought of that," said Mr. Lemon. "I can take the yacht out of Shoreham and pick you all up in Chichester bay—at night. I'll send the tender up the creek to Bosham—a little yachting centre in the Winchelsea fens."

The other men—with exception of Windy, who knew it all—were looking at the old man very suspiciously. Mr. Hess gave voice to these suspicions, for they were all con men together.

"How is it you have such an elaborate plan prepared when O'Brien's ultimatum has only just arrived?"

The old man smiled round at them, disarmingly. "It was my next job—I haven't retired yet, you know. We're searching for a sunken Trojan city under the Adriatic. I had intended to make the journey, anyway—but you are all welcome as my guests. You can be put off wherever you choose."

Windy said: "Of course we should have to arrange to have O'Brien taken care of before he can testify. I don't want to go into exile for the rest of my life."

Mr. Hess pondered for a moment, then said heavily: "I shall come with you."

"Me too."

"And me."

"Count me in."

One by one, the vote became unanimous.

"But," Sims said, "we shall all be watching you, Lemon—and you, Windy—all the time."

Windy raised his hands in innocence. "It's not my idea! I don't want your money—I've got enough." Then he added: "Incidentally, if you'd like me to smuggle your money aboard at Shoreham to save you carrying it all the way—"

The loud, ironic laughter drowned him out.

THE MOTOR YACHT *City Of Troy* moved out of Shoreham Harbour on the following afternoon's tide. Captain Lemon stood on the bridge with Windy Willow, Rene and the millionaire owner, Mr. Crakeham, who had hoped, until certain late-night visitors had got him from his Brighton hotel bed, to be sailing to find the lost treasures of the ancient Trojans. Now he was having difficulty in keeping up optimistic chatter about the weather, the calm sea, and the voyage ahead.

It had been a hectic morning for Mr. Crakeham. His entire crew had been given unexpected shore leave at double pay while a new crew had been presented to him. They were twenty in number; each man sailing without a union ticket, each man a member of the British C.I.D. While down in the engine-room Sexton Blake, Commander Grimwald, and Detective-Inspector Coutts, were messing about with oilcans and keeping their faces as black as possible.

On the bridge Windy Willow looked anxiously shorewards: "Nobody following, is there?" he whispered.

"Eh?" said Mr. Lemon.

"Oh, forget it," said Windy.

"Oooooh!" Rene exclaimed. "That was a near miss!"

The yacht had passed the harbour with a very few feet to spare.

The old man laughed. "Don't worry—good crew. I'm sure they know what they're doing . . ."

THE SUN WENT down as the ebb tide came in at Bosham creek.

The seven men in the bar of the public house watched the waters rise across the weeds and grasses to cover the road, and splash against the walls of the building. Their luggage was kept possessively by their legs: suitcases, hold-alls, parcels. Amongst the holidaymakers and the noisy yachting crowd, they made a sombre and silent group; anxious, worried, on edge.

When the sound of the approaching motor launch was first heard, each of the seven froze, momentarily; then went on drinking. They were appreciating now that they had put themselves into a desperately vulnerable position. But they could not see how Windy or Lemon could best them, since they were in a strong majority, and with their wits about them; nor what purpose it would serve Windy to betray them—for if there was a purpose, and he would gain by it, then he undoubtedly would.

In this edge of the precipice frame of mind they listened to the engine cut out. Their eyes were on the door when the young man came through, muffled up in oil-skins and with a thick sweater underneath and a woollen tasselled hat on his curly head.

Tinker stood in the doorway, looking past the noisy trippers to the group at the table. He walked over to them.

"Anyone for fishing?"

Mr. Hess stared at him steadily for a long moment, and Tinker met his gaze unflinchingly. "Who are you from?" the German asked.

"Mr. Lemon," Tinker said. He looked down at the luggage. "D'you want this stuff put aboard?"

"Just a moment, my lad," said Mr. Barratt. "Who else is on board?"

"A Mr. Willow," Tinker said, "and a bit of stuff called Rene—nice! Oh, and Mr. Crakeham—that's the owner. My boss."

Mr. Peel said: "What's the name of your yacht?"

"City of Troy," Tinker said. "I ought to know—I've been

aboard her for two years."

Mr. Featherstonhaugh asked: "Where is she bound?"

"That's a laugh," Tinker said. "She's not bound anywhere—we've been looking for some Trojan city for years. I think it's only in the boss' mind."

Mr. Hess said: "Where is she lying now?"

"Four miles down the creek. It's not deep enough to come inshore—she's got a six-foot draft."

"Very well," said Mr. Hess. "You may pick up the luggage."

Phew! Tinker thought.

Then suddenly a girl squealed with delight, and came rushing over, throwing her arms around Tinker's neck.

"Tinker! Fancy seeing you!"

"Eh?" Tinker tried to disengage.

"How's the great detective?" laughed the girl happily. "And Sexton Blake?"

Now, through a turmoil of panic, he recognised her as Jonquil Travers, the bed-sitter girl from Earls Court Square, the girl who lived below Marion and who had helped him on that last insurance case.[7] She was dressed in gay, candy-striped jeans and a bright yellow low-cut blouse, and was brimming with the spirit of the seaside and several glasses of beer.

"I'm down here on a sailing course," she said. "What d'you think? I can manage a sailing dinghy single-handed already!"

"That's nice," Tinker said wretchedly.

Suddenly she realised that he was not happy; she looked at the seven glowering, frightened-eyed men, who were getting to their feet.

"Have you caught any bad criminals lately—" she began, then caught her breath. "What've I said?"

"Too much," Tinker said tiredly.

He took out a revolver and levelled it at the seven men, pushing the girl away.

"All right—sit down—"

He got no farther. Mr. Hess crashed his glass mug into Tinker's face and Mr. Barratt kicked him in the stomach. The seven men walked over him, picking up their luggage.

Tinker, his face pressing into the floor, was almost in tears— not of pain, but of fury and frustration. This was the one little bit of the job that he might have pulled off single-handed. Now the whole thing had fallen apart—and Blake was patiently waiting, four miles down the creek.

It follows that Tinker, at that ghastly moment, was an equal distance up the creek.

> But Jonquil was a girl of parts
> A steady brain, a steadfast heart,
> She rallied all her friends around
> And knocked the robbers on the ground.

This eulogy, engraved on a silver tankard, can still be seen hanging from an old oak beam in the pub at Bosham. But like all epic poems from the *Iliad* to *The Young Lady of Rye*, its terse description does little justice to the facts.

Her beefy yachting friends took a lot of rallying, and the robbers took a lot of knocking. To her frantic cries for help as she struggled to get Tinker to his feet, the red-faced men at the bar at first refused to listen, and then became coy and embarrassed, muttering through their moustaches: "Come off it, old girl!" and "Private quarrel, y'know!" and "Don't want to make a dashed scene!"

But finally when Jonquil, feeling that the whole thing was her fault, launched herself at Mr. Peel, and got herself kicked in the tummy, the rest of her sailing squadron took heed, and in two seconds the seven men with their seven heavy loads were fighting a rearguard action.

"Avast there!"

"Steady on your beam!"

"Look out to starb'd!"

The cries accompanied hearty blows and throws and seamen's tackles, until finally the seven were lying prostrate, tied over-enthusiastically from head to foot in short-sheepshanks, clove-hitches, and reef-knots.

"There you are, Tinker," Jonquil said, now resting her foot on Mr. Peel's face, "where d'you want them?"

The landlord said: "Shall I get the police?"

"Yes," Tinker said. Then: "No. Bring 'em out to my boat—"

"I'LL GIVE YOU ten thousand pounds in cash if you'll let us go," Mr. Hess said.

Tinker sat at the helm of the motor-launch, chugging steadily down the creek in the darkness, the seven men tied up in the scuppers behind him, their money safely stowed in the cabin.

"And I'll give you another ten thousand," said Mr. Featherstonhaugh.

Huh, Tinker thought.

"And ten thousand from me," said Mr. Peel.

"And from me!"

"And me!"

Tinker became thoughtful. "How much is that altogether?" he asked.

They were offering him seventy-thousand pounds in cash for putting ashore, and leaving them.

Tinker bit his lips as the entreaties kept coming and finally thought that he would have to stuff the wool of his pullover into his ears.

"HOW ON EARTH," Blake asked, "did you do it?"

"Hm?" Tinker was watching the gang and their bundles

being hoisted aboard the yacht by the police Superintendant, by the oily-faced Grimwald and Coutts. "Oh, you know."

"No," Blake said. "Frankly, I don't know."

"I sort of surrounded them."

"But who gave you permission to jump the gun? You might have lost the lot."

"I was recognised," Tinker said. He gave Blake a summary of the events in the Bosham public house.

"You did very well, in that case." Blake gave his assistant a warm smile. "And, of course, you were very lucky."

"Where's Sims?" a voice cried dementedly.

As they turned, Windy Willow was trying to break away from the police as he searched the faces of the shackled gang. "Where the hell's Sims?"

It was a good question. Sims, the South African, having nothing to smuggle aboard, had passed all the information he could to Anny, who had passed it on to Blake, then vanished.

Sailing back to Shoreham, Blake had a chance to go through the stolen money, checking each man's share and totting it up. With the exception of the fifty thousand pounds which Sims had distributed to his creditors, it was all there.

"Do you want me to make an inventory?" Tinker asked.

They were alone with the money in the Captain's cabin while Grimwald and Coutts were busy interrogating the gang in the saloon.

"No thank you," Blake said. "I just want you to forget it."

Blake was tying up the parcels again; the young man stared at him, puzzled.

"Forget what?" Tinker asked.

Blake gave him an enigmatic glance. "Forget how many parcels you counted," he said.

Tinker's face straightened, comically. "Isn't that a little—er—unethical?"

"What's more," Blake told him, "you may have to forget it on oath."

"But that'd be perjury!"

"Perhaps it won't go as far as that," Blake said.

Tinker was watching Blake, blankly. The detective had left the remaining parcel open and was now busy stuffing bank notes into his brief case.

"Come on, don't just stand there," Blake said. "Fill your pockets . . ."

THE TRIAL OF the Dackworth robbery gang was much longer and, from the legal standpoint, far more satisfying than that of O'Brien. For, being exceedingly guilty, they all pleaded not guilty, a much more professional and dignified thing, involving the briefing of counsel and junior counsel, firms of solicitors, overtime for clerks and altogether yielding enormous profits all round. Indeed, without "not guilty" pleas, a place as big and expensive as the Old Bailey couldn't keep going; for it is a proven fact that it costs more to run than any American musical in the West End.

"Am I to understand you to say that you were not there?" asked the Prosecuting Counsel of Mr. Featherstonhaugh at one stage.

"That is correct sir."

"My Lord," said the Prosecutor, turning to the Judge, "I would like to call fifteen witnesses who will testify that the accused worked at Dackworth's for six months as a security officer—they will tell you that he was on duty there on the night of the robbery."

"*Fifteen witnesses?*" echoed the Judge. "That's *very* good . . ."

Lavish and spectacular, the trial moved on to its highly predictable ending. Anything less than seven years imprisonment apiece would have been an anti-climax.

"I'll get him! I'll get him!"

The hate-crazed voice rang across the court, and, the Judge who had series a of dull divorces in front of him, turned back to the proceedings and his face lit up at the sight of little Mr. Peel clinging to the dock rail. Wild outbursts from a convicted man, the Judge thought, happily—it was like the right vintage brandy after a satisfying meal.

"I'll get him!" Mr. Peel cried again. "We'll all get him!"

The Judge watched him dragged below, then dismissed the court.

"An excellent case, Basil," he remarked to his clerk in the robing room, a little later.

"One of the best," said Basil.

The Judge laughed, softly and intrepidly. "They're after me again. What a thing!"

Basil opened his mouth to correct this false impression, then thought better of it. It was good for the old boy's ego to believe that Mr. Peel's threat had been directed at him; but, in fact, even Basil knew that the wrath of the gang, and indeed of the entire underworld, was directed against O'Brien and his ultimatum.

THE SIXTHTEENTH CHAPTER

The Nelson touch.

"Bit unfair, surely?" Lord Quade remarked.

It was unfair, and Sexton Blake was the first to acknowledge it. O'Brien had not incriminated the gang at his own trial, he had not issued the ultimatum to the gang, he had not testified against them at their trial. O'Brien had long since resigned himself to serving his sentence as quickly and painlessly as possible, and then to come out and live on his profits with Anny.

"And there's another thing that's bothering me," Sir Martin Reynolds put in. "O'Brien's fifty thousand pounds—what happened to it? Windy Willow only produced his own share—what had he done with Anny's parcel?"

"I was coming to that," Blake said.

"Funny," Commander Grimwald said, reflectively: "Windy didn't even mention it at the trial."

"Quite," Blake said. "He was more of a gentleman than I gave him credit for. Or else Anny really had a soft spot in his heart."

"How d'you mean, Blake?" Lord Quade was getting fogged.

Blake said: "If we had found the O'Brien share of the money on Windy, and if he had admitted how he got it from Anny—then you know what the consequences would have been for her?"

"Of course," Detective-Inspector Coutts grunted; "she would have got four years for receiving."

Lord Quade said: "But she did receive it—and she's probably got it back by this time."

"No," Blake said.

Sir Martin Reynolds gave Blake an admiring glance. "I must admire your methods, Blake—you seem to be in on it, all right."

Blake's acknowledging smile was slightly strained; he had told the O'Brien story and, he hoped, told it well. He had wanted to demonstrate that O'Brien and Anny were essentially an innocent pair, guilty only of trying to meet the cost of living by accepting what fate and circumstance had laid at their door. Now came the test—had he won sufficient sympathy from his audience to ask them to sidestep the letter of the law while seeing real justice done?

Blake didn't know yet.

"I am still more than a little concerned," Lord Quade said. He looked at Blake: "You have convinced me that you had every justification for standing aside when O'Brien left Brixton Prison on Tuesday morning—no doubt you expected him to lead you straight to his wife and the money—"

"No, I didn't—" Blake began, but his lordship had not finished.

"But this doesn't help me to meet Press and public criticism. O'Brien was a sitting duck!"

Sir Martin nodded, sagely: "A sitting duck!"

"Nobody expected him to last twenty-four hours once he was released," Grimwald said. "The boys here at the Yard were laying bets on it."

"After all," Lord Quade said, "that's why he was kept in solitary confinement and why he served only two years of his original sentence—keeping him safe, protecting him, was too much of a strain and a drain on manpower . . ."

*   *   *

It HAD STARTED as soon as the gang were locked into prison. They could never be directly linked with it, for none of them was sent to Wandsworth after Mr. Peel's solemn vow from the dock—which nobody but the Judge had misunderstood. Nevertheless, two days after the trial ended a riot flared up during exercise time in Wandsworth prison yard, and O'Brien had been left lying on the ground with a knife in his shoulder.

Transferred to Pentonville, there had immediately been a "We won't eat with O'Brien" hunger strike. There had followed transfers all over the country; at Wakefield it had been a home-made bomb in O'Brien's cell, at Dartmoor a helicopter had dropped a fire-bomb on a working party, at Portland an attempted break-out when O'Brien arrived, at Strangeways the soup poisoned with disinfectant—and so it had gone on and on.

And the ultimatum was blamed for all this.

In the twelve short months O'Brien served after the gang's trial and conviction he became known as the man who grassed. The unforgivable sin. There was only one place more dangerous for O'Brien than inside a prison—and that was outside a prison.

The Press had campaigned for his protection, and one television personality had suggested during a Crime Report programme that O'Brien should be granted free plastic surgery before leaving his solitary confinement cell.

No wonder, then, that there had been a public outcry when the news of the murder got out; no wonder the Press had raised Cain, no wonder the back-bencher had stood up in the House and asked his question, and no wonder Lord Quade, at this inquiry, was still more than a little concerned.

"WHAT DO YOU mean, 'No you didn't'?" Lord Quade said now, Blake's interjection having just registered with him. "No you didn't what?"

"No, I didn't expect O'Brien to lead me straight to his wife and the money when he came out of prison on Tuesday morning," Blake said.

Sir Martin Reynolds, the prison commissioner, half smiled, suspecting a trick and not wanting to be on the wrong end of it. "But isn't that why you were there, Mr. Blake—to let O'Brien lead you to the fifty thousand pounds?"

"No," Blake said. "Quite the reverse. I was there to lead O'Brien to the fifty thousand pounds."

"I see!" said Commander Grimwald.

"That's rather different, old man!" Detective-Inspector Coutts exclaimed.

"It's quite different!" said Lord Quade.

"Couldn't be more different!" echoed Sir Martin.

Blake studied them all in silence for an appreciable period. During this silence they could hear the teeming traffic along the Embankment, the toot of a taxi horn, the wild, despairing shriek of some tiny tug rupturing itself on a string of barges at mid-river. At last Blake spoke, choosing his words with care.

"I place myself in your hands now," he said soberly. "If you put this information in front of the Director of Public Prosecutions I might easily end up at the Old Bailey—but in the dock instead of the witness-box."

Blake waited a moment, and they all stared at him apprehensively. Then he continued: "On the other hand, if you add the Nelson touch to the sword and scales of British justice, then I can promise you, Lord Quade, that justice will be done and neither you nor the Home Secretary will suffer any embarrassment at what has happened."

The Metropolitan Police Commissioner looked first at his colleagues on the board of inquiry, then steadily at Sexton Blake. And without saying a word to commit himself, he placed one hand over one eye.

"Now let me take you back," Blake said, "to the issuing of O'Brien's ultimatum."

"The one he didn't issue?" Lord Quade asked.

"Precisely," Blake said. "I had been working on him at the prison for nearly two hours without getting any co-operation . . ."

BLAKE WAS SITTING side by side with O'Brien on the bunk of his prison cell, for it was not a normal visiting period. Trying to persuade the Irishman to bring pressure to bear on the gang, he had been putting the case into its right perspective, something O'Brien could never do.

"You were the victim, O'Brien," Blake said. "They used methods on you right from the start. Windy Willow tricked you into opening the safe at Hope Brothers, then he tricked you into the belief that they had you in their power in order to use you for the big job."

"But I did get paid for both jobs," O'Brien said. "There's no blinking that. They kept their side of the bargain, and I wouldn't want to let 'em down now."

"But you're in prison, and they're out!"

O'Brien shrugged. "That's the luck of it. You must remember that I haven't the same experience in keeping out of gaol."

Blake breathed hard; this man had such a strict code of ethics, the craftsman's insistence on giving value for money, the respect for Windy and the gang on their expertise no matter in what direction; strange, conflicting, values which, infuriatingly, one could understand and admire.

"But Windy shopped you!" Blake said.

"Well, how else could he get my share of the money?" O'Brien said. "It's the regular thing, I dare say—after all, he's a fully-trained crook."

"He not only wanted your money—he wanted your wife."

"Is that right?" said O'Brien. "Well, he'd not get her if he

313

trained a lifetime."

"She had a very narrow escape."

"So did he!" O'Brien said, smiling. "She told me about it. She cracked him on the head with a china lamp. Oh, she's got a terrible temper once she's made up her mind. I have to go carefully myself . . ."

LATER THAT SAME day, after Blake had left the prison, he had an interview with Anny at the Berkeley Square offices. It was another curiously difficult interview because Anny also had twisted ethics. Because Blake was not directly connected with the police, and because she sensed his sympathy and friendship, she thought that he could try to get the money back for her.

"I can't do that," Blake said.

"I'll pay you ten per cent, Mr. Blake."

She was sitting with her legs crossed in the sunlight, and wearing one of the bright yellow shirt-waister dresses; though the skirt was noticeably less stiff and crisp. She made a pretty picture, and her eyes were large and trusting though holding a glint of righteous anger at the way she had been tricked at the safe-deposit.

"I don't think you understand your position, Anny," Blake said. "If I helped you to recover stolen property I should be an accessory."

"Oh, you can trust me," Anny said fervently. "I wouldn't breathe a word, and you could take your share in cash." She thought for a moment, then said: "And another thing, I would give Mr. Sims enough money for a fresh start—so it'd be doing a lot of good all round."

In effect she was suggesting in the most beguiling, and endearing, and indeed innocent, of ways, that Blake should not only become an accomplice in the crime he was being paid to solve, but should also help to start the South African into

314

some other highly-illegal venture by supplying the capital. And the odd thing was, because both Sims and the O'Briens were fellow human beings, and the insurance company was an impersonal machine, and because Sexton Blake was full of all the humanities, it all sounded perfectly reasonable and right.

"And you could come and visit us in the West Indies," she added, feeling that she was gaining ground, "and go out turtle fishing with O'Brien."

"Please don't go on," Blake pleaded.

"Had you something else in mind?" she asked.

"I had," Blake said.

"I'm ready to listen to any suggestion you may have," Anny said. "It's not only the money that's bothering me. My mother and her boyfriend are searching for me, and it wouldn't surprise me if they don't turn up at the prison and yell 'Antoinette' all over the place—will you see this now!"

"This" was a folded daily paper with an item in the agony column heavily ringed by pencil. Blake glanced at it.

ANTOINETTE come home all is forgiven. Ma.

Blake said: "If you follow my plan, and it succeeds, then I suggest that you disappear until your husband is released—it might be safer that way, in any case . . ."

THE PLAN WAS O'Brien's famous Ultimatum to the gang and it was, as has already been chronicled, completely successful. It was on a day some three months after the gang had been rounded up, when O'Brien was recovered from the stabbing incident and incarcerated in the solitary confinement cell that Anny paid her last visit to the prison. She had a packed case containing all her personal possessions in one hand when she arrived at the prison reception desk, and the roll of red carpet on her shoulder.

"Will I be seeing him in the solitary confinement cell?" Anny asked the reception officer.

"Yes, Mrs. O'Brien—we're not allowed to bring him out. It's for his own safety."

"Oh, I don't mind," Anny said. "There's more privacy."

She was walking on when he called her back.

"You'll have to leave those things here."

"Could I just show him the carpet?" Anny said, with a moist and winning smile. "It has sentimental associations."

The officer unrolled the carpet to make certain that it contained no files or saws or other implements that might be useful in an escape bid. He studied it very carefully, going down on his knees and taking a feather from here and there out of the thick red pile.

"Well, all right," he said at last. "I can't see the harm in it."

"You're very kind," Anny said. "I won't be seeing him again until he's released . . ."

It was two hours later that they remembered she was still there.

"You'd better knock first," said the Chief Warder as he walked with a subordinate to the cell.

THE SEVENTEENTH CHAPTER

Double-take.

"ONE CAN FEEL deeply sorry for that girl," said Lord Quade.

Blake nodded. He was relying on it.

"Losing her husband," said Sir Martin Reynolds, "just at the moment of reunion—a tragedy."

"Even so, Blake," Lord Quade said, "I don't see that you are implicated in any way—any more than the rest of us are."

Blake looked at Commander Grimwald.

"You'd better tell them," Grimwald said.

Sir Martin said: "Are the police in on this, then? That makes a change."

"We were dragged in," Grimwald grumbled. "Willy-nilly. Whether we liked it or not."

Lord Quade was staring at Blake. "Go on," he said, with barely-suppressed excitement. Deep in his heart of hearts, having heard the O'Brien story from the beginning and following Anny's adventures from the Liverpool cassy to the solitary confinement cell in a prison, after hearing all this the Metropolitan Police Commissioner was hoping for a happy ending.

"Go on," he said again.

"I'm implicated," Blake said, "because I was on the spot outside Brixton Prison on Tuesday morning when the double-tragedy occurred. It was I who told the police and the papers that the shot man was O'Brien."

Quade and Sir Martin looked at each other.

"But it *was* O'Brien!" Sir Martin said. "Wasn't it?"

"He had just come out of prison!" Lord Quade said. "Hadn't he?"

"No," Blake said, answering both questions with an astounding negative. "The shot man was Rudolph, Anny's mother's flashy thug from Liverpool—"

Now a lighter note had come into the inquiry as Blake reset the scene outside Brixton Prison on the morning of O'Brien's release. A lighter—brighter, optimistic note. Lord Quade had his answer for the Home Secretary, the Home Secretary had his answer for the House. O'Brien was not dead. It changed everything.

THERE WERE TWO wretched little cameo scenes which have their place before the drama, like curtain-raisers before the main item.

Blake did not witness these scenes but in the end he knew all about them. The first, because it happened first, Windy Willow, no longer smooth and suave but ugly and furtive looking through a wire gauze at Cyril the unpleasant youth. It is visiting day at the prison and all efforts to get at O'Brien have so far failed.

"Do you know O'Brien by sight, Cyril?"

"I fink so."

"Do you know what date they're releasing him?"

"I fink it's the forf of fiff."

"Be there—and get him! There's five hundred in it for you."

"Fanks—"

The second curtain-raiser on the day the newspapers told of O'Brien's release under the headline:

FREE TO DIE

O'Brien steps out into danger . . .

This time the characters were Anny's old Liverpool mum and her flashy boyfriend Rudolph, and they were still in the flat in Kilburn.

"She's bound to be ther to meet him out, Rudolph."

"What shall I do?"

"Follow them!"

"Suppose she's not ther?"

"Follow him!"

"Suppose he don't come out, after all?"

"Follow her!"

"She might be in a car."

"Get in with her and bring her back here—she owes a duty to me for all those sacrifices—"

AND THUS THE scene was set.

Blake sat next to Tinker in the big Bentley, not far from the prison gates. They were watching the man patrolling the pavement at a little distance as though waiting for a bus. They saw him wander up to the prison gates and read all the notices— H.M. Prison—No Admittance—The taking of photographs is strictly forbidden—Ring, and when he had finished with them he walked away, only to look at his watch and go back again.

"Do you know who that is?" Tinker said.

"Rudolph," Blake said.

"Shall we pick him up?"

"Wait," Blake said.

Rudolph again read the notices around the prison gates and was again strolling away from the prison when the old Riley car drew up by the kerb and Cyril opened the door and called out.

"O'Brien?"

Rudolph, hearing the name, turned quickly and thought fast. Of course! Anny wouldn't come herself! She had sent a car for O'Brien. He would go back in the car, pick up Anny and the money and get away before O'Brien could do anything about it.

"That's me!" he said.

Cyril pulled the trigger three times, and as Rudolph, surprised and dead, crumpled to the pavement, Cyril spun the wheel for a getaway. That's when Blake's car closed in and the bus took Cyril's car from the rear and smashed it to pieces.

And this was the moment when the prison gates opened and O'Brien came out, stretching himself and smiling at the sky.

"So you *KNEW* it wasn't O'Brien!" Lord Quade said.

"Yes," Blake said. "I knew. But in the fracas I lost O'Brien— and I saw an opportunity of protecting him. If the underworld thought he was dead then they wouldn't make any more attempts to get him—at least until I could catch up with him."

Sir Martin Reynolds breathed a sigh of sheer relief. "I think you did right—and the papers are going to have to climb down when they know the truth."

Lord Quade thought about it all before issuing a statement— for it was issued rather than spoken when at last he made it. "Yes, Blake—I think you were justified. But now the point is— where is O'Brien and the money?"

"Find Anny," Blake said, "and I think we find O'Brien—and the money."

Lord Quade suddenly exclaimed: "Good heavens! That poor girl! Do you realise, Blake, that she now thinks her husband is dead?"

"No," Blake said. "I don't think so."

They all stared at the detective.

Blake said: "If she had heard about it or read about it, wouldn't she have turned up at the hospital or the mortuary?"

Quade nodded: "I would have thought so. O'Brien must have gone straight to her."

Blake shook his head. "O'Brien didn't know where she was. O'Brien hasn't known Anny's whereabouts for the past nine months. Nobody has known."

Sir Martin Reynolds said: "In that case wouldn't she have been waiting outside the prison for him—his release had plenty of publicity."

Blake said: "She was waiting outside the prison—and that's how she knew they'd shot the wrong man."

Lord Quade said: "Well, that's a relief—did you see her?"

"I didn't know it at the time," Blake said. "But I know it now—"

He again described the scene for them . . . Turning from the wreckage of the Riley and the sight of Cyril's dead hand still holding the gun, then seeing the nun of an Anglican Order kneeling by the shot man; covering his face, then standing slowly up and walking away.

"She wouldn't have walked away," Blake said, "had it been O'Brien lying there."

"Good heavens!" Lord Quade exclaimed. "D'you mean to tell me that the girl's taken vows?"

"I doubt it," Blake said. "But what better place to hide—and after all, she needed a Retreat, so it can't be sacrilegious to use an order for the few months of novitiation."

Sir Martin Reynolds was frowning disapprovingly. "I can't agree with you, Blake. It's one thing to seek asylum, but quite another to make a pretence of renouncing the world and abandoning all worldly wealth and then go in with fifty thousand pounds under your skirt!"

Blake was shocked at such a suggestion. "Anny wouldn't do a thing like that!"

"Of course she wouldn't!" Lord Quade exclaimed.

Blake said: "Anny doesn't know where that money is. O'Brien is going to hand the money back—not Anny."

Slowly Lord Quade absorbed the situation. "Now I understand! What you're saying is, Mr. Blake, that Anny O'Brien never saw that money?"

Blake nodded anxiously. "Something like that."

"And you," Lord Quade said, "are going to show O'Brien where the money is, so that he can return it to its rightful owners."

"Yes," Blake said.

"But—" Sir Martin Reynolds began, but he broke off; Lord Quade, the Metropolitan Police High Commissioner was holding one hand over one eye.

"Ah!" said Sir Martin.

ANNY HAD SPENT the last nine months not far from the walls of Brixton Prison. It was the third convent which Blake had tried and they knew it was the right one because O'Brien was sitting nervously in the reception room, also waiting for Anny to be brought.

"There are four more gentlemen to see Sister Anny," the nun told the Mother Superior.

"Do they all claim to be her husband?"

Blake was introducing Lord Quade and Sir Martin to the Irishman.

"How did you know she was here?" Blake then asked O'Brien.

"She was waiting for me outside the prison," O'Brien said. "Just as we always planned. She's packing her things now—I had to give her a couple of days to finish off the work she was doing."

Anny entered in her nun's habit, walking alongside the Mother Superior.

THE MONEY WAS intact. By some unspecified means O'Brien had turned a key over to Commander Grimwald and the fifty thousand pounds had been recovered. He and Blake went together to the offices of Venus Life and Property Insurance in Moorgate and had a cheerful interview with Mr. Marks.

"You've done very well indeed, Mr. Blake. Although we are still lacking the fifty thousand which you say Sims has already dispersed, we must count ourselves a very fortunate company. You have earned your ten thousand pounds bonus."

It was not quite the end of the case. That afternoon Anny and her husband came to Blake's office at his request. Surrounded by the smiling faces of Paula, Tinker, Miss Pringle, Marion and Splash Kirby, Sexton Blake, with a minimum of formality, presented the O'Briens with half his bonus—a cheque for five thousand pounds.

"But for the O'Brien Ultimatum," he explained, "I could never have succeeded."

"But I didn't write it!" said O'Brien.

"You got the blame," Blake said, "you deserve the reward."

Anny's joy was clouded at this reminder: "Will there be any more trouble? We don't want to hide for the rest of our lives."

"You don't have to worry," Blake told her. "Our friend Splash here is going to splash the whole story over the pages of the *Daily Post*—if there are any repercussions, I'll get them."

"It's very kind of you," said Anny.

O'Brien was looking at the cheque, happily: "There's still enough to pay Mango for the schooner and a bit over!"

Anny said: "What schooner?"

"You remember the feller from the West Indies in the next cell—he sold me his schooner—"

He broke off, for Anny had snatched the cheque from him.

"From now on," she told him, "I'll be the business side of the marriage!"

O'Brien grinned at her. "That's all right with me, Anny—but just one thing. If you send anything to your mother, don't give her our address!"

"I won't!" said Anny.

They all watched the happy couple departing across Berkeley Square, hand in hand.

"There goes a lucky man," Blake said, with something of an envious sigh in his voice.

Tinker said: "You're pretty lucky, too, chief—you took some very grave risks that time."

Blake pondered it and shivered a little, as if looking back at a precipice just past. "I wonder why?"

Splash was studying the diminishing form across the square. There was no doubt that Anny had a way with her; several ways; the way she walked, and talked, and held her head, and laughed.

"I think I'll call her Antoinette," he said.

"She'll hate that," Blake told him.

"But it suits her," Splash said. "Romantic, exotic, historical—you know, Antoinette and Cleopatra? She's a very classical girl!"

"That was Antony!" Paula said. "And he was a man!"

"Don't quibble, darling," Splash told her. "We democratic columnists don't record history, we make it."

"By the way, Splash," Blake said. "Before you go—get your editor to pay O'Brien a couple of thousand for his story."

"Correction," Splash said. "I wasn't going and I didn't know we had to pay for it."

"The O'Brien Story," Blake pointed out, "is front page news as soon as it breaks that he's still alive."

The journalist clapped a hand to his head: "You're right! I am going—it's a scoop!"

When Splash had gone, Tinker shook his head, enviously: "They're going to be in the money!"

Blake looked at him. "You don't begrudge it to them, do you, Tinker?"

Blake's young colleague shook his head again, this time in violent denial; his conscience had been pricking him ever since that trip down the creek when he had been tempted by the seventy thousand pounds. Paula looked away, hiding a smile. Marion and Miss Pringle had followed Splash out and there was only the three of them in the room.

"That reminds me." Blake had noticed Tinker's discomfiture and already analysed it. "I'm putting through a rise for you."

Tinker flushed with pleasure. "A salary rise?"

"You've deserved one for a long time—and on this case you really earned it."

"Oh, I don't know—only did my job. I don't want a rise for that—how about the others?"

Blake said: "They'll get their usual increases at the usual time—but this is a special."

'It's a big surprise!" Tinker said. "I don't know what to say!"

"Five pounds a week more," Blake said. "Make a note of that, Paula, will you?"

Paula was already scribbling in the staff ledger.

"Thank you, chief!" Tinker went out, rubbing his hands. It was trite but true—honesty was the best policy.

BY A COINCIDENCE Anny was remarking the same truism to O'Brien as they rode on top of a bus towards Victoria Station.

"It is!" said O'Brien.

And self-consciously he ran his fingers through his prison-cropped hair.

THE END

Notes

6. The word is used as a synonym for "carefree" or "happy"; in the 1960s, "gay" was not widely employed as a reference to homosexuality.

7. This is a reference to COURIER FOR CRIME by Jack Trevor Story, THE SEXTON BLAKE LIBRARY 4th series, issue 432, published in June 1959.

BRED TO KILL

"Nope," I said, as we finished reading.

Blake and Tinker gave me questioning looks.

"Nope," I repeated. "It's all well and good, a fine yarn, but I'm still thinking about the cases involving dinosaurs."

Tinker laughed.

Blake sipped his brandy. He reached to a box on a table beside his chair and took out a cigar.

Stop! I thought. *Stop smoking! Stop drinking! You'll bloody die!*

But, of course, of all the many talents Sexton Blake possessed, dying didn't appear to be one of them.

I quashed a sigh and moved on.

"And with this next issue," I said, sliding the periodical from the binder. "I suppose I have to add the supernatural to the list."

"Or do you?" Tinker intoned in a spooky voice.

Blake said, "Perhaps you now begin to understand the nature of the Credibility Gap?" He lit the cigar because, during his absence, the atmosphere of his consulting room had obviously become disconcertingly breathable. "You see how Scotland Yard and other law enforcement agencies might struggle?"

I put a hand to my head and groaned. "If I accept that you exist—which I must, since you are expelling fumes right in front of me—then I guess I must also accept that other impossibilities can exist too."

"And horrors," Blake said, nodding toward the issue. "Martin Thomas, more correctly Thomas Martin, was particularly good at depicting the uncanny."

"He was also a staunch supporter of the New Order," Tinker added. "When the older readers objected to all the modernisations, he came out fighting and gave them what for."

Blake made a sound of agreement. "I'd briefed him. He understood the Credibility Gap and the perils that can, and did, emerge from it."

BRED TO KILL

by Martin Thomas (Thomas Martin)
THE SEXTON BLAKE LIBRARY 4th series,
issue 448 (1960)

THE FIRST CHAPTER

Dead as a fox.

DURING THE DAYS and nights of fear in the Bissett Heath countryside, the web of suspicion had two main strands. The fox-hunting feud and its alternative—a homicidal maniac. But there were also less tangible threads, more shrouded aspects. Of the Occult.

Yet what bizarre link could there be between a series of brutal murders . . . and supernatural warnings of an unprecedented threat to the human race?

What unique danger could concern the clairvoyant Mrs. Stevens, the truculent Mr. Johnson and the mysterious Mr. Ashley?

At the level of human action it was left to Sexton Blake to find a pattern and a meaning. To free a community of its terror and the Future of a dark horror.

It became the private investigator's mission to establish that even the shockingly savage killings were only a side-issue of this menace which had never before loomed over mankind.

While, behind and above the human tragedies and human investigations, brooded minds more than human.

And a killer prowled by night . . .

THE GRASS RUSTLED to his stealthy tread. In the night shadows of the coppice his eyes gleamed dully as they turned their gaze warily from left to right. Eyes set deep beneath the protruding ridge of his low forehead.

His mouth worked soundlessly. A wide-lipped, jutting mouth above a receding, almost non-existent chin. He crouched behind the cover of dense shrubbery, his body bent forward, his chest rising and falling quickly to the excited rhythm of his breathing.

Someone was plodding steadily along the earth path he was watching . . .

But from the sight and sounds of that person's slow progress the watcher's attention was abruptly distracted by a sound somewhere behind him. The faint, shrill sound of a distant whistle.

His sloping brow furrowed in a frown of painful thought. Hesitantly he remained motionless, waiting and pondering, one of his hands clutching a nearby tree-branch.

Then, as the whistle sounded again—faintly but insistently— he thrust his way back into the coppice and loped off between the trees. His feet padding silently in the direction of the imperative summons.

Unaware of having been watched, the man on the footpath went plodding on in his own direction.

This time allowed to go on living.

BILL MALVERN LEANED his muscular hands on the committee-room table and looked judicially up at the thin, angry face of Major Eyles, D.S.O., M.F.H.

Coldly and deliberately, Malvern said: "People like you should learn how it *feels* to be torn to pieces!"

The thrilled background comments of the assembled members of the anti-blood-sports committee froze into an awed hush.

Malvern, headmaster of the Bissett Heath secondary modern school, was their founder, chairman and moving spirit. And, physically, a very rugged type.

But, even after the Major's gate-crashing entry with his man Bingham—even after the last seven minutes of acrimonious argument—this climactic remark of Malvern's was of a kind to shake any resident of Bissett Heath.

The Major's opening gust, as he'd come storming into the committee-room—a front room of Malvern's house—was still fresh in their ears. Though normally even-tempered, the Major had now been furious.

"Malvern—this is your handiwork again, I suppose! Somebody's been opening up the earths again since they were stopped for tomorrow's hunt! I was prepared for it this time, though, and had my men go round again to check. They found that most of the earths stopped had been opened up again. Your damn' meddling handiwork—!"

He stood squarely in the middle of the room. A challenging, intimidating figure in twill breeches and tweed hacking jacket, his right fist gripping a formidable hunting-crop. But Malvern evidently didn't find him either intimidating or unanswerable.

"Not all of it, of course!" he said, while his wife and the committee looked on in tense expectancy. "But my personal responsibility—yes. I intended to make sure, Eyles, that tomorrow the fox you flushed would get something like an even chance to escape the kind of death planned for him! That he wouldn't be trapped in the surface coverts for your hounds to smell out and tear to pieces without a chance. It looks as though we shall have to try other methods, Eyles!"

"'Eyles'—you dare to call me that!" The Major, though less impressive now than in hunting pink, looked daggers at this familiarity. The social prestige of a Master of Fox Hounds was something only the uninitiated could fail to respect. "Your impudence is going to cost you dear one day, Malvern! You've set yourself up to destroy fox hunting in this area—to destroy something you know nothing about! I'm not sure whether you're really squeamish about the vermin or just trying to get yourself a reputation as a hero—"

Malvern grinned ironically. "Do we need another hero with you around, Major? A valiant St. George who—aided only by a pack of hounds, horses and a mob of so-called human beings—can chase one little fox to its bloody doom!"

Eyles glared. "In case you don't realise it, Malvern, foxes are a pest—a menace! A fox doesn't steal just one chicken per raid for food—he'll kill all the birds in a chicken run, for sheer pleasure—"

Malvern nodded. "Then that should give you a brotherly sympathy with him, Major! Don't you and your crowd of mounted sadists do just that—kill for sheer pleasure?"

The M.F.H. reddened. "You ignorant fool! You consider yourself fit to teach children. Don't you know that a fox hasn't the same capacity to feel pain that we have? For the simple reason that he hasn't a brain of human capacity!"

Again Malvern nodded. "Which is no doubt why you pit your brain against his—the appropriate level! His mental limitations give him an excuse for the senseless slaughter of chickens he can't eat. But you claim to have a brain of human capacity—to belong among homo sapiens, the mental peak of evolution. Yet while humanity is reaching towards the stars, the highly developed brains of your barbarous kind make an organised pleasure of terrorising and torturing an animal to death. That's a thousand times worse—a thousand times lower—than a fox's brute pleasure-killing. You make almost a religion of it with your sadistic rituals!"

Eyles, conscious of the committee members around him, gave an edgy laugh. "And because you haven't the guts to hunt, Malvern, you make a virtue out of that!"

"Guts?" Malvern asked quietly. "Does it take guts for a mob with a pack of trained hounds to chase one tiny animal to exhaustion? You've got guts for riding over rough country, Eyles—I'll grant you that. But you show it's the final killing that really matters to you, by the way you defend it and insist upon it and blood your children for it. Pest extermination is one thing; making a sensual pleasure out of bloodshed is another." His voice rose slightly. "Why the devil can't you enjoy a ride without killing something? Greyhounds chase a mechanical hare, paperchasers run after a human 'hare.' Why can't you simply chase another horseman? Do your guts demand blood?"

Bingham interrupted—jeeringly. "That's enough. Mister Malvern! The Major doesn't happen to be a ninny! He's the best rider in the county, and a D.S.O., too. What are you? Your job's to teach kids. You've only been here six months—and for about five of 'em you've been trying to show *men* how to live! You stick to what you understand, what you've got the guts for. We don't want a namby-pamby bookworm—"

Malvern's wife, pink with anger, laid a hand on the schoolmaster's arm, then ran out of the room. The M.F.H. was again orating a couple of minutes later when she came back into the room.

She was carrying a small, leather-covered box. Recognising it, Malvern tried to prevent what she intended to do. But already she had lifted the lid of the box and was exhibiting its contents.

A bronze maltese cross with a crimson ribbon attached. At sight of the decoration, the Major's eyes opened wide, and his groom exclaimed: "The Victoria Cross!" A brief, astounded pause, then Bingham added breathlessly: "Malvern, V.C.! So that's who—"

Dr. Richardson, one of the committee, broke in: "Malvern V.C., eh? Why haven't you let us know, Bill? You must be Malvern of Korea. Major Malvern—"

"Major Malvern!" Farmer Hoskins repeated. "That makes it *snap*, eh—Major Eyles, D.S.O.?"

"Not snap," Richardson grinned. "V.C.'s are trumps!" He gave a sibilant whistle. "So you're our namby-pamby bookworm, Bill? The man who led a Commando raid on a North Korean Commie camp, strangled a sentry, released a British brigadier and two colonels due for brain-washing— then blasted the camp with grenades while they got away! Remember reading the citation, Eyles?"

The M.F.H., abruptly reduced in heroic stature, muttered: "Huh! You strangle a man, Malvern, then make all this fuss about a few foxes!"

Malvern said evenly: "I didn't kill for pleasure, Eyles. I killed to save lives and the decencies—and I didn't enjoy doing so!"

Eyles' thin nostrils twitched; his cheeks still showed patches of colour. "V.C. or not, you're not going to spoil *our* enjoyment!"

"*Enjoyment*!" Malvern echoed scathingly. "I get rid of flies with a spray—but I know what I'd do to a kid I found tearing a fly's wings off for enjoyment! That's your warped mentality, Eyles."

It was now that Malvern leaned forward on the table and made his calm but memorable comment: "*People like you should learn how it feels to be torn to pieces!*"

His wife Linda had put down the case containing the Victoria Cross and came round the table.

"Major Eyles!" she said. "You're trespassing here. Will you and your man leave this house—or shall I telephone for the police to remove you?"

In a fury beyond words, Eyles turned on his heel and strode out, with Bingham close behind him.

The committee members immediately converged around the table, erupting questions and forebodings.

MRS. ELSPETH LANE Stevens, fifty, buxom and clairvoyant, sat in the midst of her Home Development Circle. Meditating.

The Circle consisted of eight members living within easy reach of Bissett Heath and Mrs. Elspeth Lane Stevens' cosy villa near the by-pass petrol station. The lighting in the room was mellow and subdued but not dim. Mrs. Stevens' psychic faculty functioned as well in daylight as in darkness. Neither was it inhibited by a blue hair-rinse, a liberal use of cosmetics or the equally plentiful jewellery adorning the medium's material form.

Mrs. Stevens had already dealt with this evening's usual quota of domestic and emotional problems troubling the assembled members. Those in need of advance information had been given the benefit of her precognition. And those impatient for the fulfilment of past predictions not yet materialised had been reminded that in the realm of clairvoyance mortal Time had no meaning.

With the routine business done, Mrs. Stevens had relapsed into a familiar silence, which no one dared to interrupt. It was now that Mrs. Stevens would seek enlightenment for her Circle upon the more ethereal questions of life, the wider destiny of humanity in general.

The five women and three men comprising the Circle waited with placid patience. There was now no need for impatience. On strictly personal problems Elspeth could produce uncanny insight and quite detailed foreknowledge; but on general human destiny and the Beyond her pronouncements were apt to repeat the accepted pattern, long familiar in the circles, societies, lodges and groups of occult research.

Tonight, however, there was to be a surprise! Tonight Elspeth had something new to say even on the fate of humanity at large. Her message was prefaced with a warning sigh. Her eyes opened half-way, with a peculiar effect of profound abstraction.

Then she said slowly, in a low monotone: "My friends . . . you know that as we now enter the Aquarian Age, mankind is due to enjoy an epoch of peace, prosperity and spiritual enlightenment. This has been revealed to humanity by the Masters, who, in their remote seclusion, have watched over the long human climb from darkness and ignorance to Light and Knowledge."

A pause, heavy with omen. "This, my friends, was pre-ordained. But, since Man has been given free will, a temporary halt or setback in human progress has always been possible and remains possible. Temporary—though, by our standards of Time, such setbacks can be long lasting through many generations.

"We know of historical examples of such setbacks and recoveries. Dark Ages followed by a Renaissance. Of an actual reversion in human personality and development. A man-made reversal of human destiny." Her voice faltered, then strengthened. "I am now given warning of a present danger so serious as to require the manifest intervention of the Masters themselves!"

From each of her hearers a shocked breath; a breath of awe tinged with fear, blended with another sigh from the medium. Her monotone continued.

"I feel I am *en rapport* with the Hierarchy. From the Hierarchy itself comes this message of warning . . . but comfort. A danger of peculiar character threatens human progress, a danger coming from those who would tamper with the inner secrets of life itself. And because this threat is against the upward progress of Man's destiny, because the threat has now crystallised, and in this country, one of the Masters, too, is here . . . more than one of the Masters . . ."

She shivered as if suddenly chill from loss of vitality, as if the strain of psychic absorption had drained the physical strength from her body. After another pause, she said slowly: "That is the warning and the comfort. A great, unique danger . . . but the intervention of the Masters to preserve Humanity's destiny, as always . . ." Again a trance-like pause. "But . . . why has this message been given to me? Why to such an obscure seeker after Light? Why have I been allowed to draw so deeply from the well of Knowledge? I . . . I feel . . . I sense . . . *it is because I am close to this danger . . .!*"

From the Circle came quick breaths of surprise and personal agitation.

". . . Because I . . . we . . . are physically close to this danger . . .! The peril that threatens humanity's path must be very near to us . . . but so will be our mentors of the Hierarchy. So will be the Masters who watch over our destiny and keep humanity moving ever forward . . . ever upward . . ."

Her eyes now opened fully. They scanned the small Circle. Unblinking, she intoned: "Tonight we of the Bissett Heath community stand at humanity's crossroads. Which way shall it be—forward or back? The danger is near, but be sure the Masters will also be near, to watch and to hear and to—"

With a quick, dwindling moan of overwrought nerves, Miss Mabel Price, who lived alone, slid off her chair and sprawled on the carpet in a faint.

WHEN THE HUNT found Bingham's body the next day, he'd been dead about eleven hours.

He was lying beside a fox-hole.

The smashed state of his body and the blood-streaks on a nearby tree suggested that he'd been swung against the tree with great violence before being strangled. He was nearly as maltreated, and quite as dead, as any hunted fox.

When the police had been fetched, Major Eyles had a brief but pointed conversation with the officer in charge, Sergeant James. As a result of this conversation, the sergeant made a personal call at Bissett Heath secondary modern school.

He wanted to see the schoolmaster who'd been known to protect a fox and strangle a man.

He was wondering whether one of those capabilities could provide a motive for the other.

THE SECOND CHAPTER

Reign of Terror.

THE DEPUTATION OF women came into Sexton Blake's private office in Berkeley Square *en masse*.

Beside his desk his honey-blonde secretary, Paula Dane, stood waiting to receive the visitors. And as the entire deputation spread around the room, receptionist Marion Lang was joined at the open doorway by junior partner Edward Carter.

"More chairs, Tinker!" Sexton Blake requested, and himself went out to help bring in further chairs from the reception office.

Marion, unashamedly curious, reluctantly returned to her switchboard. Tinker, at his chief's invitation, accompanied him back into his private office. In a couple of minutes the six ladies comprising the deputation were seated in a semi-circle centred on the desk, behind which Blake had now relaxed in his swivel chair.

"You'd like some coffee after your journey?" Blake suggested pleasantly. These women looked grim and worried. The range of their ages was fairly wide, but they had that look in common. Of grimness and worry.

A thin woman on his left was first to answer his question.

"No, thank you, Mr. Blake. We had some at the station!" She winced at the recollection of railway "coffee."

Smiling, Blake turned to a woman in the middle of the group, who was evidently leader of the party. A smartly dressed woman in her late forties. She opened her mouth to speak, then glanced hesitantly at Tinker and Paula.

Blake said reassuringly: "You can speak quite freely before my staff! Now, Mrs. Richardson—?"

The lady's immediate answer was not in words. Instead she brought from her travelling bag a bundle of newspapers, which she placed on the desk.

Impassively Blake spread the newspapers out flat before him like a hand of cards, their front pages uppermost. They were already in date order. Scanning them from left to right, Blake—with Tinker and Paula looking over his shoulders—read the banner headlines.

V.C. QUESTIONED IN MURDER INQUIRY.

With the sub-heading: Hunt Groom Dead beside Fox-hole.

Next issue: **MALVERN VC. ESTABLISHES ALIBI.**

Sub-heading: Says Police must Look Elsewhere.

Third issue: **ANOTHER FOXHUNTER MURDERED!**

Sub-heading: Ripper Atrocity.

Fourth issue: **BISSETT HEATH INVESTIGATIONS CONTINUE.** Sub-heading: M.F.H. suggests Feud by Anti-Hunting Fanatic.

Fifth issue: **ANOTHER BISSETT HEATH MURDER!**

Sub-heading: Third Victim Girl—New Motive.

Sixth issue: **REIGN OF TERROR.** Sub-heading: Is One Killer Responsible?

Seventh issue: **YARD TACKLES RIPPER CASE.** Sub-heading: County Police Baffled.

These seven issues were separated by intervals of several

days; in one instance, of a week. After his brief scrutiny, Blake looked up.

He said: "I know this is the matter you've come to see me about, Mrs. Richardson. But I'm not sure why. Particularly as Scotland Yard has now taken over the investigation. Why have you ladies personally concerned yourselves to the extent of wanting to commission a private investigation?"

Unsmiling, Mrs. Richardson looked up at him. "There are several reasons, Mr. Blake. The obvious one is that we all want this monster caught as soon as possible. There's hardly anyone in Bissett Heath who doesn't live in dread of where he may strike next. And after what happened to Mollie Chandler, you can guess how terrified the women and girls are of venturing out alone after dark—"

"Yes—I naturally appreciate all that. But now that the Yard—"

At last Mrs. Richardson did muster a trace of a smile. "You're too modest, Mr. Blake! One can hardly forget occasions when Scotland Yard has been 'baffled' and you've taken over—with spectacular success. But it isn't just that your record inspires a confidence we badly need just now. As a doctor's wife I know how badly that is—because there's been a run on sedatives since the second murder. We feel this case calls for a very special approach—"

"Oh?"

Mrs. Richardson looked at her fellow members of the Bissett Heath Women's Institute for support. "Well—look at it! The local police know our little community far better than a Scotland Yard man could hope to—yet they haven't found a motive. And it isn't the sort of case where a Scotland Yard detective can say 'Oh, Slim Jim cracks a crib like this—see where he was at the time of the crime!'"

Tinker grinned, and even Blake smiled broadly. "I'm afraid you do Yard men an injustice, Mrs. Richardson! They don't rely entirely on the *modus operandi*, you know—and they do catch many murderers!"

Mrs. Richardson shook her head. "Not this kind! *Not the kind that worries even the spirit world!*"

TINKER'S FAINT GRIN abruptly vanished. Replaced by a look of blank astonishment. Paula looked as though she couldn't trust her own ears. Even Blake's eyebrows lifted a minute fraction of an inch in acknowledgement of a certain surprise.

"The spirit world!" he repeated seriously. "Why do you say that?"

Mrs. Richardson turned to address a lady two seats away. "Tell him, Barbara!"

Barbara gazed earnestly up at the investigator. "'I—I suppose it's all right for me to talk about it. Not a breach of confidence, I mean. You see, I'm a member of Elspeth's Circle as well as the W.I.—"

"Elspeth's—?" Blake groped.

"Mrs. Elspeth Lane Stevens' Home Development Circle!" In a suitably solemn tone, Barbara—dark, thin and thirty—narrated her recollection of Mrs. Stevens' ominous pronouncement, as already recounted to her cronies of the Women's Institute. When she had finished, Blake nodded comprehendingly. The by-ways of his knowledge were extensive and peculiar, and there were few people he could not meet on their own conversational terms.

"The Masters . . .!" he commented. "Aren't those highly advanced beings thought to exist as hermits in remote retreats in Tibet—aloof from the ordinary affairs of life, in a state of *mano nasha*?"

"Not thought, Mr. Blake!" Barbara reproved him. "Known to exist! Mainly in the Himalayas, yes—though naturally the recent invasion of Tibet will have disturbed their seclusion.

They are aloof from the affairs of life only because they have already finished with a succession of human lives. They are here only to help others of us who are still on the way. To guide and protect human progress. And that's why one or more of them is expected to manifest in this country. It is in this country—near Bissett Heath—that a great danger to human progress now threatens!"

"According to Elspeth!" Tinker commented dryly—then flushed under Blake's warning glance.

"But surely," Blake said good-humouredly, "you're not suggesting that these Bissett Heath murders are a threat to human progress? They're hardly in the massacre category, are they? If they're sufficient to stir the Masters into activity, one wonders why they didn't do something about the slaughter of Passchendaele, the gas ovens of Auschwitz and Dachau and some other examples of mass extermination?"

"Perhaps they did, Mr. Blake—through human agents and the eventual course of events? Perhaps, too, a human agent is needed in this present crisis in human affairs? That human agent may be you!"

"But according to your er—Mrs. Stevens, the Masters are intervening in this affair! Why in this one and not actively in previous human crises?"

Barbara said, with great intensity: "Because this crisis, Mr. Blake, is quite unique! Nothing like it has ever threatened human progress before. Because, according to what Elspeth has been given, this threat is not against individuals but against the progress of the human race! It's a threat not against lives, but against the nature of life itself—!"

"So Elspeth says!" Mrs. Richardson broke in. "But what I'm concerned about, Mr. Blake—what most of us are concerned about—is this threat against individual lives! That, at least, is plain to see. It may have no connection with Elspeth's warning, but it certainly concerns everyone in Bissett Heath! Can you interest yourself in it, Mr. Blake?"

Blake gave a faint smile. "You've succeeded in interesting me! But let's keep our feet on the ground and consider these actual murders." He paused. "The first one—of the groom Bingham. A local schoolmaster was questioned rather personally about that?"

Mrs. Richardson sniffed. "Bill Malvern—yes! Major Eyles, the M.F.H., has got his knife into Bill because Bill founded our local anti-blood-sports society. My husband's a member of that, incidentally, and he told me about a row between Bill and Major Eyles the night before Bingham's body was found. Bingham was present at that quarrel and must have been murdered a couple of hours afterwards."

"Near a fox-hole! But what would a groom be doing at a fox-hole and after midnight?"

"Oh—Bingham was the Major's yes-man. He chipped into the quarrel. And the Major roped in everybody he could to stop the fox earths for the next day's hunt. Bingham must have been doing that when the killer got hold of him. But my husband was able to give Bill an alibi—as if he needed one! It's because he values life that Bill's against the wanton killing of even animals."

"And the second murder. That was the murder of the Major's huntsman—er—Villiers—"

"Yes. That did make it look like a feud against the hunt. But the third one was quite different. Mollie Chandler had no connection with hunting, no interest in it—and her killer couldn't have been one of Bill Malvern's supporters, because no one with the heart to care about foxes could have treated Mollie as she was treated."

Mrs. Richardson's face looked pale and strained. She glanced down at the handbag on her lap as if avoiding further reference to a subject too painful for discussion. When she looked up at Blake again, her kindly, shadowed eyes were pleading.

"Mr. Blake—my husband says that Bissett Heath needs a man of your stature and resource and—oh, everything. You can't have anything more urgent than this trouble of ours. Women and children daren't go out after dark now, and even men don't like going out alone. The police may get this monster in time, Mr. Blake—but if you can shorten the time by a day, it'll be—"

"Worth the effort! Yes—I agree. Steady now—I haven't started yet! And I naturally can't promise anything. But— perhaps you would like some coffee now? Paula?"

Half an hour later, stimulated with coffee and even more potently with hope, the deputation of worried women left Berkeley Square.

In a hurry to get back into their homes at Bissett Heath before nightfall.

AFTER HELPING PAULA escort them down to their taxi, Tinker followed her back into Blake's private office.

Blake was leaning back in his chair, thoughtfully smoking a cigarette. Tinker emitted a breathless whistle and perched himself on a corner of the desk. "Whew, chief—is this a case or or is this a case! The 'Masters' . . . a crisis in human progress . . . fox-hunting feuds . . . warnings from the Beyond . . .!" He frowned. Then he gave a sudden exclamation. "The occult! Think that could be the explanation of these killings, chief?"

"How d'you mean?" Paula asked, from her perch at the other end of the desk.

Tinker said quickly: "Black Magic! Elspeth What's-her-name may not be the only character around Bissett Heath having a dabble in the occult. And fox-hunters aren't the only people who go in for ritual killing—!"

Paula gave a gasp of excited comprehension. "Tinker! You're suggesting—"

"I'm suggesting nothing much, but I'm remembering ritual

347

killings in all kinds of black magic cults from Satanism to Mau-Mau! What other motive could there be—other than plain homicidal mania—to cover three such victims? Two foxhunters and a girl who—"

Blake said: "There could be many motives, Tinker, even if we assume all three people to have been victims of the same killer, which has yet to be proved, probable as it looks. Separately, the murders wouldn't involve any very extraordinary motives. A feud against fox-hunters would explain the first two; and a motive to explain the girl's murder has existed ever since there've been males and females. All we know of any occult associations with Bissett Heath has emanated from Elspeth Lane Stevens, and even she apparently wasn't referring to these murders in her ominous warnings. Let's forget all the paranormal suggestions unless and until we find personal reason to look beyond the normal, shall we?"

Tinker grinned. "Sure!" He slid off the desk. "Feet now firmly on the ground. But you said 'we'! Does that mean I'm coming with you?" His face wore an eager grin.

Blake returned the grin but shook his head. "Afraid not, Tinker. Too much doing here at the moment. But you, Paula, will be coming with me—what's the matter?"

Paula had given a sudden shiver. Now she gave him a smile that was too bright to carry conviction. "Oh—just felt chilly for a second. Someone walking over my—no, it was nothing. Why are you looking at me like that?"

Blake's intent scrutiny of her face relaxed. His brows were slanting as he got to his feet, and his mouth was a little straighter than usual.

Tinker broke the queer tension with a contrived laugh. "That local M.F.H. is going to feel a bit put out when you show up on his native heath!" he suggested.

"Oh —why?"

"He uses a pack of hounds and a troop of cavalry to hunt one fox—and you set about hunting a mass murderer, escorted by just one blonde!"

THE THIRD CHAPTER

Branches everywhere.

AS HER MOUNT broke into a canter, Paula Dane rose easily on her stirrups and smiled with exhilaration. Dressed in a pale lavender woollen sweater and jodhpurs, but bare-headed, she held her hands low and her back straight, her fair hair streaming in the breeze of her speed, her cheeks flushing to the fresh air and exercise.

Her knees felt the rhythmic muscular power of the grey Welsh cob as it quickened into a gallop. Then her smile widened in mischievous delight as the heavier pounding of overtaking hoofs drew close behind her and then immediately alongside.

"Easy!" Sexton Blake grinned down at her, from the superior altitude of his chestnut hunter, seventeen hands compared with the fifteen of the grey cob. "This isn't a race, but a tour of inspection!"

"Sorry, chief!" Paula smiled, looking anything but. "Must be the fresh air going to my head. Quite intoxicating, isn't it, after the Smoke!"

Taking the hint, she reined back slightly to a canter again, Blake's mount easily keeping level at only a trot.

Before them stretched the extensive heath which had given Bissett Heath its name. A broad expanse of mounds and hollows, with occasional flat stretches such as the one they were now riding over. An area of grass and bracken, shrubberies and spinnies, foot-paths and bridle-paths. A setting which had recently been the scene of two violent deaths—the other local murder having taken place on privately-owned farm-land.

It was the sort of terrain of which a tour of inspection by car would have been impossible and on foot a long, tedious, and tiring process. In this part of the country the horse was the most popular means of locomotion. Knowing this, Blake had told Paula to pack her riding kit for the trip.

Blake himself was wearing breeches and a hacking jacket. From the inside breast pocket of the jacket he now pulled out a folded sheet of paper. This was a map of Bissett Heath and environs, on which he had meticulously marked the spots at which three dead bodies had recently been found.

"Whoops!" Paula cried, as her mount suddenly shied. Then her fresh colour heightened a little as she met the gaze of two pairs of eyes at ground level. It wasn't the map which had alarmed the cob. It was the sudden sight of a courting couple, disturbed in their mid-afternoon preoccupation in a hollow of the heath. The looks which met Paula's glance were reproachful but not particularly embarrassed. The heath had its traditions hallowed by long custom, and it was for interlopers upon these to feel embarrassed!

Paula, duly flushed, murmured: "Excuse me!" Then she was safely past. When out of earshot of love's young dreamers, she slowed her cob to a walk and commented: "It evidently laughs at stranglers as well as locksmiths!"

"Eh? What does?" Blake murmured absently, studying the map.

"The thing that makes the world go round—you know!

What's happened around here doesn't seem to affect the romantic attractions! In daylight, anyway." She gave a slight shiver. "Must be a pretty desolate place after dark, though. Can't say I'd care to be on foot here then . . . alone!"

Stowing the map back in his pocket, Blake said: "Oh, you'd be all right while you were alone. It's if a certain homicidal character joined you that you'd need to worry!" They had reached the top of a slight rise, and he stopped his mount in order to look around him. Now he gestured in a leftward direction.

"Over there!" he announced sombrely. "That's where a girl died, wishing she were alone!"

BLAKE AND PAULA had arrived in Bissett Heath on the previous afternoon. Since then Blake had been busy picking up what further information was available in this fatal locality.

Bissett Heath was a bit too large to be called a village, and prided itself on being an Urban District, sparsely dotted with large country houses, secluded in their respective grounds. More than one man who made his money in London used Bissett Heath as a country retreat.

And large houses had staffs as well as families, so the possible suspects in the murder investigation were not limited to the confines of the farms and the "urban district." The range of suspects was wide enough to be a headache not only to the local county police, but to the Scotland Yard man seconded to assist them. That persistent veteran, Chief Detective Inspector Coutts.

It was over a week now since the last murder, and Blake had arrived too late to see any of the three victims of the murder series. Details known to the police were unhelpful or entirely negative. It was known that the three victims had been strangled, as well as otherwise maltreated in various ways. But there was no evidence at all pointing to any specific characteristics of the killer beyond the fact that he was obviously of considerable physical strength.

No fingerprints. No footprints—these having been obliterated in the struggle. In each and every instance this had happened.

"But at a little distance from the murders?" Blake had inquired. "No footprints there in any direction?"

"No," Coutts had answered flatly. "And that's another puzzle. Because the killer couldn't have got into a car in such places. Each murder was a long distance from any road. Each victim had been dead several hours when discovered—but surely there should still have been traces left of the way the killer departed. But there weren't any!"

"Could the killer have approached and left on horseback?" Blake suggested tentatively, looking from Coutts to the local sergeant. They were in the office of the little police station.

"Apparently not, Blake! The idea occurred to Sergeant James here, because this is horse country. But there were no recent hoof traces near the scenes of the crimes."

It was then that Coutts had offered to mark on Blake's map the exact place where each murder had been committed.

"M'm . . ." Blake murmured, studying the locations. "I see one of the murders took place on a path through a largish clump of trees! It's conceivable that a killer with some gymnastic agility might have swung himself up on a branch of the nearest tree, then have jumped from one tree to another so as to get away without leaving any footprints in the vicinity?"

AFTER A PAUSE the sergeant commented: "In this one instance I suppose it's just conceivable. But he'd have to be a very exceptional acrobat . . ." He added suggestively: "Even for an ex-Commando officer . . .!"

Blake gave him a quick glance. "You've still Malvern on your mind then—in spite of his alibi for the first murder?"

James made a grimace. "The man who gave him an alibi for that time was a close friend of his, somebody who also hates fox hunting!"

"Dr. Richardson, you mean. But even if an anti-hunting feud accounted for the first two murders, it wouldn't account for the third killing, would it? The victim, Mollie Chandler, had no connection with hunting, I understand?"

"True enough. Mr. Blake. But there's such a thing as deliberately confusing the issue. A man who'd committed two murders mightn't jib at committing a third in order to obscure the motive for the first two!"

Blake gave the sergeant a smile of appreciation. Country policeman though he was, James was evidently a man with a mind open to possibilities beyond the obvious.

James went on bleakly: "The post-mortem revealed a motive for the murder of Mollie Chandler—you can see the pathologist's report. But it doesn't necessarily follow that that motive was the only one or primary one. It could explain why he chose an attractive girl for his smoke-screen murder. A motive obvious enough to set the police looking for a psychopath, killing indiscriminately, instead of for a sane man with a special motive for the first two murders!"

"Nicely reasoned, Sergeant!" Coutts agreed.

"There's just one objection to it!" Blake suggested. "By obscuring the motive for those first two murders, the killer would also nullify their effect, if they'd been intended to frighten the fox-hunting fraternity out of their pastime! And, anyway, if the motive was to frighten the fox hunters and stop their activities, one would have expected the M.F.H. himself to be a victim?"

"Maybe!" James admitted. "But maybe the M.F.H. hasn't allowed the killer an opportunity." He frowned. "And it's still possible for him to become a victim, as long as the killer's at large!"

Blake shook his head. "I'm not with you there, Sergeant! If another hunter should be killed, it won't be for the anti-hunting motive, but because hunting people have happened to be about in the fields at night, stopping fox earths—and so been available to the killer. If there should be another murder among the fox hunters, you'll be able to stick to your anti-hunting motive only if you suggest two separate killers at large. One killing the hunters, the other responsible for the girl's death!"

James looked doubtful, and Blake pursued the point. "Don't you see, you can't credit one killer with the cunning to commit a camouflage murder and then expect him to be stupid enough to confirm the original anti-hunting motive by killing another hunter! That girl's death indicates the end of any planned hunter killings. Either because her death was intended to obliterate the feud motive for good—or because the anti-hunting feud never was a real motive anyway!"

Coutts rubbed at his ginger moustache, pondering. "Yes—that about sums it up, Blake!" he admitted slowly. "As you say, these hunting people are about in the countryside at all hours, and that could account for two of them being the first victims, even if the killer is an indiscriminate maniac. What it boils down to is this. It would be quite possible for a third hunting type to fall a victim while grubbing about the fox-holes, if there's a homicidal psycho at large. And such a murder, James, would mean either that the hunters and the Chandler girl were all victims of one indiscriminate lunatic—or that two killers are involved. One killing hunters to stop them hunting; the other responsible for the girl's death, with the obvious motive. And that's where we're left. Two killers or one? Two scheming killers—or one indiscriminate maniac?"

Blake looked at the map again. "One murder committed on a

path between trees. Two murders committed quite near clumps of trees, according to your marking, Coutts. Near enough for the killer to have jumped up to a branch in the same way?"

James answered. "No, Mr. Blake—at least, not in my opinion. He'd have to be a pretty marvellous jumper to reach a tree-branch in those two cases. My own opinion is that he ran away across the grass, and that grass had time to return to normal before the bodies were found and we arrived on the scene."

"And Malvern?" Blake inquired. "Did he have alibis for the second and third murders, too?"

James said without expression: "Yes. His wife gave him an alibi for each occasion!"

Blake's eyes narrowed. "I wonder just how you mean that! But I can hardly imagine his wife giving him an alibi for what happened to Mollie Chandler if she thought it possible for him to be responsible. That's the last kind of crime a wife would condone."

After a pause, Blake asked at a tangent: "And the people who found the bodies?"

Coutts said: "Oh—they all had alibis for the times the deaths must have taken place. I tell you, Blake, the more one digs into this affair the more mystifying it becomes. I only hope James is right about a crafty, rational killer. We've a hope of unravelling a rational plan, however crafty and involved. But if there should be another killing near here—an indiscriminate one—James and I are going to become aspirin addicts!"

That evening in the two Bissett Heath pubs, the *Crumpled Horn* and the *Piers Plowman*, Blake garnered nothing but a few half-pints of nutty draught beer and a harvest of speculative gossip. But he noticed that the local customers were careful not to leave the premises singly. And even a couple of rival Fleet Street men he recognised in the *Piers Plowman* left the pub together.

With Paula beside him, Blake, too, went out soon afterwards. They strolled along the High Street and down a dim side-street to the stables, where he booked a couple of mounts for the following afternoon. He was not very surprised to learn that the riding stables proprietor was not among Bill Malvern's supporters. The stables provided hired mounts for many people who could not afford to own horses but liked to follow the hunt occasionally as sightseers.

And now, on the following afternoon, here were Blake and Paula riding towards Sylvan Grove. The small avenue of close-growing trees in which Mollie Chandler had met violent death.

THE SHORTER LEGS of Paula's cob had to move faster to keep up with the long stride of Blake's hunter. But the two horses were together when their riders turned them into the Grove and along the footpath towards the fatal spot, Blake bending low to avoid the tree branches converging from either side.

The police had finished their investigations here. Had taken their measurements and photographs and soil samples—without any result but a comprehensive, unproductive dossier. To pinpoint the fatal spot, Blake had to count off the necessary number of trees down the path, in accordance with Coutts's directions.

But he and Paula had ridden only a couple of yards into the Grove when Blake stopped counting and his secretary's blue eyes opened wide in sheer astonishment.

Again strange eyes were contemplating her and Blake as they approached. But this time not from ground level. Not from ordinary pedestrian level. Not even from horse-rider level.

These strange eyes were looking down at them. From high among the bare branches of one of the tall trees!

This morning she and Blake had discussed the question of a man with the agility to spring up into trees, and here was a man looking much at home in a tree. A man of peculiar appearance, and doing one of the most peculiar things Paula had ever seen a grown man do. Either in a tree or anywhere else.

With his back to the broad tree-trunk, he was perched securely astride a thick branch. A brawny, shaggy, red-haired man in a wind-cheater and green corduroy trousers and with spiked climbing-irons strapped to the inner sides of his boots.

A large man who, when surprised by their arrival, had been holding up one hand, from which was suspended a fifteen-inch length of string. At the lower end of the string hung a small round object, swinging to and fro like a small boy's conker ready for a duel.

But this large male, if he was a duellist, had no visible opponent. What he did have was a visible —and audible temper!

He expressed it now in an indignant bellow.

"What the benighted demon do you mean, barging along here?"

THE FOURTH CHAPTER

Trial of Strength.

FOLLOWING BLAKE'S EXAMPLE, Paula urged her mount forward a few more yards and reined to a stop just before reaching the inhabited tree. Still following her chief's example, Paula looked up at the red-headed man with composed interest.

Then she said coolly: "Do excuse us! Are we interrupting a delicate bit of tree surgery—or are you just communing with Nature?"

"Or," Blake inquired blandly, mildly annoyed by the ferocious greeting, "are you merely on a visit to the old ancestral home?"

The man aloft on the branch spluttered with fury, and nearly lost his balance and his "conker"—which they now saw was actually a metal ring, apparently of gold.

Glaring down at them, the shaggy man ground out, in a tone of barely-suppressed rage: "Dear sir and madam, I happen to have been communing with the pulse of the infinite cosmos! And I hate being disturbed, sir and madam, by any materialistic, earthbound mortals who care to make their mundane way to the scene of my researches! Are you capable of understanding that?"

"I think so!" Blake claimed amiably. "But are you capable

of coming down to earth and explaining yourself more fully?"

"If you've squatter's rights to that tree," Paula promised, "we won't try to rob you of them!"

With an unethereal grunt, the communer with the cosmos stowed his string and ring away in a pocket of his windcheater. Then, with an oblong leather case slung on a strap over one shoulder, he suddenly dropped till he hung suspended with his large hands grasping the tree-branch.

His large boots were now on a level with Blake's head, and he opened his legs until the detective's head was between the pair of climbing irons, like a nut between nut-crackers.

"I shouldn't!" Blake said mildly, his glance taking in the threatening spikes at either side of his face.

"I really shouldn't!" Paula agreed.

Apparently the red-head agreed too, because he swung his legs clear, dropped again to grasp a lower branch, then finally dropped to the turf beside the horses.

Almost immediately, his breathing hardly quickened, he turned on his heel to face Blake. His right hand shot out to grasp the hunter's rein, but it missed and instead got hold of the throat-lash.

The horse tried to swing its head away. Blake was already dismounting. Now on foot, he stepped towards the shaggy man and advised him: "That's enough!"

The reddish, square face wreathed into a taunting grin. "Oh— is it? Not unless you're now going to clear away from here!"

His large, hairy hand tightened its grip on the narrow throat-lash. Blake's right hand came up. Its long, muscular fingers closed about the thick, hairy wrist.

Blake's grip also tightened.

FOR PERHAPS THREE seconds the big man's grin did not alter. Then, as he maintained his grasp on the throat-lash and Blake slightly increased the strength of his grip, that taunting grin faded a little and a glitter came into the angry eyes.

The two horses and Paula, like the two men, were almost motionless now. But there was tension in Paula's attitude as she watched the duel of wills and strength taking place just beneath her.

It was an odd spectacle, and from a distance it would have been difficult to discern that a duel was in progress. The men's feet were set rock-steady on the path. Their stances were now almost statuesque. On Blake's lean face there was just a trace of a speculative smile.

"No?" he asked unemotionally.

"No!" the red-haired man ground out. His teeth and open lips set into a defiant snarl and his knuckles whitened around the throat-lash.

Blake's only apparent reaction was a tautening of his jaw muscles. But that other muscles had also tautened was shown when his antagonist's teeth opened to let out a gasp and his ruddy face visibly paled.

"No?" Blake invited again.

"No—damn you!" The shaggy man bunched his biceps to maintain his grip on the throat-lash, as though that length of leather were the symbol of eternal power and prestige.

Now Blake's brows came together, his right shoulder lifted very slightly, and the fingers around the thick hairy wrist clenched crushingly together.

It was Paula's turn to gasp now—and the shaggy man's turn to yelp. Numbed, whitened fingers released their grasp of the throat-lash and uncurled.

Blake released his grip on the thick wrist. The man in the windcheater backed a pace. Blake stepped forward, paused a moment to toss his mount's rein to Paula, then turned to face the furious, frustrated tree-climber.

"You were going to explain!" Blake said softly.

"*Was* I!" the man mouthed—and swung a hammer-blow at the detective's head.

Blake evaded it easily enough with a barely perceptible movement of the head. But he did at last look just a trifle annoyed.

When the red-head tried another ponderous blow, Blake beat him to it with a left hook, followed by a right cross which connected explosively with an aggressive jaw and laid its owner flat on his back.

Red-head must have spent his formative years among mules, because even now, after a long count, he climbed up on to unsteady legs and made a forlorn stagger towards Blake.

With a grin of amused admiration, the detective gave him a push that sat him down solidly and finally on the ground.

Whistling sibilantly, Blake stood looking down at him for a patient minute while he shook his shaggy head and muttered breathlessly.

Then Blake said, pleasantly enough: "Now let's hear what you were doing up in that tree, so near the spot where a murder was committed, that made you object to our arrival on the scene!"

IT WAS ANOTHER full minute later when the sitting man spoke aloud.

"Well," he admitted, with an amiable grin, "it was a fair fight, and you seem to have won the right to question me! First you'd better know who I am." His remarks seemed to vary between the furious and the stately. Now he was in his stately mood. "My name, sir, is Volpone Johnson. Johnson with an aitch!"

"Oh!" Blake acknowledged. "I'm sure Ben 'Volpone' Jonson would have regretted that aitch!"

"Not more than I've regretted the 'Volpone,' sir! Parents can carry enthusiasm to ridiculous lengths. However, the name may be familiar to you?" The suggestion sounded hopeful but not sanguine.

Regretfully Blake shook his head. "Ben's, yes. But Volpone Johnson with an aitch—no! Should it be familiar to me?"

The beaten man shrugged. "Perhaps not. It's a small number of fellow spirits—I use the word 'spirits' loosely, of course— who know of my researches."

"Researches!" Blake eyed him with interest. Could it be possible that he himself was a fellow spirit of this fellow on the ground? That this red-head was on a similar errand to his own? "You mean," Blake asked, "that you're investigating the murder which was committed here last week?"

Mr. Johnson looked at him with scorn. "My dear sir, I wouldn't concern myself with anything so sordid and earthy! Why—I was in that tree to sever my contact with earth and attune myself with the Infinite!"

"*Not* to play conkers!" Paula commented. 'Well, it wouldn't be fair with a gold ring, would it? Even a baked conker couldn't be expected to stand up to that!"

Red-head looked up at Blake sympathetically. "Your lady friend is mad, of course! Still, with such beauty I suppose you can't expect everything. But you look sane and intelligent, sir. No doubt you recognised that I was practising radiesthesia?"

"Of course!" Blake assured him, solemnly and soothingly. "What particular divination test were you making with the pendulum?"

Volpone Johnson scrambled up on to his knees and leered at Paula with triumphant pleasure. "You see!" he cried. "You see, madwoman—*he* knows! *He* understands!" His leer vanished and he clapped a hand to his brow like an old Lyceum tragedian. "Conkers!" he repeated bitterly. Mercurially his expression changed again, to one of profound revelation. "The test I was making, sir," he breathed, "was to try to pinpoint the exact location of . . . IT!"

Paula's cob twitched its ears and inspected the kneeling man with one large brown eye.

He returned the inspection with interest. "Noble creature!" he exclaimed. "Lucky creature—to be presented with bi-focal lenses from Nature's store without benefit of opticians! How I hate the trade! One of those eye-quacks laughed when I told him I was one of the most percipient visionaries of the age. He said I had a distinct squint and—"

Desperately Blake broke in: "You were trying to pinpoint the exact location of IT! Yes. And what is IT?"

The man called Johnson got to his feet and looked at Blake as though relegating him to Paula's position in the mental handicap.

"It?" he repeated pettishly. "Why IT, of course! The direst menace to cosmic progress since . . . since *'you were a tadpole and I was a fish, in the Paleozoic time.'* I quote Langdoh Smith. The direst menace . . . and its site is not far from here!"

Automatically Blake and Paula looked at each other. Through both their minds flashed the same name. Elspeth.

Mrs. Elspeth Lane Stevens, with extra-sensory perception of a unique calamity centred upon Bissett Heath.

Here, in shaggy Mr. Johnson, was another of them.

THE PUGNACIOUS PROPHET was now stooping to unstrap his climbing-irons. When he straightened up, hefting the irons in his hairy hands, Blake kept a keen eye upon him. Those irons could be lethal weapons in the hands of a man homicidally inclined. But Mr. Johnson dropped them on to the ground beside his oblong leather box.

"A dire menace . . ." Blake repeated. "Worthy of the attention of the Masters?"

Volpone Johnson showed no surprise. He merely sniffed with disdain. Then he said: "You've heard the fiddle-faddle put about by that woman in the er—village! My dear sir—a mere

366

planchette manipulator, a tea-leaf reader! Women's intuition—hah! Psychic research is a serious business, worthy of Johnson and his radiesthesia and—"

Blake smiled satirically. "I've heard of dowsing for water or minerals with a pendulum—even for murdered bodies or lost children. How do you propose to pinpoint IT by that means?"

Johnson stared. "In the same way, of course! By the same method that has brought me here, stage by stage, from Pyecombe, where I first got the message. As I've got nearer and nearer to Bissett Heath, so the pendulum has given stronger and stronger responses, exactly as it did when I held it over a map of England. And that's not all! The etheric vibrations have got stronger and plainer on the tape, too!"

"Tape?"

"Of course!" The pendulum expert picked up the oblong leather box and opened its lid. Blake saw now that the box contained a small battery-operated tape-recorder. Johnson said: "Listen to what I recorded here only this afternoon—up in that tree! I get better results that way!"

He switched the instrument on, and Blake and Paula duly listened. From the small loudspeaker came a faint hum, punctuated at intervals by faint, distant sounds—the bark of a dog, the shout of a child, the whine of a car engine. Nearer at hand, rustling, scraping noises, which Blake took to be the sounds made by Johnson himself in his movements among the branches.

But on Johnson's face was again that look of triumph, of exaltation. "You hear them?" he exclaimed. "The sound-symbols? The impressions of the etheric vibrations? Every symbol with its story to tell. A story getting plainer, clearer, as I near the apex of the cosmic disturbance! Hear it . . .!"

With entire lack of expression, Blake and Paula glanced at each other again.

"You've certainly something there!" Blake admitted ambiguously.

Triumphantly again, Johnson leered at Paula. "I told you—he knows! He understands!"

As he switched off the recorder with smirking satisfaction, he listened attentively for Blake's next comment.

Blake said: "Ben Jonson called his play '*Volpone, or the Fox.*' Do you consider yourself a fox? There's a feud going on here against fox hunting. How do you feel about it?"

Johnson glared. "Fox hunting? '*Detested sport, that owes its pleasure to pain.*' I quote William Cowper. That's how I feel about it!"

"How long have you been in this vicinity?"

"About a month."

"Have you joined the local anti-blood-sports society?"

The prophet scowled. "I join no worldly organisations!"

"And you wouldn't carry on a freelance feud of violence against fox hunters?"

Johnson glared again. "Am I a man of violence? I leave those barbarians, sir, to their inevitable retribution. They are making their own Karma and will reap what they sow. My concern, as I've mentioned, is with the etheric, the Infinite. With principles, not persons!"

Blake gave a regretful smile. "I'm afraid my concern is with principles *and* persons! So I must ask you to come along with me to see Sergeant James. We'll see what he thinks of your explanation, shall we?"

For a moment it looked just as though Volpone Johnson would again forget that he wasn't a man of violence. But evidently practical considerations did affect him after all. He caressed his jaw reminiscently and ruefully, then picked up his climbing irons.

"I'll carry them!" Blake offered. After a slight hesitation,

Johnson handed them over. "You'll be able to walk fast enough to keep up with us," the detective said. "But not to get away from us!"

With the irons in one hand, he remounted. Philosophically Johnson started off beside the walking horses and kept level with Blake's knee.

The tour of inspection was cut short, but on the way back Blake took a circuitous route along a curving track around an extensive, shrub-grown hollow.

Suddenly the air beside his left ear twitched as a bullet missed him by an inch. A fraction of a second later there was the whiplike crack of the report.

It was over before he had time even to flinch. Then, while Paula and Johnson were still staring in amazement, Blake heeled his hunter into a canter along the rim of the hollow, peering down for a sight of the unseen gunman.

He had not far to look. Coming up the slope of the hollow was a man in tweeds. A man carrying by the ears a dead rabbit, and with his other hand a .22 target rifle. Blake recognised him.

He was Major Eyles, D.S.O., M.F.H.

THE FIFTH CHAPTER

The Tibetan.

AMBROSE LEEMING, DOCTOR of Science and Fellow of the Zoological Society, looked down at the puzzled rat.

Mowbray House was quiet. Leeming's "daily woman" had returned to her home in Bissett Heath. Croft, his resident odd-job man, was out in the private menagerie, feeding the collection of animals currently being used in Leeming's biological research.

With the day's serious work finished, and with no one present to distract him, Leeming was relaxing with a simple experiment that was amusing as well as instructive, while part of his mind pondered on a much bigger problem.

The rat was enclosed in an experimental contrivance laid flat on the laboratory table. It consisted of a maze through which the rat had to puzzle his way in order to reach the bait at the end of the correct route. By such a simple test, repeated a few times, it was possible to learn a great deal about the rodent's ability to remember and to profit from experience.

This rat, like most of his fellow rats, proved himself no fool. And his antics provided the biologist with a kind of mental doodling while his main concentration was on the other, vital, problem.

The laboratory was a room in which a nervous or imaginative person, less dedicated to its subject, might not have found it so easy to relax. Glass cases contained specimens of many forms of life; insects, fish, reptiles and small mammals.

One row of cases, fixed to a wall, contained examples of artificial modifications of type, deliberately produced by man by means of selective breeding. Preserved by the skill of the taxidermist, some of these specimens gave an uncanny impression of life. A Japanese waltzing mouse, posed as if in its frenzied dance. A telescope-eyed fish from China, its one Cyclops eye staring with almost hypnotic effect. A greyhound and a bulldog. A fantail Pigeon; a tumbler.

On the opposite wall were hung framed anatomical drawings of various species.

At the far end of the room another row of cases exhibited preserved specimens of primitive creatures still existing. The Australian duckmole, or duck-billed platypus; the horseshoe crab; the porcupine ant-eater; the opossum.

On this end wall hung a long chart, tracing the evolution of life through its various stages. From the single-celled amoeba, through the invertebrates, the fishes, the batrachian frogs and toads, the reptiles, the birds, the mammals—to the emergence of Man.

Between these four walls and the rows of cases stood the table on which the maze was now laid, and a long laboratory bench equipped with the apparatus of Leeming's more intricate researches.

Researches which speeded up the evolutionary process by artificially induced mutations of short-lived animals, the quick succession of their generations providing comparatively prompt answers to his questions. Here the humble mouse and rat had yielded awesome hints of the secrets long hidden in the genes of their species. Here significant pointers had been discovered not merely to the "why" of evolutionary changes—but the fundamental "how."

Ambrose Leeming—totally absorbed in the profound quest to which he had dedicated his years, his mind, his studies and his energies—was nearer than the world knew to answering questions which had hitherto baffled the mind of Man.

He was nearer than even his fellow researchers guessed to revealing the biological mechanism of the living cell.

Alone in this laboratory, he was reaching the nucleus of Life itself.

But now he looked up from the rat, who had successfully groped his way through his own little maze. Leeming, who was successfully groping his way through a maze aeons of years old and of immense complexity, looked up and gave a sudden shiver.

He had just had that eerie feeling which had recently come to him quite often when he'd been alone.

The feeling of *not* being alone!

Uneasily he looked all around him. The bald area of his scalp was dewed with a thin film of perspiration. Frowning, his eyes under the greying brows a little too bright, he walked steadily along one side of the laboratory and back down the other side. On the way he peered everywhere that a possible watcher could conceivably have hidden himself.

But there was no other human being in the laboratory.

No other human being visible to his eyes.

GIDEON ASHLEY, CITY of London financier, was a man of sober expression and dress. Silver-haired at only fifty, thin-featured and erect, he enjoyed a reputation for personal probity which had gained his financial house a prestige virtually equivalent to gilt-edged security. His name was synonymous with integrity, and his mode of life, like his personal appearance, had done nothing to lower that status.

He drove south-west through Exeter and kept to the A30 across Devon and into Cornwall. The speed of his Rolls never rose above forty-five miles an hour, for it was not in his temperament to hurry.

At Launceston he stopped for a rest and a meal. Then, still keeping to the A30, he drove more directly south towards Bodmin. But on Bodmin Moor, some twenty miles short of the county town, he turned off the A30 and dropped his speed to thirty as he followed the succession of deteriorating roads to his destination.

It was dusk when he stopped the car with its headlamps illuminating a pair of wrought-iron gates set back in a grey stone archway. An oak panel bolted to one of the gates bore faded lettering which the car's lights made just readable.

"*The Hermitage.*"

It was an apt name for this isolated dwelling set remotely and austerely back from the unfrequented moorland road.

Ashley switched off his engine, got out of the car, and approached the entrance archway. His right hand grasped the bell-pull set in the stone-work to the right of the gates.

There was no quick response, but he didn't ring again. Patiently he waited till footsteps sounded on the inner drive, becoming slightly louder as they drew nearer—though even then the sound amounted to no more than a patter of footwear without heels.

Then, in the light of the headlamps, a human figure was clearly visible on the other side of the gate-bars. A man wearing sandals and a monk's robe.

His head was shaven and his features were Mongolian. At sight of the visitor his slitted eyes narrowed still further as his mouth curved in a smile of welcome. Quietly he murmured the ritual words: "*Om mani padme hum.* Hail, the jewel in the Lotus."

Ashley repeated the phrase, then waited with patience while the custodian of the gates unfastened the lock for him to enter. While the monk dragged one gate back, Ashley himself pushed the other clear of the drive.

Three minutes later he was again climbing out of the Rolls, this time before the open door of the grey old house. A house which centuries before had also sheltered monks, though of a very different order.

After a wash and a very plain meal, Ashley waited for his original guide to conduct him on the last stage of his journey. To the climax and purpose of his visit.

This time he, like his guide, went on foot. Together they walked along a dimly visible path between shrubberies once carefully tended but now run wild. The present occupiers of the Hermitage had arrived here too recently to have been able to repair the neglect of years. As Ashley knew, it was only recently that these present occupiers had arrived even in the Western hemisphere.

In the shrouded dusk a darker structure loomed up ahead. On getting closer, Ashley realised it to be a summer-house. A suitable place to visit on a summer afternoon, but this was the dusk of winter.

As the cold penetrated to his bones, Ashley drew his overcoat tight around him and fastened a loose button. Now they were at the entrance of the summer-house, approaching a couple of wooden steps which led into its dark interior.

With his pupils now dilated in the darkness, Ashley could get a vague impression of an open doorway. Then, from the pitch darkness of the interior, a voice greeted him. A voice he had come many miles to hear.

The voice of Tsong-Ko-Te. The Lotus-born.

IN A LOW, thin tone, the voice uttered the same greeting which the guide had murmured at the gateway. As before, Ashley echoed it, then waited in silence.

The monk escorting him now reached out an arm and fumbled with his hand at the nearer doorpost. There was the click of a switch and the summer-house was suffused with the faint glow of a low-power lamp suspended from the domed ceiling. In this light it was possible to see that hardly any of the panes of the four windows now remained intact. Many were missing altogether; others were fragmentary or cracked. No attempt had been made to block the apertures or to repair the gaping panels and panes of the door. The temperature inside the summer-house must have been only half-a-dozen degrees above freezing point, but it didn't seem to affect the solitary human occupant.

He was a man clad in a simple saffron robe, sitting cross-legged on a cushion. His head was hairless, but his white moustache and beard were long and untrimmed. His features were Mongolian and, like his frame, gaunt to the point of emaciation.

He sat motionless, as oblivious of the frigid temperature inside the summer-house as of the material world outside it. His posture, abstraction and asceticism were like those of the "entombed ones" in caves of the Himalayan hills, almost totally absorbed in mystic meditation as they sought the perfection of the central inner consciousness, the realisation of the Absolute.

But, as Ashley knew, this was no mere monk or even Initiate, still involuntarily tied to the Wheel of Life on the long and painful quest of Enlightenment. This was one of the *Bodhisattva*, one of the Enlightened Ones, voluntarily renouncing the bliss of Nirvana, freely electing to continue on the incarnate plane as guardians of mankind's evolution to similar enlightenment.

This was one of the *Arhats* or Masters of the Occult Hierarchy, involved with human life and the material world only as one of the custodians and guides of its destiny.

That his present body happened to be Mongolian was incidental and irrelevant. Living in the world were other Masters of different physical races and traditional cultures, secretly using their esoteric influence for the advancement of the whole human race.

It was also incidental and irrelevant that Gideon Ashley was an Englishman. He was here as an Adept.

It was as an Adept that he exercised his financial power—using it as a counter-balance of finance employed for purely material ends, and helping to shape, as far as one man could, an economic system conducive to justice and integrity.

Now he stood silent, not daring to break into the abstraction from which Tsong-Ko-Te was emerging. It was Tsong-Ko-Te, himself who spoke next. In English, slowly and dispassionately.

He said: "The man is already mentally abnormal, of course; a fanatic of retrograde purpose. But what he has discovered is too dangerous to allow us compassion towards him. It is necessary that his dangerous knowledge be placed beyond the reach of even his own mind—beyond recollection or rediscovery. It is necessary that his mind be quite . . . deranged!"

With an equal lack of emotion, Ashley nodded in understanding. But still he remained silent.

The Arhat's deep-set eyes glimmered from the shadows under his brows. His thin, remote voice came again.

"You will return to the danger zone to tidy up the material aspects of the crisis. Now you wish to speak. I am listening."

Unhurriedly, himself now oblivious of the cold, the surrounding darkness and the escort beside him, Gideon Ashley began to talk.

THE SIXTH CHAPTER

Quests cut short.

A LEG ELEGANTLY draped in lovat worsted hung over an arm of Sexton Blake's swivel chair, idly swinging. A cup of "elevenses" coffee stood on Sexton Blake's desk, idly steaming. The owner of the leg and prospective imbiber of the coffee held a telephone receiver close to his left ear—and listened far from idly.

His right hand scrawled rapidly on a memo pad with a stylish ball-point pen. His blue eyes and the slight curve of his mouth expressed a lively satisfaction in receiving this call. Edward Carter, blond and rugged, intelligent and energetic, had felt a trifle aggrieved at being left out of the Bissett Heath investigation. Now the grey winter morning had suddenly been brightened by this phone call from his chief—with work for the junior partner concerning the Bissett Heath affair.

"It's purely routine, Tinker!" Sexton Blake had warned him. "Just a tedious bit of background inquiry—"

"Suits me!" Tinker had grinned. "The background's better than no ground at all. I'm in! So—?"

"Take down this short list," Blake had told him. "There are several people in and around Bissett Heath who can't be regarded as strictly local residents. I want you to dig out all you can about their previous backgrounds and personal antecedents. The first is a psychic individual named Volpone Johnson. Johnson with an aitch and—"

"Come again?" Tinker begged. "Vol—?"

"—Pone. Volpone!" Blake sighed. "Just you should see a play instead of a Bardot film! Mr. Johnson has been in Bissett Heath about a month, as the local police sergeant confirms. Johnson is a muscular character who claims to be psychic—"

"Uh-huh!"

"Yes. He also claims to have come here from Pyecombe, in Surrey. He seemed to think I should have heard of him before we met, so he should presumably be fairly well known in Pyecombe. A fellow of his appearance and temperament would be fairly well known even if he wasn't psychic!" Blake gave a concise description of Mr. Johnson's physical appearance and memorable temperament. "The question is: Is he a genuine psychic on a genuine mission here, a crank who sincerely fancies himself to be on a genuine mission—or a clever actor willing to be taken for either a psychic or a crank but with a very different motive? Details of his antecedents should serve to settle that question."

"We hope! Next?"

"Next is a biologist, with a largish house near here. Been living here about two years, but not taken to the local bosoms because he's apparently one of nature's recluses, wrapped up in his work. Staff, one resident odd-job man and one daily woman. Paula had a talk with the daily woman after 'accidentally' colliding with her outside the post office. The daily woman keeps strictly to the domestic quarters of Mowbray House, 'an' 'as an 'orror of the menagerie!'"

"Menagerie?"

"Animal specimens for biological research, presumably

guinea-pigs, rats and other creatures for laboratory use."

"Huh!" Tinker grimaced. "Risky to have four legs in that part of the world, eh? And the biologist—?"

"Ambrose Leeming. Doctor of Science, but I don't know of what university. But he's also a Fellow of the Zoological Society, and you'll be able to check that easily enough. I understand he came here from King's Lynn. Check—"

"Chief—you're considering him as a suspect?"

"Sergeant James says he and his servant Croft have given themselves mutual alibis for the murders, and also that neither of them seems to be physically powerful enough to have committed those atrocities. But who can estimate the limit of any man's strength during a spasm of homicidal mania? Find out what you can about Leeming and his servant—if the same servant was with him in King's Lynn. And if this proves to be a long job I'm giving you, ask Nick Reuter if he can lend a hand."

Tinker admitted: "I've an idea he'll be wanted! Next please!"

"Next is a person who just missed putting a bullet through my head yesterday afternoon—"

"A bullet! You really are making friends down there, aren't you? What's happened to the man who missed?"

"Oh—he's still at large! He's Major Eyles, D.S.O., M.F.H. He's given a very convincing demonstration of being more stupid than homicidal. He didn't aim at me, it appears. He was out hunting with a point two-two rifle—"

"Rifle! I thought it simply wasn't done to hunt foxes with a rifle?"

"It isn't. He was hunting rabbits—in a hollow of the heath. Apparently it didn't occur to his mind that bullets which missed the rabbits would shoot up across the path around the hollow. I happened to be on the path, with Paula and someone else, when this particular bullet missed a rabbit!"

"Lucky it missed you, too! You don't think this fellow just

thought up a feasible excuse for an 'accidental' elimination of a nosey investigator?"

"It's conceivable, I suppose!"

"Which makes two people to mark with a query! Is Johnson a genuine psychic, a crank or a clever actor? Is Eyles a thoughtless goon or a very thoughtful potential killer? Where do I check on Eyles?"

Blake said: "He has a flat in Curzon Street. See what you can find out about his pastimes in Town outside the hunting season."

"Okay. That's three of 'em. Any more?"

"Just one. A financial tycoon with a house in Eaton Square and a country retreat near Bissett Heath. He's had this particular country retreat only about six months, which makes him the most recent arrival to take up residence here other than Johnson. Make the same routine check about this man's Town life. His name is Gideon Ashley. That's the lot then, Tinker. You can phone results to the *Spread Eagle* Temperance Hotel here. The only hotel here."

"Right! How are things going down there, chief?"

"So far we're still on the spadework, trying to get level with the police regarding local information. We're under quite a handicap. The three murder victims were buried before we arrived and there's been literally no evidence for me to examine. We've had to start from scratch on a cold trail, and first we have to get to know the natives and obtain a reliable picture of the situation around here. The police had an earlier start and the advantage of reinforcements, but so far their only move has been to organise night patrols of the area by constables working in pairs."

"And your ideas?"

"Frankly pretty nebulous at the moment. The difficulty in this case is that were not up against a criminal with a known specific motive and a rational plan, which could be understood and countered. We're trying to identify a killer or killers who simply pounced on the nearest victim available. And there are other elements in the case which lift it right out of the ordinary criminal category. It has suggestions of occult associations which remind me of the Evil Eye affair in Scotland."[8]

Tinker whistled. "Whee-ew! I thought the natter about Mrs. Elspeth Stevens' clairvoyant warnings was just a bit of female superstition. But this character Johnson claims to be psychic, too, so maybe—"

Blake interrupted good-humouredly: "Leave the psychic aspects to me, old son! You get busy on the down-to-earth inquiries I've given you!"

Tinker grinned. "Suits me! Stand by for results with my well-known speed and efficiency! Cheerio, chief!"

He was still wearing a faint grin when he re-cradled the receiver and leaned back to scan his list of people to be investigated.

Volpone Johnson, Ambrose Leeming, Major Eyles, Gideon Ashley . . .

Tinker was reaching for the phone again, with the intention of calling Nick Reuter, when the buzz of the bell forestalled him. Glancing ruefully at his cooling coffee, he lifted the receiver.

"Tinker!" It was Marion Lang's voice, from the switchboard in the reception office. "There's a gentleman here who wants to see you. He apologises for not having made an appointment, but would be grateful if you'd spare him a few minutes."

Tinker frowned. He'd enough on his plate already. Then an odd thought struck him. "You say he wants to see *me*? Not the chief?"

"No—you! Mr. Carter, he said."

"Oh—you told him the chief was away?"

"No, I didn't! I—I suppose he either knew it, or prefers to see you anyway!"

Tinker's frown deepened. "Huh—then I suppose I'd better

see him! Bring him in. What did you say his name was?"

Marion answered: "I didn't! But it's Mr. Gideon Ashley!"

Tinker's phone smacked down on its cradle. His coffee continued cooling, forgotten. There was still a furrow between his brows when the door opened and Marion ushered a visitor inside. After murmuring: "Mr. Ashley!" she vanished back to her switchboard.

Tinker found himself looking at a man in a black overcoat, carrying a black, narrow-brimmed bowler hat. A man with silvery hair but unlined features. Tinker found himself being studied by dark, speculative eyes.

The visitor closed the door behind him and took a soft step across the pile carpet. On his face there was a faint smile.

Tinker took a grip on himself. He said formally: "You're Mr. Ashley? Mr. Gideon Ashley?"

"I am!" The faint smile strengthened a little.

"And you wished to see me?"

"In a way!" Gideon Ashley studied the younger man's face almost with compassion. "But only to save you unnecessary trouble!"

"Trouble!" Again Tinker took a grip on himself, feeling strangely inadequate and ineffectual. "How?"

The visitor's eyes narrowed. His shoulders moved in a barely perceptible shrug.

Then he said: "I understand that my affairs are of professional interest to you! That being so, I can surely save you a lot of needless work by putting myself at your disposal! Who knows more about my activities than I do? So . . . what would you like to know?"

IN THE PUBLIC bar of the *Piers Plowman*, Sexton Blake and Paula Dane shared a small round table with Bill Malvern, headmaster of the Bissett Heath secondary modern school.

The bar was fairly crowded this evening. Since the last killing enough time had elapsed for the local inhabitants to recover some of their nerve—to convince themselves that the third killing had been the last of the series.

But the murders were still the chief topic of conversation, and there was no better place than the public bar for hearing facts and theories—made available to the casual listener without even the necessity of putting questions. Only part of Blake's attention was on what Malvern and Paula were saying. At least fifty per cent of his attention was spared for the other conversations in audible range.

But he now put to Malvern a question that had occurred to him, a point which had almost occurred to Tinker.

"Mr. Malvern, you and your society are flatly opposed to fox hunting. Doesn't your concern for the fox apply to other animals?"

Malvern, with a glass between his hands, faced Blake squarely. "Of course! Why d'you ask?"

Blake said: "I've been told there's a man living near here who keeps a 'menagerie' of animals for biological experiments. Don't those experiments trouble you?"

Malvern's puzzled frown cleared. "No, Mr. Blake, they don't trouble me or my society. For two reasons. A case can be made out for controlled experiments on animals which are essential for the relief and cure of human suffering. And such experiments, as you know, are carefully controlled. They are permitted only to responsible scientific people, under licence, and subject to strict inspection. Such experiments, which limit the animal's suffering and utilise it only to prevent much greater human suffering, are in a totally different category from the infliction of suffering for no other purpose than 'sport.' That's one reason."

"And the other?" Blake asked, while Paula listened in silence.

"This!" Malvern said. "You're alluding to Ambrose Leeming,

385

of course. Well, I made inquiries about his animal experiments long ago, and learned that it wasn't even necessary for him to get a licence for them. For the simple reason that his experiments don't include anything which could be classified as vivisection! He doesn't perform surgical experiments on animals, for instance—or any other kind of experiment involving pain. I called on him once, and he gave me some scientific quarterlies referring to his work. That work has nothing to do with anything as crude as vivisection. It's concerned with the subtler fundamental problems of genetics and the development of species. In fact, like Gregor Mendel, he's done a lot of similar experiments on plant life. I'm sure there's no physical suffering involved in anything he does with animals!"

He drained his glass.

Blake invited: "Another?" He turned on his chair to catch the barman's eye, when the outer door opened with a crash.

Into the light of the bar a man staggered noisily. White-faced, he stood blinking while his dazzled pupils refocused.

Malvern half-rose from his seat. "Hoskins!" he exclaimed. "Farmer Hoskins—one of our society! What the—"

The farmer, standing astride in muddy boots and breeches, looked about the bar, gasping as he groped for words. Blake was now on his feet, striding towards him.

Hoskins gasped hoarsely: "He's—he's out there . . .! Another of 'em . . . Ghast—ghastly sight. Thass number four—" He swayed on his feet, trying to go on.

Blake called to the barman, now visible. "Double brandy here—quick!" To the farmer he said urgently: "A man! Dead?"

Hoskins nodded: "Dead an' savaged! Out—out there! Pinned to a tree!"

He grabbed at the proffered glass of brandy and swallowed greedily.

*　　*　　*

386

THE LAND ROVER'S headlights probed the night. Blake, at the steering-wheel, spoke crisply to the farmer beside him. "Which way now?"

"R-right!"

Hoskins had still not completely recovered from the shock of his discovery. Blake could feel him trembling with the reaction. Behind them in the vehicle were Paula and Malvern, who had insisted on coming along.

One of the bar regulars had gone to inform Sergeant James of the latest tragedy, so the police should soon be coming this way too. But the farmer's Land Rover was making easy work of the rough going, and suddenly emerged on to a smoother strip of earth road.

"Just along here a bit . . ." Hoskins mumbled through chattering teeth.

"Along here a bit" it was. Those raking headlamps speared through the darkness, illuminating a close-grown row of trees. Again trees . . .

Blake switched on the spotlight and swivelled it about so that its beam covered the trees above headlamp level. And stark in the spotlight's brilliant circle showed a grotesque form, transfixed in violent death.

Literally transfixed. Pinned to the tree not by any man-made weapon—but impaled, back-first, on a short, horizontal branch of the tree itself. Impaled by immense, incredible strength.

And the dead, open eyes that stared blankly in the spotlight's glare were those of the muscular, red-haired "psychic."

Mr. Volpone Johnson.

THE SEVENTH CHAPTER

Signs and portents.

FROM UNDER THE brim of his bowler-hat the pale blue eyes of Chief Inspector Coutts glittered like chips of ice. The Scotland Yard detective was looking down at the mortal remains of Volpone Johnson, now laid out on a piece of old waterproof sheeting, spread on the grass beside the earth road.

A photographer of the county police had done his work, and there had been no reason to leave the body in its original gruesome position. The headlamps of a police car had been dipped to bathe the corpse in a pool of white light, and the police surgeon had made his preliminary examination.

His report was that the murder victim had first been strangled and then smashed against that projecting branch with tremendous violence. It was a report which added little or nothing to what was evident to even the lay eye. In view of the irreparable internal injuries inflicted by this savage impalement, it had no doubt been fortunate for Volpone Johnson that he'd already been dead when subjected to it. The chief inspector had lost some of his usual florid colour, and there was hardly one person among the onlookers who was not noticeably paler than normally.

Coutts was looking harassed. Even his long experience gave him no shell of immunity against this shock to his natural humanitarian feelings. This was murder wanton and bizarre. Murder shorn of even any pretence at the civilised decencies. Murder that had left the victim bereft not only of life but of human dignity. The strong and stately Volpone Johnson had ended as a broken puppet, an impotent thing casually destroyed.

Now, while the photographer and doctor stood back, Coutts looked intently down at the body. It was now up to him to make what he could of the situation. His sandy eyebrows were drawn together in a deep frown. His shadow, cast by the headlights, was a long black shape joining other shadows and merging at the penumbra with the total darkness beyond.

"No footprints again!" he muttered bitterly. "The grass under the tree trampled flat, but no individual footprint to be seen. A maniac, cunning to obliterate his traces immediately after the killing. After strangling Johnson he must have gripped him by the ankles, swung him up against that branch—and then scuffled the grass to obscure his traces."

"Or," Sexton Blake suggested quietly, standing beside him, "he could have been gripping Johnson by the *throat* when he swung him against that branch!"

"Eh?" Coutts looked round quickly. "In that case Johnson would have been left upside down, not upright as we found him?"

Blake shook his head. "Not if the killer had been up in the tree, hanging from a higher branch! Not if he strangled Johnson from above, without coming down. That would also explain the absence of his footprints. He could have reached down from the tree as Johnson was passing or standing underneath. It may have been Johnson, in his death struggle, who trampled the grass. Then the killer could have impaled him on that lower branch and made off through the trees without touching the ground at all!"

"That damned Tarzan, trapeze act again!" Coutts muttered. "Let's examine the higher branches!"

Paula was sitting in the Land Rover with Bill Malvern, in the background shroud of darkness. She remained silent as Blake came over and turned the spotlight up to illuminate the top branches of the death tree. A towing rope was thrown over one of the thicker high branches and Coutts himself began to climb.

Five minutes later he was back on the ground again, knowing that Blake was probably right. In several places high branches of the tree were gouged and broken as if by a climber.

"Though we have to remember," Blake commented, "that Johnson himself was a tree climber and could have caused that damage. Look—even the trunk has marks of climbing irons!"

While a constable was pulling down the rope, the Chief Inspector returned to his scrutiny of the body.

The flesh of the face was bloated and livid. The eyes and tongue were protruding in a horrifying grimace of terror and suffocation. The exposed throat was disfigured with purple bruises and raw lacerations from the strangler's fingernails.

"May I?" Blake asked, indicating the body.

Again Coutts glanced at him inquiringly. "Huh? Oh, certainly! Have a look!"

Blake went down on one knee on the waterproof sheeting. An exploring earwig scurried away into the grass as he leaned forward to examine the throat bruises at close quarters. A moth fluttered in a crazy jive along the light-rays towards the headlamps, like a drunken air-pilot uncertainly homing along a radio beam. Somewhere in the distant darkness an owl gave a forlorn hoot, and nearby on the perimeter of light a man gave a nervous cough.

But of all externals Blake seemed oblivious as he studied the maltreated throat. Suddenly he gave a soft, sibilant exclamation.

Instantly Coutts bent down beside him, while the circle of watching eyes reflected the light and a tense curiosity. As Coutts stooped over the corpse, his black shadow flitted across it like a vampire-bat's wing.

"What is it?" he asked, in an urgent undertone.

IN THE BLEAK light the private investigator's features were etched in strong chiaroscuro contrast. In the centre of his brow his black hair made a sharp V-shaped peak. His blue-grey eyes and firm mouth were grim.

"Did you notice?" he asked, so that only Coutts could hear. "The grip the strangler got on the throat wasn't an ordinary one. It wasn't the usual strangling grip from the front, with the thumbs opposite the fingers, compressing the windpipe—"

"That's so!" Coutts agreed. "Dr. Morton noticed it too. The strangler got his grip from behind—"

"More than that!" Blake said. "He got his grip from behind— and when he closed his grip his thumbs weren't spread out from the fingers, but lying close beside them. On one side of his throat his left thumb was held close beside the left forefinger; on the other side of the throat the right thumb was held close beside the right forefinger."

The Yard man frowned. "Yes—the bruises show that! But wouldn't it be natural in a grip from the rear?" He held his own two hands forward in a demonstration. "With a grip from the rear it would be the tips of his fingers which were doing the choking. After all, whether a strangler's gripping from the front or the rear, it's the front of the throat that he wants to compress and crush. And in a grip from the rear the fingers would do the compressing, because the thumbs wouldn't come into play."

"That's so, Coutts!" Blake acknowledged. "I entirely agree with you. But there's still something very unusual about these thumb marks—"

"Oh—?"

"See how short they are! Extraordinarily short for the length of the fingers."

Coutts peered, then nodded again.

"Yes—I see that. The thumb *marks* are short—but does that mean the actual thumbs are necessarily short? Isn't it possible that the tips of the thumbs weren't being pressed down? Pressure from the thumbs wouldn't be necessary in a rear grip, remember. The fingertips would be doing the damage at the front of the throat." He paused. "Isn't it even possible that the killer had lost the top joint of each thumb?" His tone became eager. "Gosh—that would help to identify him, if it's true!"

"I don't think it is!" Blake countered in a low voice. "Nor do I think he wasn't pressing against the sides of the throat with the whole length of his thumbs. Look again! At the tip of each finger-bruise there's an indented laceration from the fingernail. And there's also a nail scratch at the tip of each thumb-mark! Not so deep as at the fingers, because only the side of the thumbnail would be against the throat. But the killer has the top joint of each thumb all right, because he's evidently got thumbnails!"

Blake looked round at the Yard man. "The inference seems to be that the actual thumbs are abnormally—freakishly—short. And that could identify the killer even more specifically than amputated joints could!"

"Huh! It's about the only item towards a physical description that we've gathered so far! Total information—a trapeze artist muscle-man with short thumbs!" The chief inspector's eyes suddenly brightened a little. "I think I'll have that description circulated to gymnasiums and circuses throughout the country! Where else would you expect to find such a killer?"

In the white light Blake's expression was speculative and oddly suggestive. He said cryptically: "A circus? *It rather depends on which part of a circus you mean!*"

AMBROSE LEEMING STOOD in his laboratory, looking down at a rat.

Mowbray House was quiet. Again, with the day's serious work finished, Leeming was relaxing with a simple experiment that was amusing as well as instructive.

The maze was again laid flat on the laboratory table.

Again the rat had worked his way through the puzzle and reached the bait at the end. But this time his reward was more than a morsel of food. This time, beyond the little lump of bait, a door to freedom stood open!

Leeming was muttering to himself as he studied the maze through its glass cover.

"One learns a good deal about a creature's mentality and adaptability even in a confined space like this. But how can one study its reactions to untrammelled freedom unless artificial restraints are removed? How can one assess the real nature of a wild creature unless it's allowed to run wild?"

He looked at the rat, hesitating at the open doorway, as if suspecting a trap outside. He gave a low, mirthless laugh.

"Even confinement in this maze has done something to this creature's natural instincts—his natural inquisitiveness and daring. Studying a wild mammal in a cage is like studying a fish out of water. A free, natural environment . . . that's the answer, as I knew it would be. An experiment with dangers . . . but the only scientifically logical one . . ."

He tapped on the glass cover. Startled, the rat made a jump past the bait and out of the open doorway. Scuttling across the table, it hesitated again—glanced back with its little eyes gleaming in the light from the ceiling strip-tubes. Then it turned and jumped from the table to the floor, questing this way and that for attractive cover.

Leeming took a step towards it. Frightened, the rat ran towards the nearest corner, seeking a way of escape. But there was no way here, and the rat sank down on its belly, cowering, its tiny eyes watching the biologist's slow approach.

For long seconds the man and the rat studied each other. Then Leeming closed his eyes and shook his head. Opening his eyes, he looked at the rat again—then rubbed a hand across his face. Once more he looked down at the rat, and his eyes widened incredulously. He swallowed; laid a hand on the edge of the bench and gripped it hard.

The rat was motionless now, but something about its face held Leeming's gaze as if in hypnosis. His mouth was unsteady now. His other hand went up to press against his trembling lips.

Again his eyes closed, this time as if in concentration. When he opened them and looked down at the rat again, a gust of breath escaped from him. The disbelief faded from his eyes, his mouth became firmer.

"Overwork . . !" he muttered to himself. "I must ease up a little. Relax with something different. It's a rat's face again now . . . always was, of course . . . I—I suppose *I* need fresh air too! All work and no . . ."

He gave a nervous, embarrassed laugh. Then he stepped towards the rat with the confidence of a person familiar with handling all kinds of creatures. Unerringly his hand went down to grasp the rodent. But it had sensed that temporary fear in the human, and Leeming yelped as its chisel-shaped incisors sank into the flesh of his hand.

Muttering an imprecation, he grabbed the animal with his other hand and dropped it by the tail into its cage.

But the rat now stared up at him defiantly, as if still sensing some change in him. Some lessening of authority . . . of mental superiority . . .

Leeming glanced nervously, almost furtively, about him as he hurried to the first-aid box.

With him went a queer, irrational fear.

THE EIGHTH CHAPTER

Private lives.

SEXTON BLAKE SPENT the morning after the murder on a sixty-five mile run to Bill Malvern's previous school, at which he had been an assistant master. It was a delicate undertaking to make inquiries about Malvern without seeming to cast aspersions on his character. So Blake was perfectly frank with Malvern's old chief during the private interview.

He explained that Malvern's known antipathy to fox hunting and the revelation of his V.C.-winning exploit had brought him under suspicion in connection with the first of the Bissett Heath murders, but that he, Blake, had no reason at all to suspect him. He admitted that he was having the antecedents of all recent arrivals in Bissett Heath investigated, and that he owed it to the others, and to logic, to include Malvern in the routine inquiries.

Malvern's old headmaster was reasonable enough to recognise the justice of this, and evidently appreciated Blake's discretion in coming straight to him for information. It was just possible that Paula Dane's charm increased his appreciation of the compliment. He certainly received his visitors with courtesy, and spoke with apparent candour about his ex-assistant.

He said: "I know there are cranks who'd pamper a Pekinese and neglect a child, but Malvern's regard for animals never struck me as being in that category, Mr. Blake. He and I had many a chat about our respective philosophies, and a cardinal principle in his was a respect for life. In all its sentient manifestations—including human life. I never found reason to doubt his sincerity."

"Some people," Blake mentioned, "have thought his record in the Korean war cast doubt upon that!"

Mr. Stock gave a short laugh of scornful impatience. "He valued human life more than most people, but he also believed there were times and situations in which resistance to aggression was a moral obligation. He realised what these peace-at-any-price folk, in their smug indifference to the victims of oppression, have overlooked or ignored. That if men had not fought throughout history to overthrow tyrannies and maintain freedom, the world and its scientists would have been under totalitarian control when the atomic bomb was eventually made. Which means that mankind would have remained under such evil domination permanently! Malvern's aversion to blood sports is quite typical of his general outlook— which is resistance to all abuses of life and its decencies!"

"He came here straight from the Army?"

"Yes, and I was sorry to lose him when he left."

"He never showed any violent streak while he was here? Any violent reaction against cruelty to animals, for instance?"

Stock hesitated. "M'm . . . he caned a boy once for shying stones at a cat, but I'd have caned the boy myself in such a case —and I don't think the boy himself complained about what he got."

Malvern evidently had an admirer in his old chief, and Blake's oblique inquiries in the vicinity of the school unearthed no specific criticism of Malvern. They did confirm that Malvern was no glory seeker, because no one Blake spoke to mentioned the V.C. Neither did anyone mention blood sports, which was hardly surprising since this was an industrial area.

Blake drove the Bentley Continental back to Bissett Heath in time for a late lunch. Beside him, Paula stared on observing the rakish car already parked outside the *Spread Eagle* Temperance Hotel. It was a sleek, low-slung, nearly new Aston Martin.

"Not coincidence . . .?" Paula murmured. "Oh, no—look at the number plate!" A minute later, as they walked into the hotel vestibule, she added: "And look who's here!"

Edward Carter, lounging hopefully near the reception cubicle, straightened up and came towards them with a grin of welcome.

"Hello, chief! Hello, Paula! Was told you'd be back for lunch, so include me in, as Goldwyn didn't say."

"You haven't run down just for a meal?" Paula suggested with a friendly hand at his elbow as they headed for the lounge.

"Not exactly," Tinker admitted. "But you two had better have lunch with me first, because this report has to be made in private!" He veered towards the dining-room.

Blake spoke for the first time. "You've been quick with your inquiries!"

Tinker nodded. "Yes. But you'll be surprised at the help I've had!"

"HE GROWS MORE like you every day!" Paula commented. "In his ways, I mean!" She was eyeing Tinker with affectionate exasperation but speaking to Blake. "Dropping these suggestive hints—then leaving me on tenterhooks!"

After a lunch more nourishing than imaginative, the three of them were in the lounge again, its only occupants.

Tinker grinned with satisfaction. It was nice to keep the chief guessing for a change.

"Item one?" Blake prompted, proffering his gold cigarette case.

Tinker took a cigarette and leaned back, perilously near a tall table supporting one of the last aspidistras in the world. The blank screen of a vintage television receiver reflected the match-flame as he lit up.

"Item one," he reported, "Mister Volpone Johnson. Confirmed a local celebrity in Pyecombe. Celebrated for his rapid-combustion temper and also for his claims to be psychic. The general attitude towards those claims varies between firm faith and ridicule. It's quite certain, anyway, that his pose as a prophet is no new one, even if it is a pose. One old lady told me he found a purse she lost four years ago, by dowsing for it with a pendulum over a map of the locality. But a barber who knew him said he couldn't pick the first three in a field of four horses even if one of 'em was lame. Maybe the barber and Volpone didn't have the same ideas about prophecy!"

Blake gave Paula a warning glance. Tinker didn't yet know of Johnson's tragic death, and Blake wanted the rest of the report before mentioning it.

"That's all for item one," Tinker stated. "Volpone Johnson didn't invent the psychic stunt just for his stay here. Item two—Ambrose Leeming. I got Nick Reuter to deal with that one, for reasons I'll explain later. Nick's report reached me, by 'phone, just before I left Town today. Apparently Leeming had lived in King's Lynn only a couple of years, and before that lived near Grantham. Nick went up there yesterday afternoon."

"And—?"

"He found that Leeming had lived *there* only a couple of years!"

Paula stared in surprise. "He's been on the move in recent years, eh?"

"Nick," Tinker said, "traced Leeming back through two

preceding moves, and is now at Penny Compton, Warwickshire. Leeming lived near there when his wife was alive. It's been fairly easy to trace his moves because he's always had a rather large house in a secluded situation. His wife died while they had the house near Penny Compton—and only a year after they adopted the boy—"

"What boy?" Paula asked.

"The boy they adopted! Nick says people in the neighbourhood still remember the family. Mr. and Mrs. Leeming and Bobby, the little boy they adopted from one of those adoption societies. He was about two years old when they adopted him, about three when Mrs. Leeming died. The household moved away about six months later, which the locals considered natural after Leeming's bereavement. Incidentally, the man Croft was with him even then, and accompanied him on each subsequent move."

"And the boy?" Blake inquired.

Tinker frowned. "He went with Leeming from Penny Compton to Lambourn Downs, but Nick has no knowledge of him after that."

"You mean he was returned to the adoption society?"

"Nick says not. He's contacted 'em by 'phone, so as to get the picture complete. Nick, of course, has been working in the opposite direction from the sequence of Leeming's moves, and it was at Lambourn Downs that he heard the first mention of the boy. When they lived there, Bobby would have reached school age, but apparently it was understood locally that he'd been getting his basic education from Leeming himself. He was seen playing in the grounds of the house, but didn't mix with youngsters living round about."

Blake stubbed out his cigarette on an ancient ash-tray. "I've heard no mention in Bissett Heath of an adopted son. But how old would he be now?"

Tinker did a rapid calculation, counting off Leeming's domestic removals on his fingers. Then: "Oh — about twenty, if Nick has his times right!"

"M'm—old enough to have taken a job somewhere. But what else has Reuter learned about Leeming?"

Tinker shrugged. "Not much. For the simple reason that, after his wife died, Leeming seems to have dropped all social life and to have discouraged visitors at his various homes. He seems to have had some sort of menagerie wherever he's been, though. So evidently his work became his hobby, too, after his wife died. D'you want Nick to dig back any further than Penny Compton?"

"No. Let's see—that's going back eighteen years, isn't it? That's far enough. What about the Zoological Society?"

"'Oh—I checked there. His professional standing's high among the other Fellows, but they don't see him personally except once in a blue moon."

"And item number three?"

Tinker's expression lightened. "I handled that myself, and it was quite a pleasant job in its way! Major Lionel Oliver Eyles, D.S.O. The man with the mask."

"Mask?" Paula echoed.

"Sure—fox's mask! He's got one mounted on a wall of his flat in Curzon Street, according to a confiding blonde I was introduced to last evening. I was told by a club acquaintance of his that this particular blonde was a particular friend of the major. Apparently the fellow was exaggerating, though. She confirmed that the gallant major had once invited her to visit his flat in Curzon Street, to see his fox's mask. But as it happens, it seems this particular blonde was *very* particular—" "

"Oh—?" Paula invited, intrigued.

"Yes. After she'd seen the fox's mask she gave the major the brush!"

"Oh—*Tinker*!" Paula winced.

Then, as her anguish subsided, she commented: "I gather the fox isn't the only creature the major hunts?"

"That's what *I* gather!" Tinker agreed. "Apparently, in the close season for foxes he comes to Town bursting with rude health and ideas even ruder. And then he hunts alone! Come November the First he's back in the saddle to recuperate in the fresh air of Bissett Heath, where the quarry grows its own fur coat."

"Any suggestions of violence to human beings while in Town?" Blake asked.

"Not that I've heard about. Actually he seems pretty popular among the perpetual adolescents. You know—the mentally retarded type who swop conquest stories when they're oiled, and whose idea of paradise is a place full of fish, pheasants, foxes and females, with themselves as the only male owning hunting rights! To that type the major's quite a hero. And even the chap who introduced me to the blonde, and who regards Eyles as the club bore, didn't hint at any faults beyond the obvious ones. No suggestion of any psychopathic urges!"

Blake's brows slanted. "Malvern regards a passion for killing foxes as a psychopathic urge! Eyles was quick to suggest a link between Malvern's Commando exploit and the first strangling here, and Malvern would be entitled to return the compliment. It's psychologically conceivable that a blood-sport mentality could run amok into a homicidal hunt of human prey and—"

Tinker whistled. "And more logical than Eyles' innuendo about Malvern! After all, Malvern's killing in Korea was done under orders and to save lives. Blood sport is a voluntary thing, for personal pleasure—"

"But there are too many hunting types in the Bissett Heath country for Eyles to come under specific suspicion on that count alone. So item number three is a blank—so far. What about item number four?"

It was now that Tinker leaned back in his chair, with that tantalising grin returning to his face.

"Item number four," he said slowly, savouring the words, "was the easiest job of the lot. Item number four did the job for me!"

THE NINTH CHAPTER

The faces.

"WELL—COME ON!" PAULA prompted, as Tinker sat studying their reactions with enjoyment. "Out with it!"

Having had his moment, Tinker became brisk again. Quickly he described the unexpected arrival of Mr. Gideon Ashley, and that person's offer of assistance.

"But—" Paula exclaimed, "how could he know you were going to make inquiries about him? You'd only just been told about the job yourself!" She looked appealingly at Blake. "You hadn't mentioned the idea to anyone else, had you?"

"Not a soul!" Blake confirmed.

"Then how could he have known, Tinker?" Paula demanded. The junior partner shrugged. "Don't ask me!"

Blake said: "Tinker—you're sure there was no possibility of him overhearing our phone conversation, on Marion's switchboard?"

Tinker shook his blond head positively. "Not a chance, chief! He didn't arrive at the reception office till our phone talk was over, and Marion says she didn't even hear it herself. As usual, she cut off her headphone connection as soon as she'd put you

405

through to me."

Blake was looking very thoughtful. "I suppose it's possible that our conversation was overheard at this end—on the switchboard of the local exchange. But that would mean he had someone at the exchange ready to eavesdrop on any calls to Berkeley Square. And there's one cold fact which makes such an explanation very doubtful indeed. You say he arrived at the office soon after our talk was finished. That means he couldn't have travelled from Bissett Heath to Town between our conversation and his arrival in Berkeley Square!"

Tinker wore a baffled scowl. "That's definite! But could he have been in Town already and have got a phone call himself from the eavesdropper in the Bissett Heath exchange? Immediately after our chat, with a tip-off as to what it had been all about?" He glanced from Blake to Paula. "Either that must be the explanation—or the fellow's a mind reader!"

Blake gave an odd smile, and drew another cigarette from his case. "More than a thought reader, Tinker, if he didn't get a message from an eavesdropper at this end! According to what you've said, Marion announced him just after I'd spoken to you about him. So unless he received the tip-off while actually in Berkeley Square, he was already on the way there *before* I spoke to you about him! Which would make him no mere thought reader—but a man capable of precognition!"

Tinker nodded soberly. "That's just what I said to myself when he showed up and made that offer of his. The man must be psychic! Heck—I said at the beginning this was a very queer case. We've had two clairvoyant characters in it already— Elspeth and Volpone Johnson. And where there's two there can be three. But how do we cope?"

Blake suggested: "By first deciding on the basic facts. In this connection they're pretty clear. To have arrived so promptly with knowledge of our phone conversation, Ashley would have had to be in Berkeley Square to receive an immediate report from an eavesdropper. But, unless we're going to accept it as sheer coincidence, even the fact of his being in Berkeley Square at the time would imply a rather unusual gift of anticipation!"

Again Tinker gave a helpless shrug. "Well, there's nothing of the crank or mystic in his appearance! He looks just what he is—a financial tycoon. I looked him up in *Who's Who*. That's how I learned about Eyles' clubs and was able to contact a fellow club member of his. But *Who's Who* doesn't mention any psychic interests or connections of Ashley's. The only societies he seems to belong to are charitable ones, for the care of refugees."

Paula broke in with impatient curiosity. "This is all very well. Tinker—but what did he say when he did arrive? Did he explain how he came to know you were going to vet him?"

"No—he didn't explain that! But he offered to let me see for myself anything else I'd like to know about him. So I made an appointment to meet him at his office an hour later. Before going there I looked him up in *Who's Who*, and also put Nick Reuter on the Ambrose Leeming inquiry."

"And when you went to his office?" Paula urged.

Tinker grinned rather ruefully. "He gave me the run of all his files—and let me look inside the office safe! Then he took me to his house in Eaton Square and invited me to look it over just as I pleased! And there was nothing I could see in either place to cause any suspicion that he isn't just what he seems to be!"

"Except," Blake commented, "his extreme helpfulness, which is hardly what one would expect of a financial tycoon knowing himself to be the subject of a private investigation! No indignation—either righteous or bogus. Perhaps he is just what he seems to be. But his peculiar helpfulness does rather remind one of a master conjurer who obligingly allows you to select the card he intends you to have!"

"You mean he showed me what he wanted me to see—so

that I wouldn't bother to dig for information myself and maybe turn up something he *didn't* want me to know about?"

"It's a feasible possibility?" Blake suggested. "Anyway, in spite of his extraordinary co-operation—or because of it—item number four is also a blank so far?"

"Afraid so, chief! But what now?"

Blake said crisply: "Tell Reuter to keep on with the Leeming inquiry. Incidentally, ask him to find out just where and when the adopted son went out of Leeming's life. If he can trace the young fellow, so much the better. He should be able to reveal more about Leeming's private life and character than anybody. And get one of Reuter's leg-men to go on digging into Major Eyles' life in Town. I find it difficult to believe that the man responsible for these killings can be entirely normal in his private life. It's not a crook we're looking for, but someone with an uncontrollable tendency to violence in certain circumstances."

"And Ashley?" Tinker invited.

"You can ask Splash Kirby what he knows about him. And also ask him to sound the *Post* financial editor about him."

"And then?"

"When you've got those inquiries going, you can come back here. Bissett Heath's the murder centre, and I may need you here."

Tinker asked curiously: "What will *you* be doing in the meantime?"

With a taut smile, Blake answered: "Oh—I'm about to beard a few lions in their dens!"

He stood up. Paula uncrossed her lissom legs, smoothed down her skirt and stood up too.

Eleven minutes later Tinker was behind the wheel of the Aston Martin, a gleaming missile streaking back to Town.

WITH AN OLD woollen scarf wound about his throat, Ambrose

Leeming left his house by the side door and walked slowly towards the building which had once been a row of stables.

The winter afternoon was grey and gloomy, with darkness only three hours away. But Leeming paid no attention to the weather conditions as he made his way along the gravel path towards his objective. The objective not only of his present errand but of his life's work. The "menagerie."

A menagerie unlike any other in the whole wide world.

Besides himself, only his manservant Croft was allowed to visit the menagerie. Between them they had cared for its inmates ever since the collection had first been started. And the collection of living creatures in this row of converted stables represented Leeming's penultimate achievement.

Not his ultimate achievement, but the essential preceding stage towards it.

With his usual eagerness he unlocked the padlock of the wide collapsible door which covered almost the entire front of the building. At his thrust, the door slid away on its bottom rail till it disappeared into the receptacle at the end of the building. Now only sheets of thick plate glass shielded the fronts of the separate compartments which had originally been stables.

Leeming snapped down a wall switch and, after a preliminary flicker, strip lighting flashed on with its colourless, shadowless radiance. And now Leeming began to pace slowly along the concrete apron fronting the menagerie.

In each compartment was a different form of life, in a setting made to conform as far as possible to the inhabitants' natural environment.

The first compartment was, in fact, an aquarium, with strange, semi-transparent fish darting through the water in fear of the sudden light.

But it was when Leeming passed on to the mammalian exhibits that fear came into his own expression.

The mammals in the first section were tiny creatures, with large eyes turned towards him as he gazed through the glass. Round eyes in small faces. Faces which seemed to change before his own eyes . . .

He stared, his mouth beginning to tremble again. But even as he stared the fact became more evident. A fact he fought against in growing panic.

"No . . ." he said. "No—not human faces! It's a trick of the light . . . or overwork . . . ! I—I'm just imagining . . . the theme must be playing on my mind . . . It's just . . ."

Dragging his gaze away from those staring little faces, he took a few steps along to the next compartment. Again mammals, but different species.

Again faces. Again faces. Again . . . *human* faces!

Human little faces with animal eyes. Animal eyes in human faces . . .!

He ran along to the next compartment . . . and the next. Before he had reached the end compartment he knew—and his lips were uncontrollable, his hands fluttering at his face, his own eyes large and round with mounting terror.

While he looked through the glass he could not evade the fact. The wondering eyes in frighteningly human faces. A sob began to rise in his constricted throat, but he fought it down.

Unable to look into the final compartment, he backed away off the concrete apron. With panic threatening to engulf him, he turned to go back to the house.

But after a few steps he had to look back over his shoulder at the menagerie. At those illuminated compartments containing . . .

He couldn't check a sob this time. He couldn't prevent his shaking mouth breaking into a babble.

From each compartment of mammals little human faces were staring after him. He dared a reluctant side-glance towards the aquarium. Through the translucent water little faces with round eyes were looking at him. But not these faces . . . not these . . . *they* couldn't be . . .

But they were! Vaguely but perceptibly. Not dogfish . . . not catfish . . . but little *manfish* . . . looking after him in appeal and reproach . . .

He blurted a bubbling cry of blind panic—and ran for the shelter of the house.

His hands were trembling as he shut the door when safely inside. Safe except for what was upstairs . . .

Croakingly he called his man Croft. Soundlessly the sombre Croft appeared in the room a minute later.

By now Leeming had fought down some of his panic. His voice was not too wild when he said: "Croft—go over and turn off the lights and lock up, will you? I—I forgot!"

Croft's blank, muddy eyes regarded him with automatic deference. The unquestioning, unflattering deference of a damaged[9] mind conditioned by long custom.

"Ess, Misser Leeming," he answered indifferently, and went out.

When he came back a few minutes afterwards, Leeming scanned his face with furtive eagerness. But that face was still a blank, unlined by thought or emotional stress; a blank on which life had yet to make any impression.

"Thass all, Misser Leeming?" he said conventionally.

Eyeing him from under lowered brows, Leeming hesitated. Embarrassed, but bound to find out.

"That's all," he muttered. "Er— everything was all right over there?"

He was watching Croft's reactions as closely as he'd watched any laboratory experiment.

"Ess, Misser Leeming," Croft replied, with the same indifference.

411

"You switched off the lights!"

"Ess, Misser Leeming."

"Did—did you look inside before you switched them off?"

Croft showed the minutest sign of surprise. "Oh—I suppose so!"

Leeming had to know. "You—you didn't notice anything? Anything . . . unusual . . .?"

Croft gave a slow, stupid blink. "Only my corn's a bit troublesome again, Misser Leeming. That means rain, don't it, Misser Leeming?"

"Croft!" The word was an angry yap. "Inside . . . behind the glass . . . you noticed nothing—*different* there . . .?"

The man's low-browed head swivelled slowly to and fro. "No, Misser Leeming. They all looked nice'n comfy, like."

Leeming was about to press home another insistent question—but started violently as a distant bell rang imperatively. A bell at the front of the house.

He looked doubtfully at Croft. Moistening dry lips, he ordered, in a flat monotone: "See—see who that is!"

While Croft was trudging along the weed-grown drive to the front gates, Leeming paced up and down in the draughty hall, exerting a tremendous effort at self-control. He was very nearly composed when the front door opened again at Croft's push and the man came stolidly into the hall.

"Well?" Leeming jerked impatiently, as Croft carefully closed the door.

The servant was facing him again. "A lady and a gen'leman to see you, Misser Leeming. A fair lady—"

"The man?" Leeming prompted impatiently. "What does he want and who is he?"

Croft humped his heavy shoulders.

"He wants to see you, Misser Leeming. And his name's . . . er—Misser Sex'on Blake!"

Leeming sagged against an antique table. In an exhausted tone he muttered: "Oh—show him in!"

While Croft was again trudging to the gates, Leeming was pressing a hypodermic needle into his left arm.

He felt badly in need of a quick stimulant.

THE TENTH CHAPTER

Grounds for suspicion.

MAJOR L. O. Eyles had shown a marked lack of enthusiasm towards Sexton Blake's request.

Blake and Paula had found him in a paddock, watching a stable hand schooling a young mare, and his welcome was trifle frigid even at their first appearance. When Blake put his request, the temperature dropped to sub-zero.

"You want me to get a list of the alibis claimed by the members of my hunt for the times of these atrocious crimes!" he said incredulously. His thin features became pinker. "Why? Aren't there policemen to do such jobs? Haven't the police already asked all the possible suspects for alibis?"

His tone and his temper climbed a noticeable amount. "And even if it were any business of mine—or yours—why, in the name of sense, should any member of the hunt be under suspicion?"

The stable hand was studiously ignoring the interview; was keeping the mare trotting around in a circle.

Blake countered calmly: "Why should any member of the hunt *not* be under suspicion with everyone else—unless he's

415

ready to furnish a provable alibi?" After a slight pause, he added: "It will be much easier to regard your shot at me as entirely accidental if you co-operate in this matter, Major. And if you include your own alibis in the list!"

The M.F.H. flared into open anger. "Accidental? You know damn well it was! But if I get you such a list, you'll only be duplicating the work of the police!"

Blake smiled. "Not exactly!" he contradicted. "Let's say the police and I are testing different variations on the same theme. The theme, of course, being murder. I know the police are very busy sifting and counter-checking the various statements and alibis of people living in and around Bissett Heath. But I'm directing my main attention to the people living in the big houses in the neighbourhood."

"But—why?" Eyles demanded, and even Paula looked puzzled.

"Because," Blake explained evenly, "I don't believe that the killer's identity would still be a secret if he lived in one of the small houses of the urban district. The nature of the crimes shows the killer to be abnormal in many respects. Each murder has been committed in a homicidal fury, and for some time afterwards the killer must have been in an abnormal temperamental condition. Yet he has evidently gone straight for cover after each murder, or he would have been caught before now." The detective's eyes narrowed. "I find it difficult to believe that on each of these four occasions he could have got to cover among the tight-packed community of Bissett Heath without being seen once. And I find it difficult to believe that if he *were* seen soon after such a killing orgy his abnormality would not have been recognised, his guilt suspected."

Paula, at least, seemed to appreciate the point. She said seriously: "It's certainly hard to imagine a killer creeping back into one of the Bissett Heath cottages and villas without meeting anyone. There's no room to spare in that kind of house—the people practically live on top of one another. And even if the killer had no physical traces of the murder—no bloodstains, or scratches, etcetera—he could hardly meet people well known to him without seeming unusual in some way—"

"Well—" Eyles interrupted. "Even if that's so—"

"If that's so," Blake said, "it's feasible that he's remained undetected because after each crime he's returned to the grounds of one of the large houses round about here! Somewhere where he could be safe from meeting strangers. Somewhere where he could calm down in privacy, and where, if he did meet anyone at all, it would only be a relation or intimate, who might shield him."

Blake's mouth was a taut line. "Frankly," he stated, "even if the killer is sheltering in one of the big houses in the neighbourhood, I find it difficult to believe that his guilt is unsuspected by anyone at all. Once or twice, perhaps, he could get back under cover and resume his normal routine without arousing suspicion. But it would be stretching probabilities to imagine him being able to do so on four separate occasions. Especially after the first couple of murders, when a general hue and cry had been raised. After each killing, everyone in Bissett Heath and the surrounding area must have been eyeing everyone else very suspiciously. Almost any unusual circumstance would have been seized upon—any unusual mood—"

"But—the hunt!" Eyles protested.

Blake told him: "You suggested that a man proficient in unarmed homicide on war service might practise it in civilian life. It's just as feasible that a man of unstable mentality, sated with the pleasure-killing of foxes, might turn to the killing of human beings for a pathological thrill!"

It took a couple of seconds for this point to sink in. When it had done so, Eyles looked several shades paler.

Then he gave an abrupt nod of the head, and spoke curtly. "All right, Mr. Blake—I'll do as you ask. Damned nuisance. Damned undignified for a Master to put his hunt through such an interrogation. But you shall have the information you want. And understand this! That shot was a pure accident! Now . . . if you'll excuse me . . .!"

Taking the hint, Blake returned his nod and escorted Paula out of the paddock.

Immediately after Tinker's departure for Town, Blake had made a trunk call to Nick Reuter and asked him to 'phone his next report to the Spread Eagle hotel, Bissett Heath. At a specified time in the morning or evening.

Now, with the distant activities of the listed men being investigated, he drove to the local habitation of the next man on his list. The country residence of Mr. Gideon Ashley.

BLAKE HAD MET powerful personalities before. Powerful for good, powerful for evil.

It was only in this personal meeting, however, that he was able to appreciate to the full just what Tinker had tried to convey. He was sitting opposite Gideon Ashley in a very comfortable room furnished as a study-library, and he was very conscious of the power and charm of his host's quiet personality.

Relaxed, there was little in Ashley's impact to suggest the energetic financial tycoon. His physical attitude was even lazy. It was in the scrutiny of his dark eyes that his strength and insight were to some extent recognisable.

Blake was able to appreciate a little more than Tinker just how rare the impact of the man's personality was. Tinker was accustomed to the superior personality of Blake himself; hitherto Blake had not been conscious of such a dominant impact from anyone. He could understand why the usually poised and confident Paula was now so subdued, a silent

418

onlooker at this crossing of mental swords by two men of outstanding character.

Blake had paid his host the compliment of not beating about the bush. Courteously, after the two visitors had been announced and shown in, Ashley had invited them to sit down.

"A pleasure to meet you, Mr. Blake!" he smiled, when they were comfortable.

"Not an unexpected one, I'm sure!" Blake suggested ironically.

Ashley smiled, and offered them cigarettes. Blake noticed that he did not take one for himself. The silver-haired man explained: "I just like to keep my palate—and other senses—unadulterated. A little foible of mine!"

The detective said, in a pleasant tone: "The results seem to justify the foible. I'm rather interested in your other er—senses!"

"Such as?"

Blake returned the smile. "I'm quite intrigued as to how you foresaw a certain routine inquiry I assigned to my junior partner! You'll forgive me being a little inquisitive about how and why things happen. It's, shall I say, a little foible of mine!"

Ashley's smile broadened. "Oh—you're entitled to ask, Mr. Blake! But dare I suggest that you shouldn't be quite so surprised at finding someone else emulating, in a humble way, some of your own feats of er—deduction?"

Blake looked disappointed. "So that's all it was? My junior partner felt quite sure you must be what he called ... 'psychic'!"

Ashley gave a soft laugh. "I suppose I can't really deny it. Who isn't 'psychic'? Don't we all possess a 'psychic'? But my anticipation hardly deserves his interpretation. Wasn't it obvious, to anyone knowing of your presence in Bissett Heath, that I would be among the local inhabitants to be investigated?" He gestured. "I could only offer facilities concerning myself, of

419

course, but it was the least I could do to make that particular inquiry as easy as possible!"

"It was very thoughtful of you," Blake acknowledged. After a brief hiatus, he asked, without change of expression: "Have you given any thought to the four recent murders themselves? Have you any suggestions to offer about them?"

Ashley's ascetic face became serious. He said slowly: "Barbaric tragedies, Mr. Blake, but one must keep a sense of proportion. Worse things can happen to the human race than individual physical deaths. But murder investigation is your province, not mine. It would be an impertinence for me to offer any suggestions regarding a matter in which I've no professional qualifications. I'm sure you'll cope with that problem with your usual skill and insight."

Blake's brows slanted satirically. "Thank you! But I'm afraid I'm not as punctilious as you are. I've a failing for being curious about many things strictly outside my professional province! Unusual abilities, for instance, interest me even when no criminality is necessarily involved." His gaze met his host's. "I suppose there's no possibility of the killer sheltering in your grounds or being among your staff?"

Ashley shrugged. "I'm quite sure there's no such possibility. And if your compliments have been sincere, you'll recognise that I wouldn't make such a statement without complete certitude. But you're welcome to the same facilities here that I gave your junior partner in London. Please inspect the grounds and any room in the house!"

Blake smiled. "In fairness to everyone else in the neighbourhood, I accept your offer. Shall we look around now?"

When Blake drove the Bentley out of Gideon Ashley's gateway and on to Mowbray House, he was quiet and thoughtful. His search of Ashley's home and grounds had produced an entirely negative result. And Ashley's small staff quoted mutual alibis.

Now remained Ambrose Leeming's house, with its resident staff of one.

When the detective entered the draughty hall of Mowbray House, Paula was at his side. While the taciturn manservant was reclosing the heavy front door, a semi-bald man was coming towards the visitors with his right hand extended in greeting. His smile was glittering, his manner effusive.

He wasn't looking at Paula, so her charming presence couldn't be the explanation of this second example of a warm welcome. Blake's glance met the gaze of his latest host's eyes—and then he knew.

These weren't eyes calm and steady with power and confidence. They were eyes much too bright, with pupils much too small.

Unless Blake was mistaken, this hectic manner and those contracted pupils were interrelated effects of one cause. A cause as artificial as the smiling welcome.

THE ELEVENTH CHAPTER

The shuttered menagerie.

"I KNOW OF you, of course, Mr. Blake," Leeming chattered, as he led the way into a room beyond. "Who doesn't!" To the dour servant, who had followed them in, he said: "All right, Croft—that will be all!" Then, as the fellow shuffled out through another door: "Can I offer you a drink, Mr. Blake? And the lady—?"

"No, thanks!" Blake declined. He was still surprised at this gushing welcome from a man who lived as a virtual recluse. It was possible, of course, that a man accustomed to seclusion might be glad of a visit to break the lonely monotony. But, if such were so, surely some attempt would be made to invite social visitors occasionally—and, according to Bill Malvern, Leeming had never been known to invite anyone to his house or to visit anyone else's.

Anyway, even the sudden release of pent-up instincts for human companionship wouldn't cause the contraction of the pupils which made Leeming's excitement so significant.

"Then at least sit down!" the biologist invited, indicating a couple of ancient chairs. Platitudinously, he added: "It's an ill wind, Mr. Blake . . . I heard from my daily woman that you were staying in Bissett Heath. But I hardly imagined that the tragic occurrences which brought you here would leave you time to visit me—or, indeed, that you'd pay me the compliment of doing so anyway!"

The detective and his secretary had sat down, and now Leeming perched himself on a chair to face them. On the extreme edge of the chair, Blake noticed.

Blake commented ironically: "I'm glad you regard it as a compliment. It's nice to feel welcome, and now I'm sure I can count on your co-operation!"

"Co-operation?" Some of Leeming's pleasure was overshadowed by a slight frown of puzzlement. "In what?"

Blake produced his cigarette case and held it forward. Leeming accepted a cigarette and Paula did likewise. After giving them a light, Blake said casually: "This is my third visit this afternoon, and I got co-operation at the two previous places."

"Previous—?"

"From Major Eyles and from Mr. Gideon Ashley!" Succinctly Blake explained the idea which had caused him to direct personal attention to the large houses on the outskirts of Bissett Heath. As he listened, Leeming drew deeply on his cigarette, but with a return of that eager smile. Blake ended: "Until a specific suspect is pinpointed, everyone is a potential suspect, of course. I understand that you and your man Croft provide each other with alibis for the times of the four atrocities. But, like Mr. Ashley, you have a large house with extensive grounds, in which a homicidal maniac might conceivably find shelter. Mr. Ashley kindly offered to allow me to search his grounds and every room of his house—which I've now done. No doubt you'll be equally co-operative?"

Leeming screwed up the butt of his cigarette and tossed it into the fireplace. Then he gave a sudden laugh.

"Mr. Blake—there's really no need to put yourself to such trouble here. Every room in this house is entered every day! There's no unused wing or even unused room in which any intruder could possibly hide! As for the grounds—my man Croft is out in them every day . . . his constitutional, you know. It would be absurd to have you wasting your time over something I can tell you already!"

Blake said, without resentment: "Mr. Ashley was also quite sure there was nobody to be found in his house or grounds, but he was very willing for me to confirm it! I even searched his outhouses, greenhouse and conservatory."

Leeming maintained a persistent smile. "And your search confirmed what he'd told you?"

"It did."

"There you are, then! It would be the same here. A householder knows whether there's any possibility of an intruder on his premises, you know. Besides, it's got dark since you left Mr. Ashley's, so you wouldn't be able to see anything outside now, anyway!"

Inclining his head very slightly, Blake returned his host's smile. He lit another cigarette and glanced about the room. "Quite a nice place you have here. Plenty of privacy for your work. Must be a little lonely for you, though? No relatives, Mr. Leeming?"

The biologist stuffed his hands into the sagging pockets of his old jacket. "No," he answered. "My wife died several years ago. Since then my work has filled my life, so I really don't miss human society very much. Human ties, you know, can bring sorrow as well as happiness—while work . . ."

Blake nodded. "I understand. But it must be very interesting and important work, to engross you to such an extent?"

"It is!" Leeming confirmed shortly. Evidently he did not feel inclined to enlarge upon it.

"Fundamental research, I believe?" Blake inquired conversationally. He explained: "Mr. Malvern and I were talking about cruelty to animals, and he assured me that no suffering was involved in your research experiments with animals—"

"Eh? Yes—that's so!" Leeming agreed. His joviality and social zest seemed to be fading a little. His edginess now had a trace of irritation in it. He stood up. "But I mustn't keep you. Mr. Blake, now you know there's no need for a personal search. No good saving you time, then wasting it on gossip, is there?"

"Oh—I'm in no hurry!" Blake assured him genially. 'Even detectives relax! I was relaxing late last night with some scientific quarterlies Mr. Malvern lent me, containing some articles of yours—"

"Yes—I gave him them to prove to him that I'd no interest in vivisection at all—"

"So he told me. He's quite satisfied on that point. Apparently you're more interested in genetics, biological mutations—"

"Many biologists are, Mr. Blake. Now—"

"Oh, before we go . . . it's common knowledge in Bissett Heath that you keep some sort of 'menagerie' here, for your research purposes. I wonder if you'd allow me to see—"

"I'm sorry, Mr. Blake!" The smile was very shallow indeed now. "I really couldn't allow my specimens to be disturbed. I've several rather delicate long-term experiments in process, which could be completely ruined by disturbance of the er—specimens concerned. I'd like to oblige you, but . . ." He hesitated, then pointed out: "It's dark now anyway, so what could you see?"

Blake and Paula were now standing. The detective's blue-grey eyes caught the biologist's evasive glance; held it for a moment.

"Never mind!" Blake grinned, buttoning his coat. "I'm addicted to idle curiosity, but I mustn't be encouraged! Ready, Paula?"

She spoke for the first time since entering the house. "Ready, chief!"

Leeming was shaking the detective's hand, with a renewal of that extreme geniality. "It's been a great pleasure to meet you, Mr. Blake. And you can take it from me that no homicidal maniac could take shelter on my property!"

"Thanks!" Blake smiled. "At least that helps the process of elimination!"

WHEN THE GATES had closed behind them, with the detective and Paula snug in the Bentley, Paula commented dispiritedly: "One more blank! Can't say I'm sorry to say goodbye to the place, though. The biological boffin was matey enough, but he wasn't exactly forthcoming, was he? Suppose a recluse gets like that— hugging his privacy like a miser with his money."

As the car picked up speed along the third-class public road, she peered out at the high boundary wall they were passing, illuminated at its foot by the car's headlights. "Glad we don't have to come back to this dreary hole!"

"Not for half an hour, anyway!" Blake admitted, easing the car round the curve explored by the headlights, then gently braking.

"For half—?" She turned to stare at his profile, dim in the gloom. He had parked on the grass verge and had switched off all road lights, leaving only the glow from the instrument panel.

"We'll wait till then," he said, "to give Leeming and his man time to settle down after our visit. Then I'm going back for another call, but this time unannounced and over the wall!"

"But—but why? What's the object?"

"The principal object," Blake answered, "is the menagerie. I'm quite keen to see it—"

"But why?" Paula sounded baffled. "Not just to satisfy

427

that alleged idle curiosity, I know! Chief—just what sort of expedition is it going to be?"

In Blake's tone when he replied there was a tantalising edge of grim satire. "You could call it a rule of thumb investigation!"

She exhaled a long breath of resigned frustration. "All right," she said, "I know I'm the dumb one of this party, so I won't press the point. What I do insist, though, is that I come with you!"

"Oh—insist?" Her pupils had expanded to the gloom, and she saw him turn his head to face her.

"Please, chief!" Her insistence abruptly collapsed, and she frankly pleaded. "Do let me come. I—I can carry the torch or something—and leave your hands free—"

"You win!" There was a grin in his voice. "Now let's get the kit ready. And don't blame me for ruined nylons!"

TWENTY MINUTES LATER, with the car in total darkness, they were standing on the grass verge. Blake was carrying a rope ladder from the car boot. Paula, true to her bargain, was carrying an electric torch, not yet switched on. And she had changed from her stiletto-heeled shoes into an emergency pair of serviceable "flatties."

At Blake's throw, the rubber-covered hooks of the rope ladder hitched silently on the top of the wall. Then the detective took the torch from Paula and said: "You'd better go up first, but wait up there for me!"

Their dilated pupils were now able to distinguish things without too much trouble, and Paula got hold of the rope ladder and groped her way up. A whisper from above notified him that she had reached the top. Holding the torch by its end ring, Blake went rapidly up the ladder, then held on tight as a rounded object hit him in the right eye. Paula Dane's left knee.

After a painful collision with the wall, she had swung the

knee up to ascertain the damage and rub the bruise. At the wrong moment for Blake's eye. Now she whispered: "Sorry! That's one stocking gone—I'm sure there's a run in it."

Breathing hard, though not from exertion, Blake got lithely astride the wall and silently pulled the ladder up. Soundlessly he hung it down on the inner side of the wall.

Masking the torch with a double thickness of handkerchief, he risked a momentary flash downwards. It revealed a tangle of grass and shrubbery and a clump of trees at a little distance from the wall.

Rapidly he went down the ladder, then held it for Paula. "Be careful!" he called softly, blinking his aching right eye.

Paula was two-thirds of the way down when she missed and tumbled in a heap at his feet before he could grasp her. He tensed as she gave a semi-suppressed squeal of anguish. Then he relaxed as she muttered: "That's both of them! This nylon's absolutely—"

"*You're* all right?" he interrupted, again breathing hard.

"I think so!"

"Then hold this!" He gave her back the torch and lifted her to her feet. "Ready now?" he asked.

"Yes! Sorry, chief!" Her meekness made him grin.

"Then come on!"

Bringing the rope ladder with him, rolled under one arm, in case circumstances should dictate a quick exit in a different direction, he led the way between the trees.

Five minutes later they were circumnavigating the house at a safe distance. It was a dark, irregular shape against a sky little less dark, and was set among a jungle of shrubs, neglected flower-beds and clumps of gaunt trees.

But a distant smaller building had attracted Blake's questing eyes—a long, low structure like a row of stables.

With a hand on Paula's wrist he urged her in a circuitous route which kept them screened from the house by the shrubbery, but brought them close to that long, low building. And when they were within yards of it his sense of smell identified it.

"The menagerie!" he said very softly, close to her ear. "Ready with the torch—but keep it masked!"

Catfooted, he approached the building from the side and felt around its edge. An exploratory hand touched metal—a padlock—then the fluted surface of a collapsible sliding door.

With Paula at his heels, he made a quick circuit of the structure, making sure that there was no one else in the vicinity. Then he returned to the padlock and shone the masked torch on it.

"M'm—think I can manage it!" he commented. "And there's bound to be some other protection behind this shutter, so that nothing can escape when it's open. Hold the torch, Paula!"

While she directed a faint, small circle of light upon the padlock, with their bodies to shield it from view, he set to work with a flexible steel attachment on his pen-knife. Picking the lock, as he'd anticipated, proved to be a very simple job.

Lifting the opened padlock off the staple, he placed it soundlessly on the ground, then took a grip on the edge of the sliding door. It slid back equally easily, and Blake rolled it away a couple of yards. The dim glow of the torch was reflected from green water behind plate glass.

"An aquarium . . .!" Paula breathed in surprise.

Without comment, Blake rolled the door back another couple of yards. Again a plate-glass protective screen, but behind this section was no aquarium. In this compartment were creatures which held Blake's intent gaze. A nightmarish creature, half-bird and half-lizard. A grotesque thing with a bird's shape and feathers, but a reptile's mouth, teeth and tail.

"Chief!" Paula whispered. "What is it?"

Blake didn't answer. He was looking at another living

creature, on the other side of a partition. A marsupial with features he had never seen before. A pouched cat!

Still without comment, he eased the sliding door past the next section, and here a small quadruped scampered back in fear of the sudden light. An animal the size of a small dog, each foot poised on the tips of three toes, and with its rather flat neck tufted with a short mane.

Paula demanded again, in blank astonishment. "What *is* it?"

Blake's answer was a laconic bomb-shell. "Unless I'm wildly mistaken—it's a horse !"

"A . . . *what*?" In her sheer amazement, Paula's voice rose in pitch.

Blake whispered a warning. "Quiet, Paula! We'll just see this last section, then get away!"

The door slid back to its full extent. Behind the glass a group of gibbons blinked in the light, and a saucer-eyed tarsier stared from a branch stretching across the cage. About these animals, however, there was nothing strange, and Blake began sliding the door back in the opposite direction.

When the padlock was re-fastened on the closed door, the detective gripped Paula's arm and spoke urgently.

"Come on, Paula—back to Bissett Heath. I've a lot to do, and no time to waste . . .!" He led the way quickly through the jungle of shrubbery and slung the ladder up on to the boundary wall.

Five minutes later, in the speeding car, Paula's frantic curiosity burst from her in a torrent of questions. "Chief—what's set you off like this? What's it all about? What were those . . . those weird . . . creatures? What—"

"Paula!" He spoke tersely, bleakly, his gaze on the road streaming towards them under the probing headlights. "There's no time to explain now. And, anyway, I've only a bizarre suspicion. I've got to make sure . . . and if I'm right, we've unearthed one of the most devilish crimes ever perpetrated!"

"The—the stranglings . . .! I know they were terrible, but . . ."

"I don't mean the stranglings!" he said coldly. "I believe they've only been a by-product of the real crime. *The crime I suspect has never before been perpetrated since the world began!*"

THE TWELFTH CHAPTER

Gathering madness.

On the *Spread Eagle* lounge telephone Blake asked for a person-to-person trunk connection, supplying three numbers by which the required person might be contacted. While waiting for the call to come through, he and Paula had a hurried snack in the small dining-room.

Blake was interrupted by a message that he was wanted on the 'phone. On lifting the lounge handset, he was surprised to find that the trunk connection was not the one he had asked for. It was a trunk call from Nick Reuter—at Grantham.

"Hello, Nick!" Blake greeted. "You've something to report?"

"Only negatively!" Reuter said gloomily. "I've been trying to trace this boy the Leemings adopted—Bobby. A double-check has only confirmed what I told Tinker. He was first mentioned to me at Lambourn Downs, but had been adopted when the Leemings were at Penny Compton. There was no mention of him at Grantham and King's Lynn, where Leeming lived after leaving Lambourn Downs. So I've back-tracked to Grantham, Leeming's address immediately after Lambourn Downs. This time I've made specific inquiries about the boy, of people who remember Leeming—"

"And—?"

"No knowledge of the boy! No knowledge that Leeming had ever adopted a child. During the move from Lambourn Downs to the place near Grantham, the boy seems to have disappeared!"

Blake was frowning. "You're sure there was no interval between the periods at Lambourn and Grantham, when Leeming could have lived somewhere else?"

"Oh, yes. People here have pinpointed the year of arrival by comparison with events in their own lives. Anyways, it seems to be fact that the boy left Lambourn Downs with Leeming but never arrived at the house near Grantham. On the way he vanished!"

"I see . . . !"

"D'you want me to carry on trying to trace him?"

Blake said flatly: "You can, Nick—unless I cancel the idea tomorrow. Just stay at Grantham and sleep on it tonight. I'll ring you in the morning."

"Uh-huh! You expecting developments somewhere else, then? Okay—I'll do as you say. Nothing else?"

"Nothing, Nick. Goodnight!"

As he replaced the 'phone Blake wore an expression that was taut and sombre. He was turning to walk out, when the 'phone bell shrilled. Mechanically he lifted the handset.

This time it was the Exchange ringing, with his London person-to-person connection.

"Sorry to disturb you, Lumsden," he apologised, when the man at the other end had announced himself. "But I'd like to have your expert advice on a matter of vital and urgent importance!"

"No trouble, Blake," John Lumsden assured him. "I was just having a drink at the club and feeling bored. But what advice in my line could be vital and urgent from your point of view? I'm flattered—but surprised!"

Blake said grimly: "I think I'm going to surprise you even more! Listen . . ."

An hour after Sexton Blake's departure, Ambrose Leeming went into his laboratory. It was not till he was closing the door behind him that he realised he was not alone. In the only chair a man was sitting.

A stranger.

The effect of the pep injection had not yet worn off, but a second after noticing the stranger, Ambrose Leeming was coldly sober. At first he couldn't have said why.

Except that he had no right to be here, the stranger looked normal enough. A man of ascetic features and silver hair. A silent man dressed in a black lounge suit with a bow tie. A man with particularly magnetic dark eyes.

"Who . . . who are you?" Leeming demanded. His voice was a husky, uncertain whisper.

The stranger did not answer. Did not even move. In the bright strip-lighting he sat there like some effigy. But his eyes were intently alive.

"Who *are* you?" Leeming insisted, in a louder tone. Again no answer.

Briefly, resentment and the remnant of the pep injection gave Leeming sufficient courage to walk towards the motionless intruder. But under that inflexible stare his courage oozed away, and he came to a halt while still three yards short of his objective. Out of reach of that calm interloper.

Suddenly, under that penetrating inspection, his lips began to tremble. His hands fluttered at his sides in indecision. The thought of calling for Croft apparently didn't occur to him.

His eyes flickered nervously and furtively from that seated

figure and inevitably back to it. His mouth opened, but could not form audible words.

He was alone in this laboratory, this temple of his life-quest, with an intruder who said nothing and did nothing. And Leeming himself was rendered dumb and immobile . . .

. . . Until the tension cracked and his shoulders hunched and his voice sounded a frantic croak of appeal.

"Don't look at me like that! Don't! Who are you . . .? What do you want . . .? *What are you . . .?*"

Then a cunning half-proud, half-resentful leer. "You know, don't you? You know I achieved it! That's why you're here, isn't it?" A triumphant, childish whisper. "But you can't alter it, can you? It's an accomplished fact—you hear?" He managed a short, sliding step forward: gave a giggling sob. "I'm the first man to achieve it, and it's been a lifetime's work . . ."

Still no reply from the man in the chair.

"You think it was easy?" Leeming demanded petulantly. "To do what no one has done before? To compress into a few years . . ." He stopped. After a long pause he muttered: "To understand just what it means you'd need to realise just how fundamental it is. To read my notes . . ."

His features showed sudden animation. "That's it! I'll read them to you! Then, instead of sitting there like some judge, you can . . ."

With an excited giggle he crossed to a steel filing cabinet and unlocked the top drawer. Into view he dragged a bulky, dog-eared file. Dropping this on the table beside the rat-maze, he opened the folder and shot the silent onlooker another triumphant grin.

"Listen . . .!" he invited in a husky whisper. "Listen to the secret no other man has penetrated since life began . . .!"

The stranger's dark eyes had followed him and were now gazing at his twitching face.

The stranger sat silent while Ambrose Leeming's mad voice began to read aloud.

IN THE DARKNESS of the séance room Mrs. Elspeth Lane Stevens sat in a light trance. Around her the members of her Home Development Circle were grouped in an awed hush, as from the medium's unseen lips came a subdued monotone.

". . . the auric vibrations are very strong now . . . the power is not far away. The carnate body lies motionless, but from its head the cord rises waveringly to the etheric body suspended above it . . .

"Now the cord lengthens and thins to transparency as the Adept's discarnate entity rises and moves away across the room in which his physical shell lies inert . . . Unobstructed by the material barrier of the four walls, his astral projection continues on its journey . . . moving, invisible to the mundane eye across the dark countryside . . .

"Again walls are no barrier, and in a long room in which evil has been brewed, the astral body settles in a chair and . . . waits . . .

"The waiting is brief . . . for into the long room comes a man whose lust for knowledge and for control over Nature has been perverted to evil ends . . .

"His eyes, opened by the concentrated power of the auric vibrations, see the presence in the chair . . .

"The man now senses accusation . . . behind this visitant he has a dim perception of unnumbered generations of mankind . . . each face a reproach for what he has done to their species in his craving to experiment . . . in his meddling with Humanity's ordained pathway to the heights . . .

"His mind fights against the accusation . . . against the awareness of evil in his achievements . . . against this invasion of moral principles in the shrine he has dedicated to the pursuit of knowledge at all costs . . .

"A conflict of wills has begun . . . and a mind, cornered with its own conscience, totters on the brink . . .

"I . . . I . . ." The medium sighed and shuddered. Her low voice, drained of its psychic energy, sank into the silence of exhaustion.

AROUND AMBROSE LEEMING, in the Mowbray House laboratory, fantasies were converging . . .

Faces human . . . animal . . . reptilian . . . piscine . . . Faces with eyes . . . staring, accusing, vengeful . . .

With a nervous giggle, Leeming appealed to the human figure in the chair. "Why do they blame me?" he demanded, with an attempt at bravado. "The origin of species . . . the unity of all life . . . haven't I proved it? Haven't I shown that that little human end-product of the life process can master life itself . . .?"

The folder lay on the bench beside him. He looked around at the converging faces in alarm—and grabbed up the folder.

"I know what you want me to do!" he said with an arch and cunning smile. "You want me to destroy these notes, eh? To destroy the record of all my long years of work . . . the years of thought and experiment and disappointment and experiment— and then triumph! You want the world to have no record of my achievement . . . no knowledge of my techniques!"

He stepped back a pace—then beat the air with one hand, hugging the folder to his chest with the other hand. "Keep away!" he cried. "Keep away from me . . ." He cringed in terror as they swirled about him in a phantasmagoria of species known and unknown.

Turning, he scuttled along beside the laboratory wall with his eyes averted, fending off threatening shapes in his way. Climbing up on to a laboratory stool, he took the wall-clock off its hook and clambered down with it.

"Destroy this!" he cried, glaring about him. "Not the records . . .!" Tucking the folder under one arm, he grasped a knob on top of the clock and began to turn it rapidly, grinning with satisfaction.

"I know what you mean . . ." he whimpered, still turning the hands anti-clockwise. "*Thou shalt not turn back the clock . . .!* There—I'm doing it, see? Years and generations . . . ages and epochs . . . back . . . back . . . back . . ." He lifted the clock high, mouthing: "Well—smash this, not my notes . . .!" He flung the clock violently down on the floor, then kicked it away from him.

But when he looked up again, and around him, his face suddenly crumpled in terrified protest. Whimperingly, he pleaded: "Aren't you satisfied now? I can't turn it back any more! No—not these . . ." He stuffed the folder under his jacket and clutched it to him.

He began to back away. Something made him look round over his shoulder. At what he saw he gave a sobbing scream: "No— don't turn *me* back, too! Not to that . . .!" He straightened up to strike a posture, clumsily dropping the file. "Not me! Don't you see—I'm *Mind!* Not just one of the primates. I'm the Science that uses the guinea-pigs—I don't belong with them! Don't send me back to . . ."

He fell on to his knees, scrabbling for the folder. Cowering, he babbled jerkily as his hands found it. "All right—I'll destroy . . . *them*. I'm no better than he was. I'm not superman. I'm a bald man with false teeth, and when I was at school I had spots. And I get frightened now. I'm not Mind over Matter . . . I'm just one of the species, seeing his own face in the . . ."

Getting to his feet, he glanced furtively towards the chair. Shaking with sobs, and with tears running down his checks, he dropped the folder on to the bench. His eyes were febrile as he slouched past the figure in the chair, muttering: "I'm doing it .

439

. . I'm doing it . . .!"

He opened a bench drawer. From it he drew a hypodermic syringe, and his tremulous hands attached a long needle. Now he went over to a cupboard containing bottles of chemical powders. With distilled water and powder from one of the bottles, he made a solution in a glass beaker.

From the beaker he filled the syringe, then poured the remainder of the solution into a glass flask. Carrying the syringe and flask, he shuffled back past the seated figure and towards the door. On his way out he was muttering: "I know . . . I know . . . But . . . they've got faces . . . they've got faces . . ."

He was still muttering as he shuffled across the outside landing and down the stairs.

Absorbed in his own plaintive whimpering and his reluctant mission, he totally ignored a heavy thumping inside another room on the laboratory landing.

A thumping that shook the thick oak door as if from blows of a great fist.

THE THIRTEENTH CHAPTER

Killer amok.

To JOHN LUMSDEN, Professor of Biology, Sexton Blake said on the hotel telephone: "Where could I find a creature that's half bird, half reptile? A creature with wings and feathers but a lizard's teeth and tail?"

"Oh—the *archaeopteryx*! Nowhere alive, of course, because it's been extinct for millions of years. It was an early evolutionary stage between the reptile and the bird. Many museums have models of it, and the Natural History Museum in Kensington has the first of the two actual fossil skeletons discovered."

"You don't know of a smaller specimen—a living one?"

"You're joking, Blake? Of course not . . ."

"And a three-toed, dog-sized horse?"

"That would be the *eohippus*, the modern horse's primitive ancestor of the Tertiary Age. The three toes became modified into a hoof . . ."

"Yes, I know that. But no living specimen exists of that primitive horse?"

"Certainly not! Blake—what's the joke? You sound serious, but—"

"I'm quite serious, Lumsden! Tell me, where could I see a marsupial cat?"

Lumsden began to sound impatient. "Hope this list isn't going to be a long one, Blake! I know of no pouched cat existing today, though there were once pouched lions and leopards in Australia. When that continent was isolated from the rest of the world, all sorts of pouched mammals evolved. Wolves, bears, lions, leopards, rats and monkeys. But the pouched bears and leopards and lions became extinct, leaving the kangaroo as the largest marsupial surviving today."

"And if you actually saw a pouched cat—the size of a domestic cat? And a small bird-reptile? And a dog-sized, three-toed horse? Alive today, Lumsden?"

Lumsden grunted. "I should think it made a change from pink elephants, I suppose—"

"Lumsden—I told you this was serious! I want your opinion as an authority. We know present-day animals and birds have evolved from primitive forms. Is it possible for the evolutionary process to be tampered with?"

Lumsden answered slowly: "It's possible for natural selection to be tampered with certainly. For instance, in the many different breeds of dog all produced from a common original stock by artificial selection for special characteristics. In cattle and horses of various types. And the siamese cat was produced by cross-breeding. We see it in plant life, too, where deliberate grafting has produced such new hybrid forms as the loganberry, and—"

"I mean more than that! Is an artificially-induced reversion to primitive type feasible? *A deliberately-produced throwback?*"

LUMSDEN PONDERED BEFORE he replied. Then: "Let's say it's just conceivable, Blake! Many of these new forms produced by artificial selection tend to revert to type, particularly goldfish and cats. Causing a reversion of natural evolution would be a much bigger problem, but its possibility is just conceivable. There's a logical basis—"

"Such as—?"

"You know, of course, that in its embryo state every mammal passes through the evolutionary stages of its species. At one stage, for instance, the human embryo has gill arches, a legacy of its very remote aquatic ancestors. If it were practicable to arrest the embryo before the completion of its evolutionary stages, it's conceivable that it might be born and mature as a creature of that early evolutionary stage. Just conceivable, I said!"

"So that if a mare in foal were subjected to the necessary arresting influence, the foal might be a primitive midget horse of the kind I mentioned?"

"Conceivably—yes. But this talk of reversing evolution reminds me of some rather advanced suggestions I heard a biologist make at a Society meeting nearly twenty years ago—and it sounded much less feasible then, when we knew so much less."

"This biologist—d'you happen to remember his name?"

"Why . . . er—yes! Leeming! Clever fellow—quite a pioneer of thought in our line. He claimed there was no inherent logical reason why it shouldn't be possible to reverse the evolutionary process at will; to cause a reversion, in one generation, to an evolutionary stage of millions of years ago."

"But you didn't think much of his ideas?"

"They don't seem quite as fantastic now as they did then, because very strange things are now being achieved. But, as you know, even such ideas as mechanical flight were envisaged centuries before they became practical propositions. I wouldn't dare to say this idea won't be a practical proposition before many years have passed, but—"

Blake interrupted. "Artificial influence on the embryonic creature would be limited by legal and other considerations to experiments on the lower animals. To produce an evolutionary reversion in a human subject, a different technique would be necessary. A fanatic determined to attempt a human reversion might experiment on a young child, say? Would that be feasible? To subject a young child to some modifying influence which would cause it to revert, as it grew up, to an early evolutionary stage?"

THE DETECTIVE HEARD Lumsden's breath sigh in the phone.

"What a question to ask, Blake! How can one say dogmatically what's possible or impossible in these times—when every day brings new advances? It's true that modifying the natural development of young creatures is already practicable. With thyroid hormone we can cause the early development of tadpoles into frogs no bigger than flies. With the pituitary hormone we can cause animals to grow to an abnormal size. By means of bio-chemistry and deep radiation we can produce artificial variations which are virtually new types of creatures. So I wouldn't put it past the ability of some perverted genius to find a way of doing what you suggest. Though I sincerely hope no one ever will."

"Why?" Blake asked, although he shared that dislike of the idea.

"Because such quirks of nature—'sports' as we call them— tend to be perpetuated. We now know that evolution itself hasn't been a slow, gradual change, but a series of large and abrupt mutations which have been transmitted to subsequent generations. For instance, the copper beech tree didn't exist before the seventeenth century. A single specimen arose suddenly from ordinary beech tree stock and has bred true to its new kind ever since. In eighteen-eighty the Shirley poppy

444

was found in a field of ordinary poppies, and has propagated its kind ever since. So you can see the danger there would be in producing even one evolutionary throwback—quite apart from the crime against the human guinea-pig himself . . ."

Blake said coldly: "I can, indeed! It would be the most retrograde step since the evolution of Man!"

Again Lumsden's breath rasped in the receiver. "Blake! Is that the possibility that's worrying you? Surely not? It's still such a remote—"

Blake asked: "What made man the dominant creature?"

"Oh—the upright stance which gave him stereoscopic vision, that stimulating his brain to develop. And, of course, opposable thumbs—which gave him the use of weapons and tools. He couldn't have become civilised man without those thumbs."

"That's what I thought!" the detective admitted. "Well, that's all for the moment, Lumsden. I'll see you in a few days' time to satisfy your curiosity—I hope! Meanwhile, many thanks for your expert opinion. It's been very helpful indeed. Goodbye!"

With his face set hard, his eyes cold, he rang off.

Twenty minutes later he was driving back to Mowbray House.

A SICKLE MOON had risen behind scudding clouds. It shed no useful light, but cast a very faint luminosity which made the shadows seem deeper.

Paula was again beside him in the car, dressed now in slacks and a sweater. And now, in her handbag, she was carrying her little .22 Webley-and-Scott automatic pistol. In a shoulder-holster Blake was carrying his heavy Luger.

He made the run in quick time, and again parked the car on the verge near the boundary wall. But now that his ideas about this case had crystallised, Paula was not going to be allowed to come into the grounds with him.

"This time," he said quietly, as he opened the car door to climb out, "I mean to get into the house itself! I don't know how long I shall be—it depends on what I find. But if I shouldn't show up inside an hour, you can fetch Coutts out here—with a few men. You know what to tell him. Now . . . keep that gun of yours handy!" The door shut behind him.

Leaving Paula and the car in darkness, he moved around the boot to the wall. There was the faint swish of the rope ladder being cast, then he was a dim shape ascending the wall. Snakelike, the ladder wriggled up the wall a minute later when he pulled it up for use on the inner side.

With a pretence of relaxation, Paula settled down in the Bentley. Every light had been switched off, but the nearside window was open an inch for ventilation. With nothing left to watch, she stared abstractedly ahead, while her pupils gradually dilated to the shrouded night . . .

IN ROPE-SOLED SHOES, and with the rolled ladder under one arm, Blake again made his almost soundless way towards the menagerie. On the opposite side of the house, a glow of light showed through the drawn blinds of an upstairs room, but on the menagerie side the darkness was unrelieved except by the dim, fugitive moon-twilight.

He emerged from a clump of shrubbery and approached the menagerie. Here a surprise awaited him. This time there was no need to force the padlock. The collapsible door was wide open, and plate glass reflected the masked rays of his questing torch. But no startled eyes looked back at him.

The menagerie was now a museum of the dead.

In the aquarium the strange fish floated on their sides . . . inert, glassy-eyed. In each of the other sections its specimens lay still and lifeless. Since Blake's recent visit, indiscriminate death had come to the denizens of this grotesque menagerie.

446

Frowning, keenly alert, Blake moved away, with the torch extinguished, towards the dark side of the silent house. But, alert as he was, he nearly stumbled over an obstacle lying invisible in the tall, coarse grass.

The touch of his canvas-covered foot told him the obstacle was a body. But it wasn't until he knelt beside it and flashed a momentary light on its contorted face that he realised the body was dead.

And that it was the body of Croft, the gloomy manservant!

CROFT HAD NOT only been strangled. His neck was broken, leaving his head lying unnaturally askew on his hunched shoulders.

Blake didn't wait to make a detailed examination. This discovery intensified the urgency of an invasion of the house. He had to see Leeming—if Leeming were still alive—and also whoever else lived in this den of warped life and blind, primitive killing.

He found a side door unlocked and ajar. He edged his way into a dark, deserted kitchen and eventually out into the hall. A flash of the torch showed that the front door was also ajar. But he padded towards the foot of the stairs, the torch casting a small, dim circle on the floor ahead of him.

He had a foot on the bottom stair when he heard the sound. Between the bannister posts of the landing above, he could see a pale glow, evidently from the open doorway of some room out of his range of vision. But it was the low sound which caused the hairs at the back of his neck to stir uneasily . . .

A low, monotonous, idiotic chuckling. A chuckling quite without mirth . . . a persistent, monotonous, insane mutter.

With the torch switched off, he crept up the stairs. On the landing he laid the rolled ladder noiselessly on the carpet. He looked about him.

He'd been right about an open doorway. Across the landing a door stood open about a foot, and through the aperture a white light streamed. But it was another door that attracted attention. A thick wooden door that had been battered to destruction and hung gaping from one hinge.

Blake stepped forward, peering past the splintered door into the room beyond, visible in the light reflected from the landing. A room with a barred window and closed shutters outside the bars. A room bare except for some sacking strewn on the floor . . . bare of all furniture. As bare as an animal's cage.

An empty cage.

Quickly Blake turned away. In three strides he was at the lighted doorway, pressing the door open wider with his left foot. He was staring down the length of a laboratory.

With reason to stare!

About a third of the way down the laboratory, a man was standing with his back towards the detective. It was from this man that the eerie chuckling was coming. Chuckling intermittently punctuated with muttered words and phrases, addressed to someone out of sight.

". . . They couldn't be allowed to breed, could they . . .? But why not . . . I forget why not . . ." A giggling chuckle. ". . . But I've done the right thing now . . . the right thing now. . . All gone . . . they're all gone . . . even Croft is gone . . ." Another giggle. ". . . And the other one too . . . I knew it would happen if he ever met Croft alone . . . it was only me he ever respected . . . grew up respecting . . ." That idiot's chuckle again. ". . . He never outgrew his respect for me . . .! But *you* don't respect me, do you . . . even now I've done what you wanted. They're gone . . . all gone . . ."

Blake had come soundlessly up behind him, was looking past him to see his companion. But there was no companion. The deranged man was Ambrose Leeming. But the chair he was looking at and talking to was empty! He was addressing his rambling remarks to a mental figment!

He started in alarm as Blake laid a hand on his shoulder. His crazed eyes turned to scan the detective's bleak face.

Blake said sternly: "Where is he?"

A giggle. A gesture towards the unoccupied chair. ". . . Why—here he is, of course . . .!"

"I mean the other!" Blake said curtly. "From the next room. Which way did he go?"

Before Leaming's bemused mind could frame a reply, an answer came from outside the house. From some distance away from the house.

At first Blake didn't recognise the distant voice, because never before had he heard that voice screaming. But when it came again, almost immediately, neither novelty nor distance could obscure the stark fact.

Those screams of sheer terror had come from the normally imperturbable Paula Dane!

Thrusting Leeming unceremoniously aside, Blake turned and raced for the door. Raced down the stairs—saturated with the frantic dread that he could not possibly be in time . . .

THE FOURTEENTH CHAPTER

The last hunt.

PAULA SHIVERED—AND REMEMBERED the shiver that had swept over her back in Berkeley Square at the very beginning of this case. She remembered the ominous thought that had come to her then.

Under the faint, fugitive glimmer of the clouded sickle moon, the night was wrapped in shadows and silence. Silence except for the little furtive country sounds that spoke of tiny life-forms going about their secret business; silence except for little rustling whispers that could mean nothing . . . or anything.

Having no light, she wished she could have turned on the radio for an illusion of companionship, but the sound would have defeated the purpose of blacking-out the car.

She was fidgeting nervily when the hand took hold of the top edge of the window, so no sound of it reached her. It was when the pressure of immense strength forced the window down another three inches, with rending damage to the winding mechanism, that she was shocked into attention. By then the hand was inside the car, reaching for her . . .

The stealthy surprise was so petrifying that for age-long seconds she had neither voice nor power of movement. Then, groping fingers brushed her shoulder, she cowered away along the seat, impelled by a warm smell reminiscent of a zoo.

At the same moment she was aware of a slight sagging of the car springs to an additional weight . . . and the soft thud of feet upon the roof. Bare feet . . .

That sound killed her instinctive urge to get away from the hand by jumping out of the offside door. It rushed in upon her whirling mind that people who'd been caught out in the open by hands like this one had died swiftly, probably without even a chance to cry out. This car, even with the hand already through the window, was almost her only protection—her only chance of life.

Almost . . .!

In the darkness, panicky with an intuitive revulsion, she scrabbled for her pistol and at the same time for the switch of the roof-light.

She reached the switch first. And as light dazzled her dilated eyes, terror flooded her bloodstream with adrenalin—gave desperate strength to muscles and voice. Her scream rent the night asunder as a vivid nightmare cameo was etched in the frame of the window.

A hand such as she had never seen before on a human being. A long arm bizarrely sheathed in a grey woollen sleeve—bizarrely because the hand that emerged from the frayed cuff was a thing of the jungle. A simian, hairy paw with long, groping fingers . . . but a stunted, rudimentary thumb!

And the face behind it, framed upside-down as the heavy body sprawled on the roof . . . the face peering in with savage determination . . .

Flung sideways, trapped behind the wheel as she groped blindly for the gun, Paula had an almost upright view of that subhuman face . . . flinched in nausea from the angry gusts of foetid breath.

A face that was neither human nor animal—and therefore more terrifying than either. A low, sloping forehead above a prominent brow ridge, and beneath that prominent ridge a pair of small eyes, feral and malevolent. A short, wide nose, squat on a jutting, chinless, hairy muzzle . . . which was opening and closing to a soft, growling mutter.

But no ape . . . no gorilla—that was the nightmare fact. The ears were large, but almost human; the nose was squat, but there was more of it than any ape or orang-utan possessed. And even the creature's attempts to get at her had little of the mechanical persistence of an animal—but a frightening proportion of human purposefulness, as in the opening of the window.

That travesty of a human face was edging through the window-opening now, canine teeth showing in a gaping grin. The weaving paw got a predatory finger on Paula's shoulder— and from her uncontrollable lips ripped a second scream.

Then the pistol was in her hand and she was struggling with the safety-catch.

The catch clicked off . . . and the pistol came up in her shaking grip. Small-calibre bullets fired wildly, and shattered window-glass sprouted stars from at least one of them.

But from somewhere out in the darkness came a cannonade of staccato blasts from a heavier gun. At least one of the bigger-calibre bullets found a flesh target. A snarl of pain and fear was accompanied by the shaking of the car as a heavy body floundered on the roof. From the speed with which the arm was withdrawn, a bullet had hit or grazed the shoulder, because the head was evidently undamaged.

This was shown when a snarling, grotesque figure bounded from the roof to the ground and ran away at a fast, ungainly lope.

A fleeting glimpse of a shaggy bullet head hunched on broad

shoulders. A bent back in a grey sweater. Long, swinging arms. Slightly bent legs in old flannel trousers. Bare, splay-toed feet.

And even as Paula's staring eyes watched the scene in the area of light cast by the car, the fleeing figure reached the belt of trees on the other side of the earth road.

It sprang. The reaching paws clutched a horizontal branch. It swung—and reached a higher branch of an adjacent tree. Then it was out of the area of light and Paula was lying limp on the car's front seats, chilled and trembling and faint from the overwhelming reaction. Dizzy, sick and unseeing as she lay half-submerged by the tide of horror.

Blake's voice reached her through time, distance and mocking echo-chambers. Then a door opened; strong, human hands lifted her; a mellow human voice uttered her name in warm concern.

What to Paula had been a monstrous, murderous presence of sound, sight and touch, had to Blake been only a vague, distant shadow. A menacing shape to be driven away at long range, and under the handicap of avoiding of hitting Paula. And then the urgent need to reach her—to make sure that she still lived . . .

Now the svelte Paula, unashamed of her terror, took hold of his two arms; looked up into his strong face, like a little girl, for reassurance. Then a brief spate of words gushed from her.

"Chief," she finished, in a sombre murmur, "you were right—and I—I'll never forget that—that creature of Leeming's wickedness. Such things should never be . . ."

"Tonight," Blake assured her, "such things are going to end!" His unintimidated gaze brought colour back into her cheeks and strength to her mind and body. "And you, Paula," he added, "are going to help to end them!"

SHE CAME INTO Bissett Heath at high speed, with headlights blazing an alarm. Bursting into the police station, she found Chief Inspector Coutts and Sergeant James trying to get rid of

Major Eyles, D.S.O., M.F.H.

Eyles, in boots and breeches, was brandishing a sheaf of foolscap papers, and complaining: "But where *is* Blake? He asked for details of their alibis, and now he isn't here to receive them! He wasn't at the hotel either. Ah—here's his secretary!" Eyles produced a smile. "Any idea where Mr. Blake is, Miss Dane? These alibis—"

"They won't be wanted now!" Paula said impatiently. Breathing hard, she spoke to the Yard man. "Chief Inspector! I've an urgent message from Mr. Blake. He wants you to organise a hunt for the strangler. He's at large now—run amok, in fact. We know who he is, and Mr. Blake—"

"You know who the killer is!" Coutts blurted incredulously. "Who is he? Where do we have to hunt? Where's Blake?"

"The chief's at Mowbray waiting in case the killer should go back there . . ." Rapidly she explained. "A man in grey cast-offs, with an apish face—that's who you've got to look out for. He's wounded, so he'll be extra dangerous. Your party had better have sticks or hay-forks or something, for self-defence in case—"

"A hunt, eh!" Eyles broke in eagerly. "Quarry last seen near Mowbray House! Inspector! Sergeant! You organise your party and I'll organise mine. A mounted hunt's wanted here—and someone who's hunted the country . . .!"

He dashed out of the office. Sergeant James left close behind him—but in a run to the *Crumpled Horn* and *Piers Plowman* to call for volunteers.

Coutts waited only to make an emergency call to county police headquarters. Then he hurried out with Paula to the Bentley.

Just as Tinker's Aston Martin came along the narrow street.

AFTER PAULA HAD driven away from Mowbray House, Sexton Blake had spent a busy quarter of an hour in the laboratory.

His task had been a vital one. A swift job of destruction.

The folder of notes he had found on the bench had been quickly scanned, then torn to shreds and reduced to ash in the laboratory incinerator. The ash itself he had raked into dust.

After a search through the filing cabinet, he had similarly destroyed any written matter with even the remotest possible bearing on Ambrose Leeming's biological experiments. And then other rooms had been inspected for written or taped records of the work. But evidently only the laboratory had contained such records, and all of these Blake had personally destroyed.

Now, KEYED-UP TO the peak of alertness, he prowled the grounds in a wary patrol—in case a wounded mass killer should come creeping back to his usual refuge.

Over by the menagerie, a whimpering madman was burying the creatures he had conjured up by twentieth-century alchemy—and then killed.

Somewhere in the dark countryside, a subhuman creature was seeking shelter from a world in which he was a lonely anachronism and every other living being was an enemy. Somewhere a bemused, retarded brain, no longer dominated by the mind which had destroyed its original potentialities, was shrinking in hiding from a species to which its own kind had yielded the world half a million years earlier.

As Blake neared the Mowbray House gates in his latest circuit of the grounds, headlight beams speared between the bars, and a car slowed to a stop outside.

From it climbed Paula, Chief Inspector Coutts and a couple of men they had picked up on the way through Bissett Heath. Behind this car another one had stopped. An Aston Martin containing Tinker and Bill Malvern. Blake opened the gates and invited them all inside.

Leaving Paula with the local men at the gateway, he conducted Coutts and Tinker to the menagerie. In the light of the police officer's torch, Ambrose Leeming blinked up with blank indifference from the job he was completing on his knees. While Coutts studied him with an incredulous expression still on his square face, Blake amplified Paula's hurried explanation.

He had just finished showing Coutts and Tinker the laboratory and the barred room, when a medley of voices at the gates announced the arrival of Sergeant James and his party, in a couple of Land Rovers. Most of the men with him carried torches and improvised weapons.

While the Yard man and James were issuing instructions to these volunteers, they were interrupted by the thud of hoofs along the earth road. Into the light from the cars cantered Major Eyles and three other mounted men, also with torches.

"More on the way!" Eyles shouted, reining to a halt. He was evidently enjoying himself. Grinning, he gestured across the heath to where torchlights bounced in the darkness to the rhythm of cantering horses. "We'll soon flush him out of cover . . .! By gosh—" He started up in his saddle as faintly in the distance a hunting horn sounded. "'Hear that—?"

Turning his mount, he dug in his heels and clattered away into the gloom beyond the lights. The three other horsemen turned to follow him. Two of them went by—but as the third broke into a trot, Blake leapt forward and grabbed at the horse's bridle.

"Get down!" Blake ordered urgently. As the man hesitated, Blake gripped his arm and dragged him bodily from the saddle. While the onlookers stood dumb with surprise, Blake steadied the horse and said quickly, for the benefit of Paula and Tinker: "Eyles seems to think this is another pleasure hunt—but there's going to be no lynching! The quarry they're after was born a human being . . .!"

Stuffing his torch into his jacket pocket, Blake put his left foot in the stirrup iron and leapt astride the hunter. As his heels touched the flanks, it pounded off after the receding torchlights and fading hoofbeats.

Tinker hesitated, then ran to one of the Land Rovers.

BLAKE HAD RIDDEN once over this heath—or part of it—but in darkness it was virtually unknown country. Country with risks underfoot and a greater menace overhead. The menace of trees, invisible in the darkness till it was almost too late to avoid them. And, even when their presence was realised, the deadly threat of low branches, to blind or unseat a fast rider.

But Eyles had both a good start and an intimate knowledge of the terrain, so for Blake speed was essential. Unfortunately, this speed lessened his chances of avoiding trees picked out by the beam of his torch. All he could do when the chase took him through some of the many clumps of trees was to keep his head low and hold the torch out before him to deflect thin branches and give split-second warning of dangerous ones.

Even the horse, accustomed to hectic chases in daylight, had little taste for this wild dash through the tree-littered darkness, and needed constant urging to keep him going at speed and a strong hand to keep him on course.

But from the third clump of trees Blake came out on to ground clear as far as his torch-beam could reach. A couple of minutes later he was overtaking a trio of horsemen going at a steady canter in the same direction.

"Major?" Blake called, riding beside them.

"He's gone ahead!" someone shouted back. "Never had any nerves. Besides, he's got a gun—"

"I spotted this thing we're hunting!" someone else broke in. "Got a good view of him with my torch. He scampered off that way—must be making for Dell Woods—"

This thing. So that was how some of these people were thinking of their quarry . . . of Leeming's victim. And Eyles had a gun . . .

Taking the direction of his informant's pointing arm, Blake heeled his mount into a reckless gallop, his torch raking the undulating ground ahead.

He saw the low stone wall at the same instant as the hunter, in time to brace himself as the horse cleared the obstacle at the stretch. There was a slight rise over a ploughed field which slowed the horse considerably—then Blake caught the momentary flash of a distant light.

If it had come from Eyles' torch, the M.F.H. must have ridden up on to high ground for just that second, then sunk out of sight in another hollow.

But the flash had given Blake a bearing, and he urged his horse across the furrows towards the firmer going Eyles had evidently reached.

Firmer going that was taking him farther ahead over familiar ground . . .

WITH A FAINT grin on his thin face, Eyles sent his mount down the incline and into Dell Woods, his torch flashing and probing as the trees loomed up.

The big moment was near now. The rest of the hunt had been left behind, and the quarry could not be far away. Soon he must be brought to bay—by Major Eyles, D.S.O., M.F.H. A big-game hunt this time, with the M.F.H. in at the kill.

The ape-man, flushed out of cover, frightened and dazzled by flashing lights, harried by unfamiliar humans astride unfamiliar animals, must be nearing the end of his tether. Cut off from his usual refuge, his prison-home; driven farther and farther from the small area he knew; pursued by an expert hunter knowing the terrain in every detail . . . Eyles felt the exultant

459

exhilaration that always came when the chase was nearing a triumphant end.

And then, as he cantered into the fringe of the woods, he felt a sudden incredible grasp close around his neck like a gigantic vice. His whirling senses were dimly conscious that he'd been plucked violently out of the saddle. He hung suspended by the neck in mid-air as his horse cantered away into the Dell.

His lighted torch had tumbled from his hand. Its protective glass had shattered, but the bulb, intact, was casting a dim, diffused radiance.

For seconds Eyles was conscious only of pain. Of the pounding in his head and the drag of his whole weight from that inhuman grip around his neck.

Then, instinctively, his bursting eyes turned upwards. His body kicked convulsively in a recoil from what he saw.

Long arms reaching down to those immense hands about his throat. An ape-like face between them, mouthing quiet snarls. Above that an inverted body—suspended from legs hooked over a thick, horizontal branch.

The hunted ape-man had not fled into the depths of the woods for cover. With primitive cunning, he had waited in the fringe of the woods for his remorseless pursuer.

Now, still snarling softly, he swung his captive by the head and tossed him to the ground.

As Eyles landed, he felt his neck break.

THE FIFTHTEENTH CHAPTER

This night extinct.

THE APE-MAN EVIDENTLY realised that his hunter wasn't dead. Dazed eyes saw him drop nimbly to the ground and shuffle forward.

Eyles lay dewed with a chill sweat. His neck was broken, and any jolt to his spinal cord would be fatal . . . He lay dizzy and sick with fear as that grotesque figure shuffled nearer . . . wary, suspicious. A night shape, dim against darkness.

Eyles remembered the service revolver in his jacket pocket. If his spinal cord should happen to be compressed by the fracture of the vertebrae, he would be paralysed. He had no option about finding out. With agonised care not to jolt his head or shoulders, he tried to move his right hand.

He succeeded. He got the hand to the pocket and slowly dragged out the gun.

The ape-man was only two yards away when Eyles raised the revolver and fired.

Even in this extremity he couldn't miss at such a range. A .38 slug thudded into the ape-man's broad chest.

It stopped him. But only for three seconds. For that space of time he stood quite still, not comprehending what had happened. Then a delayed reaction sent him leaping awkwardly for the cover of a tree . . . still active!

Eyles fired again, his hand shaking now—and missed. The ape-man was peering around a tree-trunk, then came into full view as he shuffled tentatively forward again, one paw clasped to his chest.

Eyles fired for the third time, and the bullet hit that crouching, menacing body. But still it came on . . .!

Eyles knew that in the heat of battle many a man had continued to run, unaware that he'd been mortally wounded.

But this monstrosity had two bullets in him now . . . three, as Eyles fired again . . . but still he came on. Relentlessly, inexorably, homicidally. Bigger against the shadows.

Frantically, as that grimacing muzzle loomed nearer, as those bare feet crept closer, as a weaving, clutching paw reached out, a caustic comment echoed with grisly irony in the huntsman's cringing mind.

". . . People like you should learn how it *feels* to be torn to pieces . . .!" The words of Bill Malvern in the safety of the committee-room.

Eyles sweated as another, panicky, shot went wild, and violent, brutal death filled his shrinking view. Was this how a cornered fox felt when a ravening pack closed blood-thirstily around him? Was this how it felt when your body was about to be rent in searing agony to gory tatters . . .?

He didn't hear the thudding of approaching hoofs. He didn't see a tall, lean man leap lithely from the saddle.

But suddenly the revolver was swept from his grip—and another human being was standing between his sweat-chilled body and the subhuman monstrosity.

And the two great arms of the sub-human were reaching for this nearer newcomer.

SEXTON BLAKE HAD flung Eyles' revolver away, and didn't draw his own Luger. Down the grey-jerseyed chest of this grimacing parody of humanity, blood was glistening as it oozed from three places. Only inhuman vitality was keeping this wounded creature on his feet.

"Bob . . .!" Blake murmured, his eyes filling with pity. "Bobby. . .!"

The eyes under that protruding brow-ridge flickered with recognition—then the squat body flinched with fear. This bemused creature had no cause to love a person using that name. The spasm of fear was followed by a snarl of anger. A vengeful paw reached out and closed on Blake's shoulder.

Hot pain shot through the shoulder from that grip. Then a paw fell on the other shoulder—and the snarling muzzle was only a foot away from Blake's face.

The detective looked into the shadowed, malevolent eyes of a primitive being savagely at bay in a hostile world . . . but he was seeing the original human pattern diabolically distorted by a fanatical, merciless abuse of scientific power. The evil was not in this snarling throwback. He was its victim.

Blake's hands came up and gripped the wrists at his shoulders. His biceps bulged in the effort to lift those paws from their crushing grip. His fingers ached with the strain, but he seemed to be making no impression at all. He was, in fact, being drawn nearer that gaping muzzle as the simian arms bent at the elbows and dragged at his shoulders.

His face taut, his feet astride for a firm stance, Blake exerted every ounce of his strength to resist and break that inhuman grip.

And then, through no power of his own, the grip of those paws had loosened and the broad body was tottering on its bowed legs. Internally, as well as externally, its vitality had been draining away.

Quite abruptly, the creature rocked on his heels and crashed down on his back on the earth . . .

A minute later the victim of Leeming's experimental mania was, for the first time since childhood, being treated as a human being. Blake was gently closing the lids over the dead, staring eyes.

IT WAS ONLY then that the detective turned to attend to Major Eyles. After kneeling to make a rapid examination of the injured man, Blake got to his feet and fired two shots into the air. To remove Eyles with safety, a stretcher party was needed.

As an extra guide to his location, Blake was directing the narrow beam of his torch into the air when two more men came into the woods. On foot. They were Tinker and Bill Malvern, delayed by rough country and a stone wall.

Grim-faced, they looked from the dead body to the supine huntsman.

Blake said quietly: "Yes—Eyles got to him first, I'm afraid!"

Even in the dim light, Malvern was noticeably pale. Standing over the fox-hunter, he said mordantly: "Well, Eyles—I see you made your kill. But this time there's no trophy!"

IN GIDEON ASHLEY'S study-library, on the afternoon of the next day, Sexton Blake, Paula Dane, and Tinker sat facing the man with such remarkable powers of anticipation.

Blake was saying: "You pointed out yesterday that worse things can happen to the human race than individual physical deaths. So I'm sure there's no need to tell you that, with the end of the recent series of violent deaths in this part of the country, a much worse evil has also come to an end. And you'll be glad that I helped to prevent a repetition, by destroying all documentary records of the technique."

Ashley's dark eyes expressed interest and satisfaction, but he made no oral comment.

Blake continued: "The victim of that evil is dead—and that's perhaps the least of the tragedies he has suffered. The perpetrator of the evil will spend the rest of his life under restraint, in a mental home—which is probably a case of true poetic justice—"

Tinker put in: "And a certain local resident may have lost some of his taste for blood sports when he's got over his present packet of trouble!"

"Those are the practical details," Blake went on. "But there've been less er—material circumstances surrounding this affair, which have left me wondering . . ."

"Yes?" Ashley invited, his dark eyes glimmering.

"Before I came into the case a clairvoyant lady in Bissett Heath had announced a unique danger to the human race, and claimed that it was sufficient to require the personal attention of the . . . Masters of the Occult Hierarchy, to use her own term."

"Yes?" Ashley invited again, while Tinker and Paula sat silent.

Blake gave a whimsical smile. He murmured thoughtfully: "I understand that, according to occult lore, one of the present Masters is believed to be an Englishman. An Englishman working as a business magnate, with a benevolent influence upon the use of finance."

His eyes narrowed as his gaze dwelt upon Ashley's attentive face.

"An interesting concept!" the financier suggested equably.

"Interesting indeed! One rather wonders," the detective mused aloud, as though at a spontaneous tangent, "one rather wonders just what caused Leeming's mania to come to such a sudden climax—and with such destructive effect upon the products of his life's work!"

Ashley gave the slightest of shrugs. "Life is full of matters for conjecture, Mr. Blake!"

The investigator stood up, Tinker following suit. Smiling, Blake stated: "Conjecture, as well as crime, is my business. So—"

Gideon Ashley too was now on his feet, a friendly hand outstretched. "So—if I may venture a prediction—it's quite likely that your conjectures, as usual, will bring you very near to the truth!"

Gripping his hand, Blake said: "You think so? That's encouraging—because your anticipations seem to be realised very quickly! Well, goodbye, Mr. Ashley." Blake's smile was innocent. "Oh—if *I* can venture a prediction, I doubt whether you'll find it necessary to stay in this part of the country much longer?"

As he escorted his three visitors to the door, Ashley gave a sudden warm smile. "You must be psychic, Mr. Blake! Goodbye, Miss Dane—and Mr. Carter!"

Paula and Tinker were eyeing their chief with unusual abstraction as they drove away.

THE END

Notes

8. This is a reference to THE EVIL EYE by Martin Thomas (Thomas Martin), THE SEXTON BLAKE LIBRARY 4th series, issue 415, published in October 1958.

9. The word "retarded" has been replaced.

THE FINER DETAILS of Blake's consulting room were by now wholly obscured by a blue haze. Blake's tobacco was scented with rum, spices and gunpowder, in much the same way, I imagined, that a burning pirate ship might be.

Tinker was adding to the fog. Halfway through reading the story, he'd started to smoke a Players No. 6, which was absolutely absurd, as that particular brand of cigarette ceased production back in the early nineties (I know this because my dad swore that being forced to change to a different brand had caused his lung cancer.)

If all Blake's Credibility Gap business were true, then I was obviously sitting right in the middle of it, breathing it in.

As Tinker returned *Bred to Kill* to the binder, I asked, "What became of Paula Dane and the others?"

"They retired," Blake said.

"Have you ever considered doing the same?"

Blake and his assistant exchanged a glance.

"We tried it," the detective said. "The eighties and nineties."

I gave him a look, and muttered, "Most people would consider that rather late in life."

His eyes met mine. In a quiet tone, he said, "I was referring to the decades." And unspoken: *And stop digging!*

Tinker made a face. "It was awful!"

"Retirement? Why? What happened?"

Melodramatically, Tinker clapped a hand to his forehead. "Nothing! Like I say, awful!"

Blake said, "We took up hobbies, went fishing a lot, indulged in mindless sight-seeing, tried to relax, and found it all interminably dull. We ended up immersed in study. The new techniques of detection. The new technologies. The new theories of psychology. Medicine. Philosophy. We ... *updated* ourselves." He drew on his cigar and eyed me—weighed me up—through its smoke.

I saw him reach some sort of decision.

He said, "The Craille Institute."

"Chief—" Tinker interjected.

Blake made a dismissive gesture. "I think we can reveal a certain amount, Tinker. Either it won't be believed or it will, and if the latter is the case, then perhaps it will work to our advantage, as it did in the old days." He smiled. "Tell tall tales. Twist the truth. Confound the enemy."

A short silence followed.

I broke it.

"The Craille Institute? Is that what it was called? Eustace Craille's organisation?"

"Is."

"Is? You can't possibly mean that Craille is still—?"

"Good lord, no!" Blake exclaimed. "He was an old, old man even back in the day. No, but his organisation quietly survived, though not in any active capacity. Recently, Tinker and I, along with certain other interested parties, felt the time had come to, shall we say, resuscitate it."

"Do you mean that you're back in—"

As if on cue, a ringtone sounded, the same one that had interrupted yesterday's interview. This time, though, it was Tinker who drew out an oddly designed mobile and answered it.

He spoke too quietly for me to catch his words, especially as Blake had started to fiddle with the decanter of brandy, clinking it, clearing his throat, and asking me if I wanted a refill though I'd hardly touched my glass.

Distraction tactics!

Tinker flashed a look at his "guv'nor" and some manner of communication passed between them, though what or how I wasn't able to ascertain. Some subtle body language, perhaps.

Blake stood, removed his dressing gown, and flung it over the back of his chair. He threw his half-smoked cigar into the fireplace.

Pedro gave a gruff utterance, got to his feet, and walked over to the door.

"Understood," Tinker said. "We'll be right there."

He pocketed the phone, rose from his chair, and said to Blake, "Our green-eyed friend. He broke loose during the night, stole a car and got clean away."

"Blast!" Blake muttered.

The interview had abruptly ended. I got up, closed the binder, and returned it to my briefcase. Before I could ask what was happening, Tinker reached out, shook my hand, and said, "You know those unbelievable coincidences that so often occur in the stories? This is one of them."

Blake guided me to the door.

"Mrs Bardell will see you out," he said. "It's been a pleasure. I hope we can do it again sometime soon. I'll be in touch. Oh, and yes, to answer your question —" he momentarily squeezed my arm. "Sexton Blake and Tinker are back in action!"

Disorientating moments later, I was out in Baker Street, my assignment had abruptly concluded, and my mind was brimming with questions that I thought would never be answered.

Some weeks later, however, many of them were.

I can tell you only this: Sexton Blake wanted these anthologies published.

They are a part of a plan.
By selecting the stories, I have become a part of it.
By reading them, so have you.